SAVAGE CONTINENT

Book Four of the EtharWorldSeries

BY

DEWITT C. TREMAINE

REVISED VERSION

BOOK TITLES BY
DEWITT C. TREMAINE

ETHAR WORLD SERIES:

1. **The Rise of a King** – Book One of the Ethar World Series

2. **A Time for Change -** Book Two of the Ethar World Series

3. **A Touch of Earth** - Book Three of the Ethar World Series

4. **Savage Continent** - Book Four of the Ethar World Series

5. **A Journey** - Book Five of the Ethar World Series

6. **Tallund** - Book Six of the Ethar World Series

7. **Telsa** - Book Seven of the Ethar World Series

8. **When Nothing Happens** - Book Eight of the Ethar World Series

9. **From Kendlar and Back Again** – Book Nine in the Ethar World Series

TOUCH OF EARTH SAGA:

1. Touch of Earth Saga 1 Heroes

2. Touch of Earth Saga 2 Secret Camp

3. Touch of Earth Saga 3 Janet

4. Touch of Earth Saga 4 Candy

eBook: 978-1-966954-41-5
Hardback: 978-1-966954-40-8
Paperback: 978-1-966954-39-2
LCCN: 2025910086

Printed in the United States of America

SAVAGE CONTINENT

In a dark but whimsical way the world around, him was ever changing. "I trust you to guard my back." His brother Yaun was saying, "You are the next in line to rule the clan and you don't want the job, so you will do your best to keep me alive."

"Everyone knows I don't want the position, so what difference does it make to me if you live or die," Jenyin knew his brother was right, he did not want to be at the center of politics and power struggles, "I would just pass it on, and everyone would be happy."

Yaun laughed, they had played out this debate before, "You know the rules of order, you would have to take banishment for you and your heirs. None have ever returned from banishment. The land is savage, and we must be darker than the lands around us to survive."

"We treat the farming rabble better then we treat our own." Jenyin lost interest in the debate and changed the subject, "They are fed and housed and protected and only have to do the work we tell them to do."

"They have no freedom!" Yaun stated.

"And neither do we, we are bound by our rules of order to do what we are told as leaders, upper class or whatever it is we are." Jenyin's eye caught the glint from the corner of the window that was not supposed to be there. The gesture of his hand told his brother something was up.

"Would you rather be a peasant worker, at the mercy of any fleeting urge?" Yaun chided, keeping the conversation as real as possible as they circled to identify what was there.

"You know the rules offer protection there too." Jenyin relaxed as the detection spell let him know it was just a listening bug and he smashed it with the butt of his dagger. "Spies"

"What do you think they heard?" Yaun inquired.

"The place was clean yesterday." Jenyin examined the room again, "This would more likely be an ambitious member of the youth then an enemy. It is more likely to gain an advantage by having information to compete for a position than something detrimental."

"Then it was probably one of the apprentices that cleaned the office this morning." Yaun scratched his chin, "We need to determine which one, then pull them to the side and reprimand them for getting caught. We might pull them into the fold and see if we can train them to be more effective"

"If we do, they need to maintain appearances of just being at their current status." Jenyin noted.

Yaun move his inkwell on his desk as if moving a game piece. "Another tool in the collection."

They were not human, they were not Elf, but they were creatures of the shadows whose lives were augmented by magical innate abilities. They were the Shadowkyn, feared and respected by those who knew them. The Shadowkyn were not necessarily aggressive, but much like the savage creatures of the untamed continent. They were known for being fierce and decisive even primal in their actions and ways. Their "rules of order" guided their culture protecting them from self-destruction, but they only applied to those living within their culture. Outside of their own, threats or perceived threats are quickly eliminated.

The novice spy turned out to be Lyamy, a young female Shadowkyn of thirteen years. Her skin was fair, almost translucent like all Shadowkyn of their tribe, while they appeared virtually white in light, the translucence made them almost disappear in the shadows. Her hair also like all Shadowkyn she knew could not be clearly defined by color having much the same characteristic as their skin. She was powerfully built even for a Shadowkyn female. While the build of a Shadowkyn was between that of a human and an Elf they were lean creatures, even their tails while finely defined rippled with the power of their muscular architecture.

You could tell looking at them they were descended from a cat like race, especially if they got down on all fours. Their smile if you had the opportunity so see one, at a glance looked normal, they had the teeth of an omnivore for cutting and breaking off vegetation in the front. Beyond that though, they were obviously more carnivorous with the rows of sharp shredding teeth for tearing fresh meat and combat. Their hand looked like most hands, four fingers, opposing thumbs with retractable claws. For the most part they lost most of their fur to evolution although their hair was exceptionally thick from their forehead down the middle of their backs and on the back of their tail to the tip. Protective patches of fur could still be found in discrete locations and in hereditary marking, although they did not track their heritage.

Lyamy was already one of their best apprentices, privileged to serve in the office of Lord Yaun, leader of the thirteenth clan. She was formally reprimanded and beat in front of her peers as a warning to any who would act against the sanctity of the clan. She took her beating with unmistakable submission, but pride glinted in her eyes, Jenyin noted the glint through her facade with an appreciation for her strength and conviction. Jenyin pulled her like a lowly beast from the public spectacle of discipline but did not take her to the punishment cell as she had expected. He turned off into a side room she had never before been allowed to enter.

Her eyes caught the sleeping bunk to the left suspended by chains from the wall as she walked in, "Go ahead she whispered abuse me as you must, I shall not waver from my loyalty to our clan and the rules of order."

He could taste the venom in her voice as she hissed out the words of submission. "Sit" he spoke in a totally detached manner letting go of the chain hanging from the collar around her neck. He opened the medical box on the desk lifting the flat wooden lid and letting if fall to the back side of the box… Noting how she watched his every move as he pulled the salves and powders form the box. "You have done well." He continued equally uncommitted in his voice as he rubbed the salve on her wounds and then patted the powder forming a protective scaling.

Uncertainty flashed for the briefest moment in her eyes as she raised her left eyebrow examining his eyes looking more like she was examining deeper inside his head. "You honor me with your words and the kindness of healing. I was caught doing wrong and worthy of disgrace. I perceive you are not kind out of weakness."

An almost evil sneering smile perched upon his lips, "Your perceptions do not fail you on that count and I did not bring you here for more abuse. You are never to be seen entering or leaving this room do you understand?"

"Yes, my lord."

"In accordance with the rules of order you will wear the collar and chain for five days and your peers are free to abuse you within the parameters defined."

"Yes, my lord."

"You better improve your skill of deception; at peril of life, you may not allow anyone to know the things I tell you from here forward." He looked at her sharply and lifted her chin, so their eyes were locked.

Her chest lifted with pride, "Yes, my lord." She kept her voice subdued.

"You are being initiated into the organization that does not exist, the right hand of the clan. You will receive special training, but you must continue as though none of this is happening. It will require absolute secret movement on your part and the training will be in addition to everything you are normally doing. You will feel the burden before your training is done, but you must absolutely conceal from even your closest and most trusted any indications that you are involved in anything they do not already know about."

The glint of pleasure flared in her eyes, and then slowly turned to garnet as she pulled all of the layers of her emotions under control. "I am honored, my lord."

Later in her cell of solitude, an empty room barely wide enough for her to lay down, she sat staring at the small, barred window in the door. "Give me wisdom and guidance that my path might be true and with honor." Her heart and soul reached out, in every land there are those who seek to serve a good that they hope is greater than the ways by which they were raised.

"I have chosen you." A woman appeared in front of her clothed in flames and shadows of flames. Lyamy had never before seen an Elf, but based on her education and pictures, the woman in front of her might fit the description. "ShadowDancer" the name was in Lyamy's mind and she spoke it out loud.

"You have asked for wisdom and guidance. I am calling upon you to help me in this land. If you will agree to help me, I will help you."

"Goddess ShadowDancer," she stumbled a little over the title and the name, "you are an Ancient, I will serve you unless I find you seek evil against my people. I have heard of Ancients before but was not raised to follow them and they are more myths than realities to my people, but you are real."

"For now, I will grant you two favors that will help you. First, I will double your movement speed, you will be able to move much faster, but you have control over using it. Second, I will grant you the ability to sleep in the moment, you will receive a full night's sleep in the blink of an eye whenever you need it. Go ahead and try it now, with a thought of getting rest, blink."

Lyamy obeyed, with a blink she felt fully rested, she even had the recollections of dreams as if she had slept a full night, "This will help me through these nights of dishonor, and I can see how it will help later too. You honor me with your gifts, but what can I help you with?"

"I help the outcast and those that are not normally socially accepted because they are different. I help the weak and the downtrodden around our world that they might find a place and add to the strength of their land." ShadowDancer pointed to her, "You are strong and mold yourself to the niche in your society, but you are outcast on the inside and wish for something better for your people. Here you are subject to harsh discipline and you do not ask for deliverance, or glory, or greatness you ask for wisdom and guidance. I will do what I can to help you with this." ShadowDancer vanish even as she had appeared.

Chaos ruled the world around them, Jenyin watched Lyamy, her peers treated her harshly as was expected for the five days she wore the collar. There were a few times he was not sure she would live through the abuse and noted that it was her primary competitor that instigated the worst treatment. She survived and in spite of the harshness of the five-day period proved to be a quick study in secret also. There were a couple of her peers Jenyin thought might be deliberately trying to eliminate the competition permanently while she was in dishonor. She would not forget who they were, and he was sure she would not let them forget what they did either.

Working in Lyamy's favor though, the five days gave her justification for small alterations in her personality that might help her conceal her secret promotion and training. One of her peers stepped out of line with her the day after her collar was removed, a broken nose and a foot that might never walk the same again put a quick stop to any further attempts by the rest. She was no longer restricted from retaliation and enduring punishment sharpened her senses and reflexes.

Her training was tricky to orchestrate, since she had to be trained by the best, but they could not know who she was nor could she know who they were. Identities were hidden with veiling wraps and shadowy light, voices masked when conversation was required. Jenyin was enjoying watching her skill get honed and saw great potential. Shadowkyn did not raise their children, the clan did that, but they are known to take special interest in selected apprentices bonding with them in much the same ways as might be expected by other races with their children. Yaun and Jenyin are brothers, like with all siblings they are encouraged to build a bond while they are young. Jenyin caught himself looking at Lyamy with thoughts other than those for an apprentice, but his den partners would never approve, she was way too young and he like the mates he already had.

"You will have to stop toying with your apprentice for a while." Yaun prodded, "I need you to go to our eastern border, because something has been preying on our harvest. We need to eliminate the threat to our food supply."

"By your command my liege." Jenyin, flaunted with a mocking air, doting a deep bow with the flair of his cape. "It will be good to have a change of scenery and mix with the hunters. Perhaps I can remind them that our rule is earned and not inherited."

"The young need field experience. Take three with you. One of them should be Lyamy, we need her to get maximum exposure with minimum recognition." Yaun paused and added, "Stop by the lab Nelk has a few things for you to take with you."

Nelk was a frail and weak creature for a Shadowkyn, but a master at chemistry and making gadgets. He would have expired in childhood if Jenyin had not taken an interest in him seeing potential in his ideas and stood in his defense, now his brain added strength to the clan. Jenyin often wondered how many of the weak that had died in youth would have been able to add strength in a different way had they survived. He pushed the door open to the lab and stepped in, "Hey Nelk."

"My Lord." Nelk replied but kept working.

"I have told you, Nelk, you can call me by my name, especially when it is just us."

"And you know keeping good habits can save your life when you least expect it." Nelk set down what he was working on and walked over to another bench. "I have put together a collection of things you may find useful, and a few I would like you to test."

A terrarium on another counter caught Jenyin's eye, "What are you experimenting with here?" He asked stepping over to the tank.

"That my friend is not an experiment, but a study. I have been observing the behavior of ants and aphids. It is very similar to our relationship with our labor races. The ants reap the harvest and protect the subservient aphids. Like with us, it is a mutually beneficial arrangement. It makes me wonder if they started out this way, or what led to the evolution of change that resulted in the arrangement. It also makes me wonder if our ways will continue to change and if they do where are we going as a race? After all we are as trapped right now in our social order as are the laborers. If one of us tries to leave the order of things we will be eliminated as a threat. We cannot let anyone leave with knowledge of our inner workings for risk of that knowledge being used against us."

"It is a reasonable and logical order for things, why would it change?"

Nelk laughed, "If you observe nature and the world around us that which is not growing and changing is dying. Currently we are growing as we learn ways of improving things in our society, tools and understanding. I have to wonder if we are not also in need to grow and evolve our social order in order to survive as the world changes around us."

"We have an ideal social order, one of harmony with those who share our order." Jenyin avoided questions he had in his own mind about freedoms to make choices, including his inability to choose not to be part of the line to the leadership position. It would be seen as weakness and would be grounds for some to attempt to assassinate him. "We cull the weakness out and it helps us survive."

"Ah, yes, but what we define as weakness, even you questioned at least once, or I would not be here and the strength I have added would have been lost to the clan." Nelk handed him a belt and packs and explained each item as he packed it or handed it to Jenyin. Jenyin put them on his belt and in places he would be able to access each item. "We are not a free society; we are bound by the obligations of order to follow the roles we are given and anyone stepping out of that framework is considered a threat to the security of the clan. If we observe the ant colony there is the occasional rebel, and they are killed. This helps keep their order, but" Nelk pushed a button and a liquid instantly filled the tank dissolving everything living in the tank, "if the colony gets wiped out, none survive. We are in that same place now. We have no seed colonies, sub colonies, or separated groups that operate independent of our main Clan order. We too can be wiped out in a single swipe because of the rules of order that help us survive."

Jenyin suppressed the urge to further explore the subject, "I will be taking three apprentices with me, do you wish them to come by?"

"If you would, send them individually, I will personalize what I equip them with. I'll let you know before you leave."

They had been friends for a long time and had frequently discussed matters that edged on acceptable conversation within the rules of order. Yaun would tell him Nelk is corrupting his thinking and laugh. Jenyin was not unhappy with his part in their world, but he was not happy either and he realized this too. Life just was what it was.

Jenyin sent Lyamy first, Nelk new she was favored young one. He was one of the few trusted to know that kind of information. He would take special care of her, but Nelk had a way of knowing the strengths of people just looking at them and how to customize their gear. The other two, Kye and Myrn he was not as concerned with, they were also apprentices in the clan, but Lyamy drew more significance to his eye and was being elevated in secret to a position of higher significance. Her special training sessions would have to be suspended while they traveled, but she was already reaching levels that would allow her to be sent on missions of her own.

They traveled on foot, they moved just as fast as any beast of burden and the exercise helped keep them fit. They were adjoined to a caravan carrying certain supplies out and scheduled to return with a portion of the harvest. Sleeping arrangements were their own. They had two tents, Jenyin and Lyamy in one and Kye and Myrn in the other. They would also share in the responsibilities of keeping watch and protecting the caravan. They were traveling within the kingdom; there would be no danger on the road there.

"You do not really fit, you are compliant, but your thinking is not aligned with the rules of order." She whispered to him in the dark. Lyamy like him and knew he liked her, but she knew the way his mind was working at some point he would be considered a weakness and a threat to the clan. "It is dangerous even only with the things we have talked about."

"I just cannot stop thinking about what Nelk showed me before we left, our ways do not provide for survival of our kind if we are defeated by one event. We know there are other intelligent races on other continents, and we know that an elemental disaster could also destroy an area the size of that we occupy. Yet we do not allow any break off from our society because it would be a threat to our security."

"And as you have taught me, it would in fact be a potential threat, having the knowledge of our ways exposed. It could result in our ways being exploited against us. My loyalty though is to the clan. I cannot allow myself to let these questions draw my thinking away from what helps us survive now."

They shared half the night before drifting off to sleep. Jenyin did not normally dream, but this night he dreamed. He dreamed of a place he had never been with races he had never met. Lyamy was there and he was happy. The dream slipped into tatters of memories as he woke up to the morning sun. Some of the happiness he felt in the dream survived waking up and he was in a mood exceptionally better than normal.

The journey was not long, their kingdom was not vast, and they arrived at the harvester village. There were acres of cultivated land, the majority of which was harvested and given to the Shadowkyn, but a portion was used for crops that were explicitly for the labor races. There were foods that they did not share a taste for and taking care of the needs of the races that served them made the arrangement beneficial to all.

"So, Captain, fill us in on what has been happening and what you have done about it already." Jenyin looked around the room at the people and everything in it with a very critical eye making Captain Vishi very uncomfortable.

"We have followed all procedures so far. Patrols have been doubled. We have no witnesses to any of it, but something else is harvesting our food supply. Finding random areas completely harvested."

"What about trackers?"

"There have been tracks, but they all seemed to lead to dead ends."

"Did you get a scent?" Lyamy's voice sounded sharp as she interjected.

"There was a scent." The captain's eyes turned on her questioning her authority until he caught Jenyin glaring at him. "The scent trails all vanished just like the tracks on the ground and we did not pick them back up anywhere and we circled out extensively."

"What time do they strike?" Jenyin asked almost distracted now as he started to stand.

"We do not know; the harvesters just randomly discover areas that are already harvested by these interlopers."

Jenyin collected his team with a hand gesture as he stood. "Which of your team will you send with us to show us the last few strike locations that were discovered?"

The captain pointed, "Jenks, help them with anything they ask." The over-sized hunter stepped up."

"I want to see the last three known occurrences." Jenyin gestured vaguely in the direction of the open fields and groves. As they followed Jenks, Jenyin noted that the cultivated areas could very well look like wilderness if he did not already know the plants upon which he was looking.

The fruit trees grew at random; no pattern and the ground crops were cultivated around the trees in clumps or groupings depending upon the specific crop, but it all had a natural wild look to it. Wildlife skittered around and birds flitted across the trees and shrubbery some of which were also used as a food source.

Jenks stopped and pointed. "This area was discovered yesterday afternoon."

They examined the ground. There were footprints of various sizes, but the same basic type, "humanoid" with claws, some looked to be partially clothed an indicator of potential intelligence. The scent in the area was vegetarian and the plants were clumsily trampled, no attempt to conceal foraging the area. Fruit was gone from the trees and some branches were broken. The harvesting went pretty high indicating they must have climbed the trees. The swath of foraging was about twenty feet wide and traveled about forty-five feet. Tracks went for about another five to ten feet then vanished.

"The last steps on each trail are not as deep as the previous ones." Lyamy noted as she tracked another trail of footsteps.

The second and third area they looked at pretty much fit the exact same profile. "We need to find and eliminate this threat to our food supply." Jenks stated with resolute commitment.

"That decision was made months ago," Jenyin barked, "and yet here we are with not one witness that can tell us who or what we are looking for." He watched a bird walking around on the ground foraging for bugs and food.

Lyamy followed Jenyin's eyes and watched the bird as it took a few steps and lifted off the ground in flight. "They fly." She whispered.

That night they camped in the fields. Jenyin ordered no fires, no cooking and no meat. He had everyone gather a few fruits and vegetables and pulverize them in pots of water then wash everything with the resulting water to cover and remove their scent from the air. Everyone was posted facing different directions in pairs. He was facing East and Lyamy was his partner on watch. "They are probably unaware of the fact they are stealing and just foraging for a meal."

"But that makes them a threat." Lyamy replied in a flat unemotional tone.

"If we befriended them instead of killing them, they could prove a valuable asset being able to scout from the air." Jenyin did not realize he had a dreamy look in his eyes as he looked at the horizon, "Imagine having the freedom to explore the world."

"You will get yourself killed one day for talking in so many ways against the code of honor and rules of order that keeps us a stable civilization. I like you and do not wish to see that day." Her tone did not betray her feelings.

He looked at Lyamy, he like her too, a lot, but for the first time saw she like him in the same way. "You are right, you already know enough about me to justify according to the code such actions yourself. I do not fear death, I do fear living a full life and never walking past the horizon, or never seeing beyond what we are."

"You plant seeds and dreams in my head that I like but should not have and could get me killed to if I dwell on them." Movement caught her eyes, "Look, over there."

The sky looked slightly clouded, but as he focused the cloud moved towards the ground and separated into individual forms before they landed in a distant area of the farmlands. "Quickly gather the others and we will head that way. I will go now and scout ahead."

They moved as predators, silent and quick, stalking their prey. The closer they got the more they could see of the creatures. The creatures walked upright and seemed to be gathering the harvest into containers hung from their waist. Definitely some intelligence Jenyin concluded. The wings were like batwings and they moved quickly about their business. They closed in.

Lyamy was well trained and dropped one in silence without alerting the rest, her speed and accuracy exceeded complimenting her training. She would serve the secret guard well and prove excellent protection for his brother and the clan. There was a rush and seven more of the thirty plus intruders were dead before they flocked to the air. An aura deflected the shots from the archers, so the Hunters failed to take down any more.

They pursued after them on the ground, following the flock past the edge of the harvest lands and only stopping when they reached a precipice a thirty foot drop over a rocky strewn canyon. The flock swung around and flew back facing them, out of reach, but within archer range. The hunters loaded special magic arrows, but Jenyin raised a hand and waved down the bows. "We need to find their nesting grounds and we cannot do that if we kill them."

"You still favor trying to make friends over killing an enemy?" Lyamy addressed him so that others could hear.

He was slightly stunned at her boldness and sudden disclosure of his confidence, "I may, but that is a decision I am privileged to make." He eyed her with uncertainty.

She lunged him and buried her dagger in his chest, "You are weak and your very weakness threatens the safety of the clan." She pushed him backwards over the edge of the precipice. She turned and faced the others. "I am in charge of this mission now. I was sent to protect the clan and knew this assassination may fall on my shoulders. Jenks Your captain will post a security perimeter along the cliffs and around the harvest lands to watch the skies."

"Yes ma'am."

"Kye and Myrn you will lead scout parties to follow these bird-brains and find their nesting grounds so that we can launch an attack when we are ready. They have the advantage on us here if we attack, so defend this line and let them depart." She Held up her dagger dripping with Jenyin's blood, "The disease of weakness has been cut from our clan in accordance with the rules of order." She licked his blood from her dagger in front of witnesses before cleaning it. She claimed his death, but now had a secret she could tell no one, not even Yaun.

*   *   *   *   *

Jenyin instinctively came down on his feet and rolled, but he lay still in the rocky debris from the cliff side when he stopped. '*She did the honorable and right thing killing me.*' he thought, but he was not dead. The bleeding stopped without even applying pressure. How could he live, she was too good and would not have missed? He did not know how long he lay there when he realized she did not miss; she deliberately did no real harm to him. She knew the exact angle to plunge her blade and not cut anything yet still make it look like she has killed him. She had spared his life and held onto the front of upholding the code.

Something sniffed and breathed on his neck, then grabbed the shoulder of his Leather armor and began to drag him away from the cliff. He measured the size and strength of the creature and was confident he could overtake it once they were out of sight of the cliff, just in case anyone was watching, he did not want to get her in trouble for sparing him and delivering him to a freedom he was always curious about. About forty yards into the half jungle half forest, he started to roll towards the cat when it just let go. He looked up as the cat casually strolled away from him.

"Arise Jenyin, Lyamy has asked favor for you." ShadowDancer was an Elf Ancient. He had never seen an Ancient before and had been sure they were just old superstitions, but now one stood in front of him. He got to his feet.

"Lyamy?" he shook his head, "Forgive my manners, goddess ShadowDancer." He bowed his head slightly showing her respect and taking the opportunity to gather his thoughts. Why was the title goddess in his head, he knew she gave him her name, but was not sure what goddess meant? "Lyamy asked you?"

"She is a chosen of mine and chose to serve me." With a gesture two chairs appeared and a bubble around them that cut out the distracting sounds of the forest. "Sit for a moment and we can talk."

"The Ancients have had nothing to do with us for generations, why would you choose to appear now?" He asked as he sat in the chair she had offered.

She laughed, "There was a war among the Ancients, and some are gone never to return. Some have never left, but use a lighter hand guiding the peoples of the world instead of ruling them. Some like me are new and our destiny is yet to be discovered." She paused and drew his full focus to her, the way he would with a novice, "You are chosen, if you accept, because you are a dreamer and do not fit in the hard cut edges of your people's limits. You know change is inevitable and are willing to embrace it."

"What good will it do, if I am no longer a part of my people, this may serve me, but how will it serve them?"

"It will do good. For now trust me. Will you accept being chosen?" She waited for his answer.

He pondered her request and finally answered, "I accept with reservation. I shall not be used as a vessel against my people." Just then Kye and a hunting party ran past them just outside the bubble and did not slow or seem to notice them sitting there.

"The bubble" she whispered, "they cannot see through the bubble. We are cloaked. You are not dead and talking to me in the afterlife." She laughed.

She knew his thoughts, or his subconscious actions may have told her what he was thinking. "What are your instructions for me now?

"You will find a cave two days, West of the ocean. Go there and begin setting up a sanctuary for those who will need help. Remember you are my chosen and I help those in need, I expect the same from you." She stood up, "The land will serve you most of what you need to help others, your inner strength will do the rest."

Jenyin watched her vanish before his eyes. He lost a few moments contemplating the things she had said and then looked around. He was outside the borders of his homeland. He was an outcast and could not go back, as far as they knew he was dead. The hunting party would return past here again either once they find what they are looking for, or after a day out to regroup and report back what they find or don't find. He knew it was not him they were looking for; they were not tracking anything on the ground. He assumed they were seeking the nesting grounds of the winged people.

Either way he wanted to take a quick inventory of what he had. He was fully equipped for the mission that they were on, he had full camping gear in his backpack and all the toys Nelk had provided. Nothing had gotten broken in the fall; he was thankful for that. He could not be better geared for battle or for survival. It was time to move, and he had to move quickly with as little trail as possible. He had to conceal where he was going, as best he could. Being a tracker himself, he knew what they looked for.

Since his objective was west of the ocean to the north, he headed north first then backtracked to a point where he could leave the ground and travel through the trees at an angle north west. He was fortunate to find a river and road the currents south west a distance that would have taken at least half a day to travel on foot before getting out on the western bank. The area where he chose to leave the water was a landscape of shelf rock, he could easily climb the layers as they moved back from the water.

The rock ended abruptly at the edge of a heavy canopied forest. He felt some relief stepping out of the heat of the sun into the cool damp air of the forest. It was easy traveling on the padded forest bed without leaving a trail and he was headed straight west now. Evening was approaching so he found a good spot where he could use a recently fallen branch for concealment to camp for the night.

As he sat chewing rations from his pack, he was getting familiar with and identifying the smells in the forest. A particular scent caught his attention. It was not a strong smell and it seemed to waft in, then disappear with the next breeze. He recognized it from their recent hunt. It was the winged people they drove from the harvesting fields. The forest made it hard to get a direction any breeze could wrap this way and that around a tree and alter the direction it came from. The scents also seem to come randomly from different directions.

The forest floor was matted moss, roots and dead fall from leaves and bark decomposing in a rich soil giving it a spongy surface that absorbed sounds and footsteps and left no mark of anything passing through. There were the random sounds of small animals scurrying up the bark of a tree or across a branch. A bird took wing somewhere not far away. The sounds were dampened and there was no echo. There were no signs of civilized life as far as his eyes could detect in any direction. He could see quite a distance through the pillars that supported the great canopy. Darkness fell and he slept with his ears and mind on alert.

The night passed without incident and he had no idea what time it was when he woke up, but there was enough light for him to look around. He noticed some edible herbs and berries that he did not recall seeing the night before. It saved him rations so he foraged breakfast. He finished eating and shouldered his pack when the hair on the back of his neck stood up and his hand instinctively found the hilt of his sword. A quick look around and he saw nothing, but a small gust of air and his search snapped upwards.

He was outnumbered and was glad he had not actually drawn his sword. He pulled his hands into plain sight open palms towards the winged people. He counted five of them, but they had the advantage on him and numbers. "I mean you no harm." He stated in a calm voice.

One of them landed in front of him and spoke. The language was thick, and he was not certain he understood what the stranger said, "ou er asted oun hor our hake" It felt like the first letters of their words were missing, being whistled and soft, but he interpreted as "You were caste down for our sake."

"I would be your friend." The others landed around him.

He did his best to interpret the difference in their way of speaking as they spoke, "Why were we being attacked?"

"For stealing food from our harvest lands." He thought from their movement they were surprised.

"We will go apologize; did not know we were stealing."

"No!" he spoke a little sharper than he intended and the strangers stepped back. "They will kill you. You have been considered a threat and threats are to be destroyed."

"You warn us of your own people?" asked the one who seemed to be the leader.

"You have not killed me, so your intent is not to do harm and you would apologize; that is not the way of a threat." He looked at them all with a glance, "With caution there may be hope that a future friendship can happen. For now, they, or we have you marked as a threat which means it is not safe. Threats are to be eliminated."

"You do not see us that way."

"I have been left for dead because I did not see you that way. I was marked as a weak link in our defense because I did not see you that way." He shook his head, "I am no longer a part of my people. It will never be safe for me to return." He still struggled a little with their way of speaking, but was getting more used to it, as he assumed, they were with his.

"I am Zamu." The leader stated, "Where are you going and what is your intent?"

"I now serve an Ancient and do her bidding. I am going to the coast to build a sanctuary. Zamu, I am called Jenyin."

Zamu looked at his fellows, "I see no harm in letting him pass. He has seen nothing and knows nothing that would be compromising we have no further cause to detain him from his journey." Looking back at Jenyin, "Be careful, there are many creatures in these forests and not all are of a gentle temperament."

They lifted from the ground in near silence and vanished behind the pillars of the forest. Jenyin felt justified in thinking that they would make good allies, but he was no longer in a position to make that decision. As far as the clan was concerned, he was dead and if he did not stay that way he really would be dead. If they thought, he was alive they would send out hunting parties after him. He traveled through the rest of the forest without incident.

Yaun heard Lyamy's report, and the others confirmed what happened and the words entitling the assassination. He knew too much himself about the way his brother thought. What bothered him, was Jenyin had trusted Lyamy and his judgment of people's character had been without flaw, until maybe now. Yaun ruled out trickery, they had seen his brother's corpse dragged away by a wild cat and the dagger had been buried to the hilt in his chest and the blood kept on the wipe as testimony of his death upon their return. There was no mistaking her victory fever when she licked his blood from her blade in the ritual of passing. Her eyes glowed red and the scrying showed the dagger pulling from his chest as she pushed him over the edge.

Yaun had one worry, who to fill the position as his right hand. Jenyin had not yet selected anyone, and he needed someone to immediately fill the position. Other high families would see it as an opportunity to advance, so it could not be from the families. Yaun decided to fill the position with Lyamy, at least until he found someone else, he could trust. She was true to the code, even if she was still lacking in some training. He did not want to pull the head of the order that does not exist out, he was still too valuable there, as were his other commanders.

"Lord Yaun." Lyamy dropped to one knee but did not lower her eyes.

"You have slain my brother."

"In accordance with the code!" her declaration was without any defensive posture.

"Regardless this leaves me with a vacancy." he maintained cold detachment, "He defended my back. Have you learned enough to take that responsibility?"

The line this was taking took her by surprise, but she had learned well to hold her hard lined focus. "His weakness was exposed, if weakness can serve your needs then strength should serve that much better."

"Our Code of Honor is a guideline, that has helped us survive as a people. You did right by the code and our people, but he is dead. Do not be overzealous, I would also be within the code killing you for no other reason than you killed my brother. I have chosen to elevate you to a position where you serve me, the code and our people, until I find someone to permanently fill the position or until I decide you are that person. Do not tempt me in this matter again or you may find your pride is your weakness."

"By your instruction, I shall serve according as you have chosen." She stood, "As your right hand and protector, I can no longer kneel in your presence."

"You commit yourself to my service, in accepting this position."

"I serve in honor." She knew what was required and bare her back facing away from him.

"Then I mark you with the rank of your new position." He etched a symbol in the air and the branding burned into her back the symbol of her position.

Lyamy wanted to scream but clenched against the pain. She blinked her eyes and used the rest that ShadowDancer had given her, as if eight hours of healing had passed with the rest. She pulled her garments back on concealing her back and blinked again. The pain was bearable she turned and faced Yaun, holding out her right hand to receive the ring that provided her the seal of authority. "For honor and the good of our people I serve." Her senses were sharpened by the pain, as she looked around the room, she spotted three listening devices, "You test me? No one would so soon plant the same listening device as I planted. There are two other devices different in nature also." She whispered in a message only for his ear that the devices would not pick up just in case they were real.

Yaun motioned for her to crush them all and look for any others. When she had crushed all three and indicated she saw no others, Yaun answered. "I indeed planted two the one in the windows like you planted and the one on the door hinge to test you. The third in the bookshelf, I do not know the source, nor how long it has been there."

"It has not been long, the disturbance of the dust seems fresh, and the adhesive has not had time to dry. It has been no more than six hours, by the tackiness I would say less than four. This was crafted by Nelk, it has his mark on the edge here, perhaps he might be able to identify to whom he provided this one."

"They are only provided to the order that does not exist. I will take care of this one." Yaun took the tiny device or the broken remains and set it on his desk. "If I decide to make you permanent, you will be introduced to the leader of the order and several other contacts that you currently do not know."

Her back throbbed and she thought, '*This is not permanent?*' but responded, "As you wish Lord Yaun. You know the protection I can provide is limited by what you keep secret from me."

"I need you at your full capacity, so go and recover from your branding."

"If I am to leave your presence, I am setting an alarm spell to alert me should anything threaten your wellbeing in my absence. The guards posted are also trustworthy. I will be back in the morning." she cast an improved alarm spell that she had learned by combining a few tricks she had been taught with the spell after all protection and shielding spells do not block friendly encroachments or they would block additional protection spell or handing someone a weapon or even deflect the fork when they tried to eat... She had combined the subtle under flows of magical current to make her improved alarm spell. The spell was centered on Yaun and would alert her if anything threatening to him entered within forty feet.

Lyamy, satisfied that Yaun should be still under her protection in her absence turned and left the room. She did not need rest, but Yaun did not know this. As she walked through the apprentice training yards where she would have been returned to, she made sure they all got to see the ring and noted their responses. Her primary competitors showed fear for but a moment in their eyes. Lyamy laughed inside, she would not punish them for how they treated her, she would use their fear and weakness to her advantage. She no longer had to hide where she went, but some things were still best kept at a low profile. She slipped into the administration door but vanished to all eyes before turning down the hidden hall and eventually to Nelk's laboratories.

"Hello Nelk." she said before appearing.

He flinched defensively for an instant before recognizing her voice and a moment of uncertainty passed through his eyes before he responded. "You still have much to learn. You killed Jenyin, who protected me, how can I trust you?"

"Don't be silly, you may have been weak once, but you are a strength to our people with what you do. You do not need to take sides in any political shifting because everyone wants what you can do. I had to speak to you before you found out on you own and this has been my first opportunity. You created all those devices that Jenyin carries can anyone else trace or follow him or those devices?"

"Only a couple and only if they know to look. You are a cunning one. Yaun could trace Jenyin by the mark on his back, the head of the order that does not exist has the means to trace some of the devices, but only if he knows which he is looking for and of course I can trace my own work." He paused, "Of course that makes me a potential threat to what you are doing."

Lyamy walked over and placed her hand on the now dead terrarium, "Not exactly my plan." she whispered, pulling her eyes from the glass and back to Nelk, "The plan you and Jenyin never quite made. We are going to ensure the survival of our race and make a place for ourselves in the rest of the world while we are at it."

"I am in." Nelk stated "What can I do to help"

"I have a list." Lyamy pulled down her top turning her back to him, "First when the time is right, I need to remove Yaun's ability to track me and his brother." She pulled her top back on and fastened it back up. "In time I will need to learn how to stop the leader of the order that does not exist from being able to track and follow also. For now, I need devices that will help protect Yaun to justify my coming here. In the future it may not be questioned, but for now I need to justify my every move. Now I must go to my room to recover from the branding."

"Was that today?" Nelk looked surprised, "I guess it would have had to have been. How did it get healed so quickly?"

"Some secrets I must keep to myself for now." She smiled a warm smile at Nelk, so uncharacteristic of their race he was uncertain how to take it, "Hopefully before we are done, I will be able to show you. Now what do you have for me?"

"Well, this he can wear on his belt and if he pats it firmly, he will be encased in a defensive bubble for about 7 minutes but participating in combat will reduce the duration."

"Can you capture a spell? I have improved an alarm spell and perhaps if we can combine it with a device like this, we can have it activate the device if a threat comes within 25 feet?"

"That is an excellent idea." Nelk stood a wand in a hole that appeared to be for that purpose on his bench, "Cast three times on this wand, so I can use the spell to work on such a device. If I need you to cast more, I will let you know."

"I must go to my room now, before we arouse too much suspicion." Lyamy exited with the device in her hand, heading directly for her room.

She paused at the door to her room, someone was in there. Lyamy drew her dagger and pushed the door open with her foot as she moved back. Nothing triggered as the door opened, there was no magical residue in the doorway. Lyamy could smell Freyie was in the room and while she was hidden. Lyamy threw her dagger, low enough it should strike a leg and pull her number one adversary as an apprentice out of hiding. When the other girl appeared, she had not been standing as expected and the dagger was buried an inch short of the hilt just below her left shoulder. The death of her adversary having broken into her room would be commended by the clan and without help that would kill her, she would bleed out inside. As she turned Freyie's face she watched her eyes go blank and a trickle of blood started from the corner of her mouth.

'*ShadowDancer*!' She called out in her mind, Freyie would be more use to her alive. She wanted her people to survive, not die at her hand.

ShadowDancer appeared, knelt by Freyie and pulled the dagger out, healing the wound to a scar. "Why do you wish your enemy to live?"

"She is one of my people and she has strength that will help them survive, if I have truly seen hope for the future of my people, they are all important even if they do not like me. She also came to my room and was not prepared to kill me, no weapons, just waiting for me to return."

"The poison in your cup came from her wristband."

"Perhaps, but she also knows I learned to clean my cup before I use it. Without some token form of an attempt on my life she would have been displaying weakness coming to me for anything. The poison is only there to justify her presence. She expected me to find her and attempt to kill her, so she squatted to avoid my attempt. I almost killed her trying to wound instead."

"I will give you a healing touch. This will enable you to heal wounds a little at a time."

"I am going to need further training to make up for what I am missing having been pulled out of the apprentice ranks early."

"I will get you training beyond what you would have learned." with a subtle gesture, the room shimmered "I will get you trained in captured moments from master instructors."

Lyamy looked at Freyie the drop of blood falling from her lip was suspended in the air, time in the world around them had stopped. "You stopped time?"

"Not exactly. Time is moving normal around us; we are just captured in a moment of time." ShadowDancer brought her to an empty square room with no doors or windows and introduced her to Zift. The creature had leather like skin, and a blue metallic looking head and exoskeleton around its hips. Its eyes appeared to be made of crystals and there were three of them. He trained her in Eftite combat for what seemed like a relentless week. Then they were back in her room, Freyie still unconscious in the corner. "I will meet you each night and you will get different training. For now, I will go and you can take care of Freyie, she is not completely saved yet, but you can do the rest."

Lyamy picked up her cup and dumped the powder on a piece of paper before cleaning the cup. She laid Freyie on her bed, with her torso over the edge to help drain the blood from her lung. Lyamy caught the blood in her cup, moved the cup to her stand and laid her hands on Freyie feeling the healing energy as it passed. Freyie gasped for air and coughed, Lyamy helped her up to a seated position. "Freyie, you live because I chose for you to live! You did not come here to kill me so tell me why you are here!" Lyamy was harsh, but now she had to be.

Freyie was still hazy, it took a few moments for the words to reach her brain. She coughed again and sprayed blood all over her hands, clothing and Lyamy. Mind not working right yet, she tried to wipe the blood off Lyamy's pants, "Sorry, I ..." She almost collapsed and Lyamy caught her. She looked up into Lyamy's face and fear filled her as she started to remember, still not in control enough to hide her thoughts. "You, you are too good to beat, so I," She coughed again, less blood this time and not as hard "wanted to secretly commit to you. Smart to choose loyalties early."

Lyamy grabbed her shoulder and pushed more healing energy into her rival, "You were dead, and I have brought you back." Freyie shuddered as her mind cleared and she understood what she was being told. She watched as Lyamy took the cup with her blood and held it in front of her, "This is the blood of your death. Your boldness is strong, your mind is strong, and your cunning is strong, I claim these in your death." Lyamy drank the blood. Freyie felt the essence pass from her and knew she was now bonded to Lyamy. She placed a hand on Freyie's shoulder again and pushed more healing to her. "Even as I have slain you in just battle, I have brought you back and claim you in life, bound in loyalty to me over all else as the mother of your rebirth." Lyamy pricked her little finger on her right hand and made Freyie drink. Freyie felt herself yet again bonded to Lyamy in ways that could never be broken.

Lyamy's eyes were filled with fire from drinking her blood when she looked in them. She was her master now, by an old magic of their people which they were taught had been lost. If Lyamy was hurt she would feel the pain, if Lyamy died from anything other than a natural death she would pass with her. Her loyalties were bound to Lyamy above and beyond any loyalties to anyone else including clan or code. "I am yours." Freyie whispered. A tear formed in the corner of her eye.

Lyamy liked the feeling of power she gained from the ritual but suppressed her feelings. She did not do this for power, and she did not want to hurt Freyie, she needed someone on the inside with absolute loyalty. Freyie simply gave her a convenient opportunity. "You are to maintain the air of being my rival. You will maintain that you came here to kill me, but I caught you and gave you seven lashes, which I will have to give you. Then I sent you on your way. Do you understand?"

"I do, my master."

"You will call me as you have always called me, only you and I know our bond." Lyamy stood up, "Oh, and I accept."

"You accept?" Freyie looked confused.

"I accept your willing loyalty."

"Oh. That is why I came." She opened the back of her garments turning her back to Lyamy to receive her lashes.

"You need a little more strength first." Lyamy placed her hand on Freyie's shoulder healing her a little more. Then pulled the short whip from her belt, breaking open seven bleeding welts, "Now go, I will let you know when I need any specific services. We will talk again in secret; I would know your will also that you may find some gladness in being mine."

When Freyie was gone Lyamy cleaned up the rest of the blood and looked in her polished silver mirror. Her eyes still glowed red from drinking the blood of a worthy kill. At the ritual of death, she had claimed wisdom and strength from the blood of Jenyin, but he was not dead or even near death so any bond that formed would be minimal perhaps even not felt. It made an impressive show though, the look in his face conceding to death as he fell and watched the dagger pull out of his chest. She gave him a new life and she was confident she did the right thing. She would have to face his den sometime tomorrow. In her mind she would be sorting out which of them should follow him to his new life. By right she could claim three of them and cast them down in death at the same place she had slain Jenyin. They had to have conspired in his weakness to corrupt the ways of the clan.

"Hello, Lyamy."

She saw the reflection of ShadowDancer appear in the mirror interrupting her thoughts and quickly subdued her initial instincts. "Hello, goddess ShadowDancer. How would you have me properly address you?"

"You can call me ShadowDancer, goddess, goddess ShadowDancer or Ancient ShadowDancer, although I would prefer you don't call me Ancient, I don't really feel that old." She laughed. "I am not too picky."

"I will call you ShadowDancer, I am not comfortable with the title goddess, it does not have clarity to me."

"You don't think you overplayed your hand with Freyie, do you?"

"I should have wanted her dead and some will see it as weakness that she left my room alive. It does not make sense to me that our race will get stronger by killing off the competition. I have watched the wolves in the wild, they fight and the strongest leads the pack, but they do not kill each other off after the fight and rarely in the fight. I understand killing enemies of the clan, but personal enemies within the clan will still fight for the good of the clan against real enemies."

"Indeed. Jenyin must have really liked you to teach you the forbidden magics. No more than one or two of any generation are allowed to know those skills as instructed by the Ancient Darvel."

"Who abandoned us years ago. I don't think he finished teaching me yet. I am sure I have not unlocked half the secrets."

"But you are the first to use those rituals in hundreds of years. They have been preserved for a reason though. I also perceive you care enough to make her not regret being alive." ShadowDancer sat in a chair in her room that appeared as she sat. "You are not going to stay with the clan, I will teach you the rest of craft if you will honor your clan and teach it to one that will keep the secrets and knowledge for the future of the clan. I also perceive that in the future the main clan may also split into two camps in the interest of preserving the clan ways. Your future is not bound to that."

"How can you teach me, do you even know the rituals and ways of the old magics?"

"I don't have to." ShadowDancer stood up and placed her hand on the side of Lyamy's head. "There it is done. You have all the knowledge and warnings. You know the written and gesture languages. You know all the rituals, even those lost over time. You know the fiery rage in the heart of your people that gave them the ability to survive in the savage world of the beast continent. The most important thing you now know is the sources of the code your people follow and why it was written. The old magics are a regression to the savage beasts you came from."

"And you still see good in us." her mind was reeling with the knowledge she gained and how vicious and savage her people used to be. "Maybe some of these rituals were better forgotten or lost on purpose? Like the ritual to take on the form of an enemy by eating their heart while they were still alive?”

“You should not forget where your people came from. Knowing that you can see better where they have grown and become more civilized.” ShadowDancer paused, “There was a book to preserve the old magic of your people should the knowledge passed on be incomplete. The keeper of the secrets buried it a couple hundred years ago. Here is a copy.” ShadowDancer held out her hand and three copies of a very old-style book appeared in her hand. “One you will take with you, the other you will teach your chosen enough that they can learn from the book and you will leave the book with them to learn what more they chose on their own.”

“I could teach Freyie.”

“She will be leaving with you; you need someone who will remain behind.”

“Merkyet, she is the next best among the apprentices after Freyie, or perhaps the leader of the order that does not exist when I find out who that is.”

“You will know when you have chosen, in the meantime keep the books hidden. There is one of the old magic spells to create a hidden pocket that will always be with you. You may find the pocket useful for other things also.”

“I was wondering how you expected me to hide anything in this room. I will have to get familiar with what I now know.”

“Well, I have other things to attend to. You know how to call me.” ShadowDancer gave a warm smile before vanishing, taking the chair she had created with her.

*   *   *   *   *

Yaun looked out his window. He would miss his brother; it would take time for him to feel the same confidence in another protecting his back. Lyamy did it by the book though even as his brother had taught her. Perhaps she would help him sort out his enemies. His brother and Nelk were correct, having only one center of civilization even though it was spread out into several cities and towns was a threat to their survival as a race should a natural disaster or an assault from an unknown power greater than them occur. If he were to divide the clan sending his enemies to the other side of the continent with supplies and harvesters to start a new settlement, of course still subject to the one clan it would solve two problems. It would ensure survival of the clan if a disaster event happened to one side the other would survive and it would put distance between him and his enemies, protecting them from each other.

He would need to send out special teams to explore the other side of the island. To verify his maps or update them. Yaun rolled the maps off his desk and slid them back into the hidden compartment in the back of the bookshelf moving the books to add to the concealment.

"Ambitious plans." the voice startled him, and he turned around prepared to fight. The doors had not opened he would have heard them, they squeaked on purpose no matter how much care is given to opening them and the windows were the same way.

"Who are you and how did you enter my chambers?" He exercised his long-conditioned composure, showing a hardened exterior concealing his thoughts. He saw what he would guess from lure to be an Elf floating above the floor engulfed in flames and shadows.

"You question the entrance of an Ancient?"

"A bold claim. I have no record of an Ancient by your description."

"You challenge me for proof?" She captured the moment; he would not know except for the sensation of rippling. She brought him up above the land. From the air the clan lands looked small, almost insignificant. A bubble formed around them as they flew high enough to see the entire continent. "Your entire race is barely a spot on one continent in a world with many continents. It is wise to split your people and encourage growth."

They moved down to the opposite coast of the continent. "This could be no more than a dream as I sit at my desk."

She swept them through a river valley that opened to wide plains before dumping into the ocean. "This will be a perfect place for expansion and peaceful growth." she picked a large white flower and handed it to him, "By this you will know it was not a dream." She brought him back to his office and left him standing there holding the flower as she vanished.

Yaun set the flower in his water glass and sat down. They were insignificant in size for all their years the clan was small, no more than a spec. If they were to survive, they needed to grow. Even if this was a dream and the flower was gone in the morning, it was a vision that required thought and attention. There must be a way to expand that works within the code, after all survival of the race is the first order of importance.

*   *   *   *   *

As Jenyin walked out the canopy of the forest began opening up and the sun warmed the land. He reached an open area on the ridge and could look down at the river to the south. The rocks and steep embankments were too much to climb down or up, but the ridge did appear to be sloping downward. Looking down the valley he could see the ocean in the distance. His instructions were to go to the end of the ridge.

The number of trees got less as he continued east down the gradual slope of the ridge. There was an increase in low shrubbery and flowers. Birds, butterflies and bees flitted about. The panorama would have been intoxicating for most sentient races, but he was part of a hard lined survival race and while he saw the view, he did not take the time to truly enjoy what he was seeing.

He stopped when he reached the end of the ridge. He had traveled day and night until he reached this goal. He was surprised he had not encountered any of the vicious beasts of the land, almost as if the way had been cleared for him. He had a choice now go north along the precipice or find a way down. He had been promised caves at the end of the ridge, they would be somewhere below him now. The rocky face was almost straight down, but the fall was not as great as the one he had been pushed to his supposed death. About a hundred yards north the ground dipped another ten feet making it less than a twenty-foot drop and he could jump that. He ran to the lower terrain and found that the edge was also water washed causing some collapsing and a slope of fallen stone. He descended about halfway climbing down the rock, avoiding a nest of venomous snakes and killing one straggler saving it for a meal later. He jumped the remainder of the distance with no difficulty he could have jumped the entire distance back up if he wanted to, but the climb gave him an understanding of the accessibility for other creatures to wander down.

Jenyin followed back south along the wall of stone noting a few openings in the stone that could be entrances to caves of possible use. When he reached the corner of the stone with one direction going north up the coast and the other going west up the river basin there was an opening about ten feet wide and fifteen feet high. It appeared to be naturally formed, but structurally sound. He sniffed the air, the scent of a predator was not that old in the cave, perhaps a few days to a week. "She did not say I would not have to fight for the cave." He whispered out loud. The tracks inside the entrance were familiar, they had wide rear paws and powerful hind quarters giving them stability and the ability to jump a substantial distance their front legs were also powerful, they could use them to shred their prey or dig rapidly through the ground and the tail was long and spiked in every direction at the end. They were called leophardeg and were part of the wild cats in the region. They were the worst threat the clan faced on their western border. He would not be able to take this creature in a fight face to face, he would have to count on his cunning and intelligence to outmaneuver the beast.

As he stepped into the cavern there were bones and debris that would have to be cleaned away. The tunnel entrance went back at least sixty yards before it turned enough, he could not see further and there was the suggestion of side chambers along the way. As he started to evaluate the entrance for laying alert lines and trap devices to prepare for the creatures return, he picked up another familiar scent coming from outside the entrance and turned to see ShadowDancer standing there facing out towards the ocean.

"I should probably fix that," she said without turning, "I should not let you smell me coming, should I?"

"It is not unpleasant, more like the smell of flowers on a warm day."

"You need not lay traps, the Leophardeg cleaned out the previous inhabitants of the cave when it arrived, then several days back lost footing on the ridge about a half day west and landed wrong. While recent the cave has been abandoned."

Jenyin walked up to where ShadowDancer was standing, "The savage beasts do not normally spend time in open areas where they cannot find concealment." He wondered if she had something to do with the creature coming out this far.

"And it may be another hundred years before another comes near this coast." ShadowDancer turned to face him, "The caves and caverns are quite extensive, will they suffice to building a shelter for the outcast that may come seeking help."

"I suspect you do not mean just Shadowkyn?"

"You would be correct. While I may care for and help Darval's people in his absence or until he chooses his course of action, those who follow me are scattered and free, frequently the outcast and misfits of the societies they came from."

"It will not be easy to go against the code of my people and give safety to weakness."

"Weakness? Do you call Nelk a weakness? Are you a weakness, being all ready to fight a leophardeg alone? Is it really a weakness to be different from others, or to be a half breed, a cross between races? If it were not for changes over time your race would not have survived, does that make change a weakness?"

Jenyin felt the edge in her voice. "No, the clan has gained much strength from Nelk through the many things he has done, and I have seen where the strength of the clan can be the weakness also. The same code that has seen to our survival has also kept us from growing to what we should be. While we promote the strongest and most cunning, within the code we kill each other off with competing for power among the strongest. The weaker members propagate and survive by not being a threat to those vying for power. And yes, half breeds are considered an abomination a contamination of our race with a weaker race. If you pollute the race, over time the race will be no more."

"But maybe it is the strength gained from cross breeding that will in the end result in survival. Do you know if the breeding of a Shadowkyn with a gnome, a physically small and weak race would result in Shadowkyn with the minds to develop machines and equipment even greater then what Nelk can do? But with the condemnation of the cross breeding, you will never know what might have been gained." he knew she was reproving him, but listened to her every word, "If your clan with all of its great strength went to war with a village of gnomes and you destroyed three of their machines in battle to every Shadowkyn that died would you be winning the war and proving you are stronger while no gnomes die and they keep producing more machines for you to fight? Or would you lose without a single gnome ever getting in harm's way? And in the end who then is really stronger?"

"I will have to think on your words. I protected Nelk and his value proved me right later. I believe we need to mix with the world if we are going to survive as a race, as long as we are a single target, we are easy to eliminate. The code does not cover that weakness. Me alone out here or even if my den was with me, we would still be weak against an attack by a pack of beast without the protection of the clan. What I do would be considered insane."

"Change is inevitable." ShadowDancer laughed, "You are a key to the future of your people. Build this sanctuary and learn from those you give shelter and protection." ShadowDancer faded and Jenyin found himself alone again.

He was tired not having slept for days he set an alarm at the entrance to alert him if anything came through the opening. Jenyin headed deeper into the cave to find a place to sleep. There were open areas on either side as the main tunnel of the cave. He went deeper he chose the third one to find rest. There was a shelf in the wall that would suffice as a bed for the night. He would start cleaning and working on making the place a shelter in the morning.

*   *   *   *   *

Lyamy was prepared to face the den of Jenyin, Yaun was seated behind her. Seven Shadowkyn women were escorted in and seated across from her. They would speak first and lay charges at her feet for what they had lost. They sat in order from oldest to youngest Daret, Rymnay, Karis, Chelic, Kynin, Meltose and Treska.

Daret began, "Jenyin was the strongest in our clan after our leader Yaun. You have weakened the clan taking him away, presuming his thoughts to be weakness when he only sought the good of the clan. As my protector there is none you can replace him with. I will not forgive you or accept what you have done as right." Her words were strong, Lyamy knew she would be an open enemy as long as they were in the clan.

Rymnay was next, "Jenyin taught me order and the code stood above all things. You have taken from me a mate and a house. I accept what you have done for the good of the clan." Lyamy knew she must have known the way Jenyin thought, but would not stand up for him, Rymnay may have been opposed to his thinking or may just be afraid now of being outcast.

Karis had hatred in her eyes when she looked at Lyamy, "It does not matter what I have lost, it has already been decided this was for the good of the clan. I can weep or accept fate, so I accept fate." Lyamy saw the fire in her and knew this one would be a threat to her always.

Chelic did not look up, "You have taken a dream of a better future and a new strength for our people and removed it at the base. You have taken from me that which gave me reason to keep pushing forward. I accept you did it for the honor of the code." Lyamy felt sadness for Chelic she was forgiving her for taking what gave meaning to her life.

Kynin could not have been older then twenty five, "I accept what you have done in accordance with the good of the clan, while I have lost a mate, I still have opportunity to find my place in a better den." Spoken like a true Shadowkyn Lyamy surmised.

Meltose gave a hard look at Daret, Karis and Chelic before turning back to Lyamy, "I too accept what you have done for the good of the clan in accordance with the code of honor, to lose that which is a weakness to the clan is to lose nothing at all."

Treska stood up causing the guards to shift to a readiness, "I was silenced and told not to speak of it outside our den by Daret, Karis and Chelic, I apologize for not having your strength to stand against the corruption of this weakness. You have given me cause to stand stronger for the clan in accordance with the code."

Lyamy waved to the three youngest, "They can return to the apprentice fields until they can be called to a new den or position in the clan without bias. Rymnay you will serve me and in so doing you may stay with your den until such time as you chose to be with another, or the clan needs the building for a new den." Lyamy turned to Yaun, "I chose the right of three. A Shadowkyn of such power and prestige could not harbor so great a concept of corruption without the nurturing of that corruption from within his den. The three remaining have demonstrated contempt for our ways in their words and have been charged by two of their younger den mates. So that they may not continue to nurture weakness they must be cut from the clan."

Yaun smiled at her, "Granted, and I will go with you to witness this cleansing of our tribe. You have good instincts for the good of the clan and setting an example before everyone will discourage others from standing against the code."

Lyamy could sense that she may be at risk also on this journey. She followed Yaun back to his offices without looking back at the three who had just been sentenced to death at her hand. He was wearing the device she had gotten from Nelk. She had explained the improvements she had requested on the device that Nelk would be working on for him. There had been no further question about her reasons for stopping by Nelk's lab.

He had asked her about the thrashing of Freyie. She provided the same story that Freyie was telling. The difference being Freyie was boasting of her survival, while Lyamy stated plainly that she had other uses for Freyie still. "It is good to have someone in debt to you who is disposable." she had told Yaun and he seemed to approve.

Yaun sat down behind the large desk once they reached the office, "My decision is not final yet to keep you as my protector, but I am going to introduce you to the head of the order that does not exist anyway." before he was finished with the statement, the custodian Brelk entered the room with his cleaning equipment and started working his way around the room polishing and dusting. Brelk had always been kind to her, and she had always treated him with respect and over looked the eye-patch he wore, he seemed to see as much with one eye as others saw with two. "Brelk would you mind stopping that for a minute and come over here. You know Brelk lost that eye fighting off a beast attack at the west gate. He is one of our few acknowledged heroes."

"It is always good to know an honorable defender of our clan. We should do all we can to see that our clan survives and grows stronger."

"The order that does not exist must understand that sometimes sacrifice is required for the greater good." Brelk smiled, speaking with a strong confident voice belied by his initial appearance.

"I believe I have training to finish with you." Lyamy nodded to Brelk, "Well played. May I nominate a candidate to the order? Or would that be overplaying my hand at this time?"

"We serve Lord Yaun, but business of the order is business of the order, perhaps when we meet for training."

"Lyamy is my protector, so why don't you take her for training now, she needs to know how to communicate with you without exposing you." Yaun stated "I am in my office, I have guards at the door who have proved reliable so far and I have that device you brought me from Nelk, I should be alright by myself for a while. Brelk will meet you in the training room."

Dismissed, Lyamy left the office and slipped unseen to the training room. Lyamy vanished into a corner, invisible to all but those who knew what to look for. The only light in the room was that which leaked through the ventilation around the walls by the ceiling. Several minutes went by, she assumed that Yaun had additional business with Brelk or might be giving him special instructions concerning her. It had not been her intent to get the position of protector, but it did not hurt her plans to be in a position to get things done.

Finally, Brelk came in by the other door, "You can come out of hiding, the doors are locked and it is just you and I. We will address business first then training after. Who is it you desire to make a candidate for the order?"

"She is a threat to me personally, one of my top rivals as an apprentice, Merkyet."

"This is the first time in a long time our top three apprentices are female. I don't know what you did, but you played a strong hand with Freyie and while she makes a great display of being your number one enemy, she has become your puppet. Well played. Usually only one of the top three survive very long after training. Why would you select the one person left who most wants you dead for training that could give them the means to accomplish this task?"

"By oath of the order that does not exist, I claim what I am about to tell you as secret business of the order, do you swear to that secrecy, before I speak?"

"That is an oath I rarely impose on others, this must be significant, so I will swear to it."

Lyamy paused, "I am the last holder of the secrets of the old magics in the clan. I cannot tell you how I came by the fullness of the knowledge, but the clan should at all times have at least two with this knowledge. The master and the apprentice are required. I will teach you, if you chose to learn the old magics, but they must be preserved for the future of the clan. If you initiate her to the order, I can teach her in secret, and she does not need to know who I am. The apprentice cannot harm the master, so it works out to the good of the strength of the clan. All three top apprentices live."

"Why not Freyie?"

"As you said, Freyie is already in hand and I have other uses for her."

"I will learn what you can teach me, but you will initiate Merkyet to the order. She will be your responsibility. You will have to teach her the ways of the order and the old magic. They cannot interfere with her normal daily routines, so night classes when she is supposed to be asleep. Now communications, you know most of the communications of the order already so we need to cover high level techniques. For the most part now as the high lord's protector, I will have to treat you as outside the order. You have shown your trust of the order, me, by disclosing your secrets of old magic, so I am going to trust you to the full extent allowed by the order."

Lyamy laughed, "So you trust I put the clan first and will only kill you if it is required."

"No mincing words I see. So, we are on equal footing." He showed her the communications needed between them to conceal messages in the open. She introduced him to the old magic and showed him how to create the unseen pocket and a couple other useful but simple tricks. He provided her some more training in the ways of the order. Then they started sparring. "You have learned a few moves I did not teach you?"

"Would you believe me if I told you one of the Ancients gave me training?"

"I just might with everything you keep pulling out of nowhere. You are thirteen and have the skills of hard training at least ten year advanced from where you should be."

"We are scheduled to depart in the morning. If I initiate Merkyet tonight, will you train her for the three days we are gone. That will also serve to reduce any suspicions she may have that it is me when I do return." Lyamy looked at him as if she were reading the thoughts behind his eyes.

"That I will do. I will leave here first." Brelk stated before slipping out the door from which he came in.

Lyamy took the time to house three sleep spells in her dagger before slipping back out. Lyamy went by her room, washed and changed using that as an excuse for her delayed return. She walked past Merkyet's room on her way back to the manner and kicked a note under her door without being noticed. Returning to Yaun's primary office she stopped by Nelk's laboratory to check on the progress of the special defensive device. Nelk had her cast her spells three more times on the wand, he had not yet successfully embedded the personal alarm into the device.

She scanned the door as she entered and the room when she walked in. "My Lord" she acknowledged Yaun. She walked to the corner where she was designated to stand when she was not doing anything else in particular.

Yaun finished reading some paper on his desk and looked up, "Lyamy, you know the code well and you desire what is good for the survival of our people. It has been brought to my attention recently that our clan living in one location is a potential threat to our survival. Do you know any provisions in the code which would allow for the dividing of our people into two or more distinct locations that if by some means natural or unnatural one location gets destroyed our people will still survive?"

"To do what is required for the survival of our race is the first code. Let me think a moment." Lyamy paused. "All members of the clan are required to live in lands protected by the clan. It does not specify that those lands must be adjoining. The clan can claim any lands conquered or explored as lands of their protectorate, as long as they have a means of defending them. Again, nothing specifies they must be adjoining. Regardless of location all clan report to the Lord of the Clan. This would allow for lands to be apart from the or separated by distance from other clan land. I do not know of anything specific embracing what you suggest beyond the first code. That should be sufficient to support the pretext based on the vulnerability of a single location." she paused, "Wait there is one of the codes, one thirty seven, that states under the threat of extinction to an overwhelming force, a portion of the clan is to be sent away before the threat can prevent the departure, outside of the eyes of any enemy to start in a fresh location with the potential of building the remnant to greatness."

"So, you are saying it would be in accordance with code and appropriate for us to make plans to divide our people into two bodies one that should take upon themselves the quest to establish a separate settlement perhaps on the western coast of the continent to help insure the survival of our people?" Yaun smiled a rather devious smile.

"Lord Yaun, considering the threat that has been recognized that would not only be appropriate, but required based on the first code of honor." She looked at her belt for a moment, "To prevent needless bloodshed, I will require a dozen throwing daggers before you make that announcement in a meeting, in order to stop hasty weapons."

"You will help me sort through an appropriate division of our people when we return from the executions. They will serve to slow down any attempts to contradict order and the code when we do make the announcement."

"I do have a couple requests to make this more impressionable. I think it will add to the impact you are looking for also."

"Do tell." Yaun leaned forward, appreciating the viciousness of his young new protector.

*   *   *   *   *

Merkyet arrived at her room after a long day filled with training and tasks that they had been assigned to complete. She opened her door and smelled the scent of fresh ink, but no one was there. She closed the door before bending over and examining the note on the floor. No traps, no toxins, she carefully picked the note up. There were explicit directions to go to a room and wait, an hour after they were supposed to go to sleep. She read the entire thing several times and then the paper turned to dust and vanished.

She was uncertain, this could be an attempt on her life. Lyamy had not taken action on her own against them and Freyie only received the consequences of her own actions. The under apprentices were not in a position to challenge. This could be an official request she could not ignore it either way. She would have to go prepared for anything. By the time an hour had passed she had pulled her focus to a singularity and prepared for her commitment to see this through.

She slipped out into the night, staying hidden in the shadows and made her way to the hall leading to the detention cell. She looked around making sure all was clear before opening the door and entering the hall. She paused inside and made certain nobody else was there, then moved down to the second door on the left. She heard nothing from within the room and carefully opened that door, looking and listening before slipping inside. She could see and smell nothing in the room other than a residual scent of sweat, but somehow, she was not able to identify whose. She closed the door behind her. She squatted down and waited.

A door on the opposite side of the room opened and a figure wrapped entirely in black stepped in, even the eyes were veiled. There was enough of the light from the night sky that trickled in that she could see the figure; they gave a gestured greeting and a slight bow. "You are chosen by the order that does not exist. Do you accept this choosing." The words came in a masked whisper.

She had heard rumors of such an order, but never anything official. She had not believed it was real. Now she was being asked to join. Was there really a choice. "I accept."

"Step forward to the middle of the room. You will begin receiving training at this hour five nights a week. You can tell no one and you cannot allow it to impact your normal daily activity. You must swear to the secrecy and commitment of the order, violation of this oath will result in death. Do you swear?"

"I swear to the secrecy and commitment of the order."

"You have also been chosen to be the keeper of a much greater secret of the clan."

"What greater secret can there be?" instantly taken aback by her own outburst.

"You have heard of the old magic of the clan?"

"I have heard stories, how they have long since gotten lost and the clan no longer has them."

"There are always at least two members of the clan that know the old magic at least there is supposed to be, a master and an apprentice. You have been selected if you accept to be the next apprentice. The position comes with power and responsibility. If you accept there is no turning back and the master is obligated to terminate you at any sign of abuse, which falls to their discretion. If you choose not to accept this conversation will be removed from your mind and there will be no penalty. The old magic is being preserved for the future of the clan."

Hunger filled Merkyet's eyes, "I will accept."

"You will be bound as an apprentice and you will never be able to do harm to your master."

"I accept that."

The shadowed figure made movements with their hands that she did not yet understand and then stopped. "Place your right-hand palm against mine and open your mind to me."

Merkyet opened in her mind an invitation to allow the master in and saw the eyes behind the veil glow with fire. It felt like a door to knowledge opened in her mind and at the same time a part of her being passed through their hands into her unknown master, the bond was made. "I felt the binding." She whispered

"I will teach you two things right now. First I want you to create an unseen pocket and second a spell to supplement your rest." Her new master walked her through creating the unseen pocket and explained that anything placed in that pocket would be weightless and she could access it freely like any other pocket. If she filled it with garbage, just like any other bag or pocket, she would have to sort through the garbage to find what she needed. Then they went through how to get supplemental rest which made her feel immediately better, but warned she still needs to get regular sleep or meditation for the spell to continue to be effective.

"Now we need to get your order training taken care of, we will focus on that for the next hour and for the next three nights we meet. You will have many teachers most will not know who you are even as you do not know who your teachers are. Starting next week, you will have double training, both order training and old magic training. You will only speak of old magic if your trainer brings it up first and only I can teach you the art."

Merkyet was feeling both overwhelmed and empowered. She had been warned not to let any change be noticed in her manner or behavior that might give away a change. Changes could develop over a long term which can be explained by ordinary experience. She used stealth to make her way back to her room. She used her training as an apprentice to bring herself back to a calm so that she could sleep.

*   *   *   *   *

The event was set up to be a spectacle, the three women were to be executed in disgrace and weakness. Yaun made ad lib speeches as they were stripped naked and their hands and feet were bound, their tails left unbound so they could keep their balance. Chunks of meat were tossed over the cliff where their bodies would land, and they waited not long for the wild cats to show up to eat the raw meat. Chunks of meat were hung around the necks of each of the women. Lyamy was confident that ShadowDancer was in control of the cats and the clan would be convinced the three women were dead when they were done.

She walked up to Daret and plunged her dagger in Daret's chest, confident she missed anything vital, pulled the dagger back out and licked her blood from the blade her eyes bursting with the flames of blood rage, "You have no virtue for me to claim, so I claim in your death of your spirit to add to the strength of my own." The sleep spell from the dagger was taking effect and she passed healing from her left hand as she pushed Daret off the cliff and a cat yowled with the thud of her body below. Lyamy turned raised the dagger to the crowd and then licked the blood clean from the other side of the blade.

She pulled Karis over to the edge, who looked at her with absolute hatred. She plunged her dagger again, releasing another sleep spell. As she pulled the blade out, she yelled for all to hear as she licked the blood from the blade, "I claim in your death the power of your inner rage." releasing healing into her as she pushed Karis off following Daret with a softer thud. Again she made a show of holding the blade up and cleaning the blood from the blade.

Chelic was next, Lyamy pulled her to the edge and looked her in the eyes and saw forgiveness. Her dagger plunged again, and the sleep spell released. She held her with her left-hand releasing healing into her with the thought sent out *ShadowDancer protect them.* "I claim with your death of your spirit to strengthen my own!" She licked both sides of the blade and with another healing surge pushed Chelic over the edge.

The crowd cheered like they all had the blood rage. Lyamy wished she could follow them now, but there was more work to be done. The pieces were all falling into place. She had prestige as high as there was short of being the Lord of the clan and she was Lord Yaun's tool as a hero to control the sway of the people. The cats had nothing to grab but flesh and their teeth drew more blood making the illusion of death more convincing. The crowd cheered again as they watched the cats drag what they thought to be corpses off into the woods below. The ritual executions fed the savage needs in the depths of their heritage.

As Lyamy took her placed by Lord Yaun he handed her a belt with the twelve throwing daggers she had requested, "You have done good for the clan today. I believe that the deaths have added strength to the rest of the clan. I might want to add you to my den."

"Lord Yaun, you are high lord of the clan and can have any woman any time you want including me. I will gladly give myself to you when you wish it, but I am obligated as your protector to decline joining your den, lest my judgment as protector should get clouded, by the personal closeness. Besides, women do not join a den until they have offered a cub or two to the clan."

"You are mature beyond your years."

*   *   *   *   *

ShadowDancer was waiting out of sight from the cliff side, with a feast waiting for the cats as they dropped the bodies. The taste of blood had triggered their primal feeding frenzy. A bubble went up around ShadowDancer and the bodies. She carefully examined each body healing their wounds to safe levels and cleansing them of infection.

She woke Daret first. Her name pulled her out as her eyes opened and she slowly looked around, "where, how?"

"You are not dead, neither is Jenyin, Lyamy could not tell you what was happening ahead of time. You were selected to rejoin Jenyin, not to die."

"But, how, …"

"Wait until I wake the rest, so I can explain everything for everyone."

Karis lurched to a sitting position and fell back from moving too quickly, the fire of rage still in her eyes as she looked around assessing the situation.

"Calm down Karis." ShadowDancer said in a comforting voice, "You are not dead, I will explain and answer questions after I wake Chelic."

Chelic did not wake up as easily as the others. "Chelic wake up, Jenyin is waiting for you. Let go of your despair and return to the living." ShadowDancer laid her hand on the side of Chelic's head. A few minutes passed and Chelic opened her eyes, and she took a long deep breath.

"I am back, why do you call me to return to this place when my reasons to stay are gone?" She reached up and felt the scar on her chest where she was sure a dagger had delivered her from the pain that was left in life. "Why am I not dead?"

ShadowDancer explained that just like them Jenyin was not dead, the staging of their death by Lyamy was so that the clan would not try to seek them out later. She explained what Jenyin was doing and how he was doing it for the long-term survival of their people. ShadowDancer explained that she was an Ancient and her followers tended to call her goddess and she was there to help them. She provided them with simple garments and leather boots after an elven fashion. She explained how to get to Jenyin and mentioned the winged folk of the canopy forest. "If you just tell them you seek passage and have no hostile intent, they will let you pass through their land without harm or a fight."

"Jenyin has been through and talked with them already?" Chelic asked, nothing else seemed to matter to her, she seemed focused on Jenyin with a child-like simplicity.

"Yes Chelic, and you will find Jenyin in the caves at the end of the ridge. Listen to me all of you. You may run into other things on your journey now or in the future where you will need to defend yourselves. What weapons have each of you been trained with or would you prefer to carry?"

Daret thought for the briefest moment and answered, "I would like a good composite bow, a long sword and a long knife, a dragon fang long knife if you could. We will be traveling though, so if I could have a gathering bag for herbs and such as we go, I would appreciate it." All the equipment she asked for appeared already equip with belts, quivers, harnesses and scabbards as needed.

Karis was still broody, and anger still reflected in her eyes, she could not escape the image of Lyamy licking her blood from a dagger as her vision faded before being cast from the cliff and left for dead. "I want a dagger and a rapier and a long sword and a cross bow and a blood knife and a garrote."

ShadowDancer put a hand on her shoulder, "You have to let some of that anger go out of your system. Lyamy did the best she could to make the life Jenyin wanted and give you the benefit. She selected you carefully, you were the ones who had the strongest feelings for Jenyin and would most want to be with him. I give you what you have asked for and a pack with trail rations. Hopefully you will find peace with what was done when you are back with Jenyin." The items appeared for Karis as they did for Daret.

ShadowDancer turned to Chelic, "Can we go now?" she asked anxious to be back with Jenyin.

"You need some survival equipment; you are starting a whole new culture. The beginnings will not be easy."

"I will need to help hunt for the den, maybe a sling and a bow and a harvesting stick for pulling up tubers and roots, after all we will not have the servants of the fields to harvest for us now. We will build Jenyin's dream."

"I will take care of you Chelic." A walking stick that could double for a quarterstaff appeared in her hand and the end that was up had the forked tip of a harvesting stick only made of metal mounted as part of the staff, a knife, medium length and slightly curved like an elven hunting knife and a skinning knife appeared on a belt. Hanging next to the knives appeared a sling and a bag of bullets, round metal balls and on the opposite side a harvesting bag, a backpack appeared on her back. The backpack appeared to be about half full and she was equipped with an elven bow and a quiver also. "You have been healed and taken care of as Lyamy asked of me and now you must begin you journey to meet Jenyin."

*   *   *   *   *

Jenyin sniffed the air a few steps inside the cave entrance, the scent of the carcases, bones and remains he had removed was starting to clear out. He finished sweeping the dirt off the stone floor with the makeshift broom he had made with a long bone and bundled straw from the field above on the ridge. He leaned it against the wall and walked over to the bird he had roasting on a spit over a small fire and turned it again. The smell made his mouth water. He glanced over at what was left of the pile of wood he had gathered. He had made sleeping pads in the first four caves with wood and straw. It was not the fine craftsmanship they had back in the clan, but he was not a wood craftsman and did not have all the proper tools.

He was told to prepare a shelter and he was working on just that. She had said a sanctuary, a place for outcasts and misfits. It would take time to make a proper place to live. A smell on the breeze caught his attention and he looked north in the direction the wind was coming from. The shallow gradient of the sand spread anywhere from a half mile to a mile and a half from the base of the cliff as it sprawled up the coast. There were scattered bushes and an occasional tree trying to survive in the sandy lowland, but mostly sparse field petering off into the sand of the beach. Jenyin could see for miles. Something was moving along the beach about two and a half miles away. He could not make out what or how many, but more than one. At the rate they were moving he estimated about a half an hour before they reached this far down the coast.

Whatever it was, he was downwind and they did not smell native to the land he knew. He had the cliff to his back and the grass would help camouflage his presence. He had time to eat and then he could climb part way up the rocks and blend into his background. When he got on all fours, from a distance it would also be hard to tell the difference between a Shadowkyn and the wild cats from the jungle.

After he finished eating, Jenyin put out the fire and climbed partway up the rock face above the cave and waited. Growing up they were taught two languages, their own and a language that is supposed to be common with other races of the world. It was the language he used when he spoke to the winged men. As the strangers walking along the beach came closer, he could see there were five of them two shorter one of them stocky and the other skinny, three taller ones, but there was something different about the one from the other two. They were speaking in the common language, but there were words he did not recognize, and they had an odd way of talking making it difficult to understand what he did hear.

The group stopped walking and looked in his direction. "There seems to be a cave up there." One of them said.

"Well, let's go check it out." another answered.

"Use caution the different tall one in the back stated"

"No kidding?" another laughed sarcastically.

"With all the raucous you all are making, if there is anything there it would have to be dead not to know we were here." stated one of the tall thin ones more quietly then the rest were speaking.

As the small party approached, he started identifying them from lessons about other world cultures from their library. There was a male dwarf, a male gnome, a male and a female Elf and a female human if he was right.

"There is a campfire recently put out." stated the male Elf who was advancing ahead of the rest. "Whatever is staying here is intelligent and cooks their food. It might be better if we put our weapons away." The Elf sheathed his sword, and the rest follows suit putting their weapons away.

The female Elf looked around at the ground, "From the tracks, I would say medium sized, one maybe two. They have been very busy but have not been here very long."

"That cave goes back, there could be a whole city in there. They may just not like to come outside."

"Maybe they are friendly." the gnome stated and did not wait for a response from the rest of the group, "HELLO! Is anyone home?"

The group did not appear to be an immediate threat so Jenyin dropped from the rocks above, landing in front of the cave entrance. "You are strangers to this land. This is a savage land and not friendly to strangers."

They all stepped back and their hands went to their weapons, but relaxed when he did not pull a weapon on them. These were outcasts, the purpose for his shelter and his first opportunity to do what ShadowDancer had requested of him.

"That is what the ship's crew said as they left us behind and rowed the life boats back out to sea, preferring to take their chances surviving till they could land elsewhere then staying on land here." The dwarf stated gruffly, "Apparently the captain died on the tiller and ran us aground tearing up the bottom of the ship and the crew was too drunk to know what was happening."

Jenyin did not recognize any of the nautical terminology but caught the gist that these five were abandoned survivors of an accident, that had something to do with coming from the ocean. "I am Jenyin, I will offer you the comfort and protection of my shelter if you need time to figure out what you are doing. You speak a bit differently and I am not clear on everything you say, but I understand you have been separated from what you know."

"We appreciate your hospitality." the male Elf stated extending his hand in some kind of greeting, he appeared to be the leader of the group. Jenyin extended his hand in similar fashion not wishing to ignore what might be a formality to the strangers. The Elf took a half step forward clasping his hand lifting it and lowering it once before dropping his hand back at his side. "I am Freldin I am an Elf. These are my companions the Dwarven gentleman is Desdin, he works metal and stone for a living, if you didn't notice, drawn to caves. This gnomish fellow is Grimble, he makes things from wood and metal. Then we have the lovely human lady Marrianne Brutallous, shall we say she is an, um, ah, technician of acquisitions" he seemed to stumble briefly with the job description, but nodded and went on, "and on the side she dabbles in some of the finer crafts of metal working, like jewelry. This is Chineene her and I are both elves," He smiled and winked at her, "We are adventures, skilled in many trades that aid us in our adventuring."

"So, can I check out your cave?" Desdin asked.

"Sure, there is not much to it yet, I have not been able to get too much work done yet."

"Are you here alone?" Chineene asked as Desdin walked over and started examining the entrance to the cave. "I don't mean to pry, it just does not seem normal for anyone to be on their own, especially in a hostile environment."

"Only temporarily. I do not see any harm in sharing what I am doing. I was asked to set up a shelter and start a community for those who are outcast, misfits or otherwise separated from their societies." Jenyin stated.

"That seems like an odd request for your people to make on an individual." Chineene observed.

Jenyin laughed a colder laugh then he intended that got everyone attention. "I was not asked by my people; they would have probably killed most or all of you by now depending on how much interrogating they wanted to do first. Your leaving alive would be considered a threat to the clan."

The others looked at each other with not just a little uncertainty. Freldin asked, "Then who has asked this task of you that seems to contradict the ways of your people?"

"An Ancient or goddess, however you want to refer to her. She goes by ShadowDancer. My people think I am dead, which has given me the freedom to leave the clan and pursue the dreams of securing a future for my people."

There was a long silence, each getting caught in their own thoughts and apprehensions, until Desdin still examining the cave structure spoke, "You are going to need a door and we need to reinforce the stone on the sides, otherwise the winds and salt water from the ocean will keep eating the stone away until the entrance collapses."

"So maybe it is a good thing you guys showed up." Jenyin stated, " I really do not know that much about stonework."

"We can probably make the door out of metal and wood." Grimble volunteered, accepting what Jenyin said concerning the Ancient, but more than glad to have a change in conversation to focus on. "We have an entire ship and cargo of supplies to work with."

"We were just passengers," Chineene was also glad for the subject change, "Does anyone know what the cargo was? The crew left everything except food and drink when they took off in their boats."

"I would not be very good at my job if I didn't know now would I." Marrianne laughed, "The bulk of the cargo is armor, the second largest volume is clothing and bolts of material, I think there are orders on that ship for all the merchant shops in The Merchant port of Kelleeshia, including some chests that I could not open in a discrete fashion, I would speculate they may have been headed to the specialty shops. Is there room in these caves to stash all the cargo?"

"I have not explored all of the caves and tunnels, but there are caverns large enough to house an entire clan. If you follow the caverns that go down to the southwest there are rivers of fire, but there are freshwater streams in the central caverns straight west. The caverns before that are dry and clean though."

"We should salvage every scrap of the ship," Marrianne added, "leave no scrap or sign it was ever there. We can make sure that no salvage operation can find where she landed and come looking with claim to her haul."

"The cannons have wheels; we can use those to make carts to haul everything back in manageable loads." Grimble suggested.

Jenyin looked at the long shadows from the setting sun. "I think you should all have something to eat and sort out arrangements in the caves and get some sleep and start on the salvage project in the morning."

They all agreed, Jenyin told them which side cavern was his and gave them free choice of the others, then disappeared up the ridge, while they settled on arrangements. They just finished getting the fire pit burning well when he came back down with three birds for them to clean and cook as they saw fit. Jenyin sat on a rock he pulled over and listened, occasionally participating in their idle chat. He looked forward to actually having something softer to sleep on then the stone.

* * * * *

Yaun had a listing of all the members of the clan, those in dens grouped by den and the rest individually listed including all the apprentices, children and cubs, He and Lyamy had already started sorting them into two groups. The first group would stay at their current location, and the second group would transverse the continent and set up the new colony on the other coast. The clan would supply everything they needed for the crossing and for the first month until they could start harvesting and supplying their own food needs. Those going would have to decide what of their own belongings they wanted to take or leave behind. About a third of the population would be going and about a third of the harvesters would go with them. The harvesters would be divided by number, allowing them to keep any family units together.

Lyamy suggested that the top candidates for the next two years of apprentices be sent with the cross-continent group, to help insure their ongoing survival. Yaun was surprised when she wanted her top rivals to stay, indicating they needed to keep some of their strength for the future here strong also. Lyamy went ahead to make sure the meeting hall was clean and safe, the majority of the den leaders of the clan should already be there. He pulled together his thoughts and headed to the meeting hall himself.

Yaun took his place, sitting at the head of the counsel, Lyamy standing at his right side. First order of business was to have a clerk read the record of their last meeting. There were three issues left to be resolved. After deliberated debate, the conclusion was that no den was to be excluded from contributing to the defenses of the western gates, but it would be the choice of each den who they sent when their turn came up. The dens would be held responsible if they failed. The second issue that had not been resolved was concerning the practices of enforcing the code on all ranks equally. With the recent event the accusations against the current leadership no longer held any steam and it was agreed to drop the matter completely. The third and final issue of old business was concern over the growth in population of the harvesters exceeding what the current population of the clan could reasonably control and protect.

Lyamy whispered in Yaun's ear and he stood to speak, "Let me propose that we enlist a portion of the harvesters, ask for volunteers first, to help with the protection of the western gates and to serve to help police and protect the fields as part of our field units. This will serve two purposes, one to slow down their growth and second to reduce our losses, in exchange they may feel they are contributing more to our alliance and the volunteers will be given monetary or social reward."

There was no dissension to the proposal, so the matter closed quickly, and they were ready to move on to new business. Yaun whispered his appreciation to Lyamy for the suggestion and acknowledge her to the audience for her input. Several members of the counsel had flags standing where they sat indicating they had new business to bring up for the meeting.

"Would everyone agree the first code of the Code of Honor is to do what is necessary for the survival of our race and clan?" Yaun opened as he started new business

There was a general voicing of agreement. "Perhaps a forward-thinking leader would help." came a reply from one of the more powerful dens.

"Then you would all agree, that when we discover something that may be a threat to our survival as a race or clan, we should take whatever action necessary to reduce that threat?"

Again, there was a general agreement. "True, what are you leading up to?" The audience seemed to be getting antsy. "This must be something big." was voiced among the whispers.

"It was brought to my attention recently that we are subject to a threat that could cause our total annihilation." he paused for emphasis and continued, "We live in a single fixed point, barely a spot on the land mass where we live. There are many events that could occur by nature or by invasion that would leave us as nothing more than a line in a history book if that. Can you grasp the extent of this threat? From a great eruption, from a storm at sea, from the armies of an enemy? According to our own history we once number in the thousands and other races of the world also number in such greatness. Our clan currently only numbers about twelve hundred. We have diminished over time, falling to the savagery of the land and our own petty internal fighting. Can you see how great this threat to our survival is?"

There was murmuring, but in general ascent to acceptance of the point made. Someone voiced, "So do you have a proposal for how we can resolve this crisis?"

"I do not need to come up with anything new, the answer is in the Code of Honor. Code one thirty-seven tells us what to do. It states under the threat of extinction to an overwhelming force, a portion of the clan is to be sent away before the threat can prevent the departure, outside of the eyes of any enemy to start in a fresh location with the potential of building the remnant to greatness." Yaun paused.

"So you are going to exile a handful of us, is that your proposal?"

"Not at all." Yaun smiled, "We are going to split out a third of the clan to go claim territory on the western coast of our continent. There is a great river valley with a perfect place to settle on the southern side of the river. They will take the supplies they need and a third of the harvesters with them and form a second colony as part of the clan in accordance with the Code of Honor."

Six daggers flew in a blur of motion from Lyamy and those who were going for their weapons sat quickly back down avoiding an uprising. They all glared at Lyamy pulling her daggers out of their weapon hands, disabled from turning the meeting into a fight. "The code tells us to stay united as one clan." One of them protested.

"And we will!" Yaun answered, "As I was paraphrased the code by an apprentice, '*All members of the clan are required to live in lands protected by the clan. It does not specify that those lands must be adjoining. The clan can claim any lands conquered or explored as lands of their protectorate, as long as they have a means of defending them. Again nothing specifies they must be adjoining. Regardless of location all clan report to the Lord of the Clan. This would allow for lands to be apart from the or separated by distance from other clan land.*' So, you see a third of the clan should be sufficient to settle and defend the newly claimed lands. Having two population centers will give us more freedom to grow and protect us from the weakness we now have living in a single location. The greatness of the distance will ensure survival of our clan even if one group gets completely lost."

There was a lot of murmuring and grumbling, but the tension seemed to slowly lessen. The majority consensus turned in favor of the proposal. "So, will we appoint a committee to select those who will take this brave step for the survival of the clan?"

"No." Yaun stated flatly, "This quest will require our strongest and best to make sure it is a success. I will choose what dens will go, they can choose some of the single members that have not already been given positions here. You will take the best third of the apprentices for the next two years of candidates along with a third of the children and cubs. I want you to succeed and prosper."

"How can you know of this perfect place for a settlement across the continent?"

"I was visited by one of the Ancients who has taken an interest in our survival. She showed me the risk and where to send people. She took me there. She said she will look after our people until Darvel can return."

The room went silent for several minutes, no one knew what to say. If they accepted what he said, they had no more room for debate. If they questioned it, they would be challenging Yaun for authority to lead the clan. Finally, a small female stepped forwards, "I do not question you, my lord, but is there a means by which you could help us to believe what you are saying and cleanse us of any uncertainty we do not wish to carry?"

As if summoned, ShadowDancer appeared in an ethereal form floating above the table in front of Yaun, "I am ShadowDancer. Darvel is an uncle to me. This world is much bigger than the continent upon which you live. In the past twenty-five years you have been missed by two major wars, each war has been an engagement of hundreds of thousands of troops." She waved her hands and visions of scenes of those wars displayed in a mist for all to see. "If either of these wars had overflowed to this continent, you all would be dirt beat into the ground and your clan would be no more. For those selected to cross the continent, I will give you protection. This is one of the measures I am taking to make sure the Shadowkyn survive into the future of our world. The world around you is changing, the clan will have to know change, or get lost like a whisper in the wind." She lifted her hand and the daggers returned to Lyamy slipping back in place in her belt and the wounds they caused were healed. "Do not test my anger." ShadowDancer vanished with the visions and the mist.

"It is settled then." Stated the leader of the highest-ranking den that had been previously dancing around the idea of challenging Yaun.

"Peltrhak, you are the strongest and most apt among the dens, you will lead the third of the clan westward. It will almost be like leading your own clan, you will have partial sovereignty. You will still answer to the unity of the clan, but even this will be more of a token relationship to mutually assure the survival of our people. If you wish you can come with me and look at some of the sorting out of dens we have already started. The seven strongest dens will be going with you to make sure you have the strength needed to defend everyone. The process is almost complete, Lyamy has helped me a lot, but if there are changes you wish to make, we will see if we can accommodate your requests."

Peltrhak had been thinking of this more as an exiling of a third of the clan. Leader of his own clan put an entirely different light on things. "I think I could appreciate collaborating on this work." He looked at Lyamy and her belt of daggers and back at his hand which was now healed. "You are good, I have never seen that kind of speed and accuracy before. I let go of my anger against you and respect your skill."

"You honor me with your words." She felt as much as saw his eyes appreciating her female form and smiled and wondered how he would compare to Yaun. Dismissing the thought for now, she followed the two into the main office Yaun used for all his formal business.

Yaun unrolled a map on his desk and pointed to the location on the western coast of the continent. "This is your destination. Having been there, I envy you the richness of the land. You will not be disappointed when you get there. Lyamy, we need to speak leader to leader," He placed his hand on the device she had gotten from Nelk, "You will know if I need you, but for now anyway you can go for the night."

On her way back to her room, she would stop by Nelk's and pick up the devices he had made to remove the mark that Yaun had made from her back so that he could not track her and the one for Jenyin. When ShadowDancer came to bring her more training this night, she would have to ask about training someone in the new clan in the ways of the old magic. She had other questions too, like; how was Chelic doing. Lyamy was concerned for Chelic, her precise stab in the chest was not as perfect as it had been for the others, it was a mistake that could have really killed her. It was also time to give Merkyet her copy of the book, she knew enough to be able to read it and learn even without a teacher. Lyamy would continue teaching her as long as she could. She learned the ways of Yaun and knew when he slept. That part of the night became hers to do what she desired with, only needing an occasional partial night's sleep with the rest ShadowDancer had given her when she blinked. She also started spending some time with Freyie as her personal assistant.

*   *   *   *   *

Daret was in the lead, Karis was still working on her anger issues and Chelic was following off in her own world somewhere. Chelic was starting to respond more in line with recognizing the course of events, but still had a very lighthearted detachment. Daret was determine not to stop until they reached Jenyin. There would be time to sleep once they reach the shelter he was working on, or at least she hoped he was working on.

It was not long before they reached the deep forest the air was immediately cooler when they stepped under the canopy. There was a rich fragrance of the forest mulch turning to soil, mixed with the light smells of herbs and berries that grew on the forest floor. They were all randomly gathering as they moved, collecting edible herbs, mushrooms and fungus in their bags. Another scent caught her attention and she stopped, bringing the other to a stop with her. She was expecting this encounter but was no less impressed with the flying humanoids as they descended in front of her. She gave a slight bow of her head acknowledging them as having authority in the forest. "Hello friends of Jenyin."

"You know the one who passed through here days ago. Are you friends of his?"

"We are and we just wish passage through your land that we might join him."

"Be warned there are savage creatures that live in these forests. We will be following your progress but may not be there should you find yourselves in need. If we are near, we will help should you be in trouble." The winged folk vanished into the trees around them.

Daret began her small party moving forward again. The forest was silent except for the occasional raucous of a small animal of bird stirred up by dropping what it was carrying or something else intruding in their space. They went for several hours without incident. Suddenly an alarm went off in the back of Daret's mind. She turned around and Chelic had lagged behind them about twenty feet. In an instant Daret had her bow out and loaded, but it was too late for her to bother shooting. Chelic had not stopped her casual pace or even slowed down, but three wild wolves lay unconscious in her trail knocked out with a deft precision of her staff. Chelic appeared to not even notice what she had done. "Chelic, are you alright?"

"Of course, Daret, why wouldn't I be?"

"Well, you just knocked out three wolves, rather large brutes at that. You seem as if you did not even know what you did?"

Chelic stopped, turned and looked at the wolves as if she was seeing them for the first time. Karis was searching their surrounding with her bow at the ready, as if she were expecting an army of the wolves to come out descending on them at any moment. "I did that?"

"Yes, you did. We are going to keep moving, but please try to stay up and not fall behind again. I would like it if we all made it to Jenyin unharmed." She hoped with time Chelic would return to the normal they used to know.

It was not long after that they left the canopy. The warmth of the late morning sun felt good. They had barely started across a small thicket when two birds startled out of the long grass and Daret dropped them with her bow. She cleaned the meat and hung the birds from her belt. Karis plucked the six eggs from the nest and dropped them in her gathering bag. They ate rations and kept walking. Daret noticed some of the anger was starting to fade from Karis' eyes. She thought perhaps she might be able to draw some conversation, even get her to put other things out of her mind. "We should make the end of the ridge by nightfall, then maybe we can eat something a little more than trail rations."

Karis looked at her, "I will be glad when we can sit for a bit and rest. I keep thinking we should be heading back to the den and sort things out. How are we going to survive without the clan?"

"Karis we were selected because we will find a way to give our people a place in the world that is more than hiding in the protection of the clan."

"I love that you even talk like Jenyin in private, Daret. I wish I could see his vision as clearly as you do." She laughed, "I guess now I won't have any choice to see it sooner or later."

Daret smiled, it was good to see her den-mate, laughing. She walked over and put an arm around her, "We will make a better life. You know out here we are going to have to raise our own cubs and teach them until they are old enough to be a part of our new order. They will be raised to think as we do."

Karis gave her a hug back and they separated a short space as Chelic walked up and they formed a small group hug before moving on. "I love you guys too." Chelic smiled as if everything was perfectly the way it should be.

They would reach the end of the ridge around sunset and they would all have full gathering bags and who knows what else they might find. They pressed on. The heat of the day passed. Daret was sure she could smell the ocean now. It had been almost a hundred years before that she last looked upon the ocean. She did not know how long they were supposed to live, but between those defending the gates and those killed by internal politics she had witness the shrinking of the clan. From what she could tell more of the clan died at the hands of clan then at the hands of any enemy. She knew, she had killed her share, part of the reason she so embraced Jenyin's dream of clan not killing each other.

Her worst memory haunted her, looking down at a face looking back up at her. It could have been her own face forty years earlier. The aggressive conviction fading to realization and acceptance of death. Blood ran from the corner of her mouth and somewhere she found peace and said, "I forgive you." before she collapsed at her feet. It had once been her cub, but the young woman was undermining the political advance of her den. Daret had not known it was one of her own cubs until after she had plunged the poisoned steel blade down next to her neck. That was her last kill. She had vowed after that she would always find a way that did not require killing clan. Until that day she lived by the ways she was taught, but that she knew too late was wrong. She became committed to changing and saw for the first time the clan was working towards its own extinction. Her Den leader died the next day defending the gates from a savage beast attack making the death of the young woman meaningless. It was not long after that she met Jenyin, the brother who did not want to be leader of the clan, next in line, but willing to die to keep from inheriting the position.

Daret was angry with herself for thinking about such things now when they had to stay sharp and keep moving. There shadows were getting long when they heard voices ahead in casual conversation. They stalked their way to the end of the ridge. Daret took a chance looking over the edge at the gathering around a small campfire. It was a very strange looking group, and she could feel her savage instincts rising until she recognized Jenyin seated on a rock, part of the circle. She looked over their surroundings and noticed to her left the ground sloped down to a point much closer, less of a drop to the lower ground. She led the others over and made the jump clearing the rocky slope with ease landing with almost complete silence on all fours below. The other two followed with equal ease.

As she stood up, Jenyin looked up and saw them, "Daret, Karis, Chelic, it is so good to see all of you again. No others escaped with you?"

"I have to admit, she chose us wisely and the others all would have turned on you to stay with the clan." Daret answered. All three embrace

Jenyin as he ran up. "Karis is still mad at her, but she will get over it. Chelic may take some time to recover."

"I should be dead." Chelic commented as casual as if she was talking about eating a piece of bread. "She did not mean to, but she cut something inside me, I was bleeding inside. ShadowDancer brought me back from beyond the dream. I would have been alright with being gone. I am alright with being back though too. Grimble and Desdin are going to make us a wonderful kitchen in the entry chamber of the cave." She paused with a perplexed look on her face, "How do I know that?"

The rest were all silent and looking at her. They had not been introduced yet, so the strangers and Jenyin all wondered how she knew their names. Her traveling companions were lost trying to soak in that she had died and were not even to the part where she knew future events.

Jenyin saw the birds hanging from Daret's belt. "Here let me take those birds and get them cooking on the spit, all of you come sit by the fire. You must be tired and hungry. We will feed you and get you settled in. We can sort things out in the morning."

There was not much more conversation, and most was in hushed whispers even though everyone heard everything that was said. Introductions were made. When the birds were done cooking, the ladies ate. The shipwreck survivors called it a night before they were done eating and went to their places in the cave. Jenyin led his den back to his section of the cave when they were done eating.

* * * * *

Lyamy was not in her room when the alarm went off. It just happened she was on the steps in the courtyard outside Lord Yaun's office. She was in the office like lightening. Peltrhak's sword arm was fully raised when she reached up and yanked his arm down behind his back. His shoulder made an awful popping sound as it came out of the socket and the sword clanged to the floor. Lord Yaun's shield was up, and he had sustained no injury. His weapon was only half out, and he slid it back in as he saw what she had done. Peltrhak was down on a knee looking at her with both respect and terror. She pulled his gauntlet off, pulled his arm back around, yanked it and popped it back in joint. "You would be a fool to even think about making another move against Lord Yaun or his office. Even if I did not strike you down, did you consider you would have to face the wrath of ShadowDancer?" She whispered in a soft but commanding voice.

"You were here fast." Yaun observed.

"I was in the courtyard just in case you had need of me. I knew he would not take immediate action, so I took care of business first. He is a thinker, and I knew if he were to try anything he would wait until he felt confident he had a clear opportunity."

"You said you were sending the best with me; I want her and her top rivals with me." Peltrhak requested.

Yaun laughed, "She and her top two rivals already have appointed positions, They are not available for you to pick from."

Peltrhak looked at Lyamy, sizing her up, "Maybe I will take her to my den."

Lyamy took his chin in her palm and made him look in her eyes. They suddenly glowed with flames, "Maybe I should take you as a pet. It would only require a small piece of your spirit and you would obey my every whim. Accept the offer of your high lord or pay the consequences."

Peltrhak shuddered, "You know the old magic, forgive me, I have overstepped my bounds. I am being handed a chance to be a leader, I will accept in accordance with the code."

"Then I will leave your will as your own." the flames in her eyes went out as fast as they appeared.

"I knew there was something that gave you an advantage." Yaun smiled, "You are the keeper of the old secrets. It is out of bounds for me to know or ask more. I will consider this knowledge forgotten." Yaun turned back to Peltrhak, "Return to your den, I have been told that the future of the settlement you start will expand into a city of great pride. There is no greater position you could reach for, not even mine."

"You are not to let any know outside your den of your shame this night." Lyamy stated, and placed her hand on his shoulder, "Let me relieve a part of the burden, you need to lead our people in glory not in shame." Under her touch he felt the relief as torn flesh mended.

Yaun waited until Peltrhak closed the door. "You have great power and mastery both martial and magic. You could have taken me out of your way long ago and claimed leadership of the clan, but instead even as Jenyin did, you protect me. I understood his reasoning, but you could overcome all challenges without effort. And you are still so young."

"You are correct, I could, but when it comes to matters of the clan, survival of the clan and race comes first. I will only be with you for so long and then I will be sacrificed for the good of the clan." She already had in her hidden pocket the selected bones of a savage cat and a bag of boar's blood to create the illusion when the time was right.

"You are fighting for the survival of the clan knowing that survival means you will have to be sacrificed by the clan?"

"I will not be the first, and I am sure not the last. Would you condemn your clan so you could live another day, what good is being the leader of nothing?" Lyamy laughed inside seeing Yaun actually wrestle with the decision in his mind. "It is not important once I have been used to facilitate the survival of our clan there will come a point where too much of the clan will realize I have more power than you and the clan leader must be the most powerful member of the clan. They will not know I have the old magic and it is forbidden for the master of the old ways to be the leader of the clan. That must remain a secret also, so it will be a needful thing for me to be openly sacrificed to establish your leadership above the rumors."

Yaun as usual, could not find flaw with her logic although he already knew he would regret losing her. "So why me and not Peltrhak or someone else?"

"I was taught by Jenyin there is an order to things and if we cannot get the members of the clan to do their parts, the order will eventually collapse, and the clan will cease to survive. The code of honor was never intended to have members of the clan killing each other off to the point of self-destruction. You lead the clan and uphold most of the code and it is your part to lead the clan. It is my part to protect you. If I let someone kill you, then I have not done my part and then why would I not let someone else kill them and then another and another until nine hundred leaders have been killed and only one remains. One does not make a clan, not two or three. A clan must have the strength to survive, and we have already shrunk below a dangerous number with respect to that survival."

"But you have already made sacrifices to the clan, Jenyin, the three women of his den?"

"Those were necessary. Look how much more the clan is already uniting since those events. They respect strength and order. They are attributing that to you for now and we want to keep it that way. We can build a pyre where your brother and his den were parted from the clan and you can perform a hero's sacrifice when the time is right. All will see me consumed by fire after being run through by your blade." She paused, "unless of course you do not want to take the credit. You could banish me to the savage wild, but that would not have the showmanship or leave the lasting impression on the clan."

"You have done much for me already, I will honor you when the time comes. Until then you can direct what you need to in preparation without having to consult me." He did not know that she already had Freyie taking care of all the arrangements. Lyamy had also arranged for Merkyet to be in charge of the administrative position managing the redistribution of resources to accommodate the division of the clan. This was a promotion that Merkyet knew Lyamy had arranged for her and she was set on proving she should have even better.

It would be at least a month, possibly three of four before the third of the population would be ready to begin their exodus across the continent. Lyamy recruited additional agents for the protection of Yaun, primarily based on their loyalty to him and promoted based on their ability to serve in his protection. She had her eye on three possibilities for her replacement when she was gone.

Yaun was secure again, no known threats present. Lyamy walked with him back to his den and gave a slight bow before he went in and she headed back to her own business once again. Freyie should be back, so Lyamy headed to her quarters and knocked gently. The door opened and Freyie invited her in.

"Freyie, did everything go smoothly?"

"Yes, all the pieces are in place."

"I am not going to keep you bound to me forever, Freyie. So, if you go with me, it has got to be by your choice, I am not going to make you go. When I am gone everyone will think I am dead unless you tell someone, but then you would have to try and explain your involvement. You will be safe as long as that remains secret. If you come with me, I can make no guarantee of the future, but you will be free of our things here and never able to return. You do not need to answer now, but you will have to tell me what you decide.”

“Lyamy, you have given me dreams. I would never be able to find my place here again when you leave. I chose to and want to go with you. You took a piece of my spirit and I am now glad you did. You gave me life when I should be dead. I do not want you to undo what you have done. Even now as if we were called to the same den, I give you a piece of my heart.” Freyie kissed Lyamy on the cheek and sat back again.

Lyamy gave her a hug, “Then you shall go with me, it is settled. You will lose your gem decorated metal bracer though, so we can cover your trail also. For now, we continue as we have been, Rivals who have come to terms sufficiently to work in the same village.”

“I am glad we are saving the clan, but I will be glad when we have moved on also.” Freyie laughed, “I feel things we were not raised of trained to feel.”

Lyamy was surprised when Yaun's alarm went off again in her head. She jumped up without another word and was gone in a blur of movement. She slammed against the door to his den and with a bursting sound and the splintering of wood it yielded to her entry.

It was a member of his den, she had gotten through before the shield went up, there was blood coming from his back. It was obvious she had tried again, and someone hit her on the side of the head. His den mate was crouched in the corner knife on the floor. Lyamy put her hand through the protective shielding and poured healing energy into Yaun. The injury was fatal if left unattended, but it was small and healed quickly under her touch.

"She made her way into my den in service to one of the other lords named to leave for the new settlement."

"We can send her with them, or we can hang her upside down in shame and dishonor in the main courtyard in town until she has paid the price with her life." Lyamy stated cold and detached., "She is worthy of death for the crime, but if we want to make a point now that killing our own does not serve the survival of the clan, we could cage her in a place of shame and keep her fed and healthy and send her off with those that are departing. Her true lord or den can claim her after they leave. I will act according to your judgment."

Yaun paused and let his emotions subside before deciding what to do. "Take her with you for now. See if you can get anything out of her. She was acting in accordance with the way the clan has been interpreting the code for years now, but we need to teach the clan so as a clan we can grow stronger. You will give her the mark of disgrace in private and we will cage her in the main courtyard and any who do her harm will share in her punishment. She will be released to go with those who will start the new settlement."

Lyamy stood the young woman up and bound her hands in front of her with enough cord to use a leash. She turned towards the door and saw the damage to the frame. "I'll have two guards posted outside and a repair team come fix that tomorrow."

Yaun laughed, "The door is the least of my concerns." shaking his head, "Her name is Serine."

Lyamy nodded and lead Serine out closing the door as best she could. She gestured to a guard that happened to be passing and he turned and approached her. "We need two guards posted outside Lord Yaun's door for the night. Advise one of the protectors at his office door and they will see to it."

"Yes, Lyamy." the guard made a slight bow of his head and vanished in the right direction.

"Serine," Lyamy began as she led her into the courtyard, "You are going to be in a cage on public display for a while, do you want a chance to wander around town while we talk, the closest I can give you to a little freedom before your sentence begins or would you prefer my quarters where it is private and nobody will see you are captive until tomorrow. I am good either way, you will tell me the things I need to know." She stopped and turned facing Serine who looked her in the eyes. Lyamy made her eyes burst with a flaming glow and go quiet. "You can tell me what I want, or I can take it from you. I can assure you it is easier for you to just tell me, although it is easier for me to just take it."

"I will tell you, but can I ask you one favor? Can you take me by Zenjin, that I might warn him of what I have done?"

"The schoolmaster? You belong to him? Why would he want you to attack Yaun?"

"He would not." Serine answered, "I was being foolish on my own. I thought maybe if Yaun died, I would be able to stay near Zenjin if not return to him. I did not want him banished to die with the rest."

Lyamy had a momentary puzzled look. "Serine they are not going to die. The hand of ShadowDancer will protect them, well you now also. This is not a banishment; this really is creating a new settlement to assure the survival of our people. They will live, you will live, and things will get better. Yes, we will go talk to Zenjin. We would not send a schoolmaster if they were just going to die, they provide too much value to the clan."

A tear formed at the corner of Serine's eye, "I was a fool and failed even at my foolishness."

Lyamy had never seen a tear before, she watched it break free and slide down Serine's cheek. "You need to be strong now. Let's go talk to your Zenjin."

They arrived at Zenjin's door and Lyamy knocked softly. She did not wish to wake up neighbors. She heard a rustle inside so refrained from knocking again. The door opened a few inches, then opened wider and Zenjin stepped into view. "Lyamy, what brings you here at this hour?" then he saw Serine, "Serine, come in."

"Thank you." Lyamy responded leading Serine in, noting his response when he saw she was her captive. "Serine asked if she could have your counsel before having to face the reward of her actions. I felt it was a wise choice to take lessons from her teacher in these matters. She has given me all the appropriate information that I required. If you have a room with only one door and no windows, I will allow you some time to give her private counsel that may help her learn. It is important that she gains the strength she needs continue. I will be waiting outside the room. I can give you two hours; anything longer will have to be in a public forum."

Zenjin took the leash when she handed it to him. Zenjin started to say thank you, but Lyamy's eyes stopped him before the words came out, so instead he asked "Can her hands be untied while she is in private?"

"Your words for her should not touch my ears. I am sorry, but it is not allowed for her hands to be free until her sentence has begun."

Lyamy sat patiently waiting after they went into the side room. About half the time had passed when another of the women of the den stepped out and paused seeing Lyamy sitting there alone, "Where, What, .." She seemed uncertain as to what she should ask.

"Zenjin is legally counseling one of his students, Serine. He only has one more hour before I must take her away to face her sentence in the morning." Lyamy held out the ring of her authority as if the woman did not already know who she was.

"Thank you," the woman deliberately paused before continuing, "for apprising me of the situation." She quickly slipped back into the deeper chambers of the den.

With a few minutes to spare, they came back out of the room. Serine looked much better, and even flashed an ever so brief smile at Lyamy. Lyamy did not want to know what was said or done in that room. "Thank you for taking the time to counsel your student." Lyamy stated in an official tone. And accepted the leash back from Zenjin, leading Serine out of the den.

"Lyamy?" Serine asked as she followed her back through town towards Lyamy's quarters.

"Yes, Serine?"

"When you carve the mark of shame in my face, can you stuff something in my mouth so if I scream nobody will hear it? I accept my fate, but you are right this will pass, and things will get better. Perhaps someday after we have settled the new land, you will come visit."

"That would be nice." Lyamy stated knowing she would be no longer with the clan by then. When Lyamy closed the door after they entered her quarters, she dropped the leash and went to one of her chests and pulled out a box of tools she had hoped she would never need to open. "You know you are getting off easy for having tried to kill the high lord of the clan without his dishonoring the code. I am going to do this fast; I am hoping the faster it happens the less you will feel the pain of the cutting." She held a partially wedged piece of wood up to Serine, "Keep this in you mouth and bite down against the pain and don't move." The blade she held in her hand was designed to remove strips of skin about a quarter inch wide it would take five strokes to make the mark, the corner of her eye back to the bottom of her ear, from ear to chin, from halfway down the first mark to just short of the bottom of her nose, from the corner of her mouth crossing the slash to her chin and then a stroke down the cheek crossing both of the last two, forming a lopsided pentagram on her cheek.

As soon as Serine bit down on the block of wood she maximized her speed and had all five strokes complete before the first started to bleed. Lyamy caught all of the strips of skin and had the skin and blade hidden from sight before Seline could react. She caught five drops of blood in the ritual glass that came in the kit and applied the powder to the open wounds. The powder did two things, slowed the bleeding and made sure the wound scarred. Tears were in Serine's eyes and she bit hard on the wood.

"Don't break your teeth." Lyamy whispered, "This is over, don't let tears fall from this side of your eye, they will burn." She caught Serine's tears with a small piece of linen Lyamy resisted when she found herself locked on staring at the blood in the ritual glass and feeling the hunger of the old magic.

"Only when you have to." a voice came from behind her, "it is addicting, the sweet taste, the sensation of power filling you." ShadowDancer stepped around and looked at Serine's cheek and touched her. "I will reduce the pain, but I would have to undo what you did before the scar could be taken and changing history is not allowed."

Lyamy pulled the wood block from her mouth. She held the small glass up to Serine's lips and said, "By your own blood you pay the price and drink that your honor may be restored in due time." Serine drank as she poured the glass. "No lay down on my bed and sleep until morning, this is the last bed you will get to sleep in until the caravan pulls out."

Serine laid down with her cheek up. ShadowDancer touched her and gave her dreams, glimpses of the new settlement and prosperity. "She will be fully rested when she wakes up. We need to push the schedule as fast as we can. If we can they need to be leaving by the end of a month."

"I will tell Yaun, he can make it happen. Supplies will be ready, Merkyet is set on proving she is up to any task I give her. She will be proud of her success over me when I am gone and never know I orchestrated it." Lyamy looked at the device Nelk had made to remove the arcane mark from her back. "While you are here, can I ask you a favor. Nelk made this device that will almost instantly remove a round patch of skin in one piece from my back taking the arcane mark Yaun placed there off. I will keep it with me until I leave, but I cannot reach that part of my back will you do it for me and heal the wound?"

"I will help you with that." ShadowDancer answered, then handed her a round patch of skin, "There you have the scar of your path and here is the mark for your illusion."

"I felt nothing, and you did not use his tool." Lyamy caught herself, "Thank you." She slipped the round marked patch of skin in her pocket

ShadowDancer captured the moment, and Lyamy's training continued. She was still thirteen years old, but Lyamy was sure she had received at least five years of training from ShadowDancer's captured moments. She had over eighteen years of experience plus the knowledge of the old magic and the clan that had been placed in her mind. ShadowDancer had told her she was with cub, really early stages and something about excluding that from the captured moment so she would not show before she left the clan. The males of the clan were expected to start forming a den during their fourteenth year and the females were expected to have had one or two cubs and then join a den by the end of their thirteenth year. By birth, females outnumbered males by three to one, as a society of adults it was more like eight or nine to one. The males were more often sent to defend the clan and they were more involved in the politics and wrestling for power within the clan, so more frequent they die in battle and are assassinated.

ShadowDancer kept teaching Lyamy the history of her own people along with other skills and general history of the world. The references code of honor and code of order were interchangeable, references to the same code. The application and interpretation of these codes has been corrupted over time, code that was written to prevent killing each other had been corrupted to imply the opposite in practice. Their savage roots were manipulating ways around the guidance to help them be civilized and if they kept it up, they would wipe themselves out without the help of an enemy. Lyamy began writing her expanded understanding of the intent and origins of the code. She wrote three copies, one to give to Zenjin to go west, one for the instructors that would remain in the clan homelands and a copy she would take with her when she left. She did not know the fullness of the impact that her writing would have in the future of the clan. She would become known to their descendants as the mother of civilization.

Lyamy stepped out of the moment and checked Serine. Serine was sleeping and peace and calm showed on her face. Lyamy was sure the dreams ShadowDancer gave her were filling her with hope of what would come later to give her the strength to survive what she had to do now. Watching Serine sleep was a reprieve from the never-ending activity she was now used to having in her life. When morning came it felt like it arrived way too soon, and she fed Serine in her room before taking her to the cage that was currently in Yaun's office. Once the cage was locked, Lyamy untied her hands.

*   *   *   *   *

In the morning everyone was outside for breakfast before the sun was up. Chelic looked in her backpack for the first time and discovered she had been given a magic bag that seemed to hold a volume of goods much larger than the bag itself. In the entry way of the cave to one side of the rather large chamber she pulled out enough pots, pans, and implements for cooking and eating to take care of at least ten times the number of people present. As she emptied the rest of the content, there were all kinds of hand tools they could use for working materials to turn the caves into a home, a shelter and sanctuary.

Chelic still had an air of disconnect, but a calm aura at peace with the world and it rubbed off on those around her. She prepared food and let everyone know when breakfast was ready to eat. They gathered in a circle sitting around the unlit fire pit to eat.

Desdin gesturing with his fork continued, "It should be easy to build carts from using those wheels after we disassemble the cannons. I just don't know if wheels or skids will be easier to pull stuff through this sand."

"Either way we need to pace ourselves, it will be months before any salvage operation will even get initiated so we have time for everything other than the food stores. They should be our priority." Freldin spoke in a voice that tended to sway people to his opinion.

"Even if it is month," Marrianne did not even look up from her food as she spoke, "We have to sweep away our trail and even the ground so the wind, water and time can completely conceal the fact we ever passed along the shore."

Freldin nodded, "Agreed, but that is after we salvage everything." he looked at the four natives to the land, "Have you folks any suggestions?"

Jenyin showed no evidence of opinion in his face. "We will have to see this ship to know what you are talking about, perhaps then we can offer opinion or suggestions."

"Well, when everyone is ready we can go." Freldin stood up.

Chelic took his plate, "Everyone just stack your plates and utensils, I will get them cleaned up and put away, then catch up or go next trip. That was a great idea, Grimble, wrapping the wheels with the wide banding from the ships prow so they don't sink in the sand." She set the dishes she was carrying on a small ledge in the cave and grabbed a bucket vanishing inside to get clean water.

"How is she doing that?" Jenyin pondered.

"It started after she almost died from Lyamy's wound and ShadowDancer had to pull her back." Daret answered.

Karis did not have the fire and anger she had before, but added, "She did not almost kill her, Chelic died, she did kill her. I think she has been touched by the afterlife and will never be completely the same."

"I am sure she will be alright." Jenyin stated, "The rest of us can go see what this ship we are going to salvage is. It seems it will require a lot of space to store everything."

Conversation as they walked rambled from one thing to another. They talked about improving the caves for living purposes, Some discussion of social arrangements. They discuss the differences in lifestyles and family relationships. The Shadowkyn were surprised by the ways of the strangers, including such things as exclusive relations with only one mate. The idea that sex had anything to do with liking someone or was a private issue, was alien. The expressions of the strangers said more than their words at the liberal attitude they had about the subject. The concepts were so different that the subject was quickly changed. It seemed the subject had to be changed a few more times as contrast in thinking became evident, including when Jenyin warned them again that they do not want to meet the clan.

As they rounded a curve in the coast about three miles from the cave, they could see the ship. They were less than half way there, but not by much. The tide was low and the boat was high on the beach like debris left by a storm at high tide.

"So, it is like a house that floats on the water?" Jenyin asked.

"I suppose you could look at it like that." Freldin agreed.

The closer they got the bigger the ship seemed to get. The lead end of the ship had breaks and splintering in the underside where it was pressed into the sand. It was a large cargo ship, one of the largest ships until recently on the sea.

"There is enough wood here to build a small village." Daret commented. "and you say this is like a big box full of the cargo it was carrying? You could stack five buildings on top of each other to get that height, and that is the smallest dimension."

"The cannons are inside." Freldin stated leading them to the gang planks leading up to the side of the ship. Birds took to the air as they clambered onto the deck. The captian was still hanging on the tiller and there were signs of a sudden stop obvious to the survivors, not so much to those who did not know where things belonged on a ship deck. They climbed a stairway to the next Deck down and there were the cannons aimed at windows that appeared to be boarded shut. The wheels on the cannons were about half the height of the taller members of the group."

Grimble looked over the situation. "It will take Desdin and I a little time to disassemble these and get the axles and wheels outside to start building a cart. There are enough Wheels here though to build at least three four-wheel carts."

"We will keep them simple, flat beds for now, in the interest of time and weight, considering we have no horses or beasts to pull them other than ourselves." Desdin added.

"Everyone else can just grab loads they can carry for now and we can start bringing things back to the cave. Then you are in charge Jenyin, you know the caves and where we can store things." Freldin suggested.

They all explored the entire ship before deciding on what and how to carry things. Before they actually started to salvage, they collected those that did not survive the crash and buried them above the highest waterlines. There were bags and backpacks in the compartments with the armor and weapons. Jenyin noticed that there were enough swords to arm every member of the clan and then some. They were stored in boxes of ten. The armor did not interest him as much, it seemed the weight and obstruction it caused would slow the wearer down and prevent them from moving effectively in battle, making them targets. They all grabbed bags for carrying things and agreed to start by salvaging food stores. Everyone would just pace themselves according to their own ability.

The bags he could carry did hold enough weight to be a burden to Jenyin, there was just not enough room to carry more. He was about half-way back when he passed Chelic on her way out. She smiled and waved and kept walking without a word, although she already had her own backpack. He realized she would carry ten times what he could just in that one backpack. He wondered if he would get one if he asked. He brought the food he was carrying straight back and turned into a side chamber that was consistently cooler than the rest. The back wall actually had frost some of the time. As they progressed through the day, he found he was not making as many trips as he would have chosen to, but only because he kept having to work on organizing and directing the storage of the goods and materials being brought back.

Daret and Karis pulled the first wagon load back. Initially the wagon was too heavy for the wheels to be effective in the sand. It was not until after they had fashioned the metal strapping form the ship to widen the wheels that Grimble remembered what Chelic had said. He figured it must have been the suggestion that gave him the idea. The cart had been loaded with boxes of swords and Desdin and Freldin could not get it moving very fast, so they were going to reduce the load. Daret and Karis made them wait until they tried, and they were able to get the cart up to a good walking speed and pulled it back to the cave. The main tunnel or hall as they started referring to it was large enough for the makeshift wagon to fit through without difficulty. They started warehousing the non-perishables in a large dry open chamber several times the size of the ship. It did not have multiple decks and they had not built any shelves yet. Instead they stacked things as orderly as they could in rows with space between them for navigating and retrieving items.

The second cart was complete and Freldin and Chineene started hauling it back and forth with lighter loads, but much faster than by the backpack full. Chelic was moving more than anyone else finding she could carry about two hundred and fifty cubic feet at a time in her backpack, about as much as Daret and Karis carried each trip. They actually had her carry the metal portions of the cannons because the bag reduced the weight and made it easy. The third cart just needed the flatbed added when the shadows grew long enough for everyone to call it a day. Chelic seemed to have appointed herself head chef, but Marrianne insisted on helping her with the evening meal and they prepared a modest feast for the group from the supplies taken from the ship and herbs, eggs and vegetables that had been gathered on the way to find the caves.

The second sun set and the sky lit up with stars and a sliver of moon hung high over the ocean. Looking up they all had a feeling, a sense of promise, of a new hope. Later in the privacy of their den, Daret asked, "Did you notice their females only have two breasts insstead of six or eight? They would not be much help in a nursery."

"They seem excessively large and, in the way, too." Karis added, "They would get in the way of doing things."

"They do things differently than we do." Chelic purred

Jenyin looked at Chelic, "It is good to see you so happy. You seem content with our new life."

"I am, and with where we go when we leave." she fell asleep leaving them uncertain if she had finished what she was saying or fell asleep first.

"She will be alright." Jenyin stated. They all curled around her; a den always slept in one bed. Some dens even had more than one male, but with the uneven balance of males and females it was not as common as dens with no males.

*   *   *   *   *

Yaun felt for Serine, but he did not let it show. "So, we have to force the schedule for the departure, that is the only way we can get them out of here in less than a month. I had a dream though last night. Massive amounts of the larger ferocious beasts of our lands were returning to the land from some war somewhere, and the third we sent to find the new settlement were barely keeping ahead and out of trouble. Dreams sometimes are warnings."

"Dreams or not, ShadowDancer said to make it happen." Lyamy shrugged, "Maybe telling them your dream will help, maybe it will scare them into dragging their feet."

"They had better not!"

"They know we can open a portal between places once they get there and anything, they forget they can come back for. That is basic arcane ability. It is your place to decide what we do. I will act according you your deliberation of the matter. The courtyard should be full, and it is time for us to present Serine in her punishment."

Lyamy followed Yaun out with Serine and her cage in tow. When they reach the landing outside, she moved the cage to the end, lifted it and hung it from a large hooked shaft that stuck out of the building for this purpose. She touched Serine on the hand where she clung to the bar of the cage and passed a little more healing energy. Serine gave a brief smile of appreciation that cracked the scab on her cheek and caused it to start bleeding a small trickle again.

Yaun read out loud for anyone who was passing the proclamation of punishment and the clause protecting her from further physical harm by those passing by and affixed the document to the cage. "Now to step up the schedule for departure. This really is about our survival. It does not matter if they like it or believe it, they will live longer with the distance between us and if they wait too long getting out of here, we will lose some as a meal to the savage beasts of the jungle." Yaun paused and looked at Lyamy, "You are very complicated. You spare your enemies for the greater good of the clan and yet you make examples of others to reinforce the importance of upholding the code. Now you are rubbing off on me, elevating the code to a place where it should always have been in order for our people to survive. I never was one for statues and memorials, but when you have done what you must, I am going to have a statue made to honor you with metal plates containing the full book of code."

"I am honored by the thought. If it will help the future of our people then do it, if not, I will be more honored by the doing of things that are for the good of our people as a whole." she dropped to one knee in front of him, "I am but a humble servant for the greater good of the clan." Lyamy was a little surprised when she realized she meant what she said and would in fact chose her own death if it meant the salvation of the clan.

"Come, let's get this meeting over with." They stepped into the preparation area of the assembly room and Yaun listened through the curtains for a few minutes before stepping out in view. He walked up to the podium and Lyamy shadowed him. "Give me your attention and perhaps we can keep this brief." He paused while the assembly turned and quieted down, "Foresight has been given to leaders of the clan throughout our records in the form of dreams. This has been accepted by our people forever. I am going to share with you the dream I had last night." Yaun shared his dream and then had Lyamy step up and tell them what the Ancient had told her.

Peltrhak stepped forward, "I will not be caught arguing with the Ancient's wishes again. You are correct Lyamy we only need to carry what we need for the journey. You are the Protector of the clan as appointed by Yaun and as chosen by this Ancient who seeks to help us. For conscience's sake and testimony before our people, if you declare our belongings protected in our absence until we can establish a portal from our new settlement and recover them. I will stand by that and we can expedite our departure."

"Your belongings are protected. I am confident nobody who remains behind will wish to find themselves arguing with ShadowDancer." Lyamy felt a tug of the old magic, her eyes instantly picked Merkyet out of the crowd. She averted her eyes to keep Merkyet from suspecting anything more than glancing over the crowd. She stepped back and let Yaun take back the podium.

"It is settled then; I also give my word to protect your belongings. The departure date will be twenty-five days from today. Adjust all schedules accordingly."

Lyamy knew the glint that slipped through the curtain behind them was intended for her, but she was fast, and the young guard really did not have a chance. He found himself face down on the floor with the tip of his own blade against the back of his neck. "Merkyet, come forward please. I have a job for you."

Merkyet came forward, she did not have the nervousness one might have expected from a young apprentice recently appointed to a new position, "Yes, protector?"

"Look at this guards' eyes, can you see the lost focus?"

"I do."

"He is under an influence that has overwhelmed his own thinking. You will head an investigation of this matter and report your finding back to me. Do you understand?"

"I will do as I have been bid." a touch of over confidence glinted in her eye.

Lyamy turned the hilt of the sword to Merkyet, "Take him now and do not let him do anything foolish before you can get him cleansed of this influence."

Merkeyt was a little tentative taking the sword from Lyamy, looking for the trap or device by which Lyamy was going to bring her down. The guard got up as she instructed him and she followed him out of the assembly room, performing in proper fashion as one taking their captive for questioning.

"And again." Yaun smile and led Lyamy back the way they came. "You knew something was up before it happened, I saw your look snap to the left over the crowd, then you had that guard down before he knew he attacked anyone. Then you single out your rival to investigate. If she does well, she is obligated to you for promoting her, if she fails, she must concede she is not on a par with you and accept you as her better."

That had nothing to do with why she picked Merkyet, but she would let him think that. Merkyet was the one controlling his actions. If she told the truth she would be admitting to her crime and being caught, if she did not it would give Lyamy leverage over Merkyet without letting her know she was her training master. "Indeed, strength by keeping my rivals alive and in line for the good of the clan. Merkyet is very sharp, perhaps she could serve the clan with the inspectors of the guard, her cunning might assist in exposing any plots against you. As long as you take her in before someone else does her cunning will work for you instead of against you."

"Your selections have served me well so far, but this will be the third command under me that you have placed someone who could be under your influence. It is not that I do not trust you, but in accordance with the code that is a limit I cannot allow you to exceed."

Lyamy laughed, "You are right, that is what the code says. I will restrain my future suggestions for appointments to these three commands." She closed the office door behind her as she followed him into his office. Her tail twitched as she watched him walk to his desk and she quickly diverted her thoughts to other things.

"That went much better than I expected. Peltrhak stepping up, stopped anyone else from objecting. I have the impression that he really wants to go now. It really will be like he is running his own clan; we will have little influence over what they do."

"Well, we do need to have our really hard lined methods when dealing with things outside the clan, but code that applies to a beast on the outside does not mean it applies inside the clan. Even separated by the distance across the continent, there is an obligation to help each other survive."

"Have you ever helped kill a leophardeg?"

"I have not served at the West Gates."

"Perhaps we should take a trip there and you can observe a few of the fights. I should like to see if your wonderful insight can help us to be more effective defending. I would be even more delighted if after your fashion some wondrous solution that stops the fighting and lets the beasts live to." He laughed at the idea, "You may really be able to provide some insight into techniques that will help us fight them."

"I will do whatever I can for the clan, Lord Yaun."

Twenty-five days was not a lot of time. Lyamy wanted to be sure to finish her exhaustive study on the code of honor so when ShadowDancer came to train her, she asked if she could have enough of this time in captured moments to finish her work. ShadowDancer did one better, she helped her gain more insight than she already had. For every code she wrote how it came about, if it was revised and with the "how" and "why" included, an explanation of the intent and application and samples of where it did apply and where it did not apply. When they were done, each copy had five volumes. After that, she went through all her normal training, well as normal as what ShadowDancer brought her could be.

Merkyet came for her studies as scheduled, tonight would be lessons to remember. Lyamy was actually already in the room hidden when Merkyet came in. She let Merkyet sit there for several minutes before the doors suddenly locked. Merkyet jumped to a fighting stance searching the shadows of the room. "If you had to defend yourself, you would already be dead."

"I did not see you come in."

"I was already here." Lyamy came out of the shadows still disguised, even as Merkyet was disguised. "Old magic is not to be abused."

Merkyet looked nervous, "I did not abuse them, am I not supposed to use them to achieve things in accordance with the clan and the way I was raised?"

"Old magic is a gift to the clan and a responsibility to the individual. You tried to use them for personal gain that would have hurt the clan, that is abuse. If I stopped your heart or better yet, tortured you right now you would deserve it."

Merkyet dropped to the floor with her knees folder under and her hands extended over her head and lay against the ground, "If I am worthy of death, I cannot stop you. If you spare me, I will try harder to be worthy of your teaching."

She gave a tug, letting Merkyet know she was inside her mind, "I believe you mean that Merkyet, but how can I make sure you always remember to think through the good of the clan before you use the old magic?"

"I will do my best; I do not know how to promise more than that."

"Strip off everything you wear."

Merkyet did as she was instructed and a dagger appeared in her hand, she recognized it as a sacrificial dagger, "What is this for?" She watched herself as she raised the dagger and placed the tip over her heart.

"You have evil in your heart that would make you act to hurt your clan and you must cut it out if you are going to be strong enough to wield the old magic for the good of the clan."

Merkyet trembled, she knew what she was expected to do. The thought came through her fear if this would make her strong for the good of the clan, then she would live through it. She looked down at her chest and started pulling the dagger in blood began to flow as the tip penetrated her skin, she could feel the pain as it went deeper. She plunged it hard, and the knife vanished, and she was sitting on the floor fully clothed.

"You will remember this when you consider taking action without thinking about the effect it will have on the clan first."

Merkyet felt as if her selfishness had been somehow cut out.

"It is still there, but you have a tool now to help you keep it under control. It was foolish to try and kill your master, the distorting of her trainers voice was clearing away."

Merkyet looked confused, then thoughts registered, and she looked horrified for a moment before subjecting her feelings to a cold exterior. "Lyamy? If it is you, why would you teach me the old magic at all? And even more why would you reveal yourself to me now?"

"As my student you can do me no harm, so I do not need to kill you for trying. The clan needs the old magic to survive for the future and you are the strongest and smartest left after I am gone. The codes nor the old magic were never intended to have Shadowkyn killing Shadowkyn the way it has been happening for way too long now. Rivals in the clan were supposed to compete for achievement to give the clan strength, not for survival within the clan. The old magic has to be used to protect the clan. I reveal myself now, because time has become short so I have to teach you as best I can and give you this book so you can continue after I am gone. I will not live much longer in the clan." Lyamy pulled the book of old magic out of the air and handed it to Merkyet. "Soon you will be the master, so you will have to work on your own after I am gone to learn as much as you can. You will have to find another to teach." Lyamy removed the wraps from her head exposing clearly who she was to Merkyet. "You are a secret, and you hold the secret power of the clan. You must avoid reaching levels of too much power in the clan, but you want to be in a position where you can see and feel the heartbeat of the clan."

"You are leaving?"

"You will see. I am too close to the political power of the clan. To have the power of the old magic and that of clan leader are forbidden. The rest of the clan does not know I have old magic, they do not believe it is real, but they will see I have more power then Yaun and at some point, start insisting I should be leader. So, for the good of the clan I will have to be sacrificed before that happens. I have already arranged this, and Yaun already knows he must do it when the time is right. Because of events, that time is closer than we planned. You will tell no one once you become master except the one you choose to be your student. Are you clear on everything?"

"I think so."

"Then I think we are done for tonight." Merkyet did not see Lyamy leave, She knew the trick, but it did not work for the student on the master. It did work for her on others, she had tried and tested that and other spells. Later in her room, she pulled open her shirt and looked at her chest certain she would see a wound that was healed or a scar. It was so real, but it had been in her mind only. She laughed at herself when she realized Lyamy had even told her with that tug inside her mind before the lesson had started. She opened the book and fell asleep as she started reading.

*   *   *   *   *

Lyamy left the training room and went back and fed Serine. She stood and talked with her for a while. She paused and looked at Serine for a few minutes. She was going to the west with the other settlement. They were going to need a keeper of the old magic also. *'But I do not have the time to teach her.'* Lyamy thought. "Are you willing to be the carrier of the greatest secret of the clan, to be responsible for the future of the clan you are with, carry the burden of your clan and the burden of a secret you cannot share?"

"If it will atone for my actions and do good for the clan and my den, I will do what I can."

Lyamy reached out with her thoughts, *'ShadowDancer you can read my intent. Capture us the way you do in a moment, in a place where I can initiate her and perhaps place in her mind the way you did mine, enough of the secrets that she can take them with her to the western settlement.'* She felt the ripple pass through her. They were in a room with a large bond fire in the middle. The floor and walls were covered in the language of the old magic. The tools and tokens of all the rituals decorated the room. She felt the primal power surge and fill her. Serine stood quietly in front of her.

Lyamy took her through the initiation and performed the master student ritual. They went through all the lessons required to be able to use the book. Lyamy pulled the book out and held it out for Serine to take. ShadowDancer appeared and reached over and touched Serine on the side of her head, "It is done."

"Take the book Serine." Lyamy spoke softly, but insistent. And after Serine took the book pulled out the five volumes of the expanded code, "Put this in your hidden pocket also, perhaps they will help guide your settlement down the right path."

"Thank you." Serine whispered. Her face both looking intrigued and horrified as she started sorting through the knowledge and history ShadowDancer had placed in her mind.

ShadowDancer let go of the moment and vanished. Serine was back in her cage and Lyamy let go of the bar she was holding. Neither said anything, Lyamy turned and walked away. The night air was a little cool but refreshing.

*   *   *   *   *

Every last splinter of the ship was warehoused in the caves. They had the materials now to make the caves a comfortable sanctuary for several times their number. The shipwreck survivors seemed to be in no rush to move on, more than that having fun helping with the sanctuary. As it turned out, Desdin could reshape stone with a magical touch, and Grimble could do the same thing with wood. They tried teaching their magic to Jenyin, but it seemed when he attempted what they suggested, wood burst into flames and rock turned to magma. These skills were not entirely useless, he could start a campfire easy now and melt rock out of the way, except it was really hot for a long time. Freldin stated as if he knew all along, "Desdin and Grimble are using arcane magic, but Jenyin, you are using primal power, it is much more powerful and harder to control. Usually, rituals are required to control primal magic." Jenyin did not reveal any of the secrets of the old magic, he may be starting a new community, but that was clan secrets.

Desdin had altered the entrance to the cave, making it more stable and better fit for adding a door. He also worked a counter into the stone so Chelic could start using it as a kitchen area. They discuss at length the doors for the entrance. In the end they agreed to a large door that could open and close to let large things in and out with a small door in the middle of it for normal passage. They also discuss concealing the door from the outside. Once inside the entrance, the initial cavern widened out significantly allowing them to build the kitchen area and a place to sit and eat and still stay out of the way if they needed to pull the carts in and out.

"Breakfast is ready!" Chelic yelled back through the cave. It was her turn so Daret helped set the food and plates out on the table. They all took turns assisting Chelic who insisted on being their chief cook.

"Did you get those locks open?" Daret asked as Marrianne stepped out of the cave leading back.

"No, but I did get the chests all open."

"Did you break them open like I suggested?"

"No, Daret, even better, I pulled the hinge pins out. Those are masterful locks, but they put them on chests that were not for security, so when I finally got around to looking at the back of the chest it took about 5 second to have it open. We could stock a magic item shop with what they contained."

"What items?" Freldin asked as he stepped in the room.

"From the chests, she has been working on that on and off since we wrecked." Chineene half mocked him as she followed him out.

All nine of them sat down to eat and indulged themselves in idle chat while they ate. They avoided for now topics that diverged into uncomfortable conversation. As they were finishing up their meal Desdin talking about the doors for the front of the cave added, "The hinges and planks we have from the ship are plenty stout enough I can coat the outside with stone and shape it like it was just more of the cliff, then you would have to be right on top of it and look hard if you did not know the doors were there."

"That does eliminate the aura that would show hiding them with an illusion if someone was searching with magic detection." Freldin stated

"Do you guys really think someone will come searching the coast for caves? I really think they will just count the ship as lost and when they cannot see the remains anywhere or where it landed they will move on even if they do look." Chineene trivialized the discussion of concealment with the tone of her voice.

Marrianne scoffed, "If you saw what was in those chests, I am sure you would be convinced that someone is not going to give up looking for what they lost. Everything else on that ship summed up together would pale in value to what was in one of those chests and there were eleven. I was not kidding when I said we could open a magic items shop. That crew was getting drunk thinking they were going to retire off this delivery I am sure. The excitement might have been what killed the captain, or maybe the crew poisoned him hoping to cut up the captain's share. I am thinking the crew that abandoned the ship and us left only in part because of the stories of this land, and in part because they were afraid of being cursed if they stayed with the ship and cargo."

"They may be cursed anyway if an arch Magus suspects foul play." Grimble added, "Do any of you have ways to make that stuff untraceable? At least while it is here?"

"We can put the chests into primordial pockets." Jenyin offered, "Items hidden in them are shifted through folds in time and dimension, hidden in the undefined primordial soup between realities and time."

"The undefined nonexistence" Grimble laughed, "If only someone could actually tap into that, but magic schools of all cultures have been trying for, well forever and none have managed to even touch it."

"It is said that is where the Ancients draw their power." Chineene added.

"Guys, I said his magic was primal, unlike anything we have seen elsewhere, I may even be mistaken, if the source of his magic is primordial then to him it would no more difficult than making a hidden holding container in our schools of magic. Can you set it so that all of us can have access to the chests?"

"They will be bound to Primal marks on the wall so anyone can open them by touching the mark. We can protect the room from access by strangers to keep them secure." Jenyin knew his magic, this was not even old magic, most of the clan was capable of making these fixed location pockets. They helped save space, but anyone stepping into the room knew they were there, and while there was no way to see what was being stored inside without opening them and looking, anyone could open them and look.

Marrianne shook her head, "I am sorry, but before we go putting that much loot in one of these pockets, I am going to have to see how they work."

Jenyin, made some ritualistic gestures and took a plate from the table and made it vanish in the air, "There now anyone who puts their hand on this mark," He placed his hand where the plate vanished, "can access the pocket."

"I don't see any mark." Marrianne stated.

"It is right here." Daret said placing her hand in the air and pulling the plate out.

"I do not see it either." Chineene added

Freldin looked around, "Who can see it?" Jenyin, Daret, Karis and Chelic all indicated they could. The rest of the party could not. "I am going to guess that this is a racial ability. Your race works with magic that I think comes from the primordial source and it is part of your nature to see this. We cannot touch the primordial source, so we cannot see it."

"We cannot put all that stuff where we cannot get to it." Marrianne looked upset at the thought.

"We cannot leave it all out where some guild of mages will come tracking it down and hold us to blame." Grimble shook his head at Marrianne

"I say we store it this way until we can come up with something better. There are four members of the community that can access them, and I am sure they will not keep us away. When we find a better method, we can change what we are doing." Freldin stated as if he had final say.

"Well, if I am the only one that has a problem with this, I guess I can just suck it up. There are a couple items I am going to take though before the rest gets sealed up." Marrianne disappeared back into the caves.

"She did not eat half her food." Chelic commented, "I'll just cover it, she will be back later to finish."

"We need to get a cooking surface and an oven made for Chelic." Grimble commented as he swept the last bite of his breakfast from his plate.

Desdin finishing his meal also, added, "We will need a chimney also, but smoke billowing out the side of the rocks will be a dead giveaway to our location."

"There is a vent that comes out about a halfway up the ridge on the river side that comes from the magma flows down below. Perhaps you can just run something partway up the ridge and have it look similar to that from a distance?" Jenyin asked.

"That is a great idea, for now we can just run it over to that side of the ridge, it will be at least a month after they decide the ship is missing before they could possibly get someone to this continent to look for it. That will only happen if they have reason to believe it even came this way." Desdin stated, "We should probably manage that before we put doors up though."

"You are the stone guy." Grimble stated, "I'll let you work on that, and I'll get the metal and wood up here that we will need for the stove and doors." He got up and headed back into the depths of the caves.

"I am going to go up top on the ridge and see if I can collect more eggs, and maybe gather some more herbs and vegetation for food and seasoning. Anyone else want to join me?" Karis inquired.

"Sounds like fun." Chelic answered, "but we have to get breakfast cleaned up."

"That can wait until we get back, or I suppose I can help you finish up before we go."

"I think I am going to scout the area with Chineene." Freldin stood up, "It will be good to know the area around us and what resources we have when we need them. Jenyin, did you want to go with us, you know the dangers of these lands better than we do and might be able to teach us a few things to look out for."

"I will go with you. Let me grab a couple things from my room first." Jenyin headed back to the den. He stored his gear there now. The space was large enough for them to partition it off into sections, they would later build walls to establish them as rooms. The place was starting to feel like home. He grabbed his bow, swords and a collection bag, went back and headed out with Freldin and Chineene. He did find he had to correct himself when he kept thinking of the others the way he would harvesters. They were not a servant class, they were peers in the current environment, but the code of the clan did not apply in addressing them.

The sanctuary felt like it was becoming a community. For now, they did not need rules to live by and decisions could be made by tribunal. As they grew, they would need to start laying down rules or laws. Jenyin would bring this up at their evening meal.

*   *   *   *   *

There was nothing happening at the gates when they arrived. Reports indicated that the number of attacks was way down over the last few weeks. The last few days they had picked back up to an attack every other day. The savage beasts including the leophardeg were not exactly smart. They followed more of a see or smell, attack and eat concept.

Lyamy stood with Yaun in a back tower watching the two towers on either side of the gates and the gates below. "Normally until a few weeks back, we had random attacks two or three times a day. The more common attacks were the leophardeg, but they were not the worst. Any of the savage beasts that attack can jump the height of the towers. The cage suspended over the gates is probably the safest place to be when they attack, but it is bait, the first visible target to attackers. So far they have not been able to open the cages."

"So why don't we just build metal fencing out further from the gates?" Lyamy studied the layout below.

"That was tried, but then we have to defend the metal fencing gates and they do not hold as well as the cage. The greater span allows it to bend under the weight of the attacking beasts and they can climb and jump over the fencing. The gates themselves have proven more defensible."

"Have they ever gotten passed the second set of gates and towers?"

"Only a couple times and it was when they attacked in groups. They normally hunt alone. When they attack as a pride, it is usually for territory not food. Keep in mind when you see an attack, the leophardeg are the smaller of the beasts, although the more common."

Lyamy sniffed the air about the same time she saw the guard go on heightened alert, "Something is near."

The massive creature leaped from beyond sight in the jungle, between the two towers over the gate tearing the cage down to the ground behind the gates. Lyamy could see the creature mauling the cage on the ground between her position and the tower diagonally across from the one she was in. A rain of arrows hit the beast and it reared up letting go of the cage. The mouth opened in her direction as it turned, four times as wide as her height with several rows of teeth. Without hesitation, she hurled a fireball inside before it managed to turn in the direction of its target. The blast threw it back dazed for a moment as arrows began making the creature look like it had quills instead of just fur. Lyamy leaped her way down the stairs of the tower. She wanted a closer look at the beast that was now dieing on the ground between the towers.

The individual in the cage was a harvester and while Lyamy did not normally pay much attention to them, this one was dressed as a guard and had weapons, still firing their bow at the downed creature. She started to go for the beast, but then stopped, the harvester soldier had a hurt leg, possibly broken. She shook her head and went to the cage. "You are hurt."

"It got a claw through the cage." The guard turned his leg so she could see the torn open wound running from above the knee to the ankle. The guard had long ears like a rabbit and their race still had a degree of fur instead of hair. The tail was short enough to be hidden inside the armor, but the legs were more powerful for greater jumping then her own.

Lyamy reached through the cage and began healing. She could feel the infection pushing out. She was losing the time she had to see the beast still alive, but without some healing the infection would have been bad, and he could bleed out. "I guess I can still learn what I need to after it dies."

"Do what you must, leave me the medics will come."

She yanked a rope form her belt to tie a tourniquet, "I'll stop this bleeding first, so they still have someone to save when they get here." She tied it quickly and made sure the bleeding at least slowed and then rushed the creature. She leaped quickly from one point to another, searching for places she could feel the pulse and other weaknesses and openings in the natural defenses. She could feel a level of Primal magic in the creature's fur, something that might be workable in the creating of magic items. She checked for any other residuals on the creature, but it seemed only the fur kept a residual virtue. "Skin this thing and send the fur to Nelk." she ordered without even looking to see who was there to receive the order. The anatomy was different enough, she was sure this creature did not evolve from the cat form like most of the aggressive creatures of their land.

When she was done examining the creature she leaped back to where the guard in a cage had been. Two medics had him out of the cage on a litter. With a glance she knew he was going to be alright, so she headed back to Yaun.

"So, what did you discover?" Yaun asked confident she would have something helpful.

"First the fur on that creature retains magical qualities. I am having it sent to Nelk to see if he can render anything of value from it." She pulled a stick of charcoal from her bag of tricks and drew the creature front and back on the wall with markings and notes. "These are the locations where it is vulnerable to attack. The places where our archers should aim to take it down more quickly. You saw how effective that one spell was in disabling further destruction by the creature. We should keep a caster in each of the towers to aid. Our people have these skills, they are not a secret, we should use them. Has anyone thought of stringing razor wire between the towers the beasts will not see it and it could prove to have a fatal impact even if only on some of the creatures?"

"I knew you would be able to help at least some." Yaun stated.

"I would like to go out there and find the different creatures alive."

"I can send you with a team," Yaun started.

"Alone," she interrupted him, "I can watch out for myself, but I cannot defend a team on the hunt and keep the prey alive. I also can not reveal some of what I am going to do to others. It will be easier not to cover up with explanations."

"Well, I can track you if you get in trouble."

"And then what send people out to die with me? If I make a mistake it is on me out there, there will be nothing you can do." She looked back out the window, "Have you tried cutting the jungle back far enough that we might see them before they jump through the gates?"

Yaun shook his head, "It grows back to quickly for cutting to be effective and those cutting or burning it back get caught without any defenses dyeing faster than the guards letting them get to the gates. If you must, go out there, but only if you are very confident you will survive to come back. There is a difference between being brave and being foolish and sometimes that line can get blurry."

"This is not particularly brave, nor is it foolish. I will return with knowledge and unscathed. I will first inquire of the men of every type of beast they have encountered at the gates and the ones they have only heard about."

"I hope it proves worth the risk." Yaun conceded.

Lyamy knew when she got out there, she would be using old magics to keep herself out of trouble. Her people were once as bad or worse than these savage creatures. She got descriptions and names of all the creatures she could from the guards. There was little of any value to the descriptions of behavior, according to the guards, all the beasts behaved the same. She took into consideration they served their duty assignments and left. No one knew any extended stay at the west gates. She would talk to Yaun about this too, they did not have time to learn to know their enemies. New guards repeated the same mistakes of the last new guards with nobody getting smarter by experience.

'*I should have gotten blood from that fallen beast, while it was still alive, or at least fresh.*' It was too late for that now. Lyamy heard the whispers of disbelief as she slipped out the gates and had them closed behind her. She vanished to the eyes; a spell not unfamiliar to her people. What she did next they could not see, but she would leave no trail and no scent. She sniffed the air; she was on the hunt and she could feel all the savagery she had learned about her ancestors swelling inside her. It was no surprise that the first scent she picked up was the leophardeg, they were the most common of the wild beasts.

Lyamy moved in the direction of the scent. It was actually moving in her direction. She moved with caution. The beast stepped into sight, sniffing the ground and the air, it too was hunting. She maneuvered around until she was directly in front of the beast as it started lifting its head from the ground. Her eyes filled with fire and she captivated the eyes of the beast. It was not as intelligent as the clan folks she had used this on, but what was lacking in smarts was made up for in determination. She started to sweat from the effort to keep the creature dominated while she did what she had to.

She drew five drops of blood from the creature and performed the ritual of the old magic. When she was done, the beast was hers. She climbed on the creatures back making herself invisible and without scent again, she listened to the creatures' mind. '*Go back to what you were doing, I am just here for the ride.*' The beast went back to the hunt. She paid attention to the leophardeg's likes and dislikes. There were plants he avoided and would not cross. He survived mostly on the small creatures that made the mistake of being seen. He would run things down, dig through anything, for a larger meal.

Lyamy saw a lot of the ways of her own people in the beast. She was ready to jump off at any moment when her pet came upon a female. They circled each other for a few minutes communicating their desires, both in agreement, they gave Lyamy a rough ride while they took care of business and when they were done went their separate ways. Not unlike the clan she thought to herself. When she felt she had gained as much information as she could about the creature, she slid from his back and thanked him for the ride, watching as his walked away. She felt the permanent bond in the distance, he would answer her call whenever she was in range and wanted him to. The ways of the old magic were usually permanent.

The ground shook from the footsteps of something very large. Lyamy pursued the sound and the shaking of the ground. When she caught up with it, she was looking upon something larger than any of the guards had seen. It was related to the creature at the gate. It emanated fear using old magic. If she had not been trained in old magic, she may have been frozen I place by the repeating waves pushed out from the fur of the creature like waves of dust. The mouth was massive, usable in battle swinging it back and forth would effectively shred anything in its path. Horvalka is the name of the breed, the one they took down at the gates was smaller and this larger one made the first one look tiny.

This creature was thirty feet tall and stood on its hind legs most of the time. Lyamy used a sparkling light glamor to get the creatures attention and stop it from rampaging onward. She was up a tree in a heartbeat and played with minor spell casting until she managed to get the beast to look in her direction. This beast was massive and could crush her by accident, but she dominated its mind as fast as her eyes lit up with fire. Not much of a mind, this one relied on brute force and instinct to survive. The creature reached out at her command and she stepped out on the extended arm and walked closer keeping eye contact.

She used her dagger and drew just enough blood to do the ritual. The old magic she used was similar to what she did to Freyie. The difference was the bond was not to the extent of feeling pain or death. Once she had control and was securely perched on the creatures neck, she instructed it to continue the hunt. This creature fed on anything, while it preferred other creatures, if it was not getting enough, it would eat massive portions of the jungle canopy. This creature avoided the same plants as the leophardeg and her own people as far as that goes. The plant was pelekura and if you wanted to insult someone you told them they smelled like a pelekura. It seemed this beast was an eating machine and the only fear it experienced was of the winged beasts somewhere in the distance near the middle of the continent. Images of jutting high peaks came to mind when the beast thought about the creatures it feared.

Lyamy over a period of five days tracked down five additional different creatures in the jungle that were on the list of gate attackers, before deciding she knew enough to head back. She dismounted before she got in range. She commanded the beast she rode back into the jungle and ran towards the gates. She called and the guards let her back in. They were sincerely surprised to see her return alive.

"Yaun headed back two days ago." The captain of the hunters that guarded the gates stated, "He decided that you knew what you were doing or something like that. He said to heed anything you instructed us when you returned."

"Great. Well to start with here are seeds, plant pelekura all around the outside of the gates for as far as you can."

"That stuff stinks."

"Yes, and none of the savage beasts will cross it so this stinky plant will make the gates safe and save the lives of those protecting us." she paused, "Get me paper and I will draw these creatures and their weaknesses. You will have copies made and send copies back to all the lords of the clan." Lyamy knew she had to get back and do her job protecting Yaun.

*   *   *   *   *

Merkyet was having an internal battle. The way they were raised said they should kill or be killed in the competition for the top position of their training group. The way they had been taught the code for years agreed. Lyamy had opportunity several times to eliminate both her and Freyie, but she had not, she used the code to justify all her actions. Merkyet knew she was not stupid, yet Lyamy saw right through every attempt she had made without punishing her. To make things worse, the more she learned from reading the code and studying the old magic, the more she agreed with Lyamy against their training.

She had released the guard and went through the motions to placate the legalities required to settle the situation. She sufficiently covered the trail of evidence and provided misdirection indicating a possible outside influence was involved. Then she was promoted to the investigative group of the guard because of Lyamy's recommendation. This put her in a position that fit what she needed. Merkyet was able to go anywhere and justified in questioning anyone. A perfect position to keep track of the "heartbeat" of the clan as Lyamy had put it. She had even forewarned the protectors of a plot against Yaun and it was thwarted with minimal impact on other clan activities. The guilty parties agreed in secret to compromises adding to the strength and stability of Yaun's leadership.

She stepped into the pet and food shop. She really did not know for certain what she was looking for other than pet not food.

"Pet or dinner?" the merchant asked from behind the counter as she stepped in.

"Something a little fierce and untamed." she thought a moment as she looked around, "but small enough I can put it down if I have to."

"So smaller then a leophardeg, but meaner than a domestic. Have you considered a canine, perhaps a wolf, wild, but not savage?"

There was a natural distaste between canine and feline and Shadowkyn were the latter. Her hair stood on end slightly as she approached the cage, a challenge to her focus, but controllable, "Should be a nice challenge." she whispered. She stood back up after examining the wolf, "I'll take him."

The merchant seemed please and gave her a special discount because he liked her. The standard discount that he gave everyone using different flattery on a case-by-case basis. It was good for business to make each customer think they were getting special treatment. She walked out with the cage and carried it home.

Merkyet had not yet drank fresh blood, so she had not yet experienced the blood lust that brought flames to their eyes. The first time she had summoned the old magic alone, she startled herself in the mirror when her eye lit up with flames. She had used it in training and a few times as discrete as she could, including the time she got caught by Lyamy. This time she was learning to apply techniques and it was better to practice on a creature that would not bring attention to what she was doing.

She placed the cage on the table in her living area, got on her knees and looked the wolf in the eyes. As she summoned the old magic, her eyes burst with flame and the wolf began to growl a deep throaty rumble. She focused and subjugated the animals mind, then opened the cage and placed a cut on the wolfs front leg, just enough to catch at least five drops of blood in her glass vile. She kept her eyes focused on the eyes of the wolf and began the ritual. She drank the blood and felt the savage rush fill her and then the sweet energy as the piece of the animal's spirit entered her own. Things she had read about their savage history fell into place in her mind.

She could feel the wolf's mind, she could control it. She brought the wolf to a howl from within and felt it as the wolf howled out loud. She did not make the wolf do anything, she made it want to do what she wanted it to do. She had a control, the wolf was a part of her, like an extension of her own body. She could feel everything the wolf felt, and keep it separate at the same time. *'And this is a wolf, one of the least compatible creatures.'* She thought to herself as she felt the surging within her from the experience.

It was after dark, but she went to the streets to find what she needed to bring the power under control. Seven encounters later, she returned her urges satisfied and a calm control forming over the power and lust. She could still feel and control her wolf as she let it out of the cage free to do as it wanted in her home. Merkyet wondered how Lyamy maintained such absolute control, how she had never seen her on any rampages. She noted that even with the public sacrifice of Jenyin's den mates Lyamy had maintained control.

She used the rest Lyamy had taught her with the old magic to help her calm down and eventually got some sleep before the night was over. Part of her knew that Lyamy could have this same control over her.

*   *   *   *   *

They were all outside appreciating the work Desdin and Grimble had put into the door. From as close as ten feet, you had to know what you were looking for in order to find the door. Their entryway was secure.

"What about the obvious trail in the sand ending at this point?" Jenyin pointed out.

"True, any tracker would notice that." Freldin added.

"We can make some base stone come out, covering the ground, but if we do, should probably do it here and there along the base of the cliff for consistency of appearances." Desdin observed

"There will still be tracks in the sand around the base stone and the stone will get worn with time too. I would say anyone seeing the tracks in the sand will already be on foot on the beach and looking for something." Chineene looked around the group, "I say we move on to other things for now. If this becomes an issue later, we can address it. For now, nobody in a boat or down on the beach will not see the entrance if we see them first."

"That is a good point," Freldin said, "IF we see them first. We are not keeping any particular watch. We should probably come to an agreement as a group as to what kind of security we want."

Jenyin held up a hand to focus their attention on him. "At our evening meal. I have some other things I was also planning on bringing up this evening. We can formalize our time a little and use the evening meal to discuss issues of common interest or concern. We are still a small community and we have no written laws or rules, but in order to live together we have to have some guidelines and agreements between us even if they are not written."

Marrianne added, "Very true, we also have cultural differences and even if they become uncomfortable, we should discuss them so that we can learn not to offend each other even by accident. We seem to be expecting others to join us over time, so we should probably try to be prepared for that before it happens."

"Tonight then." Freldin agreed, in a manner to conclude the discussion and move on to something new.

"I think we have food warehoused sufficiently to accommodate several months. We can probably take a few days off from gathering and focus on other things." Jenyin put out there.

"I'd like to set up for blacksmith, stone and metal working down by the magma flow." Desdin piped up.

"I'll help with that; we will need several crafting setups as we advance." Grimble started towards the door to go back in.

"Daret, can you or Jenyin do something to shield the room where the chests are being stored." Marrianne inquired, "I would really like to start sorting through those goods. I am sure that we all could benefit from things that are there once we know what they are. I cannot work on them unless they are out in the open and we cannot do that if they are not shielded from discovery."

"Jenyin, do you remember what we did in the den back home? The room that nobody knew was there?"

Jenyin nodded and looked back at the cave. These strangers would never know when he used old magic as opposed to normal Shadowkyn magic. "We can do that, everyone will just have to remember where the room is or run into the wall a few times until they get used to it." he laughed.

That evening they all sat down slightly anxious about the conversations that would pursue. The fact that they all wanted to get along helped avoid arguments. They also found that once they got past some of the taboos and personal hangups the conversations they had previously avoided were not as uncomfortable as they expected. Those born and raised on the continent agreed to be more discrete at taking care of their natural urges.

They all agreed on distribution of mundane maintenance, like keeping things clean in the general areas and organization of storage.

Over the course of the next week, Jenyin secured the room, and everyone tested their magics to see if they could detect anything through the barriers he set up. It worked well. The opening to the room disappeared and looked like the rest of the hall stone wall. Desdin could see the door and tried to explain as a dwarf it wasn't that he could see the opening as much as he could see the real stone. Nobody really cared why or how. Shelves were built and Marrianne took on the responsibility of sorting and cataloging everything from the chests.

Jenyin was not sure when he started discovering he was gaining abilities as a follower of ShdaowDancer. He only knew the reason because of what Chelic said when they were up on the ridge together and he asked how she could gather eggs that were not there till she picked them up. "As followers of ShadowDancer, the land will yield it's bounty to us. The more loyalty we show her the more we can do." She stated it as if he should have already known

"Daret and Karis are doing this without even knowing aren't they?"

"When they gather," Chelic smiled, "and there is always more there to be gathered. We will not be disappointed when we move to ShadowDancers homelands."

"Homelands? Never mind." He was still not completely used to her random comments. He knew some were prophetic of the future, some he just did not understand and let them go, filed somewhere in the back of his mind. "I have the hunger you know."

"I know." Chelic stated calmly, "You have done well keeping it hidden, but it is only the two of us. I am yours already, but if you just wish to subdue the needs of the old magic, you can taste of me. You really should find a creature of the land here though and make it familiar with you."

"You are not supposed to know the old magic is real." he laughed.

"I didn't until I died and came back."

"Keep watch for the others and let me know if someone is coming." Jenyin sniffed the air and slipped through the underbrush. Any creature would do, but predators were preferred. He followed the scent and overtook the small striped cat with gold and brown striping. The cat was about the same size as Jenyin. He subdued the animal with ease, and felt his eyes fill with fire as he drank the blood and performed the ritual. The surge of the small piece of the cat's spirit was what he hungered for. The cat was now an extension of him. He stood there and watched the cat run off. At the same time he was in the cat chasing down a small animal, the pounce, the kill, feeding to satisfaction. Jenyin turned heading back to Chelic, the wild cat now a part of him. His hunger was satisfied.

Chelic was waiting where he left her, her long tail swat playfully through the air. "My gathering bag is full, but there is no rush to head back."

*   *   *   *   *

"So, you managed to find a way to avoid the fight after all." Yaun laughed at Lyamy, "Pelekura, the captain must have loved that."

"We are only ten days away from the grand parade west. We should use the plant to protect the caravan."

"That would be wise, but we will have to suggest it and leave it up to Peltrhak. I have given he full control over what they do."

"Did you two already do the ceremony"

"Yes, and we can now both feel where the other is and send messages back and forth inside each other's heads when we use the leader's ritual. We will be able to consult with each other across the continent. It has built more trust between us."

"The buildings of the top two dens have been converted to storage for everything that new settlement will be coming back for protected by your word and mine. I don't think anyone will violate that trust, but the buildings have been added to the guard assignments for the protectors."

"You are going to remain stoic to the very end, aren't you Lyamy?" Yaun did not hide the fact he was impressed. "I do not know if I would handle it as well knowing in twelve days I would be sacrificed."

"I only ask that I have freedom to get my affairs in order before the time comes. I have known the path I follow and accepted the consequences."

On her way out she stopped by to check on Serine. The scar was healing nicely, it would be a clean mark, no infection or festering. Their eyes shared more than their words and Lyamy was confident that Serine would do well for her new clan. Her next stop was Nelk.

"So, when I was out with the creature, the fur emanated fear using an innate primal magic that remains residual in the fur." Lyamy explained based on what she felt when she was out in the jungle.

"You are right the magic is there, but it is not focused on any specific aspect, like fear, so it must have something to do with the movement or configuration of the fur." Nelk was busy working as they talked.

"Well, I don't know if you can find a use for it, but the essence of the magic was there so I had you first in mind."

"I can appreciate you thinking of me. Some I prefer they forget I am here." He looked up and laughed. Then his expression sobered, "Don't forget me when you are out there in the world. You said I am needed here still. I accept that, but someday maybe you will pull me out and I can see the ways of others in this world."

"I will remember you Nelk." She smile a warm smile, a rare site in the clan, then turned and continued back towards her private Den.

She heard and felt something coming at her fast from behind and to her left. As she turned Lyamy saw the blade in the air and five of her daggers found their marks as she stepped out of the path of her attacker. Her instincts were good, and her skills trained beyond her years. The young apprentice did not know she did not have a chance against Lyamy. Rolling her over Lyamy looked in her eyes. "In your death I honor your courage," making sure the young apprentice saw her lick the blade while she still had life. She felt the fire burst in her eyes from the blood rage, and felt the young apprentice surrender a part of her life to Lyamy.

Lyamy did not let the tear form until her eyes closed and she would not see. '*This has to stop ShadowDancer, an apprentice two year younger than me seeking a place in the clan a name, by attempting to kill. The teaching is wrong, now what would have been a strong member of the new clan is lost.*' Lyamy pulled her blades and placed them in a case so that blood they drew could be used in a ceremony to honor, she didn't even know her name.

"Guard," a hunter, member of the guard came over. She told him what happened and walked away. She would not miss the killing, for that alone she no longer belonged with the clan. Without change, the clan would perish. That change was in motion, she hoped it was not too late already. Who else would she have to kill before her last ten days were over?

She could feel Merkyet was still up, and she needed someone to talk to. She rounded the corner and knocked on the door. Merkyet opened the door ever so slight, then stepped back and invited Lyamy in. "Hello, Lyamy."

"You have tasted, I knew when it happened. My manners, Hello Merkyet." Lyamy looked in Merkyet's eyes, "You like it, you feel the addiction and want more."

Merkyet saw more in Lyamy's eyes than she wanted to know about. The hard cold power, the untamed savagery burning beyond anything Merkyet knew, but held in control. "It is sweet and makes me hungry."

"Let me show you what I just did." Lyamy was instantly in Merkyets head. She brought Merkyet through the events after leaving Nelk's, the attack, defending, looking in the dieing girls eyes, the bitter-sweet taste of victory. The death weighed heavy, Lyamy made it a little more than it really was. "This is what tastes so sweet Merkyet."

Merkyet shudder for a moment when she was back to herself. "She died."

"Only minutes ago, Merkyet, but understand that surge you get, that rush of power, that sweet tasting essence is paid for with death. Sometimes in part, sometimes in whole. In this case it was complete death. With you as a student to me, that was in part. A part of your freedom died giving me freedom and dominance over you."

"I wanted to know how you controlled it, why you did not take the pleasure you could have in drinking the life out of Freyie and I."

"It is balanced by the price that is paid. You carry the old magic for the good of the clan. If you lose control the clan loses. Every death even in part is a death of a part of the clan." She pushed the image of the clan shrinking over time, killing each other for honor and greatness within the clan until the clan was too small to survive.

"That could never happen." Merkyet protested.

"It is already happening, look where we were only one hundred years ago." she entered her mind again and took her back in time in a vision to see the population of the clan was more than double what it was now. "It was not something on the outside that killed us down by the thousands until we stand now less then twelve hundred strong."

Merkyet swallowed hard, "I see how this helps you keep the hunger under control. I will surely go insane before I am done." She looked in Lyamy's eyes, "You have a hundred years' experience in your eyes."

"You will not go insane; you will learn and grow stronger. I was chosen by an Ancient, so I was given the experience and knowledge needed to be her avatar. If you look inside you have also gained the two years experience of your wolf. Did you know there is a horvalka to the west of here that is over seven hundred years old and you can see that in my eyes too if you look close enough."

"How have you done so much in so short a time?"

"Do not envy me, Merkyet. Live a long life on your own and enjoy it as much as you can." Lyamy embraced Merkyet, "I am not here much longer, you should pick who you are going to claim as your student. I am going home now, you should get some sleep, but remember what we shared this night."

"I will." She returned the embrace.

Again, Lyamy found herself on the streets headed towards her place of rest. All the pieces were in place and their plans were near completion. She wondered for a moment where she would have been if ShadowDancer had not taken an interest in her. She would not have had the wisdom, experience or training she currently had. That young apprentice might be alive instead of her. Yaun might be dead, Jenyin might really be dead. The more she thought about it the more people might be dead. It did not remove the burden of killing the young apprentice, but it did make it a little less heavy to carry. After all it was self-defense and by any standard she was justified. She made it to her door and slipped inside, she sniffed the air and scanned the place with all her abilities, no traps, no intruders, just some welcome quiet.

She dreamed, mostly good dreams, caves on the coast, Jenyin and strangers. She had dreams of traveling to other parts of the world. She had a very strange dream about having a cub with the horvalka, not a bad dream, just a dream, somewhere in the dream she realized it was not her dream, it was the horvalka dreaming and she could feel there was more thought than she had seen when the creature was awake.

*   *   *   *   *

Peltrhak was there with the sealing of the doors protecting their belongings until they reached that promised settlement. He had confidence in the word of Yaun and Lyamy, of course he did not know that two days after they left Lyamy was scheduled to die. He was there when the houses were sealed because his people wanted him to be there. Taking on the responsibility of leading his people somehow made their opinions matter.

They all knew there were not enough of them to fight amongst each other, they needed each other to survive. The idea of decorating themselves and their belonging as they traveled with pelekura was repulsive, but if Lyamy was right and he was starting to think she always was, it could save their lives. After returning from the West Gates Lyamy changed the route, they were to travel so that it arched to the north avoiding the jagged mountains in the middle of the continent. She said something about flying beasts that even the horvalka feared. He did not ask how she knew; he would just go with it. The distance increase was made up for by the easier terrain, so it would have almost no impact on their schedule.

There were two clans of harvesters, the long ears were the larger of the two clans. They all had a meeting and when they were done, they wanted to keep their clans united so they agreed the long ears would stay. The bandit clan would go across the continent. They called them bandits because the natural coloring gave them the appearance of wearing a mask over their eyes. They were just as humanoid as the others, standing upright their tails were bushy and they too had more fur then the Shadowkyn, they appeared to be descended form raccoons if you knew what a raccoon was.

There were legends about how food became friends with the Shadowkyn. Both legends had members of the weaker clans saving the lives of leaders in the clan and gaining audience for peaceful arrangements. The legends could not happen in the present-day clan, an injured clan leader brought back to the village would be slain by his competition to gain position and power. This made Peltrhak have to give serious consideration to Lyamy's interpretations of the code. Peltrhak had killed his own brother born the same time to the same apprentice and expected to be close. The assassination had earned him position and power, but forever lost him trust. If he would kill his brother to get ahead, who would he not kill, but that was how they were raised.

A new start, a new reading and understanding of the code, he really was looking forward to the new settlement with hope and expectation.

*   *   *   *   *

Something triggered an alert, Jenyin and the other Shadowkyn grabbed their weapons and raced out of the caves. The others followed suite only because of the sudden urgent movement. Jenyin let out a yowling roar that was answered from somewhere off in the underbrush. Jenyin lead the way up onto the ridge and then headed north and slightly towards an inland direction. He waved everyone to a stop, pushed his hands outwards and then down, the den scattered and vanished in the underbrush, the others followed suit. Jenyin appeared to vanish where he stood. Marrianne turned a ring on her finger she had found in a chest and also vanished if anyone was close enough to see.

There was a scream of death not that far away off in front of them, followed by glimpses and the sounds of humanoids rushing pass them in the underbrush. Then a massive creature leaped landing about twenty-five feet from Jenyin, mouth wide open. With a few quick gestures and a whisper under his breath Jenyin appeared to throw something towards the creature and flames bust in its mouth. The creature stammered backwards; arrows flew. The creature's legs seemed to lose strength, just as Daret appeared and lightening cascaded down upon the creature. Jenyin barely heard Marrianne's string of expletives from behind the creature as it finished collapsing to the ground.

Jenyin Leaped from where he stood to land behind the creature, searching the area as he came down. A few feet to his left there was brush and grass compressed to the ground in the shape of a person with no trail in or out of the spot. Marrianne moaned and appeared as she turned her ring back. "Someone should warn a girl when they are going to bring down the wrath of the heavens on something we are attacking."

Jenyin looked her over. He found no visible wounds. "I think you are going to be alright. You did not take a direct hit from the lightening."

Chelic was the next to appear leaning over Marrianne, using healing magic, "A little shaken, may take a few to get your balance back."

"Can someone grab my knives from that things back? I am pretty sure they are why it collapsed." Marrianne tried standing and fell back to the ground.

Jenyin pulled her knives from the creature's spine for her and returned them. He quickly returned to the beast and plunged a dagger pulling it out bloodied. He licked one side of the blade and whispered the words, "In your death I honor your strength and claim a portion to add to my own." He did not clean Marrianne's blades not knowing if she honored those she killed. He started looking for those that were running from the beast.

Daret headed to the beast. "Karis and I will dress it out and salvage what we can from the horvalka."

Freldin had an arrow notched and was facing the deeper wooded area. Jenyin placed a hand on his shoulder and said, "He is mine. He will not harm anyone here."

Freldin lowered his bow, "I did not shoot as long as he did not appear threatening. I knew that the cat saw us but did not seem either afraid or aggressive."

"Let's see if we can gather our new friends. At least a couple of them looked something like Grimble." Jenyin looked towards the caves, "I hope they did not over run the edge of the ridge; they did not look like they could make that jump."

Freldin waved to Grimble and the three of them went to seek the fleeing strangers. They found them regrouping at the end of the ridge above the caves. "Horvalka are not normally found in these parts, they usually stick to the deeper jungles." Jenyin was saying as they approached.

"Greetings friends." Grimble waved as they approached, "That was some run, are you staying nearby?" They were indeed gnomes and there were five of them gathered together on the ridge.

"We have been staying in the forests north of here. We need to go back and see if anyone else survived."

It turned out they were second-generation survivors from a gnome ship that caught a bad wind in a storm driving it blind into land before most of them were born. They brought them to the caves first and got them fresh clothing and weapons that might help against any larger beast they may encounter. Jenyin, Freldin, Daret and Desdin went with the lost gnomes to help search for survivors. It was not hard to find their way back to the village, the horvalka left a path of devastation giving chase to the gnomes. It was early evening when they arrived. Tree houses were pulled down and huts at ground level were flattened.

There had been twenty-five in the village, two returned from another direction after they arrived, and one was found under a collapsed building with minor injuries. It was a vegetation food storage shed, so the smashed fruit overshadowed any scent the beast may have picked up. Jenyin invited them to come stay in the caves. They helped the gnomes gather things they wanted to keep. The only carrying mechanisms they had where baskets made from surrounding materials. They placed signs with messages around the camp for after they left. If anyone else returned they would know where to go. They all slept the night in the remains of the village.

In the morning it looked like there were only the eight survivors five female gnomes and three males. With as much as they could carry, they headed back to the caves at the end of the ridge. The sun was moving downward by the time they made it back. The gnomes would be the first occupants of the houses they were building in the largest central chamber. Grimble took on the responsibility of helping them settle in and letting them know the rules of the land, at least what was established so far.

"So, Jenyin, the way we are currently governed, you are the leader of this community. The rest of us here are your council, so anyone else who joins our community more or less needs to come to one of us with concerns." Freldin stated more than inquired.

"There is one more member of my council then as you put it. She has not yet arrived, but she made this possible." Jenyin did not forget what Lyamy had done for them.

"As you wish. If you want a member of each new group that joins us to represent them that is an option too, until we get too big for that."

"I am sure things will evolve as they need to." Chineene added, "we can discuss and plan, it will help, but things will keep changing."

"We may want to build doors and walls and restrict open access to the supplies we have. They are abundant for now, but the bigger we get the more in demand everything will be." Marrianne pointed out, "We also need to start working on ways to build on supplies. The wood is easy we harvest from the forests, but cloth, well we have to figure out what fiber is good here and how to set up equipment for crafting the raw bolts of cloth and thread."

"Everyone in the society will contribute." Chelic aired optimistically.

"Our new friends have no skills." Karis complained.

"They have some skills." Grimble objected, "and we can teach and train them."

Jenyin had been practicing drawing the bounty from the land, although he was still not sure of all it meant, he had learned he could even draw metals from the stone in the cave, "We do have some ability to rebuild our resources beyond the normal means." he offered, "As followers of ShadowDancer we have enhanced ability to draw the bounty of what the land has to offer."

"But we are not all followers of ShadowDancer." Grimble was the first to object. "We learned a long time ago not to rely on the Ancients to take care of all our needs." The others seemed to agree but did not express it verbally.

Jenyin held his hand against the wall and a small iron ball formed in his hand, "This is what I mean. It seems I have earned my way in her favor sufficiently to have access to a lot."

They all stared, contemplating the implications of what they just saw. "We still need to maintain an inventory." Marrianne shrugged, "I don't think it matters so much how we get the materials to maintain the supply."

"It really is not a worry yet." Freldin shrugged, "at least not until our community grows to a level that may tax the inventory we have."

Jenyin stood from their meal, "I have a few things to do before I sleep." he headed to the den alone. Closing the door as he stepped in. The space was clear, and he began going through his ritual combat practice. It was relaxing, reinforced his training, and helped him clear his mind. He had completed a few of the routines when he heard a knock at the door. He opened the door and let Marrianne in. She seemed a little nervous concerning whatever she wanted to talk to him about.

"Jenyin, you folks are open and less personal about certain behavior." She stumbled a bit over what she was trying to say, "um, I am not sure how to approach this, well here it goes. I don't want or need any attachments, you know guys that think they have some kind of business with a girl,. Well, maybe you don't know. Anyway a girl has needs, and," She paused embarrassed, "oh, never mind, I am just being silly." She turned and Daret was standing in the doorway.

Daret stepped in with a friendly laugh, "I am sure we can help you."

"How long have you been there?"

"Long enough." She laughed. Daret looked at Jenyin and twitched her tail, "She just needs some of your time."

"Oh," Jenyin, recalled their conversations on the subject. "I guess as long as it is not something of a personal bonding for you. A community is supposed to take care of the needs of its members."

*　　　*　　　*　　　*　　　*

Yaun and Lyamy walked with Peltrhak as far as the gates. The day had come, and all were ready. "I am actually excited to be setting out." Peltrhak's expressions did not reflect his words, but he meant it.

"Your journey is protected." Lyamy nodded. ShadowDancer had promised so she felt safe in restating the promise. "Do not let anyone stray or linger behind. If they leave the protection, whatever happens is on them."

"I look forward to hearing your progress and success." Yaun also meant his words. The society was changing for the good without changing their code. It was the same rules, but with more care about people then stuff or power. They went out through the gates before stepping to one side and watching as the entire caravan walked by. Lyamy smiled to Serine as she walked by with Zenjin. Yaun even gave her an approving nod.

They watched as the last vanished into the jungle. About a third of their population just left and they felt a slight vacancy on the inside. Walking back home the impact could be felt in the streets. There were houses temporarily not occupied. Every member of the clan could now feel the importance of keeping each other alive to survive. They would feel the weakness of their smaller numbers. It felt like the vision she had given Merkyet coming true.

"It is on your shoulders to bring the population of the clan back up to safe numbers, perhaps five thousand or more in your lifetime."

"You could stay. We could find a way to explain you to the people." Yaun did not want to lose her.

"I was chosen for what I do, and I accepted that choosing. I pay a small price to insure my people will grow to greatness." If she stayed now it would change everything. She was the avatar of her goddess and she had to go out in the world to make a place for her people and their future.

"I could easily build an argument for your remaining."

"Are you arguing with the Ancient now? If you saw what was inside me, would you be willing to risk everything with what I can do? You know I went out in the jungle alone and came back with the knowledge of the horvalka. To do that I have everything that it is inside me"

Yaun reconsidered his thinking. He did not want to risk that, she was right. He would honor her as he had promised. Their conversation dropped off at that point and it was a long silent walk back to town and leaving him at his den. It was her last night in the clan. She walked around, committing everything she saw to memory. The morning sun was rising, and she blink a full nights rest, ready to face the day.

She walked at Yaun's side the distance to the harvesting fields and the cliff where she was known to have slain Jenyin and his den. It looked like everyone had gathered to watch the event. Lyamy excused herself for a minute when they arrived presumably to prepare. With no body watching she created the image of herself with magic and the items she had collected and placed the patch of marked skin in the middle of her back on her image making her complete.

Lyamy vanished from all eyes and detection. She followed her replication back out. She had never performed this spell before, but she could see, feel and speak through her construction. She stayed back about ten feet, while her persona stood next to Yaun.

Yaun gave a wonderful speech on her virtues and gift to the clan. He told everyone she was responsible for their salvation. He spelled out many of the feats she had accomplished for the clan. He finished and everyone cheered for her and shouted.

Then he began again. He shared that she had accepted a responsibility with a price and knew she would have to pay this price. Her acceptance made it possible for her to gain the power she needed to be the clan hero and perform the wonderful works to save the clan. He explained that this was raw power from the primal nature that made them. It was dangerous power and there was a limit to how long she could keep it under control. She deliberately burst into flames and pulled it back in for emphasis. There were sounds or sympathy and understanding from the crowd.

Yaun went on, "It is time for that sacrifice and our hero willingly gives herself for our good." her form stepped forward and turned to face Yaun, "We honor you in death for the love of your people." He pulled his sword and touched her chest, looking in her eyes as they lit with flame. The burning seemed dull to him, but he considered it was because she was conceding to death. He hesitated, but she moved the tip of his blade over where her heart should be and pulled the blade as she pushed herself towards him.

The audience watched as they saw Lyamy pull herself from Yaun's blade a trickle from the corner of her mouth and the blade dripping as she turned and stumbled her way to the pyre, falling once before she reached the great pile of wood. Two hunters stepped forward and helped her climb until she dismissed them, pulled herself the last distance and rolled over flat on her back on top.

Lyamy felt her heart racing, she was feeling everything that was happening to her construction. She could not lose consciousness, or all would fail. Her form raised a hand and the fire started. She had to maintain the construction until the flames hid her on the pyre. Tears formed and she held on as long as she could before letting go and taking a breath of relief.

Still invisible to everything Lyamy turned to go to where Freyie waited. There was a cheer from the crowd in her honor, she could feel the touch of sadness in the cheer. "In death I give you honor." she whispered.

She grabbed Freyie as she ran off the edge of the cliff they landed on the back of the horvalka. Freyie smacked her on the chest with her fist. "You could have told me about this." They both clung to the fur as the creature took them forward faster than they could move on their own. They sped through the canopy forest and out the other side uninterrupted. Halfway down the ridge they stopped and climbed down. Lyamy sent her savage companion back to the jungles and they continued on foot.

Lyamy paused and opened her shirt to look at her chest. There was a scar where Yaun's blade had pierced her construct. She wondered if it would really be her blood on his sword. She lashed it closed and reached the corner of the ridge before the sun had reached high in the sky. She looked out at the ocean and took a deep breath. It was the first time she had ever seen the ocean and she could smell the salt in the air.

"Lyamy, welcome home." Looking down Chelic was waving to her.

She jumped down next to Chelic, it was an easy jump, less than thirty feet. "It is good to see you well." she gave Chelic a big embrace. "I was afraid I faltered too much when you forgave me. I thought you were going to die, and I so wanted you to be happy, not dead."

"I did die, but ShadowDancer brought me back." Chelic smiled as if she were talking about the color of a flower. "Don't pull a weapon, Lyamy."

Lyamy suddenly went on full alert, the only thing stopping her from drawing her sword was what Chelic had just said. "A dwarf." she spoke as if sending out a warning.

Desdin looked around and said, "By the Ancients, where?" acting all shocked and worried.

"You are silly." Chelic and Desdin both laughed as Lyamy pulled herself together.

"Forgive me" she whispered, "I am not used to being away from the clan."

Freyie leaped down next to her, "We will learn."

Freyie's shirt was slightly open from the jump, and Lyamy saw a fresh scar. "How did you get scarred?"

"What happens to you, happens to me, remember?" Freyie smile, "but we are together, and it really was worth it."

"And you really do not want that eased at all?" she whispered in Freyie's ear

"Not at all!" Freyie gave her a hug and pushed her away, "So where is everyone else."

Karis stepped out and saw Lyamy, she could not suppress the mixed emotions that danced across her face. She walked up and slapped Lyamy across the face hard and then hugged her, "You stole my purpose, then you killed me in front of the whole clan, then Chelic died and I hate you so much. Now you have given me a life returned to me my purpose, gave us a freedom we would never have known, and I love you." She let go, turned around in tears and went back inside.

Freyie laughed and rubbed her cheek. Chelic smile, "I won't tell anyone Lyamy. I know things I am not supposed to after coming back from beyond the dreams."

"Please, show us around and introduce us to the friends we do not yet know." Lyamy hoped she could sort things out with Karis but was anxious to see Daret and Jenyin and meet the other people ShadowDancer put under their protection.

"Well to start with this is Desdin a 'dwavish' friend we met who has been working with us. He works with metal and stone."

"A pleasure to meet you, miss …?"

"Lyamy"

"Well, Lyamy, welcome to your new community." Desdin turned and headed off, "Have to check the stonework, the kitchen stove is backing up a bit of smoke."

As they were led in through the door, she noticed a cloud of smoke forming above their heads in the cave. She was introduced to Grimble a gnome currently assisting Desdin with fixing the stove. Karis was sitting at the table, pulling herself together and nodded acknowledging them as they walked by and then deeper into the tunnels. Lyamy and Freyie were given a full tour and introduced to everyone that now lived in their sanctuary. Lyamy and Freyie chose to live in the same cavern near the Den of Jenyin, Doret, Chelic and Karis.

Everyone offered to help them with walls and anything they needed. It felt strange not having to check their room for traps and spies when they came and went. Lyamy did it anyway, some habits even if not necessary were safer to keep. She had to convince Grimble several times, they only needed one bed, a den always slept in the same bed.

"Freyie, yes, it is nice being one, feeling and having this bond that no one else can see, but don't you want some freedom to do some things without me knowing every detail? I mean I do not pay attention to everything you think and do, but if I think about it, I can remember how you stepped in the door and what you thought about it, even as I can remember my own thoughts and actions. If I make the change, you will stop feeling my pain and you will be able to have private thoughts. You will be able to take time to be alone or share time with someone else without me being in your head with you. We will still be linked and know when the other needs us. We will still be able to share when we want to."

Fryie knelt in front of Lyamy, "I am happy the way we are. It makes me happy to be a part of you, but if you are not happy, I do not want to make you unhappy so do what you must." Lyamy felt Freyie's passion and desire to keep their bond the way it was.

"Then we will stay this way," she pulled Freyie to her feet and gave her a hug, "but if you ever change your mind, or find you might be happier if I ease this bond we have, you let me know and I will give you as much freedom as you want within my ability." No den could have one of them without having both.

"You are with cub." Freyie said as they pulled apart, "and you have known for a while." She placed her hands on Lyamy's tummy filled with excitement as she looked up. "Soon, very soon."

"The horvalka picked up on it, that is why he dreams about it." Lyamy took a sigh of relief, "It is not that he wanted to have cubs with me, it is because he knew I was having cubs."

"The horvalka?"

Lyamy pushed the dream into Freyie's mind.

"Oh. The same one that gave us that ride?"

"Yes, and while he does not think when he is awake, he does think when he sleeps. It is like his mind sleeps when his body is awake and his body sleeps when his mind is awake."

A knock came from their door. Lyamy barely opened the door and looked out before opening the lock and letting Jenyin in. "So, are you settling in? Anything else I can do for you?"

"She is with cubs!" Freyie said showing more excitement than a Shadowkyn would normally display outside of their den.

"There is no community nursery yet, we have to raise our cubs within our den now."

"That is the way it used to be anyway." Lyamy replied. "The nursery was designed to harden us so that we would not have attachments holding us back in our drive to compete."

"Along with any sense of bonding to the community or family ties that would have placed the community bond above the self-centered achievement." the bitterness he felt was subdued from outward evidence. "Anyway, it is time for the evening meal, and you are considered a part of the council of those responsible for the creation of this place, so please join us in the dining area by the entrance. Freyie you are invited also." with the slightest bow of the head acknowledging their den he departed.

The two of them changed into something clean and left their weapons in the room, with the exception of a knife each. As they stepped from the room Lyamy was on full alert out of habit, Freyie while also on alert was more attentive to Lyamy. They walked the short distance to the entryway and joined the others. Jenyin's den sat to his left, Lyamy and then Freyie sat on his right.

"She may not have been here, and it may take her time to be a comfortable fit here, but without her, there would be no sanctuary. Lyamy will be the right hand. She arranged for this to come about with ShadowDancer Ancient or goddess, who has taken a care for those in need and those who are separated out from their people. If there is ever a time to come when the clan can be friends with outsiders, it will be because of what she has accomplished."

"I am honored." Lyamy replied, then looked at the others, "I serve the goddess ShadowDancer and I serve my people. The Shadowkyn and clan are my people and those who serve ShadowDancer are my people. Those who are friends will be treated as friends, and no one should choose to be my enemy." She realized she was suddenly comfortable calling ShadowDancer "goddess".

"Well spoken," Marrianne lifted her drink, she was obviously in a better mood than she had been since her arrival, maybe longer, "I chose to be your friend and if this ShadowDancer takes care of her people as I have seen so far, I just may choose that too."

Some of the other seemed uncertain how to take either one of them, Lyamy with her dominating manner and you are with me or against me attitude or Marrianne smiling and being in a good mood. Lyamy realized she was not in the clan and may have over spoken her position with these softer strangers. "We will get used to each other with time."

They all relaxed a little and continued eating. "I am going to move down with the other gnomes." Grimble stated, "I am just more comfortable with flat walls and a house with a kinda inside outside feel to it. Besides, those youngsters need someone to teach them, they barely know how to talk. They have sharp minds, just no experience or training."

"That is good Grimble, you will be able to represent their interests then also at our meals."

"We have more people coming." Chelic stated out of nowhere. "They will think they should be in charge because there are more of them then us."

Everyone looked a Chelic and waited a few moments to see if there was more. "Sounds like it is time to set up a watch." Jenyin stated.

Freldin looked at Grimble, "We should each pair up with one of the younger gnomes to pull watch shifts, we'll have to do a full set of shifts, day and night."

"I can cover eight hours a night." Lyamy volunteered. Time on the planet Ethar is different than on earth, eighty minutes were an hour, and sixteen hours made a day or roughly twenty-one and a third earth hours. An eight-hour shift was half the time from one sun up to the next sun up.

"We can share the load." Freldin shook his head, "No reason for anyone to take an imbalanced share of the load. There are eleven of us and sixteen hours. Everyone can do an hour and a half with a few minutes of overlap."

"Each shift will watch from the top of the ridge above the cave. There is a good view in most directions from there." Jenyin instructed, "We can officially start in the morning. Chineene, you can make the schedule and you can favor personal preferences as long as they don't conflict. Lyamy and I will watch from the sunset hour until the first hour of morning tonight. We have some catching up to do."

"There is nothing else we should know about?" Desdin asked, kinda gesturing at those at the table, more indicating those that arrived with him.

Jenyin could sense the tension and surmised it was the more authoritative tone that was brought in with Lyamy and carried over to some degree in his manner. "No, we are still the same as we were. I am not going to dictate changes, and neither is Lyamy. All of us are the governing body of this sanctuary. I may make decisions to break conflicts, or for action in the urgency of a situation, but discussion and consensus after can change those decisions. The only things that are not up for change by the group are those that come from ShadowDancer."

There was an obvious relaxing and calming effect from his words. "For clarification," Freldin spoke up, "I tend to speak in an authoritative manner also, it is not my intention to override anyone or negate the option of speaking up if you disagree with something I say."

"We do not need conflict to harbor amongst the group of us. Speak your mind and we can talk things out. I spent enough time in the clan where everything was secret plots and scheming for power. We do not need that here. We all need each other and have done well in finding compromise where we have needed to so far. Let's keep it that way." Jenyin did not want this group going the way of the clan.

"We have buildings to house maybe twenty more family units built and materials to build more. They are all basic, should we keep building or wait and see who arrives?" Grimble asked.

"I would think we can wait." Freldin offered.

"We still need to find a way to produce other products we will need." Chineene spoke up, "We need things like paper, ink, clothing, our new friends have weaving skills for mats or storage containers."

"It would not be a bad idea to start setting up the structures for workshops and other buildings before we need them, but perhaps in one of the other larger chambers for a merchant center?" Freldin pitched in.

There was more discussion of general things they could do to prepare for expansion. Conversations included food storage and organization of space. Jenyin let Freldin lead the engineering of their planning and development of space. Jenyin excused himself and headed out and up onto the ridge. Lyamy and Freyie followed. They got comfortable sitting in the grass in a circle so between the three of them, they could see anything coming from any direction.

"I conceded you did right by the clan when I thought you killed me." Jenyin looked in Lyamy's eyes.

"It had to look real, I could not risk you giving any hint. I also did not think you would have agreed in advance."

"Is Freyie your student?"

"I am not her student, unless she decides to teach me, but I am hers."

Jenyin raised an eyebrow looking at Freyie, "I never taught you this binding, Lyamy. I know I did not because I do not know it myself. If she is bound to you like this, we can talk freely in front of her. How much more have you learned that I do not know."

"I know all of the old magic from the beginning to now. The knowledge was given to me and I have a copy of the book restored." She pulled the book out of her unseen pocket and handed it to her teacher.

"May I keep this and study it for a while?"

"You are my master and teacher; you do not need to ask that from your student. I am bound to you even as my students are bound to me."

He looked up at Lyamy again, "Students? You have more than one?"

"Well," She paused, "Yes. Merkyet is chosen to continue the old magic with the clan, bound as my student she cannot do me harm and I did not have to kill her. Serine of your brothers' den was really of Zenjin's den sent in, to spy, she is the carrier of old magic for the new settlement. Then there is Brelk, he is a student in that I taught him a few tricks to help in his trade."

Jenyin laughed, "So you did not kill any of your rivals. I was sure you would avenge the treatment they gave you while you were under punishment. You have proven stronger than I judged you to be, and that was already exceptional. You may be bound as a student, but you are in knowledge my master. I would be honored if you could teach me."

"We can teach Freyie also, the free bond she gives me is even stronger than the bond of magic that holds her to me. She would do anything I asked of her." Lyamy looked at Jenyin, "There is one more task I must do, that will hurt you."

Jenyin looked uncertain, "Oh?"

"You are marked and your brother if he checked would find you are alive and could track you down." She pulled the device Nalk had given her out.

"You are right, I have not figured out how to remove it."

"This will hurt, but it will be quick, and I can start you healing right away."

"Do what you must."

Lyamy pulled the block of wood she had used with Serine out and handed it to Jenyin to bite, then placed Nalk's device against his back and triggered the mechanism. Immediately she started pushing healing repeatedly into his back until the round patch of missing skin filled in with a cover of scar tissue. "This must be destroyed." She handed Jenyin the patch from his back. He could destroy it in his own way.

"So now we have matching scars?"

She smiled, "Yes we do. Apparently, you survived well enough to still have humor."

As they sat guarding the sanctuary through the night, they all shared their stories. They fully disclosed even their thoughts and answered freely each other's questions. They shared a trust that normally only happened within a den as the night passed.

*   *   *   *   *

They were on their fourth day out from the clan lands, stopping to sleep and recuperate every other night. As they pulled to a stop Peltrhak sent word back for the leaders of each group to come forward for a meeting to assess their travel. They had not been attacked at all by the beasts of the land and they did not need to slow down for anyone who could not keep up the pace. There was no record of clan ever going this deep into the inner continent.

He had a large bonfire built and as the leaders straggled up the found places to sit around the fire. He walked from group to group, listening to their stories of what they had seen in the jungle, occasionally ask a question. When all had arrived, he took his place and called for everyone's attention.

"We have been out for four days now. We were promised protection by ShadowDancer. We were promised the same from Lyamy. We were instructed to stay together and for none to leave the protection that is being given. It was suggested that we use the pelekura to keep the beasts of the jungle away. I have heard some of your stories and I have seen it also for myself. The savage beasts have come close enough that we have caught glimpses, but they have not threatened our passage."

"I would not come near us with all this pelekura," One from the audience jibbed and they all chuckled.

"That may be all that keeps them away, but even if it is, the promise is still kept. Lyamy has shown us all a new way, that is the old way of our people. She showed us we can live by the code and not kill each other off. She has proven to us that we need each other to live if we are going to follow the first code which is to do whatever it takes for the clan to survive. We have about two months of travel to get to our new land."

"The time will pass quickly." Someone yelled

"Indeed. We need to get our minds clear on the code and how it was written so our people would live. With that in mind our apprentices need to continue their training as we travel. Our children need guidance and teaching, and our cubs need nursing and care. We will all have to share in this responsibility because we cannot have a nursery while we move, or a classroom. Every den is to adopt an apprentice or two and a child and a cub until all have been distributed and can be cared for. I also want each den to adopt a family from the harvesters. They will travel mixed with us so we can better protect them, and they can help us with foraging as we go and caring for our new responsibilities. We may keep this arrangement for a while even after we arrive, at least until we can get our community built."

There was a little murmuring and conversation among those gathered, but the general consensus was in agreement. It caused some delay in the next morning's start time, but it was worth it. Peltrhak was actually starting to think of the harvesters as his people too. He mixed with his people as they traveled, and the mood seemed to get better with each passing day. He did not know if it was because they were moving away from where they came from or towards a new promise. Maybe it was just the time bonding and not trying to kill each other or getting to know the harvesters who were usually happier and more at peace then the clan. It didn't matter, the future he saw was good for his people.

*   *   *   *   *

Yaun wasted no time having a bronzed statue of Lyamy bigger than life built in the center of town. His new protector was diligent and watchful but could not replace Lyamy. There had been no assassinations, not even an attempt since Peltrhak and a third of the clan departed. With the number of the harvesters down, members of the clan took time to go help them harvest.

The opening up of abandoned houses allowed apprentices who were willing to pair up or group to move into these building before they were establish as dens. The understanding was that new dens would be given favor over just roommates.

There was a sense of fear that Yaun felt was healthy, about what would happen if the clan was too small. The west gates were quiet now that they had fields of Pelekura between the gates and the jungle. They still reinforced their defenses with casters in each tower and magic was more openly used as a part of normal activity. Yaun could not figure out why they had not used it more before. Magic made mundane tasks easier.

Merkyet was doing well with the investigator division, success had gone up significantly since she was there. He was surprised she was not making a bid for Lyamy's old position, but it seemed that she found her place talking to anyone she wanted. Freyie had disappeared the day Lyamy was sacrificed, her bracelet with blood and marks of a horvalka were found at the edge of the cliff near where Lyamy was sacrificed. It appeared she had wandered too close to the edge and became lunch to the savage beast. The investigation of her disappearance stopped there.

The mark on Lyamy he felt it destroyed in the fire when she was sacrificed. He felt a tug at the destruction of the mark on his brother and decided it must have been the mark being destroyed in the belly of some savage beast that ate him. Yaun felt alone. He still had his den, but Jenyin and Lyamy were just the last of a long series that had vanished from his inner circle. Now even his enemies were gone and those rising up were neither inner circle nor enemies. They were just what they were.

His people needed something to help them keep their edge. It was good they were not killing each other, but something had to be done to keep the beast alive inside them. Perhaps hunting raids, or maybe more advanced training games where they could work as teams and compete. *'Whatever I come up with, it has to be team building and competitive, nurturing the strength of the beast within.'* he thought to himself.

He was ready to get up and leave his office for a stroll around town when a knock came from the door. Merkyet carrying an armload of books was let in by his protector and announced. "What can I do for you, Merkyet."

"It is what I can do for you, Lord Yaun." She set the stack of books, five large volumes on his desk. "This is a gift to the clan, from our late Lyamy. It is her comprehensive dissertation on the code of honor that belongs to our clan." The magic pen she learned from the old magic helped her finish the copy quickly.

"From Lyamy?" He picked the first book up and opened the cover reading the title and author of the work. "When did she find time to do this?" He was obviously impressed with the volume of work. "It reads just like she thinks. I will have to read the full work before I can approve it as official." He eyed the five volumes. Perhaps I can endorse them one at a time as I finish them."

"She did a lot that no one knew about." Merkyet stated matter of fact.

"It was sad she had to go. She had to convince me several times. She even pulled my sword herself when she saw me hesitate." Yaun stared in his mind back at the event.

"I do not blame you for what had to be done. I don't think anyone does. I even wonder if Freyie may have given herself to the savage beasts because she could not deal with losing Lyamy."

"You and Freyie would have worked well together." Yaun commented, more distracted thinking about Lyamy then what he was saying. "I will start reading these right away. If they are as true as she was, we will start making them the new order very soon." Yaun continued reading and Merkyet excused herself and left the office.

*   *   *   *   *

Movement on the distant horizon across the water caught Lyamy's attention. She pointed and Jenyin turned and saw it also. "One of those houses that float he whispered."

With a thought from Lyamy, Freyie jumped down and went inside to get the others. They all came rushing out. "Where, what do you see?" Freldin asked.

Freyie pointed to the horizon, "It is out there."

"I don't see anything." Desdin sounded a bit gruff from just waking up.

Marrianne pulled a telescope like a captain's glass from her belt. "There is something out there, might be a boat. I would guess they cannot even see land yet without their captain's scope from the crow's nest."

"May I see?" Freldin asked. He took the scope as she handed it to him, "How the blazes are you guys seeing that when we can barely see it with a scope?"

Lyamy and Jenyin jumped down from the cliff, "It is there, we see it." Lyamy shrugged.

"How well do you guys see at night?" Grimble asked.

"Sometimes shadows and peripheral vision gets tricky, but we see pretty much the same at night as during the day." Jenyin sounded as if he thought it was normal.

"Unless there is something making it pitch black." Freyie added. "Then we can only see ghost images and heat"

Lyamy put her hand on her tummy, the cubs were stirring. Jenyin caught her movement, "How soon?"

"I am not sure; I have never had cubs before." She put her other hand on her tummy, "They are moving."

"We better get you inside." He looked at the others, "How long for that floating house, um ship as you call it?"

"Another day before they see land, a day and half before they might see us, perhaps three days before they weigh anchor and can come ashore." Marrianne estimated looking out through her spyglass.

"Let's get you inside then Lyamy, you will be back before we need you." Lyamy, Freyie and Jenyin went in. Jenyin left the two of them when they went into their room.

"They are coming." Lyamy said as Freyie spread some clean worked hides on the bed. Lyamy laid on the cover. Freyie lost her balance and sat on the edge of the bed. The first cub was coming.

An hour later, Lyamy was inspecting the five cubs. At this age the fur balls would be hard to differentiate from ordinary cat cub. Freyie had helped her clean them and was laying down now corralling the cubs between. There were five cubs, four of them healthy and strong, the fifth was not well balanced and she had to direct its movement for it to feed. Training told her she should remove the weak one, one bite to the back of the neck and it would not weaken the clan.

Lyamy stated as she looked over the weakest cub, "The clan is not made stronger by killing each other." She looked at Freyie and she agreed. Five cubs, the two of them fell asleep while the cubs nursed. Having been there through the experience with Lyamy, Freyie also was able to feed the cubs and share the roll of nursing them. Both purred as they slept.

Desdin and Grimble managed a back entrance that opened above the ridge so that they could come and go without being seen from the sea. It was well concealed and anyone who did not know where and what it was would miss the hidden entrance. Today the ship should reach close enough to shore that it might anchor and send boats ashore. Lyamy was taking her shift on the ridge watching the approach with one of the younger gnomes. Freyie was taking care of the cubs while she was away from the den. The ship dropped anchor and at first there was no more activity.

Lyamy saw the splashing that began off the side of the ship. "Go tell the others, they are casting people off the ship. They have changed the flag to a black flag with a falchion and a rum bottle. It looks like the people are swimming towards shore."

The gnome slipped off through the tall grass and disappeared. A short time later, others started showing up laying low in the grass and looking out at what was happening. After dozens of people were in the water, the ship pulled up anchor and started moving away. "We have to help them." Jenyin lifted up to all fours. "Those on the ship are not looking back." He headed down off the ridge and towards the beaches where outcasts from the ship would reach shore. The rest followed.

It was a long swim. As the strangers got closer to shore, they all pitched in helping them out of the water to rest on the beach. There were several that gave up but were close enough that members of the sanctuary could swim out and pull them in. In the distance there were three bodies floating in the water. Lyamy looked at Jenyin, "We cannot leave them."

"The strangers can not tell when we use the old magic." Jenyin agreed. Both of them suddenly had eyes filled with fire and they ran out over the surface of the water. They each grabbed a body without slowing down.

Lyamy made a gesture and the third body lifted off the water and followed her back to shore.

"We must flush the water from them." She rolled the one she was carrying over, facing away from her and on their knees embraced their tummy and squeezed as she pushed them forwards water surged from his mouth and he suddenly sucked in air and started coughing. Jenyin followed suite with the female he was carrying. Lyamy dropped the guy she was carrying on his side and rushed to the girl who was still floating behind her.

Attempting the same technique on the young female, the water came out, but there was no cough and breathing. She made several attempts without results. Lyamy could feel the life still in the girl but was at a loss as to what else to do. Determined not to lose the life of someone under her protection, Lyamy nicked her with a claw and drew just enough blood to do the ritual. drinking in the few drops on her claw she pushed herself into the youngster's mind. The heart was still beating, she made it beat stronger. Lyamy pushed the girls mind to take a breath and she did. Suddenly the girl was coughing and gasping for air.

Lyamy pulled out of her mind, but with the working of the old magic, there was a bond between the two of them that would always be there. She gave the young girl a hug, "You will be alright, Shelby Dune. We will take you to our sanctuary."

Freldin had a large fire started on the beach in front of the entrance to the cave. They escorted the group a few at a time to sit around the fire. The ship they had been dumped off was taking passengers and a cargo from the Walled City of Talmorg to the Merchant City of Kelleeshia. They were met by a pirate ship from the southern kingdoms of the middle continent, and it turned out that a couple of the crew and passengers were members of the pirates. There were on sixteen of the ship's crew still alive, others were killed or throw overboard out in the deep sea. There were twenty-three passengers that survived the swim. The pirates kept four of the women locked in the captain's quarters and four men that they started calling new crew members.

One of the women they kept was Shelby's mother. The young girl's father was among the survivors and they clung to each other sitting by the fire, "Thank you for saving my daughter." the man said for the tenth time to Lyamy.

"You are welcome, Brandon. You will be able to think more clearly after you eat drink and get a little rest."

Chelic and Chineene were busy making sure everyone had something to eat and drink. Slowly the castaways began recovering a sense of presence. They were starting to think clear enough to realize what had happened to them. Waves of fear and panic were visible in their expressions along with the myriad of other emotions. The captain of the ship stood up, "We need to find shelter and a way to defend ourselves in this savage land. The day is half gone and this land is the most savage in all Ethar."

"We can offer you shelter until you find a way to move on or decide to do something else." Jenyin offered.

"Your cave may be fine for the small handful you have living here. These people are civilized and cannot be living crowded in caves. I am their captain, and I am in charge until I can get them back to their civilized homes." the crew was starting to gather around the captain.

"We pulled you all from the water and have assisted you in recovering from whatever happened to place you in this misfortune. We will continue to help anyone who wants our help, but if you stay here you follow our rules. You are free to move on when you are ready with any who choose to follow you. We will take care of any who choose to stay. We have room in our shelter for many times the number here and are willing to share with you, at least until you are able to follow your own choices."

"Did you not hear me mate," The captain stepped forward, chest puffed in Jenyin's face, "I am in charge here, and if we have to use your cave for shelter, that is the way it will be, but we will build real houses and protect these folks until we can build a ship and take them home or find a port city in this savage land where we can hire passage." The rest of the castaways were getting uncomfortable and those of the sanctuary shifted to alert postures ready for a conflict they wanted to avoid.

"I am Jenyin and I am the leader of this sanctuary. You are a guest and disoriented from recent events. Perhaps you have forgotten yourself, but those wishing to stay in our sanctuary are welcome to follow our rules while they are here." The hairs on his shackles were standing, but with effort he maintained a friendly manner without backing down.

"Well, I am Captain Dave Williams, and these people are my responsibility. So, you are going to have to get used to listening to me as long as we are stuck here." He moved towards Jenyin with an arm extended to emphasize his point. Lyamy had him pinned to the ground with a roar before he made contact. Her claws gently pressed into his neck.

The crew started to move, but Jenyin, Daret , Chelic and Karis were instantly between them and their downed captain and the rest from the sanctuary were moving into place with weapons drawn. "You will back down and apologize." she whispered in his ear, loud enough for the crew to hear, "You and your crew are not enough to challenge me, let alone all of us. So accept our hospitality or move on." She climbed off him and helped him back to his feet.

"Anyone wishing to stay," Freldin spoke up to the crowd, "Please follow me and we will get you settled in with a place you can stay and sleep while you are here. All of the passengers got up and followed Freldin, five of the crewmen broke off and followed also.

"Knowing what is in the jungles here, I would recommend you stay at least for the first night." Jenyin stated, "but it is up to you."

"You will regret having turned on me you deformed beasts." the captain glare back and forth between Jenyin and Lyamy, "What say ye, my loyal men? Stay or make for our own."

"It might be good to learn something of the land before we go out unprepared." his first mate piped up, "and we have no weapons to defend ourselves out there or tools to make anything. It is not easy to hunt with a stick and your bare hands. We do not know the vegetation or animals. Perhaps when we do head out on our own these people can provide us with tools and weapons at the least and some sense of what to watch for?"

The rest of the crew grumbled their agreement. "Very well, we will stay the night, and see what tomorrow brings." Jenyin led them down to the chamber where they were building the places for people to move in.

"The rules here are pretty simple, everyone helps out and looks out for each other. Being new your needs will be provided for. If you stay it will be expected that you find things to do to help the community. So far we have not had a problem with anyone that has moved in." Jenyin expounded on the rules that had been agreed upon and let the captain and his ten crewmen move into three of the buildings.

The new members of the community or visitors were a mix of outlander races. There were humans, elves, dwarves, gnomes and some less recognized. The already established members of the sanctuary helped provide the new guests with a change of clothing. They were given a tour of the portions of the caves they could use as guests. Everyone was invited to share an evening meal in the meeting hall that had been built in the same cavern as the residential structures.

During the first two hours they were there, crewmen under instructions of the captain were caught three times trying to get into the storage cavern or other areas that were restricted. Jenyin and Freldin went together to speak to Captain Williams about these discretions.

"If you cannot keep your crew where they belong, we will be forced to expel you and them from the caves." Jenyin stated.

"You have been extended exceptional hospitality already and you keep abusing the situation." Freldin supported Jenyin.

"So, you are saying my men are not free?" Captain Williams scoffed deliberately acting offended.

Jenyin had enough "They are free to leave and free to do whatever they want outside of our community. Everyone follows the rules inside. Next time we will not be discussing anything further."

"You don't have your girlie here to protect you." The Captain challenged, standing a few inches taller than Jenyin. "This is a nice racket you have going on here, maybe we will cooperate if you cut us in on the action."

Jenyin's eyes lit with flames, "I do not need protection." He turned his hands facing back and upwards giving off a brilliant flash of light, stepping sideways as two crewmen fell to the floor. Then with one strike of the heal of his hand on the captain's chest he sat him back in his chair. "Next time we won't be nice." Freldin followed him out the door.

*   *   *   *   *

Lyamy was on the bed nursing the cubs. She could feel Freyie opening the door. Something hit her on the head, and she lost consciousness.

Lyamy was on her feet in a heartbeat grabbing her daggers on her way around the partition.

"Someone else is in here, just grab her sword and let's go."

Both daggers flew as she leaped out the door passing Freyie sprawled on the floor. The crewman fell down bleeding. The one with the sword got away, because Lyamy stopped to make sure Freyie was alright and push healing into her companion. As Freyie started getting up, Lyamy went to the downed crewman and pulled her daggers. He was dead. "You die with no honor." She whispered, then raced in the direction in pursuit of the other crewman. She sent a mind link to Jenyin with an image of the crewman, from behind, that she saw, *'He knocked out Freyie from behind and stole her sword. His partner is dead.'*

'The captain made an attempt on me when we went to talk to him. I told him one more incident and they were out of here. I am coming back towards you from the housing.' Jenyin answered.

Lyamy moved forward quickly, she saw no trace. Her connection with Freyie let her know that Freyie had moved into their den and was now taking care of the cubs. She made the turn towards the residential cavern and Jenyin was coming the other way. Lyamy quickly went through Freyie's memories to see which sword was taken. "It was the sword personally crafted for Freyie when she became an apprentice in the clan." Lyamy stated as her and Jenyin stopped where they met.

"He did not go by me, so I would assume he may have ducked off in an alternate path or possibly used magic to slip away." Jenyin stated.

"The sword has clan primal magic in it forged into the blade and hilt, it is attuned to Freyie. Freyie and I are one now, so I should be able to activate the magic in the blade if we are close enough."

"Follow me." Jenyin turned heading back the way he had just come from, "I have an idea." He led her to the street by the three residence structures the ship's crew were occupying. "Try here and activate maximum fire, use the old magic to amplify the effect."

Lyamy reached out in her mind and activated the sword, her eyes burst with flame and she augmented the fire of the sword with the old magic. There was a resounding yelp of pain came from the captain's house and they headed for the door.

When they walked in the captain was cussing holding his wrist. His hand was a bright pink with some blistering. There were burn marks in the floor around where the blade had fallen. "You should not mess with things you do not understand!" Lyamy was still burning with the primal drives of having used the old magic. She held out her hand and the sword jumped from the floor into her grasp. The blade told her who had recently touched it. She turned on the crewman, "Your buddy is dead, would you like to join him? If not, then take off your shirt and offer your back to accept punishment for striking my companion." She pulled her short whip from her belt in her left hand.

One of the other crewmen made a move in her direction and flames burst from the blade causing him and everyone other then Jenyin to take a step back. "You cannot barge in here and beat my people." the captain bellowed as he stepped backwards.

"You can bring your complaint to a tribunal if you wish to stay that long." Jenyin glared.

Having no choice, the crewman dropped his shirt and faced away from Lyamy. Lyamy lightened her strokes knowing this was a weaker skinned race but left seven stripes as a warning on his back. "Do not do wrong against the people of this sanctuary again." She turned on the captain, the sword in her hand blazed harder, "Remember these words, you will be held responsible for the actions of your crew from this point forward and will share in their punishment. This is the last time you will be spared."

Jenyin looked at the crewmen in the room, "Loyalty is a good thing, but following a fool to a foolish death is not loyalty." Jenyin turned and kicked the door open. In the street outside the house were the other five crewmen holding random objects they could use as weapons from sticks to shovels. Jenyin did not bother pulling his weapon. He jumped the first one and knocked him out with his own stick and used him for a shield from the second crewman's swinging shovel. He gently pulled the shovel causing the second crewman to take the blow from the spiked board of the third and drop injured possibly dead. He leaped with a somersault in the air behind the last two banging their heads together. The third crewman was the only one still standing as he stared at the board, he swung with the spike stuck in the neck of his shipmate.

Lyamy backed out and closed the door. The flame went out in the sword and in her eyes. She pushed the crewman that was standing to the side and pulled the spiked plank carefully out of the others neck. Placing her hand over the injury she blocked the flow of blood and pushed healing energy into the man. She licked his blood from the spike and whispered, "I pull you from the gates of death and claim a piece of your spirit in life." The crewman standing there heard her whisper, but not her words. The bond was there, and she would be able to use this one to see and hear what he was involved in. She stood and stated, "He will live, which is more than any of you deserve."

"They can clean up their own mess." Jenyin walked away with Lyamy.

At the evening meal only five of the crewmen still sat with their captain. The meal went without incident, there was some celebration.

Survival and hospitality made it a great experience for most. Jenyin called for a meeting with the council after the appropriate social interactions were done.

It was well after sunset when they met around the table in the entrance area. Lyamy brought her cubs with her in a carrying basket lined with silk one of the young gnomes made for her. They discuss the attempts to get into the storehouses by the ship's crew. Freldin and Jenyin shared what happened with the captain earlier. Freyie, Lyamy, and Jenyin shared what happened with the sword.

"We need to keep an eye on the crewman that have deserted their captain still. It may be a ploy." Marrianne stated, "That is something I would do in their place, well in a situation that might call for it. They are just fools not accepting their place here."

"We were planning on giving them weapons to survive if they left to do their own thing, but now we cannot trust them not to use those weapons against us." Freldin expressed his concern.

"So, is everyone in agreement with the way we have handled the situation so far?" Jenyin asked.

"I would have slit their throats and been done with it." Marrianne offered.

Chineene was a little more passive, "I think we have been more then generous in giving them a chance to come around. We should invite them to leave in the morning, perhaps a basket with a few days' food. If they have further problem with it they can leave without the food."

The rest agreed the captain should be put out and any who chose to go with him.

Chelic stood up, "They will be gone by morning and we will need to get more kitchen knives. The ones we have in storage are better anyway. It will be a year before they trouble us again."

Peltrhak looked at the ravine. There was no way they were going to be able to leap the distance. How were they supposed to continue? It seemed their only choice was to head south deeper into the inner continent, but that was what they were avoiding with the whole arching their trail north. '*Lyamy was the one with the direct line to an Ancient.*' he thought to himself.

A single winged creature appeared some distance away coming towards him. The closer it got the more he could make out that it was humanoid. The wings were separate from the arms and had a powerfully large span. The creature glided in and lighted on the ground next to him. '*ShadowDancer promised us protection, so I am assuming this is not an enemy.*' he hoped as much as thought to himself. The creature was scaled, even the wings appeared scaled when they were open.

"We were told you would be coming. We greet you as friends."

Peltrhak looked around uncertain. "I appreciate your friendship. You say 'We' are others coming?"

"I am Zarathu, leader of the dragon men and I am not alone." He lifted his hand and for every member of the caravan there were four dragon men that appeared, both male and female.

Peltrhak laughed, "I am glad you are friends. What can we do for you?"

"For now, friend it is what we can do for you. You need to get to the other side of the ravine; we were asked to help. It was suggested that you may be interested in a trade agreement in the future, perhaps trading food or materials for metals from the mountains. We can discuss that at a later time after you have established your settlement."

"That sounds like a proposition with promise. Your help is appreciated."

"We have to fly invisible, so as not to draw attention from anything else in the sky. As you may have noticed we can take care of that also." Zarathu lifted him up under one arm without difficulty.

Peltrhak watched as the rest of the caravan lifted off the ground and vanished in the air. "Are you what the horvalka in the jungle fear?"

"Perhaps to some extent, but I would guess more likely one of our cousins to the south. This is a land where the Ancients came and experimented with creating new races. They made the mistake of cross breeding races they created with materials like scales shed by their masters the old ones more commonly known as the oldest race of dragons. We are one of the forbidden creations, but there are others much fiercer then we that have no respect for anything that steps in their path. I am sure those are the creatures that cause even the horvalka to fear."

Peltrhak noticed they were going much further than the other side of the ravine, "How far are you taking us?"

"The savage beasts of the continent were taken away to a war and recently returned. They are redistributing themselves across the continent and you were not moving fast enough to stay ahead of the wave. We are taking you about eight hours flying. It will put you days ahead of the beasts that almost caught up with you."

Peltrhak estimated as they landed the dragon men had carried them half the remaining distance to the other coast. It would save them weeks of travel, not just days. "Thank you for the assistance. I will look forward to future friendship and trade."

"You will find that this side of the continent is far less savage. Perhaps part of the reason the Ancients created the great ravine." The dragon men lifted back into the air and vanished.

The landscape was different. The jungle around them seemed to be filled with more fruit and a much greater number of smaller animals. They set up camp and the leaders gathered. There was discussion and arguments as they arrived.

"They could have eliminated every one of us, how much more of a threat can there be?"

"They helped us, they did not attack, so they are not a threat unless we make them one."

"We would not stand a chance if we called them a threat."

"We are friends with the bandit clan, why can't we be friends with someone else for mutual benefit?"

"Isn't that what got Jenyin killed?"

"Who are we to argue with the Ancients." Peltrhak began, "We travel west under the protection of an Ancient, obeying the instructions of an Ancient. We have new insight into the Rules of Order because of an Ancient. The first rule of order is to do whatever it takes for the survival of the clan. These dragon men were sent by the same Ancient we are already listening to for guidance. To do less than accept their friendship would be contrary at this point to the first rule of order. To turn away from this friendship would be to turn away from the Ancient that is protecting us. Who is still foolish enough to argue with an Ancient?"

"We have not seen anything of this ShadowDancer since we left, how do we know she is doing anything for us?"

"Has anyone died to the savage beast or even been injured? Who do you think sent the dragon men to help us?" Peltrhak defended.

"The pelekura keeps the beasts away and we are convenient for now to the dragon men, so that they can get food or other materials from us."

"Why give credit to an Ancient for the natural course of events?"

Peltrhak was getting irritated, "I see we have fools that would argue with an Ancient among us. Take your Pelekura and wander away from the caravan and protection of the Ancient and meet us at the new camp if you survive. If you are so confident that is what is saving you then prove yourself or keep silent. We lost the strength of Jenyin to the clan because of the savagery of our interpretation of the code. The power of those events carried out in perfect execution of the code have given our clan the drive and strength needed to evaluate the way we have been doing things and see the truth in the code for the survival of our clan. I will not give criticism to anything Lyamy did. She was focused on achieving what was best for the clan without consideration for her own good. She exemplified doing what was best for the survival of the clan above all else. At least a dozen of the lords here are alive because she chose the strength of the clan over her own gain."

The rest were silent. ShadowDancer appeared in the middle of the circle. "You speak with wisdom Peltrhak. The rest of you. I have nothing to prove. I give you a future if you choose to spit on it, your loss." She vanished.

"This meeting is over." Peltrhak dismissed the gathering.

*   *   *   *   *

Yaun had twenty apprentices making copies of the five-volume expansion of the code. He made it required reading for every member of the clan. Killing clan members would be the exception, not the rule. Even dealing with those outside the clan required an evaluation of perspective threats, although still allowing immediate protective action based on the immediacy of the threat.

She came and went like a fireball. Yaun stared at the statue, it was fitting still that the gold leaf book of code held in the hands of the statue was the original she had learned from. She had brought the clan together again in mind and purpose. He would honor her and do all that was in his power to make the clan stronger without the bloodshed of their own people. He would award apprentices each year for coming up with ways to improve the strength of the clan with better equipment, methods of doing things and means of assuring and protecting population growth.

Discipline was still important, so punishments still had to be strong, just not lethal, or crippling. He stepped into the meeting hall, as always, his protectors flanked him. They were not as good as Lyamy, but he was not in as much danger anymore either.

"Lords of the clan, I call this meeting to order." Yaun sat in his usual place, "what old business is there?"

The minutes were read. Some of the dens wanted to move to the fields with the harvesters. This provided better protection and increased interaction and strength to the bond between the clan and the long ears. The growth of pelekura had been extended along the entire western portions of the clan lands and exceeded a swath of twenty feet in most places. It was working to protect the city without having to fight. Warehouses were full of crops and groups of clan members were actually finding time to go on hunting adventures and bring back meat from of some of the larger creatures. Skins and portions of the beasts they could use were also brought back.

Study of clan histories discovered the clan used to farm animals also. Attempts were being made to control and herd grazing animals and also birds for eggs and meat. Yaun felt like daily clan life was becoming much calmer.

It was time to introduce the idea of competitive activities that would help keep skills sharp without death being the mechanism of winning. The idea was received well, and they were all instructed to come up with ideas for competitions.

*   *   *   *   *

Lyamy, Jenyin, Freldin, Daret, Chineene, Marrianne, Desdin and Karis hid along the route between the entrance and the house of the captain and his remaining loyal crew and watched. A couple hours after everyone was supposed to be asleep, the captain and crew slipped out of his house and started working their way to the cave entrance. The intent was not to stop them, just make sure they did not get supplies they were not supposed to access. It was already agreed they would let them take the knives from the kitchen, giving them a chance to survive.

The captain was following his crewmen and when they paused outside Lyamy's den, he barked at them in a whisper, "Leave her alone or we will not make it out of here. We need to search the beaches north of here and report what we have found. There is no sign of the wreck here and the Magus will not care about these people. They only care about their magic treasures. Their detector either doesn't work or it isn't here."

"Aye captain, we would be loyal even if you did not share your secret mission with us after last night."

"Well, I had to know who was loyal and who were fools before I let it out the ship was returning for us."

"What they lost must be worth a lot if they are paying for a covert operation to track it down."

"You will all get your fair cut." the captain stated gruffly, "Now, let's get out of here."

They reached the kitchen and the captain called out to them, "Grab the cooking knives, they will give us at least some means of defense. When we get our booty, I am going to come back with an army and take this place over. They will regret not yielding to my command while I was here."

Jenyin held back the urge to kill the captain and avoid any future conflict... As soon as the captain and crew were out the door and it was closed, he dropped down from where he was hiding and gathered the others.

"Well they did what Chelic said they would."Jenyin stated.

"They did not know we were there. They spoke freely." Marrianne noted, "They are looking for a treasure from a wreck and using some kind of detection device they got from a Magus. We can guess what they are looking for."

"It is a good thing we kept them out of the storage areas, the ship parts and cannons would have been a sure give away." Freldin looked at the rest.

"I heard part of that conversation. The captain was the only one who knew about the mission and just shared it with those who had proven loyal to him last night after the big fight. And after the meal was over." Karis added.

"We still cannot trust those left behind." Marrianne interjected, "At least not until they prove themselves."

Lyamy hesitated, but decided it was better to share, "I have created a bonded link with the one that was hurt and I healed. He is totally unaware of my presence in his mind. He has stayed with the captain so I can track their movements and I can see what he thinks. They are going up the coast looking for any remnant of a shipwreck."

Freldin nodded, "They are looking for the ship we came in on and the cargo, specifically the chests full of magical items. It is a good thing none of us mentioned anything about the shipwreck or salvage operation."

"That was not an idle threat the captain made about coming back with an army." Jenyin stated, "I don't think the rest of the crew has the same attitude, but we cannot let that captain leave with that intention."

"We want him to signal the ship nothing found, so they do not come back here looking again." Freldin stated.

"Anyone else notice that they came looking awfully quickly," Marrianne pointed out, "and they did not land way to the north and start searching or even where the ship actually wrecked. They were dropped off outside our door, as if the location was pinpointed and they only came to confirm."

Chineene added, "If that is the case, we may have a visit from some very powerful people even without confirmation. The Magus who hired the captain may have already gotten enough information just using a crystal to watch the captain. They could come through a portal any time they wanted to investigate themselves."

"They would be more civilized than the captain though," Freldin shifted uncomfortably, "If they were tracking their cargo to start with, they would already know the detection device had very little chance of finding anything. That much magic does not vanish only to be easily discovered again."

"These people place great value in certain metals like gold and platinum, the same as you do correct?" Jenyin asked.

Marrianne looked at him trying to evaluate his question. "That would be the reason they have so many items being shipped, to sell for money, rare and precious metals like gold and Platinum. You are scheming, please share."

Jenyin pressed his hand against the wall of the cave and pulled out a bar of gold and a bar of Platinum, each about two inches in diameter and about twelve inches long and placed them on the table. "The rock here is filled with these metals, well, there are like rivers of these metals deep in the rock. If this is what they want, we have more use for the items themselves, I think."

Marrianne was having trouble not staring at the bars, "So you are suggesting when the Magus or his representatives arrive, we just buy the cargo off them? Those two bars alone may be sufficient to cover a full purchase, with the possible exception of a few items that they may choose to keep."

Freldin rubbed his chin in thought, "This could be a good opportunity. These people did not come here by choice and many of them may wish to return to their homes or the destinations they previously had. The Magus could set up a portal between here and Kelleeshia, something we can set up as a transport between locations. It would also be a means for us to travel back and forth with the rest of the world."

"Only if we can put it somewhere, we can control the traffic and only if we can have absolute confidence they will keep their end in a guarded location also." the idea was enough to pull Marrianne's attention away from the metal bars. "Although the two bars would also cover any cost associated with that too. Can you do that as much as you want?"

"I am not sure how much I can do this. I would assume that ShadowDancer would not want me abusing the ability." He pulled a couple more bars of each out of the wall.

"You know these people may be better off here then where they came from or where they were going. Some may choose to stay. They have food, shelter, clothing, and an opportunity to make a future of their own." Desdin pulled a coin out of his pocket and looked at the bars. "Currently we do not need coinage in our community, but we should come up with a name for this place and mint coins for dealing with outsiders. It will help us establish some kind of respect."

Freldin thought he knew the answer, but would ask anyway, "So I am going to take it from the way everyone here is talking that we have all decided this is our home, even if we have a means of passage back?"

"I am here at least for a while, and Grimble has already told me he would stay even if a ship did come to take us back." Desdin answered, "We have all we need here and opportunity to make anything we want."

"We already talked about it, Freldin and I are planning on staying and being a part of this sanctuary." Chineene smiled.

"I am in." Marrianne answered, "Where else would I ever be able to hands on with this much hot loot?"

"You don't even have to ask any of us." Jenyin half shrugged, "It is nice to have your commitment to stay and help with what we are doing. We could use the first cave in the hall for your portal room. Put a metal and stone reinforced door with locks. Once the portal is built, we can shield the room, the magical link should still hold through the primordial shielding, making it working but undetectable."

"Do we want to bring the Magus here on our timing?" Marrianne smiled a devious smile, "There is one item in the booty that I am sure was not intended to be sold and they will not waste time when they detect it independent of the rest."

"Tomorrow, after everyone is rested," Jenyin gestured towards the door, "down the sand towards the beach."

"I will summon a few companions I made in the jungle, they are savage beasts, but they are mine and will not harm anyone in my protection. Do not be afraid tomorrow when you see them." Lyamy said softly, with a slight dark edge to her voice. "I will keep watch tonight, the rest of you get your rest."

No one argued. As the rest turned back heading to their places of rest, Lyamy slipped out the door. She reached out to the jungle and called to her companions. They were all closer than she expected, almost like they were waiting for her to call. She had them follow the river down to the sands just south of the caves where they could wait.

Lyamy called to Freyie and she brought her cubs out. They met the horvalka a few hundred yard from the entrance to the caves and Lyamy introduced Freyie and her cubs. The creature sniffed and she could sense that it was happy to meet Lyamy's companions and cubs. There was a total of seven savage creatures present and Lyamy introduced them all to each other. They would recognize each other in the jungles and not harm one another possibly even help each other.

Freyie headed back to the caves with the cubs, nursing them as she walked. They were growing and their shape was developing more to the form of the Shadowkyn. Soon they would no longer be cubs, but children. Shadowkyn were only cubs for about the first three months of their lives. Once they had the Shadowkyn form they were children for about nine years when they started developing their adult characteristics and became apprentices or young adults. By the end of their thirteenth year, they were fully functioning adults in their society.

Lyamy went up on the ridge and waited. The captain and his five crewmen had pushed their way about eight miles north, well beyond the location where the ship had been washed up on the sands, Lyamy could sense the movement of the crewman she had healed. The sun was rising in the distance over the ocean. She could see the ship in the distance out to sea and to the north. Based on the thoughts she was picking up from the crewman, they were signaling the ship. They were telling them there was nothing to the south of their current location. Lyamy blinked and was fully rested.

The others were starting to come out of the cave entrance. Lyamy jumped down and accepted the breakfast that Chelic brought out for her. Leaning back on the stone near the entrance she quietly ate. She saw Jenyin recognize the ship to the north on the ocean, she nodded when he looked at her. There was no sense telling the others until everyone was out and ready. Freyie was the last one out, the cubs were back in the room they would be safe until one of them got back.

"Everbody," Lyamy called, "There are seven beasts to the south of us only a few hundred yards away. These will not hurt you, because they are mine. Normally if you see one of these creatures it is too late, you are their next meal. The creatures came up closer so everyone could see them. Today they are on our side and will protect us should a fight break out."

Even Jenyin shuddered at the sight of the horvalka, looming taller than the ridge above the entrance. The other creatures would have been terrifying on their own, but that was diminished by comparison. "You will have to talk to me about how you did this later in private." Jenyin told Lyamy.

She laughed and reply, "You actually taught me this. Just like the cat you have waiting on the ridge."

"Are we ready?" Marrianne asked.

"Let's do it." Freldin replied. The Shadowkyn spread out and vanished. Marrianne ran back in to get the item she was sure they would respond to. Jenyin stood by Freldin with Chineene on the other side of Freldin.

Marrianne came running back out and stopped about fifteen feet in front of Jenyin, Freldin and Chineene. She assembled the pieces she was carrying, and it formed a staff that glowed with power. She stood it in the sand and moved back a few feet behind the leaders of the sanctuary. "This should not take long; they will not want anyone to find this power before they have it in their hands. The surge of power should have tingled their arcane senses even if they do not have alarms set looking for it."

Lyamy could smell the exotic essence of the arcane before the portal started opening. It was in tune with the staff. Two armored warriors stepped through and took positions on either side of the portal. They were followed by four magic users of some kind in robes and attire. Last through was a Magus, a caster of obvious power and stature. Lyamy could sense the limitations of their powers as if they only use a small part of the power. They were limited to primarily arcane and anything they used outside the arcane was not with direct knowledge. She could see that they were powerful with what they knew. She related it in her mind to a warrior who only used s stick, and did not know how to use a sword, but was good enough with the stick it was all he needed.

The Magus walked forward and picked up the staff. The glow subsided making the staff appear more mundane. "This was no accident, so I am going to guess you called for me. It is strange that I just got a report telling me there was nothing on this portion of the coast. Obviously, you figured out we were looking for some things we lost and seek some type of negotiations." He looked at the horvalka, "Obviously we did not come with sufficient force to make you agree to our terms, but then neither have you chosen to attack either."

"You are welcome to our sanctuary." Jenyin stepped forward, "You are free to come and go. You are required to maintain appropriate behavior as guest while you are here. We have something you lost, that we have rights claim having salvaged it. As testimony to our good will in this matter you are already holding the one item which we estimated to be of the greatest value to you regardless of price."

Freldin stepped up next to Jenyin, "Please come in and we can discuss our proposition. We can offer you something to drink or eat if you choose while we talk." Those that were hidden appeared.

"I would be honored to accept your hospitality. There is obviously more to you then can be seen through normal means." He looked at Lyamy, "I perceive that if you had wanted us dead, we would already be there."

"Your entourage is welcome also." Freldin waved to those still standing by the portal.

The Magus lifted his hand and the portal closed. "Come let us accept these people's hospitality."

Jenyin led the way in with Freldin, Chinieene and Lyamy. The Magus and his entourage followed and then the rest of the governing body of the sanctuary. They went all the way to the meeting hall in the residential area. Chelic had already prepared for this and had drafted people to help with preparations and serving. At first the conversation was idle chat. The Magus was impressed with the caves and what they were doing. There was slightly more seriousness when they discuss the captain and his abuse of their hospitality. The Magus indicated that the captain was not supposed to act independently, and he was supposed to report if anything was here, not go after the treasure himself.

About the time they were done eating, the conversation moved around to the subject that had brought them together. "Speaking of treasure, that is a sizable cache you lost." Freldin stated. "Enough to stock a new magic shop."

"Indeed that was the intent. That and a few items of personal request." the Magus answered

"So aside from a few items, your intent is to sell the whole lot?" Marrianne piped in.

"That is the plan." the Magus stated, "and for recovery of the property we are willing to generously offer twenty percent of the value to have it all returned."

"We do not have a lot of use for money here, in case you didn't notice we have been cut off form the rest of the world." Lyamy stated sipping from her drink, "What would you say if we offered to buy the lot, minus of course the personal items, along with requesting certain other services from you?"

The Magus raised an eyebrow, "If you don't have money how would you pay for it?" He paused. "Ok, if you can pay the price minus the twenty percent reward and pay for any other services you are going to request, then that would save us the time of selling everything in the shop and we would have the money to restock. We could deal with that."

Freldin set down his drink, "The twenty-three passengers on that captains ship did not ask to come here. They were destined for Kelleeshia. We currently have no use for coinage because we have no passage of exchange. I do not hold you responsible for the five of us that survived the shipwreck, but you hired the captain who had the passengers thrown overboard, as part of his ploy to find your items. A share of that burden is yours."

"I suppose in fact I can be held accountable for taking part of that burden."

"So then would you be willing to establish a portal between here and a location you can protect in Kelleeshia. It would serve you on two counts. First it would pay your debt to these passengers of misfortune and second it would give you a new line of business."

"You are capable of creating a portal, both of you anyway." The Magus looked at Lyamy and Jenyin, "However this proposition does sound advantageous to all of us. We also both want this passage to be protected from random travelers from both ends."

"We have never been off this continent." Lyamy stated, "We would need a location we have at least some familiarities with or a focus the way you used your staff in order to open a portal. You know where it would be safe at your end to place a portal, that is not in the general eye of the public and will not draw attention as people go in and not out or come out that never went in."

"There is sound logic in what you say and worth considering. I have to ask though how will this give me a new line of business if you do not use coin?"

Freldin answered, "Because we do not use coinage currently in our small interdependent community does not mean we do not have any or that we cannot provide other resources perhaps worth more than coin."

"I agree to your bargain if you can give me payment for what you have salvaged as you say."

"This should cover everything and generously more for miscellaneous other favors or details needed getting established." Jenyin pulled out one bar of gold and one of platinum out of his hidden pocket, so for appearances out of the air, "It is not coin, if you wish to wait, we can turn it into coins, or you can take these two bars as payment in full. And still recover the few items that were not intended for sale."

The Magus dropped the bars into a con bag on his belt that did not look big enough to hold more than a twelfth part of one bar. "Then the bargain is sealed. Shall we pull the five items from the collection first or see where it is you would like the gate between continents placed?"

"We will pass the storage room first, Marrianne has organized that so she will be best apt to help you find what you seek. Then we can continue on to the room for the portal."

Lyamy lead the way and stopped by the entrance to the room that almost no one could see. Marrianne turned and walked through the wall. The Magus cast a couple spells then laughed, "I have no means to see this opening or door."

Lyamy held an arm through the wall so he would know where the opening was and he followed Marrianne in. A few minutes later they came back out and Lyamy continued to lead the way up the hall. "Our magic is different than yours. The power source is not arcane, or a source you are familiar with seeing used throughout the world from what I understand."

"I am truly pleased to see new and different magic that I do not understand. We cannot learn if we never see more then we already know."

As they approached the room for the portal Jenyin wondered when Desdin and Grimble had finished the metal and stone door to the portal room. "This is where we had in mind for the portal. Once it is complete, we can conceal it the same we we did the room full of magic items. The portal will stay connected, but not be detectable."

The cavern and the door were a good size, the horvalka outside would not be able to get in this room, but you could probably get an elephant in and out pretty easy. "Do you have anyone who can shape stone and someone who can forge or manipulate metal?"

"That would be me," Desdin stepped up, "Was expecting to be called upon."

"This will be an arcane portal; I have an Arch Mage at the other end. The mechanics will maintain and recharge. The portal can activate from either end with a thirty-minute duration and two way passage with a thirty minute recharge time between uses." the Magus looked at everyone standing there, "This will take a while, probably most of the day, you may want to carry on with normal activity."

"We have a problem," Lyamy stepped up, "Captain Williams has threatened to get the resources and return here with an army to claim this place for his own. He was going to use the reward for that purpose."

The Magus paused and stroked his long gray beard, "We will not allow the portal used for anything like that. We can send resources to assist you in defense, but I would say you have the means to defend against anything he could bring by sea, even if he did entice other captains to come with him. Or you could track him down up the coast and eliminate him before he becomes a problem. That is the problem with posting jobs for free lancers, some of the takers are less then honorable."

Lyamy turned and headed out. The rest of the world it seemed may not be as different from the clan as they first appeared. It seemed there were times when the elimination of members of the society worked towards preserving the future. "Thank you." she said over her should as they left the room.

Outside Lyamy instructed six of her companion beasts to use the river for travel and head back into the depths of the jungle. The leophardeg stayed with her as she walked down to the beach. Lyamy reached out with her mind to the crewman with the captain now close to twenty miles up the coast. She looked through the crewman's eyes.

Captain Williams was directly in front of him. They were still searching for any signs of a shipwreck. No message had been sent back to them letting them know the search was off. Lyamy had not notice before, but the Captians skin had a greenish hue to it. From the crewman's thoughts she learned he was only half human. She also learned that the Captain did have the means to gain the following of an army and starting a new colony on this continent would give him prestige among his people. He was unquestionably a threat to the sanctuary and to the clan. She checked and her crewman had a long kitchen knife on his belt carried like a small sword.

It is time to end this Lyamy decided. She pushed her will into the crewman. She tested, reflexes were a little slow, but workable. Body responded to her thought. Using his body, she jumped up, plunged the dagger down on the left side of the captain's neck, kicked off into a back flipped pulling the knife back out and landing feet first about ten feet behind the captain.

The captain fell forwards, turning halfway with a look of total surprise on his face. Lyamy looked around to make sure the other three crewmen were not coming after the one she was controlling. There was a pause as the rest looked back and forth between their dead captain and the one standing there, knife in hand. Suddenly the First mate started laughing. "I wanted to leave him back in the caves, but I was honor bound to hold true to my captain. You have just delivered us from our oaths. I say we go south, forget this quest and see if those cave people will forgive us."

"Aye," one of the others added, "We don't want to go back to that ship of pirates from the southern kingdoms, they will have no use for us now. Their part of the deal was to get the weapons and armor as compensation for their armies."

Lyamy let go of the control she had over the crewman. She put an arm around the leophardeg, "We are not so different. Just between you and me, we both kill for survival." She knew the beast did not understand her words and sent him off to the deep jungles also.

Jenyin walked up to where she stood staring out at the ocean, "If you hadn't, I would have. The others should know he is dead, they do not need to know how. There is a balance between not killing and necessary killing."

Lyamy shook her head, "You did not tell me, but I learned. Every time we take a take a piece of someone, and bond them to ourselves or anything, we are killing in part. We kill a part of their free will. It is a part of life though, not just the old magic. The agreement between the clan and the harvesters has killed both in part for the overall good of the whole. Part of the harvester's freedom died and part of the clan freedom died in exchange for the rewards of the relationship. In this case, the death of the captain has given his crew the chance to trade off gaining a freedom at the sacrifice of being a part of what they were."

Jenyin put a hand on her shoulder and walked her back towards the caves, "I may have been your Master of old magic, but you have learned more than I ever knew. Speaking of which, a Student is not supposed to be able to attack and kill their Master, how did you manage that one?"

Lyamy laughed, "Are you dead? Intent influences the magic. If I had intended to do you serious harm, I would have been stopped, but the intent was to give you freedom to do what you wanted. Even if I miscalculated and you died, it is not the results that the old magic works on, but the intent. If I rolled a rock off a cliff to clear the way for passage and it fell on you the rock would kill you not the magic and the intent was not to do you harm. If I tried to roll a rock off a cliff to kill you, the magic would stop me."

"That knowledge was lost by the time I was trained. All there was left was the rule a student cannot kill their master." Jenyin laughed, "It seems that there has been a lot of knowledge lost by the clan over time."

Desdin came out the entrance of the cave, "The Magus is asking for you two." he shrugged and held the door for them as they walked in.

They walked in the room and the portal was open. The Magus turned and saw them, "Ah, there you are. Can you see the arcane working and how we have configured the portal, what holds it open, and what will trigger it to open again?"

"I can see the magic," Jenyin began, "but I cannot see the working that refined."

"I can see it." Lyamy answered.

"Then you can use the magic you know and adjust things so that the gate will be always open and only close if we need to close it. Let me offer that as an option, I do not wish to force this on you if you do not want it."

Jenyin nodded, "There is no reason not to, what do we need to do?"

"I will have to defer to your Lyamy for that." Magus glanced at her.

Lyamy studied what she saw, "We will need one of us at each end." She paused and pushed what she saw and what they needed to do through the bond with Jenyin her master. "We will be replacing some of the arcane threads with primordial threads and the power will cycle instead of being spent. I think the same thing can be done with arcane, but I have not worked with it as much."

"Your primordial magic will be more stable than the arcane."

Jenyin stepped through the portal. There was a pause and then Jenyin and Lyamy started working as one from both ends of the portal. The wavering of the portal slowed and steadied. The sound stopped and when they were done the portal had a much cleaner appearance. Jenyin stepped back through. He was impressed with what Lyamy could do and how much he was learning from her.

"The Lever at either end can close the portal or reopen it." Lyamy stated. She looked at the Magus, "You know and understand magic you cannot see. You have been touched by this magic before." Somehow, she could pick up on some of his thoughts. "We are not bonded, but I can sense some of what you think."

"I have been touched by an Ancient, and you wield the same power. I recognize it. I am sure there is more to what they do, but it is said that all the common magic threads from the same source." the Magus looked at the portal and then back to Jenyin and Freldin who were now both in the room, "It is a pleasure doing business with you. We will talk again soon. For now I have business I need to get back to this was not exactly a scheduled event for me and I will have to make up for the scheduled things that fell to the wayside."

The Magus and all but one of his entourage went through the portal. The sorcerer that remained turned and said, "That was the High Magus of Kelleeshia, David Kremlern." He bowed and left through the portal.

"So, he was the top of the magic circles in Kelleeshia. He commands more respect than their High Lord." Freldin stated, "There are only a few in the world out there that command more respect."

"He seemed to esteem Lyamy's power over his own." Jenyin observed.

"Yours too, she just seems to have even more then you. Personally, I would not want to be on the wrong side of either of you."

Chelic stepped in and looked at the portal, "We were ready when the soldiers came up the beach. The Magus is powerful, but he cannot see the lines that bind us. Lyamy likes Mellina, but what she is scares her too." She seemed oblivious to everything she said but smiled and went back out the way she came.

"Do we have anyone writing down everything she says?" Freldin asked, "If we don't, we should."

"I think her mind is crossing the threads of time." Jenyin smiled, "She even enjoys things as if they already happened before doing them."

Lyamy's eyes also followed where Chelic had departed, "I am not sure, but it may not be so much that she touched death, as who brought her back. If ShadowDancer can transcend time she may have accidentally imparted some of that when she reaches deep enough to pull Chelic back. Our history is filled with those who have been brought back from beyond the dreams, some of them came back with abilities or changed, but they knew what they were doing and had control. Perhaps ShadowDancer imparted some of herself into Chelic to bring her back."

The others stared at Lyamy, "How could you possibly know such things of an Ancient?" Desdin asked.

"I have spent a lot of time with her. She can capture the moment and experience months or years in the twinkle of an eye. I know because I have been there with her. She has filled me with knowledge, and I am sure I have seen an overflow of things beyond the specific knowledge she was imparting. Those of us who have shared minds with others, know what I mean."

Desdin stared at Lyamy for several minutes, then decided not to pursue the subject. "Well, there is always more work to be done." He headed off about his business.

*   *   *   *   *

Merkyet sat in her office. She was troubled. Lyamy was gone, but she did not feel her master die. She was master now and her student was coming along nicely. They knew who the other was, there was no need for the secrecy Lyamy had used with her. Lyamy's words were starting to haunt her. *'I will be sacrificed...'*, "If I share a portion of my food with my wolf, I have sacrificed, or if I leave a few birds in the wild when I capture a flock for the farms they are sacrificed." she accidentally spoke out loud.

Merkyet realized that sacrificed does not mean dead. *'Everyone saw Yaun's bloody sword, just like she said they would, and the flames envelop her on the pyre.'* "I was there, and I did not feel her spirit pass from this world."

'I will be dead to the clan' she said, but Merkyet realized she never said she would be dead without some kind of qualifying attachment. Merkyet searched everything she knew of the old magic for a way to come back from being burned or doing what she did taking a sword and climbing in a pyre without burning and could come up with nothing.

They found bones that had not been fully consumed by the fire and brought up the image of what form they had when they were burned, and it was unmistakably Lyamy. *'Why do I question what my eyes have seen, and the records have witnessed. I would be considered either crazy or still in mourning if I said anything about my doubts to someone else.'*

Merkyet was beginning to question her ability to see reason. Freyie had died the same day, torn apart by a savage beast her bracer bloodied and left behind with the teeth marks in it to prove what ripped it from her wrist. The blood verified it was Feyie when the vision was summoned. She already examined the possibility of Lyamy killing Freyie and animating her body to take her place on the Pyre. Lyamy had traveled to her own sacrifice with Yaun and was out of his sight for less than a minute behind a bush while she relieved herself. He would have seen if she went anywhere else other than the bush or if someone else was there with her. There was no time or place for her to have made a swap and according to the evidence Freyie died while Lyamy burned. It was suggested that Freyie was bonded to Lyamy and if it was with old magic, the magic would have brought her death since the heroes sacrifice was not a natural death. That would explain why a beast came and only took Freyie.

Merkyet gently tugged the thread in her student's mind, they both had time, she could use more study. "The thread, that is it." Merkeyt reached around in her head, remembering where she had felt that thread when Lyamy tugged at her. The bond was still there. If she was still bound to Lyamy, then Lyamy was still alive. Merkyet smiled and sat back. Another secret she could tell no one. Unlike the others this secret made her burden lighter. By the old ways of the clan that raised her up, she should hate Lyamy, but Lyamy changed that and now it made her happy to know her mentor was not dead.

Was Jenyin, or... she pushed the thought aside. It did not matter the one who mattered to her was alive.

A knock came from the door.

"Come in Treska."

"Chief inspector," Treska bagan as she walked in the door, "What can I do for you?" closing the door behind her.

"We both have some time, I thought perhaps you could use more instruction."

*   *   *   *   *

Nelk had a store front on the street and an apprentice tending to the business. He still made secret items for the order that does not exist and for Yaun and his protectors. Now he could do so much more. He had orders for special items from harvesters to lords. He even drafted a couple of the younger members of the clan who may not have survived the old ways to study and help him with his craft.

The village always had coins, but they were not used often before, but with markets opening on the streets, the value of the coins became real. There were measured portions given to every adult and apprentice as they became an adult. Everything that was done was checked against the expanded code, even if there was nothing specific it would be balanced against the good of the clan as a whole recognizing the whole was made up of the individuals.

The dominant members of the clan were still those with the physical strength and prowess to provide protection to the others. The minds of the others were starting to be recognized as having virtue that also belonged serving a part in the running of things even if it was just as advisers and consultants. Lyamy had taught them act quickly and decisively when they had to, but to look for the good of the clan in the things they did.

Nelk re-examined everything Lyamy did and said around him. She was to sharp and had demonstrated to him she would find a way for clan not to die. He knew she had gotten Jenyin and three of the women of his den out to be free in the world under the guise of killing them. She had him make devices to prevent Yaun from tracking her or Jenyin once they were out of the village and the devices made it to Jenyin.

How could she not have found a way to escape her own fate when she planned it. All the evidence said she was dead. Everyone witnessed it, but Nelk was sure she was out there, and she was just smart enough to cover her tracks better then he could figure out. He was confident that one day she would be back for him. She told him the clan still needed him, but the promise was there that one day he might see the world beyond the clan.

*   *   *   *   *

Brelk talked with Merkyet occasionally, knowing she was the heir of the old magic from Lyamy, he let her know he had some training and was interested in more if she was willing without adding another bond. She agreed, but part of him felt that Lyamy was still his teacher. She was supposed to outlive him. He saw her uphold the code to the greatest of degrees, so he was not completely surprised she put the code ahead of her own life.

A part of him did not believe it, she was cunning and found ways not to kill her rivals, surely, she was cunning enough to save her own in spite of what his own eyes told him. Something inside him felt that she was still out there, but he dismissed it as some kind of wishful thinking which was not healthy for the head of the order that does not exist.

The order was not as vital currently as it had been in the past. Politics was fickle though and it was still important to keep eyes open on the events that are hidden. It was nice having a lull in the backstabbing cutthroat behavior, but that made it harder to keep his agents sharp. It made more work for him, but that was alright. It was much better to have to work at keeping the order sharp then having to replace agents that vanished of turned up dead.

Splitting the clan had no small part in reducing the violence. He designated the highest-ranking order member being sent west as in charge of that division of the order. Lyamy did ask him who from the order to send and found an alternative justification for picking them to go. Lyamy really did know way too much to be safe for the clan. She knew the leaders of all the major secret parts of the clan including those that lead the split to the west. If she were captured by an enemy the information, she had could provide devastating advantages against the clan. Perhaps Lyamy knew she was doing the right thing.

*   *   *   *   *

They made it to the main river as they moved down the lush valley that seemed to get better as they went. The volumes of herd animals and more docile creatures meant an abundance of food for the clan. It seemed that all the plant life they were familiar with was here and many lush and fruit producing plants that they were not familiar with. There did not appear to be many if any predators at least none large enough to be competition for the clan.

'You will not be disappointed.' Yaun, and Lyamy had both told him and they were right. This was a land of promise. They would do well, and they had not yet reach the point where ShadowDancer had told them. She had given instructions to set their village where they could see the ocean and the river. The first thing they would do would be to mark the land and open a portal. Looking at the land they were entering, Peltrhak understood now what Yaun meant when he said he envied him this journey.

It was obvious the entire caravan was impressed and in high spirits. It would fall on his shoulders to make sure his people continued to work together for the good of the growth and strength of their clan. It appeared that defending the settlement as it developed from savage beasts or outside threats was not going to be a worry. They would be able to focus on building and developing their village.

*   *   *   *   *

Jenyin examined the coins. It had been decided to name the Sanctuary after him, they called it Jenyin Sanctuary. The name was stamped in all the coins. One side of the coins had the value and year, the other a relief of the founding eleven members sitting at a table. They had a full range of coins made from copper, silver, gold and platinum. Everyone living there was given a base amount to start with and they were working on means to make sure everyone had an income and balancing prices of goods. Some of the price balancing came from market rates through the portal.

It had been about forty days since the portal was setup. The next day the crewmen that had left with the captain returned and left immediately after returning the knives they had taken form the kitchen. Freldin gave them each five gold coins to get a new start when they went back to Kelleeshia, but they did not want to stay for fear of repercussions for standing with the captain. Only one family from the passengers chose to go to Kelleeshia, but they were going there to join family already. The family that left was also part of the noble class and had more reason to return to the established parts of the world.

The rest of the passengers were there because they wanted to see a different part of the world, or wanted a new start, but none had anything to lose by staying. They liked the idea of being a part of something new. Many of them were already followers of ShadowDancer. There were others who visited from Kelleeshia and some of them also chose to stay. Traders came back and forth through the portals on a regular basis, buying some of the crafted work and offering deals to shopkeepers for other goods.

There were adventurous groups that were intent on setting up business procuring raw materials like wood and mining up the coast. A wide variety of people came and went, and Jenyin Sanctuary actually had to set up a legal system to settle issues and enforce rules. There population was growing pretty steady, according to Freyie they were over two hundred now. Some of the arrivals simply said when they arrived ShadowDancer had suggested they come here.

"I was thinking about exploring the cliffs on the southern side of the river." Jenyin was telling Lyamy, "Did you want to come along? Karis is waiting with a boat. We could take Freyie and the cubs, they would probably like to get out for a while."

"They have changed enough we have already started calling them children. They have started talking too." With a thought she let Freyie know, "Freyie will be up shortly with the young ones."

"They are growing quickly and learning quickly for that matter." Jenyin said as they stepped out of the caves into the open.

"I think that they are catching up with time, not sure how to explain it. Just my life was touched by ShadowDancer and I think that is affecting my children too. That feels different, my children, not children of the clan. I also used a lot of things," she paused, the reference to old magic they had decided not to use openly, "that may be impacting them while I was carrying them."

"I suppose, I never considered how that might effect unborn cubs."

"Did you know, when we raise our own cubs, they can learn from what is in our minds. There is a natural link, like the bond between a student and master. It was in the knowledge that ShadowDancer gave me, but I did not think about it until I started feeling it. The link will fade to a controllable link as they grow to adults. Our people have lost the advantage this gave us by sending our cubs to the nursery and not raising them ourselves. That is how they learned to talk as much as they do now."

"We used the nursery to control how the cubs and children would think. To keep their thinking in line with the concepts we held as following the code." Jenyin pondered.

"And look how that turned out to be corrupt..." Lyamy turned as Freyie came out with the five children holding her tail, "Morning Freyie, children."

The voices gave a discorded "Mmorninging m,momomy." Three of the children moved over and took Lyamy's tail and they all headed down towards the river and the boat where Karis waited.

Karis Held the Prow of the boat as they all got in. It was a medium sized rowboat built by their own craftsmen. It would hold the nine of them comfortably. They shifted towards the back of the boat lifting it out of the sand. Karis pushed them off into water and then leaped landing gracefully in the front of the boat. Each of the adults grabbed an ore, Karis did the steering, she turned the boat towards the cliffs south of the waters.

There was no beach, just a sheet rocky drop into the water. There were small caverns in the stone they could see as they approached. The children were all excited and wanted to look in every space and hollow. "Stay back from the edge," Lyamy instructed, "we don't want to tip the boat and fall in the water."

There were a variety of crystals that were occasionally evident in the stone. They eased the boat long the base of the rock wall. For no apparent reason one of the children, Drustle, jumped up about twelve feet on to the rock wall grabbed something and dropped back into the boat. Lyamy started to address him when she saw what he was holding in his hand. It was a very large crystal that seemed to be pulsing with energy. "It is like the one in your mind mommy that can hold and channel great magic."

They were all examining the gem as the momentum carried the boat past the next cutback in the cliff. Freyie was the first to look up. "I didn't know the harvesters used weapons?"

"What are you talking about, Freyie?" Jenyin looked up and the rest joined in looking around. They had entered a cove the eddy current pulling them in. There were long ear harvesters with spears and bows in a half circle around them.

Savage instincts rose inside Lyamy, all she could think about was protecting her children and her eyes filled with fire.

"Lyamy?" one of the harvesters called out, "I thought you were dead?"

Lyamy looked, it took a minute, but she recognized the guard. "How is your leg?" her question confirmed who she was. They eased the boat to the shallows where he stood.

"Renninger, I never told you my name. They say you saved my life. The medics would have been too late if you had not taken care of me." He waved the others to lower their weapons.

"We are dead, and you never saw us." she stated. The tunnels behind them caught her attention, "Have you always had tunnels down to here, or are you working on plans of escape?"

Renninger laughed, "We have always had these and others we can leave any time we want without a trace. You guys protect us in exchange for food and never venture into our tunnels. Things are changing though; we are getting more notice and the clan is starting to know us by name."

"I hope the changes are for the better."

"We are getting respect, and there is less killing, so I would say yes. The only drawback will be they might start wondering where we have kids and things like that. You are the first to see us this side of the fields. We cannot have them knowing we are actually serving by choice; they may feel the need to take that choice away."

"We will not tell the clan; they would kill us if they saw us."

"They made a statue of you Lyamy. It stands in the middle of town and Yaun looks at it every day."

Lyamy looked at the tunnels and thought of Nelk, "We need to see if we can work out some business arrangements, but just you and me when I don't have my children with me, will that work?"

"I owe you." Renninger said, "but we have to convince the elders now that it is safe for us to let you go. We have never had our secret compromised before."

"Let me show you a little something you can share with the elders. We are here on peaceful terms and do not wish you any harm." Jenyin would you shape that stone, she pointed to a stone about the size of a bowling ball, he touched it and it turned to magma and steam billowed up where it flowed into the water. Lyamy pointed out over the water, spears of flames danced on the water then plunged into the water creating a cloud of steam on the surface. "So, you know these are trivial demonstrations, but you cannot take us or keep us unless we are willing."

Renninger raised an eyebrow, "Noted. It is not our way to kill if we do not have to, but it would be nice to have some way to give assurances that you can keep our secrets. Would you come with me to speak with the elders?"

Lyamy trusted Freyie to get the children back to safety if anything started to go wrong. She looked at Jenyin, "I'll be back." Then followed Renninger into the cave. The cave opened up to a large warren, there must have been at least five times the population that the clan had been aware of just from what she could see. "So now you show me more of your secrets."

She followed him into a large, shaped chamber. Renninger gave a bow to the elders, so Lyamy followed suit. There was some whispered discussion in a language she did not know. "Step forward." one of the elders commanded.

Lyamy stepped forward, "You know our secrets. Renninger says he thinks they are safe with you, in part because you saved his life. I say that makes him bias. What assurances can you offer that our secrets will be safe?"

"I am not with the clan, and neither are my companions. The clan thinks we are dead and if they found out otherwise, the changes that have been happening might collapse and we would be recognized as a threat or even enemies to the clan. I have children now, not clan children, but my own the way it is supposed to be. I will risk your knowledge of my secrets in exchange for you risking yours with me. It is better for both of us and the clan if they find out nothing about what either of our secrets are."

The elders reverted to their other language and talked for a few minutes, obviously not in agreement on all points. "You threatened us and that is an act that makes it harder for some of us to trust you."

"We were surrounded by a display of force, weapons, spears and bows. I was not threatening, I was merely demonstrating that this show of force was not what kept us here to negotiate terms of understanding, because if we chose to, we have the power to leave. Our willingness to negotiate demonstrates our desire to come to peaceful terms, and not follow the path of destruction."

There was more talk she could not understand. "We are in agreement. We note you also have a means to travel on the water. We would be interested in possibly acquiring some of these, we are not sure what they are, but water floating devices."

"Boats. Perhaps we can come to a deal. There will come a time when I will need to help others of the clan escape in secret. When the time comes, perhaps you could help. I could have them come to a location we can agree upon. Then you could blindfold them and sneak them out through your tunnels, and we could take them away by boat. Only if this is agreeable when the time comes." She turned to Renninger, "I will not comprise your integrity. I will honor your vouching for me."

Renninger nodded, "I will lead you back out. You were fierce with the clan, and you have changed their future. I trust your intent." They came back out into the daylight.

"You and another can come with us and when we get back, you can take this boat as a token. I suspect we will share more between us then has already been agreed."

Renninger gestured to two other guards and they all pushed off back into the waters. When they got back the long ears took the boat and the adventurers walked up the beach. "We will not take the children anywhere we have not already explored again." Lyamy could not get it out fast enough. They all laughed, partly from relief, partly because it was funny seeing Lyamy that emotional.

As they reached the cave, Freldin and Chineene were clamoring down the the rocks from the ridge, obviously exited and anxious to share.

"We went exploring," Chineene shared, "We used caution heeding your warning, and we discovered the forest with the high canopy. Did you know there are flying people that live there?"

"We did." Jenyin answered.

"Well, they would like to trade with us." Freldin picked up where Chineene left off, "They seem really friendly and they showed us some of the things they craft and can use for trade."

"Seems we have a day for building relations with the neighbors." Karis laughed and went inside.

"Sounds great Freldin, Chineene." Jenyin responded.

Freldin looked out at the ocean, "The comment Chelic made the other day about being ready when soldiers come up the beach, has been nagging at me. We have the cannons from the ship, and we could make this place very defensible from any assault coming in from the sea. That ship also had weapons and armor and I suspect that word is out we are here and dealt with the Magus. There may be others who decide to try and come for their own piece of the action here.”

“Then we should do it.” Jenyin agreed, “I don't think we need to meet to discuss this, get with Desdin and Grimble and we have plenty of people willing to help. Lyamy can arrange for a watch and help with security concepts. We need to divide responsibilities so that we can make quick decisions and improve efficiency.”

“I agree.” Freldin added, “We can still discuss things when we meet, but we are going to have to be able to act and make changes on the fly.”

Freyie continued inside with the Children. Lyamy stayed, “We need to recruit every willing body to take turns pulling guard duties and organize defensive measures. Everyone needs to have training even if they are not serving as part of the security. We have magic here now that I am not familiar with, I will have to inventory for defensive purposes, the skills and equipment we have at our disposal.”

Lyamy slipped off into the caves, on her way she stopped by her den, to make sure Freyie and the children were alright. As she stepped in through the door and closed it, she felt a ripple she had become familiar with, “Hello, Lyamy.” ShadowDancer said as she appeared in front of her. And stepped as if walking with her to see Freyie and the children. “They grow up fast and we can get caught up in life and the time we want to spend with them is gone before we know it.”

“Hello, ShadowDancer.” Lyamy noticed that Freyie and the children were all caught in the moment with them. “Freyie, you may not remember ShadowDancer except through shared memories.” She turned to ShadowDancer, “Children, this is ShadowDancer, she is the Ancient that has been guiding us on our path.” Gesturing back at the children, “This is

Drustle, Shahani, Nozomi, Kasha and" she paused ever so briefly and smiled "our little guy, Nelk."

"Yes, Nelk named after the craftsman of the clan who represents, acceptance of weakness as having the potential for other strength." ShadowDancer smiled at the youngsters, "As you probably already guessed, I am not just here on a social visit. Hi, Freyie, it is good to see you are doing well."

"It is my honor," Freyie bowed her head slightly.

"Freyie, you really should let Lyamy lessen the bond. You can still be just as close and still share everything you want to share, but it would be healthier for both of you to be able to live your own identity also. You do not want to lose the sense that it is you that loves Lyamy do you?"

"I do not want to lose that, but I do love being a part of her too. My life is hers."

"You can keep that ability, without being bound every second. You still need to be able to function as separate people. Will you give me permission to change the bond so that you share only what you want to share between you? If you still want to share what she feels at any given time you will still be able to do that, but you will not feel it every time she bumps her head or has a breeze blow across her face."

"If you feel it is the wisest thing I can do, ShadowDancer, then do what you think is right to me." Freyie had a touch of sadness in her eyes.

"Dear Freyie, trust me in the long run you will be happier, you are not losing your bond, you are gaining back some of your freedom." ShadowDancer placed a hand on each of their shoulders and they experienced a sensation of a lifting of weight from the bond that held them together, "There, now you should both feel better."

The sadness left Freyie's eyes, she had not realized how much she was losing her own identify until she had it back. "Thank you, ShadowDancer. Lyamy offered this to me a long time ago, but I told her not to. I was afraid we would not be as close."

"Was this why you came?" Lyamy asked.

"No, although this was important. You all are not the first of your race to escape or survive away from the clan. There is a small pride not far from where the gnomes lived, that has survived using their ability to stay hidden. There are only just over twenty. The problem they are having that keeps their number so small is why I want you to invite them here."

"If they are staying hidden, what kind of problem are they having?"

"Your children are maturing to adulthood quicker than normal, because they were touched by some of the time distortion capturing you in the moment as much as we did. Your cubs would normally be cubs for closer to three months and you cannot start using your magic until after you have developed into your true form." She paused, "This means the cubs cannot hide and for some the ability to start using magic does not come until after the first year. Most of their offspring do not survive."

"That is sad," Freyie said and looked at Lyamy, "We have to help them."

Lyamy placed a hand on the back of Freyie's comforting her, "There must be some reason you did not just tell them to come and join us."

"I am not one of you and they do not trust anything that is not Shadowkyn. It is more complicated than that. Even you will have to earn their trust and it could take a couple weeks to a couple months. It will involve magic and ritual. You will know everything you need to know; it is in the old magic you learned. They have forgotten much, but they freely share the ways of the old magic with each other to survive unprotected in the jungles."

Lyamy shuddered at some of the old rituals and wondered how savage this pride had reverted. "Will they be able to fit in this community?"

"They can still speak both languages, they have not forgotten life in a clan. As you have learned, when you raise your own cubs, they learn directly from you mind. You always knew your clan as just '*the clan*', but you are the white leopard clan if you notice, there is a spotting to your skin and while the translucence gives you a whitish hue in the light, the base color is that of a leopard. These are from the golden tiger clan. You have memories of them. They were the golden tiger clan."

"We were not exactly on the best terms. They may not be so happy to see me."

"You know what you need to know and alone they will take you in and give you a chance to earn their trust. Then you can persuade them to return with you. I will tell Jenyin they will need their own place in the caves for a while and you will need to work with them to help them integrate into the sanctuary."

"That is a long time to be away from my Children."

"You can still spend time in Freyie's mind. Your children are connected with both of you. When Freyie has her own, you will have the connection with them also. Anyway, you will still be able to communicate with your children then too. I know this is a lot to ask. If you say no I will find another way."

"I will do what you ask, I just wish there was a way I could be in two places at once," Lyamy, laughed, "I am being selfish. I would not even have my children if it were not for you helping me."

"There may be a way." ShadowDancer made a slight gesture.

Lyamy felt the quivering sensation again, "Are we out of the moment?" then she noticed that Freyie and the children were not moving.

"No, I captured a moment within the moment. I have never done that before." ShadowDancer seemed to check things that Lyamy could not see. "We are good. Like I said there may be a way. I am going to pull you into my mind, so you can see what I do. Are you ready?"

"I am." In an instant Lyamy was in ShadowDancer's mind and standing in front of her at the same time.

"I am going to split myself into two. This is not written in your book of old magic, so pay attention." It was simple, Lyamy felt ShadowDancer think it and it happened. There were two ShadowDancers standing there, but both were still her and then with a thought she was one again. There was a myriad of other things going on in ShadowDancer's mind and Lyamy tried to keep her focus where she was directed. She knew when it was time to pull back to herself and she was out of ShadowDancer's mind. "Now, I am going to enter your mind and guide you as you do the same thing."

Lyamy did as ShadowDancer had showed her and in the process, she learned that the rituals they did could be done on the inside as fast as thought. She did not have to go through the physical motions on the outside. With a thought she stepped out of herself and she was two. "This is amazing." They both spoke at once. "We are separate." one said, "and we are one." the other finished.

"Now pull yourself back together." ShadowDancer guided her through the process, "You already have some experience, being two people at the same time. It is not totally unlike the relationship you and Freyie had, and you were doing something very similar with that crewman. It will be more like what you did with the construct at your own sacrifice, you were both, you moved independently, acted and spoke independently, remember every detail of both, because they were both you."

"You would know about that." Lyamy had some sense of guilt about using the crewman to kill the captain.

"You had a hard decision, and you made a choice. It is never easy to make a choice to kill and if it ever is, then you need someone to talk to you about what is wrong. Are you comfortable with being able to do this so you can be here and there at the same time?"

"I am." she hesitated, but decided to express her concern, "I have seen things and learn things I don't think you intended for me to know. I can keep secrets, but I just wanted to be sure you know what I know."

"What do you know that makes you so concerned?"

"Your birth name, who you are, were, before you were ShadowDancer."

"I trust you to use good judgment. There is one other thing I want to do while we are here. I may not always come on my own, so I want you to meet my messenger." A young girl appeared, to Lyamy she looked like something between an Elf and a human, half Elf like some of the recent arrivals. "This is Melina. When she was alive, she was a half Elf and her sister who still lives as a priestess of mine in a different land."

Melina smiled and said, "I am pleased to meet you."

Lyamy looked a little uncertain, the girl was dressed in appearance similar to ShadowDancer clothed in Fire and shadows like fire, "I am pleased to meet you too."

ShadowDancer nodded and Melina vanished, "There may be times when I cannot come see you myself and I will send her."

"How can she come see me and me see her, if she is dead?"

"You know how you take a piece of a person's spirit to bond them to you. Well, I drew her entirely out of her body, and she lives in a different place now. It is complicated, but she is dead, and I have given her new life within me to take on form when she needs to. I would show you, but it would compromise secrets of the Ancients, so I cannot."

Lyamy thought about how they took a piece of someones spirit when they did many of their rituals, that sweet feeling and rush of power. She thought about how Freyie wanted to giver herself entirely to her. Melina seemed really nice, but what she was, a spirit taken completely from her body, was like being dead, but trapped. Lyamy found it a little unnerving. "I really do not need the details. She is your messenger; I will honor her as such."

"Move back just a little so we are where we were, I am going to let go of this captured moment and we will be back in the moment with Freyie and your children." There was a rippling sensation.

"So, I will stay and go." Lyamy made an attempt to continue the conversation from where they had been.

"How will you do that." Freyie asked.

"It is something like what I did with the construct at my sacrifice. ShadowDancer just taught me something new."

"I thought you already knew all the old magic." Freyie started, then thought about who Lyamy and ShadowDancer were, "I am sorry, if the two of you worked it out, I should not question what you are doing. I am just glad you will still be here with us. I do not know how we will find a male for our den who is strong enough, especially out here away from the clan, but I will be yours no matter what happens." Freyie smiled with all she was at Lyamy.

"Strength is not always what we see on the surface. There are also many males in the rest of the world that are not Shadowkyn and we still do not know what the future will bring us. We still have hope in all things." Lyamy smiled back.

"We have taken care of everything that brought me here. Is there anything either of you would like from me?" ShadowDancer asked.

"You have done a lot for us already. Thank you." Freyie responded.

Lyamy looked at her children, "I want my den to be safe."

"Very well then, let me know if you need me." There was a rippling sensation then ShadowDancer faded and was gone.

"How are you going to stay here and go?" Freyie asked

"Like this." Lyamy became two in front of Freyie, both spoke as one, "I am both of me," then one continued, "or I can act," she let the other finish, "separately." Then she immediately merged back into one. "I can now really be in two places at the same time."

"That is amazing, and that is something new with old magic?"

"Yes, and I need to go up top through the back entrance and one of me will come back and the other will head off to find the golden tiger clan. It is almost time for me to take watch anyway."

"I will be up to relieve you in about an hour and a half." Freyie acknowledged.

Lyamy slipped out of their room and headed to the back entrance to the surface above the ridge. She stepped out into the evening air. Slipping out of the clump of bushes, she sniffed the air and looked around. There was nobody close enough to be watching so she became two. One of her stood up and headed to take her turn pulling guard duty.

Lyamy moved with stealth through the grass and underbrush heading north. She used the same techniques she had used at the west gates of the clan, vanishing and then losing scent and trail. She would pass undetected until she reached the territory of the golden tiger clan. She headed north until she reached the old horvalka trail. There was still enough evidence of the creatures destructive passing for her to easily follow the trail to the gnome's old village.

It was much faster traveling alone then with a group. She was pleased that when she split into two all her equipment seemed to also replicate. It was into the morning when she reached the gnome village. The gnome village was getting quickly overrun with plant growth. Rain was a daily occurrence across the continent. Tropical sunshine and surrounded by ocean. She sniffed the air, there was a gentle breeze from the west and now that she knew she was looking for it, she could pick up the scent of her own kind. They were a distance away still or using a method of reducing the scent they left.

With a little more caution and less speed, she headed towards the scent checking the air regularly to be sure it was still coming from the west. She started sensing a tingling of the old magic, indicating old magic was in use nearby. Sharpening her sense, she could see auras of the forms of others moving in the area. Lyamy lowered her invisibility.

"Greeting cousins. I can see you are here, and I have come to counsel with you. I am here alone." Lyamy waited, watching the golden tiger clan circling her. She could see only the glow of the old magic defining their general presence nothing specific, but she assumed they were examining her, so she kept her hands clear of her weapons. One stopped in front of her so she focused on that one, assuming that at some point they would appear and talk with her. A projection from the glow started to reach in her direction. Lyamy dispelled the cloak of invisibility and grabbed the wrist to the individual, who looked extremely shocked that he had been so easily foiled. "I have come to you in peace. If I wanted you all dead, I could have killed you all without you even knowing I was here. I can see you cloaked in the old magic, something you obviously have not yet learned, but I can teach you this as a token of my intent."

"Those cloaked cannot be seen." The other countered.

Lyamy did not bother to explain, she used the contact of holding his wrist to push the instructions of how to see those invisible to his mind. He looked around and she could see that he could now see his companions also. "So, as you can see they are not hidden from me." Lyamy continued, "now will you accept that I came with peaceful intent?"

The other stood up straight and pulled his hand back sheathing his knife. "She is not here to bring us harm. So why are you here?"

"You have been surviving a long time, but not living. You lose your offspring to the jungle and the jungle has not been kind to your clan. I wish to offer you an easier life, more than mere survival."

He looked at her hard, she knew he was searching his own memories, and the memories passed on from his clan. "You are white leopard clan, why should you care about the survival of any other clan? I can remember the history, if only in part, but your clan was never before friendly to our people, although we are probably no longer at war."

"The clan, white leopard clan, has long been thought to be the only surviving clan, so there is no more war. I am no longer part of the clan, a sacrifice I made to save the clan, perhaps someday I can tell you that story. The important part to you is I am no longer part of that clan. I came for one purpose alone, to help you. I am Lyamy."

Another of the tiger clan dropped their invisibility, "She is exiled and seeks shelter as a member of our clan." an obvious disdain in her voice.

"And if she has, we can use her strength." The first snapped, "I am Wujin, leader of the golden tiger clan, this is Shenji, my first."

From the histories ShadowDancer had taught her, Lyamy understood the structure and order of the golden tiger clan. "I am the first in the Jenyin sanctuary clan and avatar of the Ancient ShdaowDancer, ambassador to you.

I will accept the position of shadow in your clan until such time that you can accept me as counsel to provide wisdom and a hope of a future to your clan." she picked up the scent of a leophardeg in the air. The first of the golden tiger clan vanished. Lyamy located the beast with old magic, and it was headed their direction. "Vanish, I will handle this."

Wujin vanished and Lyamy leaped sideways as the Leophardeg landed where she had been standing. As is turned she caught the eyes of the creature with her own and projected the illusion of her companion horvalka into the mind of the leophardeg. The creature yowled like it had been stepped on and bolted away as fast is it could go.

Wujin appeared again at her side, looking at her with some respect, "What did you do, she looked at you and yowled in terror and ran?"

"I projected the illusion of a horvalka into her mind." Lyamy stated as if it were nothing. "I have a horvalka companion, so I drew the illusion from that."

"We have companions, they are lookouts for us, but we can only make companions of creatures we can dominate or subdue." he looked at her from head to foot, "We are not big enough to subdue a horvalka."

"There is more than one way to dominate." Lyamy filled her eyes with fire for a moment and let it go.

"You have greater power in the old magic then I have seen in others." Wujin stated. "There is more to survival then old magic though and it takes a clan, not an individual."

"You are correct, and I apologize if I offended the proper order. When you have accepted me as a shadow, I will do my best to learn and respect the ways of your clan." she bowed her head slightly to his authority, "I have learned over time that killing is not the best way to resolve most issues."

Shenji appeared again next to Wujin, "It seems you may have knowledge of the old magic that has been lost to our clan."

"I can teach some things to the clan in general, but I can only fully instruct one in your clan and then only if they accept me as their master. This will first require I am an accepted part of your clan with enough elevated status to be trusted with that much authority over another member of the clan."

"I accept you as shadow." Wujin stated, "Everyone come and meet our shadow. You will have to go through the rights of recognition."

"Understood, I know my part." Lyamy responded.

"I am starting to think you may know our ways better than we do." Shenji responded

"We have a place we use for the rituals; it is not far from here." Wujin dropped to a somewhat stealthier stand and started heading to the north west. Lyamy and the rest of the clan followed. It was getting close to evening when the approached the base of a rock formation. Lyamy could sense it was not natural. The threads of power the pulled it up were old and more powerful than what she could summon. Perhaps it was the work of an entire clan or one of the Ancients. She did not ask why they didn't just jump up the rings to climb the cylindrical stone formation as they started the spiral upwards. It was better not to dishonor any perceived customs or ways of their clan.

"Watch your step," one of those ahead of her warned, "the ledge is narrow in some places."

"Thank you." she acknowledged seeking to keep good manners. The sun was a glow on the horizon when the crested the flat stone top. There was room for the entire clan to take positions circling around the edge to keep watch. Wujin directed her to follow him and Shenji to the middle. There was a small monument with the emblem of Darvel. Lyamy recognized his symbol from the histories of their people.

"You still serve the Ancients. I am glad to see this." Lyamy stated.

"We are dedicated to Darvel." Wujin stated, "It is said that when time has passed, he will return."

"You must accept dedication to Darvel to be a shadow of the golden tiger clan." Shenji stated, setting up for the rituals.

"I am an avatar of his niece, I must have her allowances before I can dedicate to another Ancient, or Darvel's acceptance of my dedication to his niece. They will answer if we call upon them."

Shenji had doubt reflected in her eyes, they were obviously not as hard lined about concealing their emotions as the white leopard clan. "If the Ancients come and grant you these dispensations, then it will be as they choose. If not, we follow clan custom." She started the ritual to summon the presence of Darvel, all three sat on the ground facing the monument, "Come Darvel and give us guidance."

Lyamy thought '*ShadowDancer, please bring Darvel with you to this place. His people ask for him but have forgotten how to reach him.*' she only uttered out loud, "Come." and placed her hand upon the base of the monument pushing a trace of the old magic into the emblem lighting the emblem as a beacon.

Shenji watch the flames burst and her mouth dropped open slightly in disbelief. She had not seen Lyamy place her hand against the base of the monument. "They hear you." she whispered.

"I have only lit the beacon; we will know when they answer." Lyamy stated.

There was a whirl of wind accentuating the flames up from the monument and two figures appeared in an ethereal form. Lyamy decided the one must be Darvel and the other was ShadowDancer, but she had assumed the appearance of a Shadowkyn overlaying her normal appearance. Darvel appeared in the same manner both Shadowkyn and Elf forms.

"Shenji," Darvel spoke, "Lyamy belongs to my niece, accept her as she is, the future will show you why and you will be given a time to choose when the path of your clan meets the time appointed. Until then ShadowDancer also represents my best interest for you. Listen to her as you would me. ShadowDancer is my niece."

ShadowDancer spoke, "Change is inevitable, Lyamy is here to respect your ways, before leading you to change. From the things that are weak will rise greatness and what you know as strength will find place in its shadow."

Lyamy bare both her shoulders. Darvel placed a finger on her left shoulder there was a popping sound and the smell of lightening and burnt flesh and the mark of Darvel was branded on her left shoulder. ShadowDancer touched her right shoulder and after the same manner her mark appeared. Lyamy blinked and again a second time and a third, healing the scars into place. She could feel the thread that now connected her with Darvel, she had permission to call upon him to help his people.

"Darvel," Lyamy began, bowing her head in his direction and looking back upon his form, "The golden tiger clan has forgotten how to call upon you. Do I have your permission to teach them this? Or," she looked between Darvel and ShadowDancer, "Should I teach them to call upon ShadowDancer?"

Darvel smiled at her, "My niece takes care of her people, but you can teach them both and they can choose who they call on when they need help. When she accepts you, you can teach Shenji everything you know." He turned to Wujin and Shenji, "Is there anything you would ask of me at this time?"

Wujin looked upon Darvel, "I would that my people had a place in this world again to find shelter and grow strong again."

"That is why Lyamy has come to you."

"I would know what we did wrong that you departed from us for so long, that we might not make the same mistakes again." Shenji said with as much humility as she could muster.

Darvel looked upon her, "We are Ancients, and we are not perfect. You did nothing wrong it was I who failed you by getting caught away in affairs of the Ancients that kept me from you. If you are angry with me, I will not be angry with you. Listen to my niece, she cares about you, not the conflicts between Ancients." Darvel waited and then vanished.

"There are none among you who care more for the success of your people then Lyamy. Listen to her and she will help you." ShadowDancer touched Lyamy's temple, and her mind was filled with the history of the golden tiger clan. "I should give you more knowledge, there are other remnants scattered around the continent, but I will wait until the time is right for each."

Lyamy knew she received again more then ShadowDancer intended her to know when she saw the blue-white blazing blade of an ancient and realized she could summon the same in her blade. "Are you making me an Ancient? That I should gain the ability to make the weapons wielding their power?"

ShadowDancer smiled and laughed, "It would not be the first time, but if I do this time, it will not be by accident and you will know what you are getting into. You are my avatar now and can use any power I grant you. You do not need to hide what you are any longer."

Lyamy placed her hand upon the stone column and drew from the stone a golden medallion on a chain. On one side of the medallion was

ShadowDancer and on the other was the universal symbol of the Shadowkyn. "This symbolizes who and what I serve. I will wear it as a reminder and a sign to those around me."

"I will go now; you have much to do." ShadowDancer vanished.

"You talk to the Ancients as one does to their friends." Shenji said with great uncertainty.

"We are friends, but so are you and me. Do you not respect your friends? If so, then you can be friends with those you respect." Lyamy stated with no emotion expressed as was the manner by which she was raised. "You respect Wujin who is in a position of authority to you, but you still talk to him as a friend, and this makes it easier for you to have an open conversation."

Wujin was anxious to finish the ceremony, "Shenji, have you found Lyamy accepted to be a shadow of the golden tiger clan by the will of our Ancient?"

Shenji looked for a moment then realized he was completing the ceremony, "I have found she is accepted." putting away her branding tools she did not need since the ancients gave her their marks directly.

"Then, I mark you, Lyamy as accepted among our clan." He hesitated, but Lyamy leaned forward exposing her left cheek to him. He swiped her cheek with his four claws leaving four marks about an inch and a half long. He looked at the blood on his claws, "By your blood I bond you to the golden tiger clan."

Lyamy felt herself linked to the clan. She could feel their presence even as they could now feel hers. She wondered for a moment why the white leopard clan had stopped this practice, then thought about the backstabbing and realized it would have been in the way of cutting each other's throats. "I am honored to be one with the golden tiger clan."

Shenji's eyes opened wide, "You are in two places at the same time."

Lyamy laughed, "I am ShadowDancer's avatar. I will teach you,because Darvel gave me permission to teach you everything I knew at that point in time. Anything I have learned since or learn in the future I will need permission before I can teach you." she paused, "but first things first, I cannot be elevated to a level of trust to take you as a student until the clan can officially accept me which is at least two weeks. Things your whole clan should already know based on what I know of your history, I can freely teach all of you."

"Like how to see where our magic has been used?" Wujin asked.

"Yes, like that." Lyamy added, "That does not give you the ability to see things hidden by arcane, there is an arcane spell for that. Do any of the golden tiger clan dabble in arcane?"

"We only know clan magics." Shenji answered.

"Perhaps then I will teach you some arcane also, at least enough you can tell when it is being used."

Wujin looked at her, "Our females have been endangered in bearing offspring and are protected by the clan. Our males outnumber the females because of this, which is not natural. We only send males to face danger now."

"I cannot violate the rules of your clan while I am with you. That is part of my evaluation for full acceptance. If I tell you something is not dangerous for me, I will have to differ to your judgment."

"Who is the Jenyin sanctuary clan? I heard you say that earlier." Shenji asked

"I died to the white leopard clan, as have several others. We were instructed to build a sanctuary for those in need of shelter and protection and for followers of ShadowDancer, so we did. We have taken in many who are not Shadowkyn at all as we were told to do. This is what I refer to as Jenyin sanctuary clan."

"So, they are not really a clan, but live in the same village, so you used the term to express the concept lacking another way to embody all the people as a group." Wujin suggested.

"They will defend each other as a clan, they share as a clan, they have politics as a clan." She paused, "I think they are as much a clan as any other clan. You accept me as part of your clan now, but I was not of your clan, it is very much like that."

Shenji interjected, "It does not matter, they are your clan and you still think of yourself as part of their clan. You are even there now like you are here with us."

"I understand your hesitation, Shenji. I am an avatar of ShadowDancer first, I am here for the good of all Shadowkyn second, then I serve my clan. These things should never really be in conflict, but that is the order. When the time comes, you will have to accept me for what I am. I do not wish to hide that from you." Lyamy pulled open her leather tunic and shirt, exposing the scar of Yaun's sword, "I took this that the white leopard clan should be saved from their own destruction." She turned around and showed them that the scar was on her back also. "We are Shadowkyn, and I put our survival ahead of my own good."

Shenji put her ear to Lyamy's chest checking for a heartbeat. "How can a sword scar you front and back and not stop your heart?"

"Because it was a construct of me, not me that was run through with the sword." Lyamy paused, "You are missing what I am saying, getting caught up in details. What I am telling you is everything I have done has been focused around saving Shadowkyn."

Wujin motioned them to follow. "Let's get some sleep. We can go invisible at the bottom of the ritual grounds and sleep in the grass. The men will take shifts keeping watch."

Lyamy sat and meditated. At first, she started reviewing the knowledge of the golden tiger clan that ShadowDancer had placed in her mind. She felt the web of the golden tiger clan and it distracted her as she explored each thread. She could sense the feelings of each clan member as they slept without prying. She did not try to see any further out of respect for their privacy. She would know instantly if any of those on watch went on alert. Someone was moving towards her.

"Hello Shenji." she said without opening her eyes.

Shenji sat in front of Lyamy facing her. "I would start taking lessons from you, if you are willing. I understand you are limited in what you can teach me until the proper rituals have been done, but as you said there is a lot you can teach me that every member of the clan should already know."

Lyamy opened her eyes and smiled, "You can sense the urgency, that is good. You cannot see me, but you can sense more than where I am, or you might have sat behind me or next to me, so you have a natural strength in clan magic and that is good. Give me your hands and we can speak without words."

Shenji held out her hands, Lyamy knew from the movement of the magical aura where they were and took them in her own. They could not talk through thoughts. *We will start with communication, so we can do this without having to touch. And then I will show you how to see the aura of our magic so you can see those using invisibility and things that have been effected by magic.*

The lessons began and Lyamy committed to teaching her for an hour each night. This would be very much like the way it was done in the white leopard clan.

* * * * *

Official trade had been opened with the long ear clan and with the winged clan of the canopy. Buildings were being started outside the caves. It made sense that milling needed to be done above ground. They had built smaller boats inside, but they needed docks for larger boats and a building on the water if they were going to build larger boats for fishing or exploring the coast. Some of the members of the community hoped to make a trading port in the mouth of the river. The foundations were being built in stone.

Lyamy was seeing to the best security they could provide. There were one hundred members of the security forces now and they took shifts patrolling inside and outside the caves and consisted of about twenty five percent of the population. They were being paid fifty silver per week, which was very generous. This was the average pay for anyone who was working in the sanctuary. Those selling their crafts of harvested goods made more, or less coin, depending on the efforts they put into things. Basic housing was free, but if you wanted something more elaborate, you could pay craftsmen to build for you and buy materials.

The security forces only worked five-hour shift, four hundred minutes, which was established as an average work week. This did give them time if they chose to do other things for additional income. Everyone was provided weapons and training that could use them and was expected to step up in defense of their village if they came under attack. The cannons from the original shipwreck were mounted in positions to defend the entrances and every caster was registered and knew what their job was should the sanctuary be attacked.

Lyamy was busy the doing routine tasks the day she split. The second day she left her security chief in charge and took the day off from other tasks. In the morning she took her children to the merchant district and bought them new clothing along with purchasing supplies for their den. Freyie took the morning off to do other things but was back with them by the afternoon. "Freyie, this evening I am going to need you to watch the children for a while. I know you do anyway, but I will be going through the rights of acceptance with the golden tiger clan."

"I thought you were functioning separately. I haven't noticed anything different."

"You remember the construct, how even you have the scar?"

"Yes." Freyie answered tentatively.

"Be glad you are not experiencing what I will experience tonight. If you want, I will share it with you, without you having to actually go through it." Lyamy smiled and placed a hand on her shoulder.

"I will be there; you can just step away when you need to."

"The children are studying right now and will be busy for a couple hours, so tell me about this morning."

"He was really nice, and I enjoyed the time with him, but he did not understand our ways really and the more we talked the further from being compatible we were."

"Oh, like how? he seemed nice enough when he was here." Lyamy inquired

"Well, like most the races out there, the gnomes only have one partner and while he seemed to like the idea of having to be with both of us if things went that far he was getting irritated if I looked at other guys. He could not separate the concept of den and sex. He would not be a good match for us, and he realized it would not work too." Freyie shrugged.

"As long as you are having fun exploring and we don't cause some kind of rift in the sanctuary." Lyamy left it hanging. "I want to go down to the beach, maybe we should give the children a break and just go play for a while. This swimming is something we never did back with the clan, we had no deep water."

"The children enjoy it," Freyie stated, "and they already swim better than we do."

"We can add to our collection of shells."

They gathered the children and took them out to the beach for a while. Swimming close to shore collecting shells and having fun together. Lyamy had a quiet calm as they went home with the approach of evening. It was time for the evening meal and meeting as they entered the cave. The children were always welcome to join them. Discussion was routine about the current events with the sanctuary. Nothing exceptional happened today.

Freyie and Lyamy were back in their den, children in bed, casually chatting when Lyamy braced herself. "Here it comes."

"What?" Freyie asked, then saw the scar form on her left shoulder and then her right shoulder, "oh."

"Burned in by the ancients themselves." Lyamy said after taking a breath, "This one won't hurt as much." suddenly the four scars appeared on her check. All of the scars were fresh and pink. "Just like the scars we both bear from Yaun's sword, they are the marks of our path. I can show you the memory of the ritual if you would like?"

"It is a big event; I would like to share it with you."

"You will not receive the scars or pain, but you will share in everything else." Lyamy pushed the memory to Freyie and let it play out.

"You are more than just chosen, you are her avatar, and you can be called upon at any time to manifest her power, not just the power you have already gained."

Lyamy did not know how to respond to the observation, "They will be coming here. We need to find a section of the caves they can occupy and give them an alternative exit of their own. In time they will merge with the rest of sanctuary, but they need to maintain a center of their own culture."

"You need to tell Jenyin and the council."

"ShadowDancer said she would tell Jenyin, so I will wait until then. We can still explore the caves and see if we can find a section ideal for their needs, but not too far from everything else."

"Did you really learn to wield the power of the ancients in your weapon?" Freyie asked.

Lyamy pulled her sword, "I have not tested it yet, so here we go." She held the blade out in front of her and it glowed blueish white, she pushed more power into the blade, and it burst in flames of the same color. The brilliance would have been visible for miles outside.

Freyie shielded her eyes, "You are going to wake the children."

Lyamy subdued her blade and slid it back into her scabbard, "I don't hear them, maybe they did not wake. Now we know, yes, I can wield the power of an ancient in my weapon. Do not share this with anyone else. This power is even greater than the old magic, primal or the primordial sources that we use."

"Not even the children." Freyie promised.

Lyamy gave her an embrace, "I must report for my shift at watch. I will be back later."

Lyamy relieved Jenyin standing guard above the entrance to the caves, "Where did you get those scars?" He caressed her cheek as he looked at the four claw marks, "They are too perfect for a fight."

"You will know in due time, Jenyin. I am not at liberty to tell you right now of my own. You could exercise your authority over me as your student and find out, but it would be better if you wait."

Jenyin had no desire to force his will upon Lyamy, "I will not push. I trust your wisdom. Do we count as student and master here, or have you found a student to teach yet?"

Lyamy was not sure how to answer, "First, having children and raising them myself, well with Freyie, my mind is an open library for them to learn from, so I cannot keep that knowledge from them. They will grow up knowing old magic. Then comes the part of things I cannot tell you about that goes with the scars."

Jenyin laughed, "Is there anything we can talk about that you can tell me without being cryptic?"

Lyamy looked at Jenyin, then gave him a hug, "Soon, I will not have to keep these things secret form you. Yes, there are lots of things we can talk about, I think we just covered everything I cannot talk about."

Jenyin returned the embrace, "We could be one den if you and Freyie would like it."

"There are things coming ahead, and it will be better if we stay as we are. Freyie and I have discussed the possibility but agreed it would be hard on the den you have and we still need room for our remnant to grow. Freyie has been testing to see if we can find compatible relations with outsiders, but so far, they are not ready to think our way and we have trouble with theirs. Maybe in another generation or two."

"Not as cryptic," Jenyin snickered in her ear, "At the very least both of you come by and visit our den."

"We will." Lyamy promised. She watched Jenyin walk away and turned to face the ocean.

The power of the Ancients was in her now, she could feel it. Like the old magic, once you had it you had it.

Lyamy looked out over the ocean and contemplated her new power source. She now had access to two of the power sources that the ancients used. *'Maybe three,'* she thought to herself, *'there was that power surge she felt when she received a piece of another spirit. Was this yet another source of power she could access if she needed to?'* The thought made her shudder. Even with her savage heritage using a spirit as a source of power seemed evil to her.

The power of the Ancients that lit her sword with blueish white fire was another layer to the existence around her and now that she was aware of it, she felt like a child just beginning to learn the world around her. She thought about how she taught a brand-new student of old magic, starting with simple little tricks that lack any significant effect. She rehearsed in her mind the feel and look of the power, the threads and weaving that gave her sword power and began pulling them apart.

She began applying this new power the way she would the old magic. A gentle weave and a blue flame perched on the tip of her finger. Then she carefully pulled it back as if she were following instructions from a cautious master teaching her the art. She built a hidden pocket using this new power source, very much like the one she had from the old magic. Lyamy put a few things in this new pocket and when she reached in whatever she wanted seemed to be the first thing in her hand every time. She sensed that this pocket could hold a significantly greater volume then the one made from the old magic.

Lyamy looked around the way she would with the old magic, only applying the new source of power as she looked. She took a sharp breath, amazed at what she saw. She could see the effects of the old magic and the threads that joined things, like her to Freyie. She could see the ebbing and flowing of the arcane powers. She could only guess at what some of the other things she saw were. She could see the natural bonds between plants and the ripples of power in the ground and waters. Everything seemed to have power or energy around it joining it to everything else. She could see the weave of the portal that could not be seen with either arcane or primordial magic. It arched up from the ground above the chamber and headed over the ocean to the other end.

She reached out and touched a random thread with her mind and immediately felt the purpose, what it was doing and how it worked. She started reaching out with her field of perception and realized she could sense everything around her in all directions. She reached out over the ocean and perceived the creatures under the water and pulled back when her mind touched land across the sea. She started to reach the other way across the land, but suddenly she saw Chelic floating in front of her. It was, but it was not Chelic, she was ethereal and had wings of white.

"You have powers that do not belong to mortals and you are learning to understand them and use them on your own. Do not abuse what you have discovered, and you will be allowed to keep it." Chelic smiled a happy smile, without any concerns that might bring her down in anyway. She held that peaceful aura that calmed those around her.

"Am I supposed to use this power, or should I stop studying what I can do?"

"You are meant to have the path you follow, but the time will come when you are tempted to do things you must not do. Use wisdom and understanding of the weave of existence that you do not make things unravel. If you use this power to undo the existence of a grain of sand, you pull the thread from the beginning. The thread of that one grain may impact the balance of all things, so you must know all the consequences of pulling one thread out of existence before you give it consideration."

"What about my sword?"

"That use does not undo what is, it cuts and shifts and moves what is there, as with any weapon. I only deliver the warning." Chelic's ethereal form passed back down through the ground to the caves.

Lyamy contemplated Chelic's words and decided not to explore the inner continent with her newfound power, at least not until after she talked with ShadowDancer about it. There were enough trivial things she could use for practice, like summoning food and water, making sounds or lights in the night. She could work her skills and master manipulating techniques refining what she knew. She was contemplating her systematic developing of her skills and the words Chelic left her with when Freyie came to relieve her watch.

"Your eyes are glowing a blueish white, like your sword." Freyie said walking up.

She had not considered that activating the magic would behave similar in fashion to the old magic, "Thank you, I did not know." Lyamy subdued the magic within her. She headed down to the den.

*   *   *   *   *

They built the platform and erected walls around it. This would be the center of the new clan territory. Peltrhak used the leader ritual to contact

Yaun and let him know they were ready to open the portal. Members at both ends began the casting to make the portal stable enough to last awhile. They had to move all their initial materials through and the personal belongings of all those that made the crossing. They were all encouraged to set their tents up where they would want their dens to be built on one side, the rest of the first village was already preplanned how it would be organized.

Zenjin was one of the older schoolmasters and he chose to mark out where the school should be built and offered to teach history to the young children and cubs while the others of the clan made ready and used the portal to bring the rest of their belongings over. Zenjin may very well have been one of the oldest members of the clan. He had avoided falling victim to political assassination by staying out of open politics and finding ways to stay aware of what was happening on the inside of the higher political families.

Zenjin remembered being raised by his mother. She had been one of the last hold outs. He was one of the last of the clan to learn from the minds of his den growing up. This gave him knowledge of history long lost to others. Normally he told the stories of family and lessons of history relating to heroism born from this knowledge when he was alone with the cubs in private. Today was a new day and he told his stories in the open to cubs and children who may have some grasp on the concept of den family. He liked to think that some of the changes that were happening now were in part because he taught what he knew to the clan when they were young, and it promoted free thinking outside the harsh framework of emotional suppression.

Serine stayed with Zenjin while the others of their den brought their belongings over to their den tent. She was too close to time to have cubs now, to be traveling back and forth, possibly even today. She sat and listened to the stories and helped guide the cubs from wandering off or getting overzealous and hurting each other. Serine was liking the idea of raising her own cubs, this would not be her first offspring, just the first she would get to know as hers. She remembered the ache she had giving up her previous litter, "a sacrifice for the good for the clan" was what she was told like they told everyone.

Peltrhak passed through the portal to meet with Yaun. "Meeting with me is a formality that we will keep," Yaun was saying, "for the good of our people. We will keep communications and trade open, but I am not going to tell you how to run your clan. I will give you advise when you ask and ask you for advice."

"You know at first I thought you were just trying to get rid of me. This journey has changed me, and I would say for the better. I see hope for our people, even though we have those who are slow to embrace change."

"Things are changing here too. I am going to guess that you got the expanded version of the code written by Lyamy?"

"Yes, Serine had copies made while we traveled, and I have required everyone read it and learn from her. Where is Lyamy anyway?"

Yaun looked out his window, "She gave herself as a sacrifice for the future of the clan. It was not what I wanted, but I cannot argue with the results. The clan here has never been more united and the ways of corruption that had us destroying ourselves have been falling away like old scales to make way for something new and better."

"She is dead?" Peltrhak almost looked alarmed for a moment, "It was her word that protected our belongings while we traveled."

"And her word was good." Yaun stated, "My word and honor were bound to the same and the people here respected her and her word for what she did to save our clan."

"You have honored her word and yours." Peltrhak looked back for a moment remembering how Lyamy had taken him down when he attacked

Yaun, "I still find myself pulled by our old ways, or perhaps I should say the ways we were taught."

"Let me take you on a tour, we have had lots of changes, there are markets in the streets, and it is safe to walk the streets."

"It seems this has been very healthy for the clan and both portions are changing in the same direction. I was thinking of calling our location west Lyamy in her honor."

Peltrhak followed Yaun out and was very impressed with the changes, starting with the statue in the courtyard.

*   *   *   *   *

Lyamy was awake when the golden tiger clan started waking in the morning. She had food stores in her hidden pocket. She had discovered that if she put food in the pocket back at Jenyin sanctuary, she could pull it out where she was with the golden tiger clan. She waited and observed. They all seemed to have their own stash of food, from what she could see without looking too hard, they all had their own containers, perhaps secret pockets, or bags that were enhanced with old magic.

Shenji came up to her, "Do you have food? I can scrounge enough from the others if you are lacking this morning."

"Thank you, I am well supplied and can offer up from my supply if other needs some." Lyamy offered.

"We are due for a hunt today, so some may be low. I will check and let you know." Shenji started around to the other members. When she came back two of the other clansmen were with her, "Rukyo and Nunji are low and could use what you can supplement for them. We will need our strength for the hunt."

Lyamy reached in and pulled out two leaf wrapped packages of cooked eliko(one of the native herd animals related to the elk) and two packages of fruit and vegetables. She dropped her invisibility cloak and held the packages out to the other two members of the clan. The packages were more than a meal for each, perhaps even a couple days food supply. "This should help."

"You are generous with your offer."

"ShadowDancer is generous with her follower."

"You will want to cloak again. We do everything cloaked, it is part of how we survive and avoid danger." Shenji whispered before heading off towards Wujin.

Wujin signaled that the hunt had begun. Lyamy sent a whisper to Wujin's ear, "There is a herd in a clearing to the northeast about twenty minutes out."

She could sense from Wujin's response that she had done something she was not supposed to but did not know what. He went in the direction she suggested anyway. The scent grew stronger as they approached. The clan closed in on the small herd, from what Lyamy could tell, Wujin was targeting a two-point buck on the fringe of the herd. She focused her attention on another buck in the herd, ready to draw. Wujin and Rukyo appeared as they leaped with daggers drawn to take down the buck.

Lyamy loosed two arrows, the second in the air before the first one hit. The second buck hit the ground almost as fast as the first. The rest of the clan dropped their cloak and appeared startling a bird from a nest in the grass. Lyamy loosed one more arrow and the bird fell next to the buck Wujin and Rukyo were dressing out. She slipped her bow back in place on her backpack and headed to the second buck and pulled her arrows. Then walked over to the bird and pulled her arrow form it also.

Others were already dressing out and cleaning the meat from the second buck and the bird, so she walked over where the bird had startled form the ground and picked up six eggs and brought them back to Shenji. She performed the ritual honoring both the creatures she killed, then cleaned her arrows and returned them to her quiver.

Wujin waved her to the side, "We will overlook your transgressions, since this is the first hunt you have been on with us."

"What did I do wrong? Did I miss something in my understanding of your ways?"

"Remember I said some things we have changed because of the need for our females to survive. There is also the matter of speaking once the hunt has started. I am not sure how you did that so I could hear you whisper from the back of the party to the front, but we do not talk once the signal is given to begin the hunt. It does seem that no one else heard the whisper so I am letting it go this time. Females are supposed to stay back and wait for the kill or kills from the hunt to keep them out of harm's way. I did not know that was a weapon before you used it. So, these are not so much clan ways as they are survival under current conditions, so we will have to council and decide."

"I did stay out of harm's way."

"You did, and I hope you can craft more of these weapons. I see how they can make the hunt more efficient. We will also ask you to teach at least a few of us how to use them. I am sure we will be tolerant of your mistakes, but we will have to go through the formalities." Wujin paused, "You have made fast friends with Shenji, ask her before you do anything, and she will tell you if it is acceptable under our current order of things."

Wujin went back to helping divide the meat. They were efficient, using almost every part of the any creature they killed. Lyamy requested the intestines and began dressing out the sinew to use for bow strings. She explained what she was doing, but also stated she was not experienced with crafting bows and weapons, so she was going to use her gift to pull finished bows form the trees she knew where used to craft them. When all was said and done, they had eight bows and twenty arrows for each bow, using the feathers from the bird she had taken down and others they could find. When they were out of feathers, she used feathered strips of wood for flights.

After taking the time to teach everyone how to use the bow, the eight who proved most skilled were given the bows to carry and responsibility. Lyamy took the time to cook and season her meat, explaining that it would last longer in storage that way. She also selected with care what leaves she used to wrap the meat. Some of the others tasted her meat and chose to follow her example, others chose to continue in their own methods.

The golden tiger clan had no shelters and did not sleep in the same place twice. They were ever on the move. Nunji was with cubs, she was scared and Lyamy could smell the fear. Lyamy asked Shenji if she could talk with Nunji about this the next time they stopped. Shenji insisted that she be there for the conversation. Back at the sanctuary, Lyamy placed the cub carrier she had used in her hidden pocket.

"Nunji," Lyamy started, "You have to bring your fear under control. Anything that comes close enough can smell the fear and will be drawn to hunt for you."

"Our clan needs cubs to survive, but having cubs is almost certain death. The cubs are born in blood which calls out to the savage beasts that hunt us. If that is not bad enough, cubs cannot yet hide themselves with magic and we do not have a way to cloak others around us. The cubs cannot move fast yet either, so having cubs is like giving easy food to predators."

"Anything we wear goes invisible with us, right?" Lyamy asked.

"Well, yes." Nunji answered, Lyamy noticed the distracting conversation lowered her fear and she could smell the difference.

Lyamy pulled out the cub carrier, "I will give this to you so you can carry your cubs, like your backpack and your weapons you will be wearing it, so it will vanish when you do along with your cubs. It will protect you and them." amazement and relief fill Nunji's eyes. "The clan will protect you while you give birth, and we will move immediately after. We should keep moving until then also."

"I am impressed." Shenji stated, "We never considered a carrying device."

"It was a gift from a gnome. We need to find water and wash the scent of fear out of your fur, Nunji. You do not have to be afraid any longer." Lyamy turned to Shenji, "Will Wujin take us to water? I know there is some risk staying by water since all the beasts go to water to drink."

"Let's go talk to him." Nunji was smiling as they walked away and put her invisibility back on.

"Wujin." Shenji called as they got close.

"Yes?" Wujin noticed Lyamy was in tow.

"We need to get to water where Nunji can wash the scent of fear from her fur and avoid being tracked. She is near time for her cubs, and Lyamy has talked her down from her fear."

"There is a stream not far to the east, we can head there, but we need to leave again as soon as we can."

"Lyamy has also told Nunji the clan will protect her while she gives birth."

"How can we give protection?" Wujin looked hard at Lyamy

"We can protect her if we use precautions, make sure the area is clear first, and we have the ability to defend against the lesser of the savage beasts." she saw that both of them still had doubt, "I told you I have a companion that is a horvalka. The code of all clans starts with 'do whatever it takes for the survival of the clan.' I can bring my companion to protect the clan while she is birthing her litter. And send it away when we are safe again. I am here for your good, so far you have not had a successful litter in a very long time." Lyamy didn't realize her eyes had lit up with the old magic.

Wujin hesitated and Shenji whispered in a hardened voice, "We need these cubs, if we cannot keep Nunji and the cubs alive, we will run out of hope for survival."

Wujin let his anger show, not wanting to be told how to run his clan, "Bring your companion and we will judge if it can help us defend during her time."

Her companion was not as far away as she had expected. The golden tiger clan went to the water. Nunji was bathing when Lyamy's horvalka was close enough for her to announce him. He waited downstream just out of site until she called him.

Lyamy dropped her invisibility, "Everyone, do not panic at what comes up from downstream. It is my companion, and he is here to protect our clan that Nunji can have her offspring in safety from any threat." the ground shook a little from the footsteps. Lyamy could sense the fear in the golden tiger clan, but they stood their ground with her in front. She held up her hand and took the finger of the beast. "Please everyone, come up one at a time and I will introduce you, so he knows who he is protecting."

Shenji still a little unnerved was the first to come forward. She built enough courage to touch the hand Lyamy was holding. "ShadowDancer did say you were her avatar." she went back to the others and encouraged them each to go up one at a time and make the introduction.

Wujin was no longer angry. He was more conceding to accepting that Lyamy was there to help them now, rather than joining for the protection of their clan. He even decided they could make camp here until Nunji had her cubs. The horvalka sat and played a little in the water. As long as he was there, nothing else would challenge their safety. Lyamy summoned food enough to keep her companion fed and happy for a week. It did not take too long for the members of the clan to start accepting their protection and start to relax.

This was the first reprieve that they had received in a long time, a chance to put their worries and fears aside and take time for personal pleasure. The entire clan was playing in the water, Lyamy stripped, stacking her gear and clothing in a nice pile and immersed herself in the golden tiger clan. The entire clan slept comfortably that night and it was shortly after sunrise when Nunji called for Shenji.

The cubs were born, nine of them. There were two male and seven female cubs. Shenji helped Nunji clean them all and the clan celebrated, welcoming the new members. As soon as the welcoming ceremony was complete, Lyamy could feel the cubs like she did the rest of the clan. Happiness prevailed throughout the clan, a new sense of hope for their future. Nunji tried the cub carrier and all the cubs fit. When she cast her cloak of invisibility the carrier and the cubs vanished with her bringing a wave of relief to the clan.

They spent seven days getting to know each other on a personal level outside of the survival mode. It was an experience none of them were familiar with, but they did not want to let it go either. Wujin and Shenji after a private discussion decided it was time for the clan to move on. They did not want everyone losing the edge that helped them survive. Once they were in motion again, Lyamy sent her companion back into the depths of the jungle.

Lyamy had noticed during their reprieve that the golden tiger clan did not have swords, their weapons were knives and daggers. As they traveled, she asked Shenji, "Is there a reason none of you use swords?" She placed her hand on the hilt of her sword to be sure she was clear in what she was asking.

"We pounce by nature and daggers and knives work better for that, but I think the real reason is we can no longer make our own weapons being on the move all the time and any swords we had have been long lost." Shenji shrugged, "Constantly moving we do not have the luxury of a forge or metal to make weapons."

"Do you enhance your weapons with the magic of the wielder?"

"What do you mean?" Shenji asked.

"The ritual to make a weapon an extension of the owner." she put her hand on Shenji's shoulder as they walked, "Let me show you." When Shenji lowered her mental barriers, Lyamy pushed the details of the ritual and the effects to her mind.

"No, this must have been lost to us over time. When we stop, can you show this to the entire clan, or help me take everyone through the ritual for one of their weapons?"

"I will be glad to, it will make a great difference in how effective the weapons will be."

The pride suddenly stopped moving and went on alert. They were all invisible, but there was a scent on the wind of another leophardeg. Lyamy could feel the creature was close and moving in their direction. As she heightened her senses, she perceived it was following the scent of the cubs, she could be mad at herself for not noticing the scent later. She sent out a mind message to Shenji and Wujin that it was following the cub scent and moved herself into a position closer to Nunji and the cubs.

'*Can you give me permission to defend Nunji and the cubs?*' Her thoughts whispered in Wujin's mind, '*right now I am her best defense.*'

'*You have permission.*' she could sense that he only gave her permission because he could not think of any other option.

The creature came into sight. It was for the most part a large cat walking on hind legs and about four times her size. There was animal cunning in the creature's eyes, Lyamy used old magic to conceal her scent and tracks. The creature sniffed the air swaying back and forth slowly finding the path to the intended prey. Lyamy followed the pattern of the over-sized cat's movement and appeared eyes glowing just as it turned in her direction. It fought for control as she dominated the will of the creature. "Nunji." She whispered, not lowering her focus, "Come here."

Nunji came up next to Lyamy, "Yes?"

"Draw the blood, a drop on each claw and perform the companion ritual now!"

Nunji obeyed, "With your blood, I claim a piece of your spirit to bond you as my companion." The bond was made, and the creature would serve and protect Nunji and her cubs.

"She is yours now. You can call upon her to protect you and command her just as you would one of the smaller companions of the clan." Lyamy turned to Shenji, "I need to teach you all now, how to cover your scent. I tracked you by scent when we first met, and this creature tracked the scent of the cubs. Just because they cannot see you, does not mean they cannot kill you by accident following your scent."

"I remember one other who tried to subdue a leophardeg," Shenji stated, "What happened was enough for me to never make an attempt."

Wujin made his way back from the lead while Nunji was performing the ritual. "Is there any chance she will break the bond?" he asked pointing at the creature.

"Old magic is almost always permanent." Lyamy stated, "Nunji, introduce her to the rest of the clan as your family and tell her to help protect them too. This will prevent her from attacking anyone who get separated from the group, she will recognize them as friends. Only you can do this, she is your companion."

As everyone gathered, Nunji did the introductions to her new companion and guardian. When all were gathered Lyamy became visible. She demonstrated the ritual and explained the actions, thoughts and words used to apply the magic hiding both scent and trail. Then she pushed the instructions through the web of bonding the joined them all. When everyone had performed the casting, she sniffed the air. It was clear, the scent of the cubs was gone also.

"We are good." she said and vanished with the rest. They continued their movement through the jungle, Nunji's new companion stayed about ten feet to her right and traveled with the group.

*   *   *   *   *

"It is like they have divided me up and each one is specializing on different areas of my knowledge." Lyamy said to Freyie, "I mean they are all overlapping and getting general knowledge. It would have been so much easier if we were raised this way."

"I do not have as much in my head as you, although I have noticed that the children do each have their own areas of interest. Shahani has taken a keen interest in learning weaving from the gnomes that joined us from the north. The have found ways to make a wide variety of different cloth materials from the fibers of the multiple frond leaf bushes that grow everywhere."

"They are so much more advanced than we were at their ages, even adjusting to the time distortion of their development, and mostly because this is how we were meant to be raised."

"You know Lyamy, we have time today and you did promise Jenyin we would visit his clan one of these days."

"I did promise, and I will honor that promise." Lyamy slipped into garments so she could go out in public, "We have picked the caves out for the clan, but we cannot have an entrance opened until we can talk openly to Jenyin. I hope ShadowDancer has talked to him." She straightened the chair she had been sitting in, "Children, we are going to go visiting."

She heard them dropping what they were doing in the other room and they came running up and formed a line in the order they came out. "We are ready, mommy Lyamy and mommy Freyie." Drustle said being the first one in line.

"I'll follow." Freyie said, she put her hand on Nelk's head. Nelk was never in any particular rush, but when he had to move, he was much faster than his siblings. Often times he would prefer to sit and examine things that had no interest to the others, like a bug crawling across the floor or a bird fluttering around across the sand foraging.

Lyamy led the way out in the hall and to the next entrance, knocking on the door when she got there. Karis answered the door, she was laughing, "Chelic said you enjoyed dinner, so I am going to invite you to stay for dinner now. Come in, make yourselves at home."

Daret stepped out, "Jenyin will be out in a minute, he is taking care of community needs." she snickered

Marrianne stepped out just a few moments behind her adjusting her sword belt, "Hi, Lyamy, good seeing you. I was just discussing a few things with Jenyin. See you at tomorrow's meeting, if not sooner."

Lyamy sensed a touch of embarrassment, "It is always good to see you Marrianne. We can talk about that merchant security issue you mentioned earlier at the meeting." she figured trivial conversation might relieve the embarrassment. Not that long ago embarrassment would have been a tool to use and exploit to gain advantage. Now, Marrianne was a friend, and they were not competing in a cutthroat life.

Marrianne smiled appreciative of the distraction, "Alright, I have places to go and things to do." See you all again soon, this time her smile was more one of relaxed satisfaction as she slipped out closing the door behind her.

"How long?" Lyamy asked more curious than anything else.

Daret answered, "Oh, she comes by once every week or two, sometimes more often if she is frustrated. We take care of her. It is mostly because she is not ready to commit to anyone. She is getting more comfortable though, she has actually stopped by a couple times just to visit."

Jenyin came out, "Lyamy, you came to visit." she stood up into his hug, "and Freyie," she also accepted his embrace, "and children." The all ran up as he knelt to a big group hug. When he stood back up he turned back to Lyamy, "ShadowDancer said you would want to know she stopped by and paid me a visit."

"Good then I can talk to you again." Lyamy laughed.

"She said you will be bringing the golden tiger clan to stay but need special provisions." he sat across from the visiting den, "Something about needing a certain degree of privacy and their own entrance."

"They have been living wild for generations. There are twenty-eight adults and only seven females. They just had their first successful offspring where the cubs and mother did not get eaten by one of the savage beasts of the jungle in years."

"How do you know what is happening with them now?"

"Because I am with them right now, just as much as I am here with you." She saw he did not understand what she was saying, "I am in two places at the same time." She got up and touched his shoulder using the bond she had with him as her teacher, she gave him the memory of her splitting apart, one pulling guard duty and the other heading north to find the golden tiger clan. She did not give him enough to know how to do the split just enough to see it happen.

"Oh." he stared at her for several minutes. He started to speak and then paused, "Alright, I am going to have to think on that one, something else I did not teach you." he paused again, "Anyway, that does explain how you know what they are doing."

"I have been through their rights of acceptance." She showed him her scars, "This one I got from the ancient Darvel, this one from ShadowDancer, and this," she put her had on her cheek, "is from Wujin, Leader of the golden tiger clan."

"Ah, I see, and the other questions, teaching them survival skills." Jenyin raised an eyebrow as if passing a secret message.

"She is a good student," Chelic just threw it out there, "fighting for survival has not allowed her to fill her mind with any social corruption that would pull her focus off what she needs to learn."

"The golden tiger clan is different than we are when it comes to the old magic. As a clan they actually use everything they know to survive. They were all raised by their dens, so they assimilated knowledge from the members of the den. Actually, the entire clan is joined like a den, so they may have been able to learn from the entire clan the way it is natural for any cub or child to learn from their den. They have all learned at least some of the old magic."

"But the rules of a master and student," Jenyin started, but Lyamy interrupted

"Were developed within the white leopard clan, just like sending our children to the clan nursery to be raised. There is still one master and they will pick their student, but it is not clandestine, no secrets within the clan. I cannot totally hide any knowledge I have from my children. Every member of the golden tiger clan has a bond with every other member. It is for their protection. Each of them knows the location and movements of the others."

"If we had done that." Jenyin started, "We separated our children from our dens, and we separated the members of the clan from each other. It is almost like someone was trying to divide us and destroy us from the inside."

Freyie leaned forwards, "But, doesn't this mean that the members of the clan had to be convinced to go along? I cannot imagine giving up the bond I have with the children now that I know how good it can be."

"It was something they were used to." Daret suggested, "We are used to having a door on our den. If there was a general consensus that giving up doors was needed for the good of the clan, we would not know what we were losing until it was gone. We may not even know what we lost until we at some later point got them back."

"I don't see that not having a door would be a problem?" Karis was not following the argument, "So our door is gone no big deal."

"It is a big deal, but you are proving my point," Daret continued, "See it would not take much to have a general consensus. If you did not have a door, you could not have anything in this room of value for anyone to see that passed by. Where we are now, you would always have to where clothing like you were in public, you could not lounge like we are right now. Anyone walking by could hear anything you said, so you would have to watch more carefully your words."

"And we would not really know what we were missing until we got our privacy back." Freyie finished the circle.

"We were at war." Lyamy put out for consideration.

"Yes," Jenyin was thinking it through, "which means anyone captured knew all the clan secrets as long as there was that universal bond, but what about separating the children?"

"The emotional bond is a weakness that can be exploited by an enemy." Daret quoted, "We were taught that in the nursery growing up. A mother who raised her own children would die to try and save them. We were living a wartime society long after the war was gone. It was never intended to last forever."

Lyamy sighed, "And even that was corrupted to what we became. Without an enemy on the outside of the clan we made our own enemies on the inside."

"We picked out the caves." Freyie was ready to change the subject for now.

"Yes," Lyamy was ready too, "We needed to be able to discuss it in the open before we could make arrangements to add a private entrance in and out of the cave system."

"That should not be a problem, but that is one more concern if we should get attacked." Jenyin pointed out, "Although that would also be one more escape route if we were being overwhelmed by an enemy."

They discuss the impact and implications of the golden tiger clan joining. Conversation straggled to other matters of public concern within the sanctuary. Eventually discussion turned to a more friendly and personal nature, discussing like and dislikes and idle conversation of trivial things.

Chelic prepared food and they all sat around eating, watching the children distracted and playing. She had sliced small strips of meat, dipped them in egg and rolled them in seasoned flower from the seeds of the same plant the gnomes used for their weaving fiber. She cooked the strips to a golden brown in boiling oil, serving it with sliced tubers cooked in the same manner. Lyamy could not stop telling her how good they were. It was after the youngster's bedtime when they finally went back home to their own den.

They were just slipping off to sleep when ShadowDancer appeared capturing Lyamy in the moment. "You are my avatar; I need to take you to the western settlement. Serine and Peltrhak need your help."

*   *   *   *   *

Enough buildings were erected to give the entire clan shelter while they continued working on others and expanding out building the den homes. Peltrhak was in the central office. It was not fully finished, but sufficient to run the village business. A knock came from the door and Zenjin stepped in with Serine and one of his other den mates Shaariy. "Come in Zenjin. I have the plans for the school right here." He laid them out on his makeshift desk. "Does Tsulin know you are here?"

"This was a scheduled meeting." Zenjin nodded. "I am still surprised that you trusted the second strongest den here to handle security. The previous ways of the clan are not completely let go by everyone."

"I trust him; we have gained an understanding and a respect for one another. Not unlike Jenyin, he does not want the position I have. It does not have enough freedom." Peltrhak smiled.

"I see you have made the modifications I asked for." Zenjin stated, "It is important that we build a library of knowledge, any history or knowledge that members of the clan can share to help the rest."

Serine stepped up, "The school is important, but we have a pressing problem."

Peltrhak looked at Serine, "What problem is so pressing that it needs to interrupt schedule discussion and cannot wait for an appointment of its own?"

"I cannot tell you how I have this knowledge, but there is plotting against you." Serine looked around and made sure no one was close enough to hear, "There were tent ropes cut almost threw on your den tents. They were replaced when they were discovered. There were planks pried loose on this building where they would compromise your safety. They have been refastened."

"How come I was not informed by Tsulin?"

"This button was found in the grass near the damaged tent ropes, and this knife dropped in a bush behind this building." she set the button and the knife on the desk.

Peltrhak examined the button, it bore the symbol of Tsulin's den, as did the handle of the knife, "You think Tsulin is behind this?"

"He has everything to gain, if you are removed." Zenjin pointed out.

Serine did not look as sure, "I sense there is still a lot of deception in our clan. There are several who do not like the changes and think we are becoming weak."

"They have been given open opportunity to speak their minds." Peltrhak protested.

"They spoke out against the dragon men and were put to silence. They are not used to an environment where they can express themselves without consequences."

"Then I need to start balancing power. Zenjin, I am going to appoint you to lead the investigative agency, at least until you can find someone else, I can trust to do the job."

Serine went on alert, the old magic in her tingling a warning. She suddenly started looking around examining everything around them. Facing away from Peltrhak her eyes lit with fire and she started casting. She pushed the gas back out of the room, but not before Shaariy fell asleep and collapsed to the floor. Six members of the clan burst in, wrapped in cloth so they could not be identified. Two had swords drawn and blazing. The others pulled theirs as they saw everyone was not asleep.

"Kill them anyway; we just cannot be as neat about it. I thought you had this place full of gas?"

"They should have been asleep like everyone else in the village." They lifted weapons and headed towards the Peltrhak, Zenjin and Serine. Serine screamed in her mind for ShadowDancer and Lyamy.

Peltrhak pulled Zenjin and Serine behind him. Serine called to her wolf, and then pushed the image of a pack of wolves into the eyes of one of the assailants in the lead. Fear filled his eyes and his companions had to avoid the random swinging of his sword as he fought off attackers that were not there. Peltrhak parried the blade of the other lead attacker, his own blade also burning with flames.

Lyamy appeared in the room to the side of the combat. She quickly assessed the fight and six daggers hit their marks. The attackers dropped their swords and the door slammed shut behind them blocking them in. Serine, grab some chairs, Zenjin you have cord to bind them, tie them to the chairs."

The attackers looked at Lyamy with terror in their eyes, "You are dead." the leader of the group stated.

"Then unless you want to anger the dead, you better all sit down in separate chairs." she grabbed him and threw him in a chair with one hand.

Zenjin tied each securely, "Is that really you Lyamy?"

"I am the avatar of ShadowDancer, you may be the only one in the village who knows what that means." She looked at the six would be assassins, "Before we unmask them, go get Tsulin." Zenjin left quickly. Lyamy knelt down and checked Shaariy, "She is just asleep."

"Thank you for coming." Serine said as Lyamy stood back up.

"You look like the move has done a lot of good for you." She turned to Peltrhak, "You are unhurt?"

"Yes. How did you know you did not have to disarm me also?"

"Well first you were only using defensive moves, and second if you had killed one of them they really did deserve it." She glared at the six watching her every move, "They still might die one or all of them if that is what it takes to carve this corrupted way of thinking out of the clan."

A few moments later, a groggy Tsulin came in with Zenjin. He looked at Lyamy like he was seeing a ghost. "What is going on?"

"It seems," Lyamy began, "like you missed a plot against Peltrhak. The village has been put to sleep with the exception of these six and they seemed to be set on the assassination of your leader." Tsulin braced himself on the corner of the desk, "Well, who are they?"

"We left the unmasking for you."

Tsulin walked over to the first and pulled the wraps from his head, it was the junior leader from the third den. "Kren? You wish to go back to the clan killing each other for power? That has been voted as a crime by the majority of the village to make sure there was agreement."

He stepped up to the next and unwrapped the disguise. There was a stunned look on his face, "Loetin, you dishonor our den. Do you wish your blood claimed for the crime you would have committed or for the dishonor you bring on us?"

When he unwrapped the third, the girl's eyes pleaded with him, "Really, Errinin, you too, have you no respect for your own den or your clan? You two are of my clan and I am charged with protecting Peltrhak and you seek to shame me, the clan and our den by plotting against me."

The other three; Chelt, Kylee, and Antak were all of the third clan. Tsulin stepped back from the group that was tied down. "Why?"

"The clan is not following the rules we have had for years." Loetin protested, "We are becoming weak, and you would run the clan with a much firmer hand."

"Kren, Why?" Tsulin asked again.

"The rules of order and the way we were is how we survived as a clan. This softening up makes the clan weak, look how easily we almost succeeded and everyone but these three were asleep, they could have been just as easily dead."

"Do you think for a minute the head of your den will approve of what you did?" Tsulin asked.

"When he is clan leader he will approve." Kylee stated defiantly.

Lyamy could see their thoughts through their facades, "Koetin and Errinin you were played as fools. It was the plan all along to kill Peltrhak and blame the Tsulin den. Then the third den could step up and save the day leaving you in dishonor. You were going to leave all Tsulin den marked weapons, making it appear the crimes were committed by the den with no evidence of any other help. Tsulin would be dishonored for failing his job. Your entire den would be dishonored for committing the crime and if you stepped up and implicated the third den in any way you would have only added disgrace to dishonor."

It registered on the faces of Loetin and Errinin that they had been played as fools, "We are sorry." Errinin stated.

"Unfortunately, you are only sorry you were played and used, not that you made an attempt on your leader's life." Tsulin breathed heavy.

"Kren and cohorts, you too disgrace your den leader Doulon. I know he has other responsibilities that would keep him from accepting the role as leader even if it were to have gone that far. All your little performance could have caused at best would be to weaken the clan and make fools of your dens. You conspired on arrogance and foolishness and did not bother to take the time to think about what you were doing. How can anyone in this clan trust any of you again?"

Peltrhak spoke up, "You have made a very bad move. The village is not set up to provide for the proper punishment if we let you live. We should execute you all and save the burden it would place on the clan having to deal with you. Do any of you have a suggestion as to what we should do as punishment for your crimes?"

Kylee was the only one that still had defiance in her eyes, "What crime, we followed the code according to how we were raised. There is a punishment written for getting caught, if you cannot provide for that you are proving the weakness we were acting against."

Lyamy laughed at Kylee, "The means are here without even leaving this room of providing the punishment you are talking about, but you are being foolish to think that is the only crime you have committed and that there is only one punishment option for anything. Even more foolish, you think you will find glory in dieing for an already lost cause."

Kylee glared at Lyamy, "You died, and you live on in glory and all you did was destroy what we had. You have no place here, you are of the eastern clan, and you are not even part of our clan."

"You are still of the eastern clan." Lyamy stated, "They still have cages to hang you in the streets and let you receive your just punishment for the crime you committed, which was a crime long before the corrupted interpretation of the code you were raised with. Do you really want to be left in a cage until dead? Where is your glory in being spit on and shamed until dead?" She touched Kylee on the temple and gave her memories of a long history of punishments given for attempted assassinations in the clan before and during the corruption of the code. "The clan grew in number and strength before the code got corrupted and has almost diminished to non-existence by comparison following the corruption you embrace so dearly."

"We should get Doulon, perhaps he can talk sense into his own." Peltrhak stated, "Perhaps chaining them and making them serve doing the lowest labor for the clan or requiring them to each individually be attached to and serve an elder of the clan."

"I'll get Doulon." Zenjin slipped out again.

"Most of the clan wants to go back to what they know. It is these new ways that are corrupt to them." Kylee still protested.

"These are not new ways, Kylee." Lyamy felt some sympathy for Kylee, "These are the ways of the clan before the clan wars. We no longer have other clans we are warring with, and the continued practice of wartime ideas has turned the clan against itself, not having an enemy to stand against. Enemy was never intended to mean another clan member."

"I wish you could stay with us Lyamy." Peltrhak almost pleaded, "We have so much to learn about who we are and who we should be."

"I cannot. I serve ShadowDancer as her avatar. I am bound to that commitment." Lyamy turned to Peltrhak, "There is a clan that will join you, the lion mane clan. They will be able to teach the history of the wars. Take them in and make them a part of this clan."

"If you say it should be done, then we will do it."

"Perhaps making these youngsters help them will teach them more then we can here."

Doulon came in not hiding his anger, Zenjin had obviously explained what was happening. "You dare to defy me, our den, the safety of our new settlement, and the clan and use the pretense of doing it for anything other than yourselves? Banishment in these lands would be too kind for what you have done." He clawed the mark of shame on the cheek of each of his clan that were tied down using his claw.

Serine placed her hand on her own cheek without thinking.

Peltrhak set a box on his desk. Doulon opened the box and used the white powder on the open wounds to make them permanent scars and stop the bleeding. Tsulin pulled the tool out and did the same to his clan members with the blade instead of his claw.

Doulon addressed his clan members. "You will live in the streets only and have no shelter for at least three months. You will only eat whatever scraps you can find in the streets. You will not carry any items or wear any clothing. After three months we will see if you have learned any understanding of the need to keep members of the clan alive and not kill them. If you have learned, then you will submit yourselves to whatever additional punishment the clan sees fit. This is just your den punishment."

Tsulin addressed Loetin and Errinin, "This seems a fitting den punishment for you two also. I will add one more thing. During this time, you are not allowed to speak with each other either."

Doulon added, "That applies to all of you also." and the two den leaders stripped their members of all belongings, Doulon returning to Tsulin all the items bearing his den mark.

"We will wait until the rest of the clan is awake and we can announce this before we release them to the streets." Peltrhak concluded the matter, "The clan reserves judgment until they have served their den punishments."

"I will call to the lion mane clan." Lyamy stepped outside into the star and moon light, lifter her head and gave a series of roaring yowls into the air. An answer came from not far away.

A female Shadowkyn appeared twenty feet away walking towards Lyamy. She had a light brown hint to her color, but with the same evasive translucence common to all Shadowkyn. Around her neck there was long fur that blended back into the hair that ran down from the top of the head to the tail. "Greetings Lyamy."

"Greetings Kyamy of the lion mane clan. Welcome to the white leopard clan. Let peace join our people for common good." Lyamy gestured to Peltrhak, "This is Peltrhak, leader of the clan here in their western settlement. Peltrhak, this is Kyamy leader of the lion mane clan. Their numbers are dwindled because they have not had any male children in a very long time. The last male died of old age about twenty years ago. They have always been a nomad tribe, traveling and living off the land, but not without resources and means. As you already know this land is generous."

"I am honored to know you Kyamy." Peltrhak acknowledge her position in her clan with a slight nod of the head.

"It is indeed an honor for me also. We have been told in part about your clan and would petition to join you and become one clan. We can offer knowledge and experience in these lands and ourselves to add to the strength of your clan and dens."

"I have done what I was sent for." Lyamy bowed slightly to both, "I must let ShadowDancer take me away."

"Wait," Peltrhak turned to stop her, but she was already fading away.

"She is a guardian sent by ShadowDancer in our times of need. We will give her and her Ancient honor and respect." Kyamy stated

Peltrhak looked at Kyamy, he knew there was supposed to be some ritual of acceptance for bringing someone into the clan. It was something he had heard of long ago as a child that was done when children were born to the clan a long time ago, "We lack in some knowledge and history and I am not knowledgeable concerning how to bring others into the clan, but we will accept you as part of our clan. I have been told you can teach us much of our own history and that may help even with some recent division in understanding among some of the clan."

"Thank you." Kyamy bowed in submission to Peltrhak's authority and on hundred thirteen other members of the lion mane clan appeared, bowing in submission to Peltrhak. "We are yours; direct us in how we may serve our new clan. This is Lattia, she is my second and master of the old magic. Perhaps she can work with your second to help give the clan strength and understanding."

Serine stepped forward to Lattia, "Our clan has kept the old magic hidden even from our leaders. I believe it is time for that to change back to the old ways again. I am Serine, second of the western settlement of the white leopard clan."

Peltrhak raised his eyebrows. This was who Lyamy had chosen to carry the old magic for him and the western settlement. "It looks like we have a good start; Tsulin, Zenjin, Doulon and Serine shall give you a tour of what we are doing and introduce you around. You can probably best determine where your skill will benefit the whole of the clan."

Peltrhak returned to the office and sat behind his desk. He looked over his would-be assassins. "You should really think about this. Did you see that the Avatar of Lyamy had the branding of acceptance on her shoulders of the ancients Darvel and ShadowDancer?" he paused, not expecting them to answer. "She sacrificed herself and her own gain for the good of the clan and her people. She did it so we would stop killing each other and she did so by our own code and the will of the Ancients. She has been exalted in life and death to glory she was not seeking for herself. Now, regardless of what you think, or I think the clan should be doing, even if our laws did say to do things or to act this way or that, when the Ancients that created us say stop doing this or start doing this we are obliged to obey. Do you understand, if you had succeeded in killing me, Serine and Kenjin you would had removed the promise of protection that was given to us. There would be nothing then stopping the dragon men or the savage beasts from coming and wiping out our entire settlement. The biggest thing Lyamy tried to teach us was to think, if I do this what does it mean to the entire clan, what will the chain reaction of events result in and will it be good for the whole of the clan. You acted out of anger, envy, and selfish power lust. I know these things, because I was raised, trained and lived that way. I resisted these changes also and took actions that I have since learned were wrong."

"The Ancients left us without guidance for generations." Kylee answered, "We were taught to hold on to the code as it was taught to us and it would assure the survival of the clan, now you tell us cutting the weakness out of the clan does not make the clan stronger. It is like a rope, if a portion is weak, you cut it out and rebind the remaining rope back together stronger then it was."

"The clan is not like a rope; it is more like your body. Your body has weak parts, but do you cut them all off? If you remove your weakest finger because it is weak, then you cannot control your sword as well in battle. If you cut off your weakest toe, because it is weaker than the rest, you will stumble and fall, taking away from the strength of your body. In training, why do you think we make a fighting dummy out of bundles of weak straw instead of a solid stick? The stick would break, but the weakness of the straw becomes the strength of the dummy, bending and absorbing your blows, pushing back and giving you a real feel of combat. You are acting like the single stick standing strong on its own, but one hard hit and it is broken and gone. We need to stand as the bundle of straw a full clan made up of its weaker parts giving us the flexibility and strength we need to survive. Do you understand I am a hardened warrior, and I could have killed all six of you with no difficulty? You were all fighting as individuals, not even depending on each other for strength, I chose not to kill you."

Kylee went silent, thinking about all Peltrhak's words. She did not want to believe him she wanted to find fault so she could hold onto what she believed and had committed herself to. She did not want to be wrong, but the more she thought, the harder it was to not change the way she was thinking.

*   *   *   *   *

They had circled around back to the stone and earth pillar and spiraled their way back to the top. The two weeks had passed since her initiation and acceptance as a shadow. The decision was already made and none of the golden tiger clan dissented, she was voted in. Shenji held a ritual bowl, she pricked her finger with her own claw and put one drop of blood in the bowl, Jenyin did the same, followed by each member of the clan in turn. Last Lyamy shed one drop in the bowl and Shenji stirred with a flat stick. She lifted the stick and touched her tongue, "By the blood we are bound as one." Her eyes lit with the fires of old magic. She passed the bowl to Lyamy, then Wujin and around the circle until every clan member had tasted.

Every eye glowed, "By the blood we are one."

Lyamy felt what the old magic was doing. Each individual shared a tiny thread of themselves, they merged into one, then threaded back out to the rest of the clan. When the bond was complete, it was stronger than what was there when she was just a shadow. "We are one." she whispered.

"You can now take me as your student, my old master has long since parted." Shenji stated. She squeezed another drop of blood from her finger and held it out to Lyamy.

Lyamy took the drop and placed it on her tongue, "By your blood I bind you as my student, that I may share with you all the ways of the old magic." Lyamy reached in her hidden pocket and pulled out another copy of the book of old magic she had crafted. She had added the pages in her own writing teaching how to use the old magic to do what ShadowDancer had already taught her when Darvel approved taking Shenji as a student. "This contains everything, that you might learn still should we become unable to continue training. You are not an initiate to the old magic so you should already be able to read and study the book." The thread of master student between them felt stronger than that she had with her other students.

"By the blood I accept you as my master." The old magic in Lyamy's mind opened to Shenji as a library, much like the way her mind was open to the children of her den. Lyamy also found that Shenji's mind was also open to her in much the same fashion. They could feel what the other was looking at and they could block things they did not want to share. Lyamy chose not to look outside of what Shenji knew about the old magic. There were gaps in knowledge, but what she knew was accurate even if some of the superficial words or ritual were different.

"You are good with what you know, there is nothing to correct, and you now have full access to everything I know about the old magic."

"You know more than the old magic." Shenji smiled.

"True," Lyamy shook her head slightly, "but you need time to consider before you ask to become a student avatar. You sacrifice yourself for your clan now, as an avatar you have to be willing to sacrifice all for your Ancient. While you can serve more than one Ancient, you can only be an avatar for one."

"So, I will have to wait until I can be clear on choosing ShadowDancer or Darvel for that." Shenji looked at Lyamy's shoulders, "but you are marked by both?"

"I serve both, but I am avatar to ShadowDancer."

Shenji turned to the clan around them. "Lyamy has honored us in all ways as the golden tiger clan. It is time for us to hear the reason she came to us."

Lyamy stood and turned passing her eyes over every member of the clan. "It is true, I did not come here to join your clan. I did join you to better serve you. I am a part of a bigger clan and I came to offer you shelter and opportunity when you are ready to consider joining us. We will give you shelter that is yours even if you chose not to join us, you will have our protection and your freedom. You will have a place to go and raise your children without fear of losing them to the savage land."

"How can we know what we are considering?" Shenji asked.

"I can take you there, you can enter through your private entrance. You can take your time and observe. You have no obligation. We will let you mix in and out as you choose. In the end the choice is yours."

"I would say we should follow you to this place." Wujin stated, "clan vote, those in favor?"

Everyone responded through the bond of the clan in agreement to follow and see what they were considering. "We will begin our journey in the morning. Shenji, is it alright to rest here in the hands of the Ancients for the night?"

"We have never slept here before, but I do not know any reason we cannot." Shenji, had never considered that option before.

Lyamy showed Shenji the ability to get enough sleep in a blink through their mind link. It was old magic, so she knew it was safe to share and she had written it in the book. "Shenji and I will pull watch tonight so everyone else can sleep without worry about taking watch."

"Yes, Lyamy and I will keep watch." she confirmed her agreement with everyone. While the others turned to matters of eating and rest, Lyamy and Shenji started lessons, they would take watch when the others went to sleep. That night, ShadowDancer would fill the clan with dreams of hope.

*   *   *   *   *

Freldin and Chineene were visiting with Lyamy and Freyie when Jenyin and his den stopped by for a visit also. "We should go." Freldin started saying, "so you can visit freely."

"Stay," Lyamy stopped them, "there is no reason we cannot all visit at the same time."

Marrianne actually came in with Jenyin's clan. "If they can put up with me, I am sure you are welcome."

"Well, it is nice to spend time with everyone and not have it a meeting." Chineene laughed.

"Welcome and everyone please come in, get comfortable and relax." Lyamy waved them all to sit down. "Jenyin, I hate to start out with something of a matter of clan, er community business, but I am going to anyway, before I forget."

"It must be important, or you would not have such a sense of urgency." Jenyin responded.

"The other clans I have spent time with, practice something the white leopard clan stopped a long time ago. They have a clan bond. It is a light bond, but it allows them to function as one when they need to. This is a perfect group to attempt what I want to try. We can try the not permanent bond, the shadow bond. I know it will work between Shadowkyn, but I am not sure if it will work with others. With the shadow bond we can try it and remove it if it is not wanted."

"You can try if they are willing to try." Jenyin shrugged.

Freldin looked curious, "I do not know what you are talking about, but it will help, and it can be undone, I am willing to see what it is."

"I am too," Chineene agreed.

"What does this bond, do or mean?" Marrianne asked.

"We will be able to sense one another and do some communicating." Lyamy explained

"You are sure you can undo it if we don't like it?" Marrianne was uncertain.

"I am."

"Then I will participate."

Lyamy took a bowl and dropped a droplet of her blood in the bowl and passed it around, "Everyone needs to put one drop in the bowl." The bowl was passed around the circle until it got back to Lyamy. She stirred it with the tip of her dagger, then touched the blood to her tongue, "With this blood we are joined in a shadow bond as one." she passed the bowl and felt the thread from each person added as they tasted the blood. She was not completely surprised when the eyes of the elves and the human were lit by the old magic. When bowl and her dagger were returned to her, she set them down. "by the blood we are shadowed as one."

The bond was there, Lyamy could feel it with everyone. She knew Freyie and Jenyin's den would feel it. "Freldin, Chineene, Marrianne, can you feel the bond and sense where each of us is in the room?"

"I can see the magic." Freldin answered, "It is not one I have known before. Yes, I can feel everyone in the room, where they are and how they are feeling."

Chineene added, "It feels like I could use this magic now that I know it is here."

"This is insane." Marrianne expressed her surprise, "I could never pick your pockets as long as this was turned on."

'We can speak with thoughts. You have to push the thought through the web that joins us.' Lyamy pushed the thought through the web that joined them. "You can push it to one person if you want also."

'Hello.' Marrianne tested pushing her thought, "Can we share images this way too?"

"More than that," Lyamy laughed, "You can share memories." She pushed out the memory of when she first saw the ocean. She could see they all received the memory. "You receive the memory, but like a dream you can keep it separate from your own."

"But everyone cannot just look through my mind, now can they?" Marrianne had concern edging her voice.

"Not because of this bond." Lyamy started, "It will not stop anyone with the ability to probe others minds from doing so, but they will not be doing it through the bond, they will have to use their own ability."

"There is some comfort in that." Marrianne conceded.

Freldin rubbed his chin, "With this or the permanent bond, if someone leaves the community does the bond go with them?"

"Yes, you can follow where they are no matter where they go. This, the shadow bond can be removed, the full bond cannot."

"For our community, we would have to limit this to the shadow bond then." Chineene was sure of herself, "People will come and go at all levels, leaving for other lands. This would be an imposition on their privacy. All races have things they do in private and would choose not to be traceable for everything they do."

"I don't think that even Shadowkyn that have been free from it would want this open bond with their entire community. We have over four hundred living here now and I have met some that I do not want to know anything else about. I am not even sure as the Shadowkyn population expands that I would want this bond to reach far beyond selected groups I wanted to share with." Karis questioned the virtue.

Marrianne added, "I would not mind this with a small group of friends. This with you guys is alright, but I have to agree I do not want this kind of bond with the whole community. I also prefer that it stays removable."

"We can keep this for a few days anyway and decide if we like it?" Chineene asked.

"What about Desdin and Grimble, should we ask them if they want to join us in this. They have been with us from the beginning?" Marrianne asked.

"I can add them easy enough." Lyamy answered as long as they respond to the primordial magic as well as the rest of you."

"I will ask them, and they will come to you when they are ready." Freldin offered

"I can see you in both places now." Chelic laughed.

"How are you doing that?" Chineene asked

"Some things I have to keep secret." Lyamy answered. "They, we will be here soon. At first observing activity on the outside, then coming in through the entrance Desdin and Grimble built and observing before they are ready to be introduced."

"You have opened us up to your magic source," Freldin broached the subject, "now I feel like I should have seen it there all the time. I am thinking we might actually be able to use this magic now that we have touched it. You know those symbols and location-based storage areas you tried to introduce us to that we could not see, can we try that again?"

"I don't see why not." Jenyin stood up and traced a symbol in the air and put one of Lyamy's shell crafted decorations into the pocket.

"I can see the symbol now." Marrianne stated, stepping up, placing her hand on the symbol and pulling out the room ornament.

"Is the manipulation similar to arcane?" Freldin asked.

"There are similarities but be careful sometimes the primordial source runs a little hotter and more random."

Freldin vanished and then reappeared, "It seems you have granted us access to the power Magus Kremlern would pay a fortune to know. We should probably not offer this to everyone in the community unless we can find an arcane way of performing the bond."

They all agreed, "We will still bring Desdin and Grimble in though." Lyamy wanted to be clear on their intent. "We can talk to them at our dinner meeting tonight, as long as we do not have anyone else showing up." Lyamy looked over at the corner where the children were quietly playing. She saw Mellina sitting on a cushion with her legs tucked under her, watching the children play.

"That will work." Jenyin stated.

Lyamy stood up and walked over to the children and bent over as if talking to them. "Hello Melina."

"Oh, I am sorry. You were busy and I was going to go deliver the message to the other you, but your children are so sweet, and I got distracted. ShadowDancer says you are doing well, and she will come by and visit soon."

"That is all?"

"She said you handled the western settlement better then she would have and thanks you for taking the time. The lion mane clan has blended in well and is teaching the rest a lot they needed to know. Oh, and make the sanctuary leaders wait until the third day before introducing them to the golden tiger clan. They need the time to observe the sanctuary first."

"Thank you." Melina vanished.

"Lyamy?" Jenyin was calling.

"I am sorry," she said turning back to the group, "I missed what you were saying."

"I was just asking if you would bring the children over. They are growing up quick and we would all like to say hello."

"Sure, I am sure they would like to say hello to everyone too. Come on Children, say hello to everyone here." The children rushed over excited and talked with everyone. Lyamy followed them back to the group and sat down again. "About the golden tiger clan, you will all know when they arrive, because you will see my double returning with them. Please nobody go welcome them or greet them until I make the invitation to do so."

"Not a problem." Freldin responded and went back to listening to the children excitedly telling their stories. Jenyin's den offered to take the children and bring them back at the dinner meeting later. Marrianne stayed a little longer after Freldin and Chineene departed.

"Lyamy, Freyie, I don't have anyone else I can talk to about this. I am not even sure if I should ask, but can you keep in total confidence the things I am about to ask?"

"Of course, we can." Lyamy answered for both of them.

"I didn't mean for this to happen, but I find myself really liking Jenyin and his den. I feel at home with them, and I feel free when I am with them. They tell me I can stay whenever I want." Marrianne paused, "It goes against the way I was raised and all that." She realized she was avoiding her questions, "I don't want to offend Daret, Karis of Chelic, I like being with them too. Are they going to be alright with it if I am there all the time?"

"I am sure they would have told you openly if they did not want you around or sleeping with their den. We really do not hide our feelings when it comes to things like that." Lyamy smiled.

Freyie added, "They seem to all like you too."

"Is it allowed for someone of another race to become a part of a den?"

"We looked for a male mate among the other races, we just did not find any we felt were compatible or we would have taken them in. They seemed overly possessive and seemed to cling to one of us over the other, which made things awkward. Anyway, to answer your question as far as I know and I know more of the codes, ways and rules of our people better than most, it is alright."

"Half breeds were considered abominations by our clan though, Lyamy."

"Our clan corrupted a lot of our ways, Freyie. There are no codes, customs or rules that say that. Other clans do not have those attitudes either."

"I care about what you think and what Jenyin's den thinks. There are others in the sanctuary that will be offended, and I really do not care. If those in my circle of friends are happy for me, that is good enough for me. Is there a process or does someone specific have to ask me to join?"

"How many nights have you slept with the den this week?" Freyie asked.

"Three." Marrianne seemed a little uncomfortable but determined to make sure she was doing things right.

"I only have one question; have they all kissed you when you were um, preparing to sleep?" Lyamy asked

Marrianne blushed slightly, "Yes."

"Then they already think of you as part of their den. If you are happy to live by den rules, you know how we are about things your people consider private and personal, then you can stay with them from now on as part of their den. You can still keep your own place as long as you want."

"Thank you, both of you. I just wanted to be sure I was not doing something wrong or cause any problems. I know the whole relationships are not the same as with other races. The problem with that would be the males and married women of the other races would not understand, so unless some other Shadowkyn males come long." Marrianne left the statement hanging.

Marrianne stood up to leave, Lyamy and Freyie each gave her a hug, "I think Freyie and I will go do some cave exploring. I want to take a closer look at the area we have set aside for the golden tiger clan." They all stepped out, Marrianne turned to go back to Jenyin's den and Lyamy and Freyie headed the other way.

Marrianne walked light on her feet. She had fallen in love with this den and apparently, they felt the same about her. She was relieved to know that she had been accepted, and they were not just being courteous to her. She walked in, they told her she did not need to knock anymore and placed her gear and garments on the shelf they had provided next to theirs for this purpose. You do not normally wear anything in your own den, as much as the den belongs to you, you belong to the den... For the first time she did not just feel like she was making herself at home in their den, she felt at home in her den with her den family. She wondered if she was carrying a baby or a cub.

*   *   *   *   *

Even Kyamy was surprised that Peltrhak let his would-be assassins live and for the most part the lion mane clan was much less harsh than the white leopard clan. Those punished were required to depend on the kindness of others for their food and any comforts they might get. The clan was pleased to have more members, but still tried to sort out how they could even exist. They had spent their lives knowing that their clan was all there was of the Shadowkyn. Now they not only find out there are other clans, but this one has joined them.

The lion mane clan was all female, but better than half of them were already in their own dens. They were being brought into other dens, but those already joined had to join dens together. The ration of females to males had already been between seven and eight to one, now it was closer to ten to one. On top of that there were now one hundred and fourteen females who spent the last twenty years without male company.

The first few days after the arrival of the lion mane clan progress slowed down, but the more they were assimilated the more progress stepped up to an even faster pace than before. There was an increase in the free use of magic, the new members did not have the inhibitions about using it or sharing knowledge with the clan. Bonds grew within dens and the children of the clan were not moved to nurseries.

Zenjin was key in keeping the children with dens, insisting that the nurseries were only built for the wartime society and the future of the clan depended on the young being raised by the dens. Instead of nurseries, the buildings were used for schools and libraries, places for learning outside of what could be taught in the den. School participation was free and voluntary. There were awards for educational achievements, but anyone who did not want to go to school was not required.

The exception to the school voluntary rule was combat training. It was required for every clan member to train in hand to hand, weapons, and archery. This was for the protection of the clan. A clan sword was always forged for each member when they became the age of an apprentice. The sword was attuned to the individual and would activate into a flaming blade when drawn by the owner. This was new to the lion mane clan, but they all accepted swords and training.

Loetin found that he was generously rewarded when he provided services for members of the clan, so he worked hard and ate well. He even found places to get some shelter from the elements when he slept. Errinin followed the example of her den-mate. The two of them did not talk but worked together and looked out for each other. Before being put on the streets to survive, their wills were easily bent by Kren, they were younger and felt less noticed in their den. Now they were learning they had their own worth and together they added to each other's strengths.

Kylee struggled for days with the words of Peltrhak and the memories of one punishment after another. She conceded to herself that she had been wrong. She had stood for what she thought was right. She was not convinced to do what she did by another and her motives while for position and gain were not selfish as much as driven by the system, she was taught was right. How could she have been so wrong putting everything she was into what she thought was right? How could she trust her own ability to think again?

Kylee turned inward, her own guilt eating away at her form the inside. She often forgot to eat even if she had scraps available. Tears filled her eyes until there were no more tears to come. Thinking became more difficult until she felt her last thought coming. '*ShadowDancer, Ancient of Lyamy, I am not worthy to live. Come and take me that I may not hurt my clan again.*' She drifted into the cold darkness. She welcomed oblivion.

Time had no meaning. There was a light. '*Am I dead?*' She was in a room, prostrated on the floor in front of a woman, an Elf dressed in flames and shadows, ShadowDancer. "I am not worthy to face you." she whispered.

"Look at me child." Kylee obeyed. "You made a mistake, a very strong-willed mistake. Would you choose to make things right, or give up and let the wrong you did become all you are?"

"If I could, I would make them right."

"Would you concede to being defeated by your error and weaken the clan, or turn the strength of your will to overcoming your inner weakness and do good for your people?"

"I would choose to do good, but my judgment of what is good has failed me."

"Given a chance to live again, would you embrace love or hate?"

"I would choose love so much that those with hate might only know that love should they torture and destroy me, that love might live beyond that which has consumed me."

"Will you give yourself to my service and live strong for the good of your clan?"

"In life or death, while I am not worthy, I give myself, I am yours."

"I claim you as mine. Stand." Kylee stood, "When you have endured your punishments, I will teach you and make you my priestess. Return to your body and chose to live again."

She opened her eyes, and she was looking up into the face of Peltrhak, his eyes filled with concern for her. Her chest was heavy and strained to breath. Looking into his eyes she whispered, "I am sorry Lord Peltrhak. I beg your forgiveness."

"Her fever is passing." Serine's voice echoed in her mind. A wet cloth was placed to her lips. She sucked in the moisture. She wanted to cough but did not have the strength.

"Yes, ShadowDancer, for you I will live." she coughed, her breathing came just a little easier. Someone wiped something wet from her cheek "I must finish my punishment." she tried to sit up but had no strength and someone pushed her back down.

"When you are healthy enough, we will decide concerning your punishment." Peltrhak's voice was filled with compassion. "Is that from the fever on her shoulder?"

"It looks like the symbol of ShadowDancer." Serine answered, "I have never seen a fever brand a clear symbol like that before. It looks like a mark of acceptance. Kyamy may know this better than I do. I just have a library in my head, she has the practice of her clan."

"Go find Kyamy." Peltrhak instructed. The footsteps of someone small took off. "Can you drink yet, Kylee?"

Her voice came out in a rasp and she pushed her lips forward to receive the moisture. A dripping cloth was pressed to her lips and she drank in the water. She slipped back into sleep, filled with random dreams. She dreamed of Lyamy walking out of a fire with a sword through her chest, the blood cooked on the blade where it came out the back. She dreamed she was wearing holy fire and blessing the followers of ShadowDancer. She dreamed she was crying as her clan lay dead around her, with her sword in her hand covered in the blood of her clan. Her sword became a scepter with flames and shadows dancing from the top. She poured her spirit into the flames and the clan rose from the dead. Dreams of wars and changes around the world, then quiet.

She could hear birds not far away. She opened her eyes and tried to sit up but was not yet strong enough. She looked around; she was in a basket in Peltrhak's office, and he was sitting at his desk working away on things to make their village a better place to live. She tried to kill him, and he labored to keep her alive. She examined what she was feeling, it was love. '*I chose love, not hate.*' she thought to herself. Fresh from deaths door, still sick in a basket covered with a cloak she felt stronger now than she did when she came charging in, hating change and set on killing. Now she felt the strength of the support of those around her and the love that filled her and brought her back to the living.

There was a bowl full of water and a balled-up cloth in it within reach next to her. She summoned enough strength to grab the cloth and bring it to her lips. The water felt good on her lips, tongue and throat. She could breathe easier than last time she was awake. She cleared her throat.

"Hello, sleepy." Peltrhak looked at her with a smile from behind his desk.

"Hi." She rasped unable to get more than that out.

"You probably should not talk for now. Not until you feel a little better." he saw the distressed look on her face, "Yes, I forgive you."

Kylee smiled; she was going to be alright. She would heal and then finish her den punishment. She would endure the clan punishment and then she would serve ShadowDancer and her clan. She would be a priestess to those who chose to follow ShadowDancer. She would be a servant, to her people. She smiled with hope as sleep over came her again.

Peltrhak had seen others concede to their own death when punished and shamed, without even getting as sick as Kylee they just gave up and died. The punishment had been harsh though caged and beaten hanging in shame for the entire village to abuse. Kylee had punished herself more than they could have. She was truly repentant of what she had done and been a part of, she was changed. He had also never before seen anyone surrender to death and come back. There was more to this than he could see right now. He could see that Kylee now had the will to live as strong or stronger than it was to stop change before.

Kyamy stepped in and walked over to Kylee. "That is a branding of the Ancients. It was placed by ShadowDancer not branded like it was done by the first. There is no damage around the mark. The mark is clean and made by lightening, but it did not extend beyond the mark itself. She was way too weak to have endured this from anyone else."

"So, it is not a fever scar?"

"A fever scar? At best a fever scar might take on the general shape, not the detail."

"She did not have the scar when we brought her in, but it was there when she woke up." Peltrhak shrugged.

"What an Ancient does to us when we are asleep is done when we wake up. Unless it was a vision, but then we watch and are not a partaker." Kyamy stated. She turned and looked at Peltrhak and her tail twitched, she tried pulling back the thought, she was not here for that. It was too late to conceal, Peltrhak saw and gave her a nod indicating he would take care of her need.

Serine and Lattia spent a lot of time together and with Zenjin. Every den was taught how to build a den bond. Cubs and children within dens adapted to the den they were in and built the bonds needed to learn from the den members. The bonds united the clan, lion mane and leopard became one. They also knew it would not be long before the clan doubled or tripled in size.

*   *   *   *   *

Yaun was in his office when Merkyet stopped by, "You summoned me?"

"No." Yaun answered.

"I did." ShadowDancer appeared in the room with them. Melina was with her. "First this is my messenger, Melina. When I send her, you will accept her words as mine. There will be times when I am not available to come myself."

"Hello, Yaun, Merkyet."

"Hello, Melina." Merkyet responded with formalities.

"Hello, Melina." Yaun gave her a once over, part Elf messenger, dressed just like her master, flames and shadows. Melina vanished

"Now to the business at hand. There is a clan that has been surviving in the jungles outside your walls. They survive by hunting savage predators before they do the hunting. There numbers are small, but they are hardened and strong. They are a mix of Shadowkyn clans that joined forces to survive. I am sending them to you. They will join you and you will accept them. They will teach you and you will teach them forming one bigger and stronger clan."

"I understand." Yaun looked at Merkyet, "but why do you bring her here?"

"The ways of Shadowkyn clans are more open than the practices of the white leopard clan. The master of old magic is the first of the clan and is the magic leader of the clan standing at the side of the clan leader. You have to return to that practice now. Merkyet is your master of old magic, so she is your first so that the two of you can balance decisions and work together."

"Does their first have the book of old magic?" Merkyet asked.

"They do and you will both fully share. You both have pages that are missing from the others book. You will both work with their leader and first, sharing responsibility, but having final say if you disagree. They will accept this. Their clan was cut to less than half when the savage beasts were returned to the continent when the war they were dragged to was ended. The number of beasts that came through was too great at one time. They only number about four hundred and ten. They are experts at scavenging and hunting. They are to be treated as equals and den buildings will be repaired and built for them in equal grandeur to any others."

"I will not be found to argue with anything you ask of us." Yaun responded

"I owe you and Lyamy what I am." Merkyet bowed

"You have two days to prepare your people. On the third day the two of you and appropriate support will meet them at the west gates." ShadowDancer touched Merkyet on the temple, "That is the list of spells you are to teach everyone in the clan. You will need every den to build a den bond and include the children and cubs they care for."

"How do we explain that there are other Shadowkyn? Where and how did they survive without us knowing?"

"When the white leopard clan was at its height, over a hundred thousand strong you were feared by all clans and you were at war to rule and conquer. It was the arrogance of the white leopard clan that almost brought an end to all Shadowkyn. You were infiltrated and the bonds were used to channel information. As a result, the other clans were able to avoid being overrun. You broke bonds and started sending cubs and children to nurseries and only remnants of other clans escaped the movements of the white leopard clan that they could not follow."

"How did that almost destroy all Shadowkyn?" Yaun asked.

"The savage beasts that wander this side of the continent used to be contained in a single valley where the ancients tested their creations. The white leopard clan was tricked into opening the seals of the valley in pursuit of other Shadowkyn, but instead released the wrath of savagery on the rest of the continent that they knew. The size of the clan dropped below forty thousand before the fortifications that protect you now were built. It was assumed that any clan outside the protection of the white leopard's would parish. Secured from the threat and no longer having an enemy but living by the practices of war the need for an enemy turned inward and you know the rest. You were diminished to less than two thousand by your own hands."

"We will convince our people." Merkyet looked at Yaun, "and we will share equally with this wild clan. I will call upon Treska to assist me. You better organize the Lords to prepare for this joining of clans, Yaun."

They worked hard and on the third day everything was in order and ready. All empty dens were repaired, and new ones built. Merkyet and Treska taught everyone all they were instructed to share. With the den bonds built any residual thoughts of restarting the nurseries vanished. Merkyet and Yaun waited at the gates, their seconds remained in town preparing the welcome.

"The last we met these clans we were all enemies. She must have spoken as strongly to them as she did to us, just to get them to come this far." Yaun observed.

Merkyet laughed, "Not everyone in the world is as stubborn as we are. They may be coming because more than half their clan was wiped out and they need our shared strength to survive. Or because behind our fortifications they can get some rest they have long done without. Or just possibly they are coming just because ShadowDancer asked them to."

"They are approaching." a Guard yelled from above the gate.

"Open the gates!" Yaun commanded.

The gates opened and the arriving clan was still two hundred yards out. "All I sense is they seek shelter." Merkyet commented.

"Look at the size of their front guards, did they cross breed with leophardeg?"

"Watch your manners,Yaun. We do not want to start a war by insulting them."

Greetings and welcome, I am Yaun and this is my first Merkyet." Yaun greeted when they were close enough.

They began stopping, "I am Khandric and this is Cantese my first, we are honored by your welcome and accept the hospitality of your clan."

"Let us keep moving until all your clan is within the walls of protection before we stop." Yaun suggested, "I assume, ShadowDancer explained to you also the terms of our becoming one clan? Based on those terms, clan members being equals, we share rule and if there is a disagreement, we have the final say, but are required to consider compromise as an option, I invite your clan to join us." They talked as they moved.

"Indeed. We accept these terms as they were also spelled out to us. We thank you and honor your invitation." Khandric came to a stop and turned to Yaun once they were far enough for the gates to close behind the last of their clan. He visually evaluated their situation "I trust ShadowDancer so we are here. You will have to understand that you the white leopard clan are known as the enemy we needed to hide from for as long as any of us can remember. It will take time for us to build a mutual trust."

"We have been through a lot of changes lately and faced with things we would not have faced on our own." Yaun replied, "We did not know any other Shadowkyn existed, so it will take time for us to overcome the amazement that we were not the only survivors. We do not remember the war. Arrogance no longer serves any Shadowkyn."

Merkyet and Cantese both stepped up. Merkyet spoke, "We can sort things out back at the office in the central village. Your people have free choice of the open housing. We can show the den leaders around and they can choose and help their dens settle in. I would suggest we can let ritual and ceremony wait until tomorrow when everyone has had a chance to get some rest and clean up. Our clansmen will serve meals at tables in centralized areas and partake in meals this evening."

"Merkyet, you and I will take some time for just the two of us to compare notes and work on agreeable arrangements for what we do." Cantese added, "and how we will bond our clans together."

They proceeded into town. The leaders went to the office, which had been expanded to provide for both with equal stature. Merkyet and Cantese led the den leaders around first to choose their den homes, then the unattached members to pick from other housing if they wished. The dens were happy to have a place to set their belongings down and rest.

Cantese asked Merkyet to talk with her in private. Merkyet still lived alone with her wolf, so she offered to meet with her in her home. Something about Cantese was making her uncomfortable, but she was attempting to be compliant with ShadowDancer's wishes and cooperate.

*   *   *   *   *

The golden tiger clan reached the coast and worked their way south staying invisible and leaving no trace as Lyamy had taught them. Lyamy was in the lead with Shenji and Wujin. They were using the bond to communicate in silence as they traveled. Using thoughts passed between individuals, selected groups or the whole clan communication was quiet and efficient. This ease of communication was what was missing in the shadow bond. Communication could be done in a similar fashion, but it took more articulate effort and skill.

Lyamy showed them their private entrance hidden in the forest. They were impressed with how well it was hidden without the use of magic. Before entering she gave them a tour of the outside, avoiding actual collisions with people. They saw the boat docks and the mills and outdoor structures, and the cultivation done by the foreigners that had taken up residence with the sanctuary.

Lyamy led the way as they descended into the cave reserved for them. A couple of buildings had been erected for them to use, but for the most part it was open space for them to do as they pleased. There was a stack of woven mats with padding and covers stacked near the passage that led deeper into the caves. The bond that webbed through the clan let Lyamy feel how much safer they all felt hidden and sheltered from the savagery of the jungle. A few of them sat or laid on the stone and Lyamy indicated the mats and suggested they use them to sit on or lay down.

'*Shall we go and explore the rest of the community?*' Lyamy inquired of Shenji and Wujin

'*Just the three of us should be safe.*' Wujin responded

' *Follow.*' inflections of courtesy and emotions cannot translate to words, but Lyamy thought in a well-mannered and respectful way.

Lyamy lead the way down the tunnel into a larger chamber of the caves still not used with several tunnels out in different directions. Wujin and Shenji appreciated the availability of space. They passed through the next tunnel and Lyamy slowed down as they came out in the merchant cavern. The three of them browsed the shops avoiding getting bumped into or disturbing anything that would give them notice.

Lyamy gave them a full tour of the residential area and the craft shops in their separate caverns. She explained the storage area on their way by. She brought Shenji and Wujin into her den. Freyie knew they were there, but deliberately avoided seeing them per Lyamy's instructions. '*This is where Freyie and I live with my, our children.*'

'*You left your children to help us?*'

'*Not exactly.*' she said as her other self, stepped from behind a partition to talk to Freyie. '*Both of me know you are here. This is why you sensed I was in two places because for now I am. I will merge back to one soon. When it is time though.*'

They slipped back out of her den and followed the tunnel to the kitchen-entrance chamber to the caves. Then returned the way they came back to the cavern set aside for the golden tiger clan. Lyamy dropped her invisibility and spoke out loud, "We are safe here. We are under the protection of ShadowDancer." Suddenly Lyamy grew tense, "Merkyet!" she looked at Shenji, "I'll be back." Summoning the old magic, she teleported herself to Merkyet.

She appeared next to Merkyet and the wielder of old magic who was dominating her mind. Lyamy backhanded Cantese knocking her to the floor. "You dare act against one of ShadowDancer's protected?" Rage and fire filled Lyamy's eyes. She saw the bond Cantese had made over Merkyet, the same bond she had over her savage beasts. Her eyes went from red flames to blue-white flames. "You will not rule over my student and the chosen first of the white leopard clan, protected by the hand of an Ancient! I am her avatar and I reverse your bond." she reached with her mind and literally turned the thread of the bond end for end giving Merkyet full dominance over Cantese reversing the exchange of life.

"Impressive." Shenji said from behind her. "Sorry I was curious and followed you."

Merkyet hugged Lyamy and Cantese cowered in front of them. Lyamy introduced Merkyet and Shenji and laughed, "You are both my students."

"That was not old magic." Merkyet observed.

"No, it was more powerful than old magic and more dangerous to know." Lyamy said, "This is knowledge I cannot share." she looked at Cantese and backhanded her again, "You were given a great opportunity and you tried to use it for a selfish power gain. She would have shared everything with you, now you can serve her as you intended her to serve you. If you utter one word against her for what has happened, or one action, I will be back, and you will pay more of a price then you know. You can tell everyone that you were smacked down by the avatar of ShadowDancer for offending her."

Shenji laughed, "I am glad I have your protection, not your anger."

"We better go back, before I do something I will regret. Merkyet it is good to see you again." She gave Merkyet a hug and a kiss on the cheek. Stepped back, touched Shenji on the arm and vanished with her back to the caves with the golden tiger clan.

When they appeared back with their clan there was a clear sense of relief around them. "Can you tell us when you are going to take off like that?" Wujin sighed

"We have a couple wandering?" Shenji noticed

"Yes, I told them they can explore a couple at a time as long as they don't mess around or get caught."

"They all need to at least take a glimpse at what they are considering becoming a part of and in a couple of days everyone will be able to meet the leaders of the sanctuary." Lyamy spoke openly. "You will see that more of the people here are not Shadowkyn then are."

"That might change." Nunji said letting her cubs run free in the cave around the clan. "We will not be losing our litters if we stay here."

Lyamy could sense that Wunjin really wanted this to work, being leader of the clan fell to him, it was not by choice. He would not come short of standing up for his clan in every way, but if he could trust passing the mantel of authority to someone who could lighten his burden he would. "Wujin, Shenji, the three of us should go and sit in the shadows and observe the dinner and meeting of the sanctuary leaders this evening."

"We should eat before we go." Wujin suggested and several of the golden tiger clan began preparations of food for a community meal.

"They will know we are observing because you are with us won't they?" Shenji asked

"They will, but they will not do anything different, and they will not address you until I have allowed them to introduce themselves to you." Lyamy thought a moment, "I can leave you for now and return to my place in my den and with Freyie, so that I do not know you plans and movements. I can honor you by not looking at the bond that joins us, so you have freedom to observe in secret."

Wujin held his hand up while he thought, then responded, "Your willingness to do so, gives me reason to trust your words and those you trust. The three of us will go after we have had a chance to eat."

*   *   *   *   *

Jenyin sat at the head of the table where he normally sat. Chelic and Freyie served the meal, baked fish, a mix of mashed tubers, some bread and a salad. They knew when Lyamy's other self, came in and they assumed the others were with her but chose not to let it distract them.

"Not that we really need the money," Marrianne adjusted her seat, "but we are collecting three percent on everything that comes and goes in trade. The Magus of Kelleeshia thinks we should be charging two or three times that much."

Dresdin pointed with his fork, "The sanctuary owns and controls all the mining operations within the caves. We redistribute ten percent of that to the population. None of our citizens really have to work for money. The rest is being stockpiled and used for resources."

"The sanctuary also runs all the harvesting operations. Fifty percent of the food is distributed twenty percent is stockpiled and the rest we use for trade. Wood and other resources we harvest are distributed as needed to the people with additional supplies purchasable to those who want more, and a lot is being warehoused." Freldin added

Chineene set her fork down to speak, "We allow anyone who wants to to do additional harvesting outside of the sanctuary operations. We also let them do prospecting and whatever they want in areas outside of the limits we set as sanctuary lands. We still offer them shelter and protection, so we are not limiting what they can do either. We have no poor people and no bad parts of town. Like most places."

"We are a young community; we do not want to let overconfidence breed corruption. We have crime and we have punished according to Shadowkyn law. There have been complaints that our ways are to harsh. I would hear the judgment of those who are not Shadowkyn here on this matter."

Grimble spoke up first, "The strength of the enforcement of the laws we have make a clear message and protect us and the community is generous enough there is no excuse for the most part for criminal activity. We do need to balance that with compassion though, it is better for people to learn and love their community then to feel fearful and oppressed. I would rather give someone the wealth they need to get a new start and send them back to Kelleeshia then have them stay and harbor or brood on doing evil here."

"I agree." Desdin nodded, "We have already sent some away, but we do not want them to well off when they leave, and we want them to tell the world how hard we are on those who do wrong. It will discourage others from coming just so they can be kicked out richer then when they got here or to come here thinking they can pillage our people and get a light slap if they get caught."

"I think we have done well so far." Freldin stated, "but I would say this is something we should keep as an open discussion to be sure we do not get corrupt in our application of justice."

"We have a general consensus then, for now we continue as we have been." Jenyin concluded the topic.

"They have left port this hour with a month to our shore." Chelic spoke as she ate seemingly oblivious to what she was saying, "In forty-two days as the sun comes up, they will assault our beach. Men in metal casing like bug shells. We will be ready. Don't worry about your plates, I will clean everything up tonight." she grabbed other plates as she got up and brought her own to the counter where she would wash them in the water basins that were already warmed for this purpose.

Lyamy cleared her throat, "So now we have a date. We need to clear all our boats from site at least seven days prior. Knowing when gives us even better ways to prepare. If everyone agrees, I want to avoid killing them. We can send them back home on their ships with food only, strip them and their ships of anything they can use as weapons. Send them home naked and they will not return."

"The only place armies like that could come from on that timetable would be the southern kingdoms of the middle continent. They are humans, so they are unpredictable, no offense Marrianne." Freldin apologized, "They could brood until they seek revenge, or they could plot, or they could get the message and not return."

"No offense taken." Marrianne laughed, "Those kingdoms are opportunists. They are only coming now because they think we might be an easy target. I think with that kind of embarrassment they will not risk it again. The stories they tell when they get back will be exaggerated to justify their failure."

"Then that is settled too." Jenyin looked around the table, "Is there anything else we need to bring up tonight?"

"Some of the engineers," Gimble voiced, "want to work on piping water in and out of the residential areas, convenient central areas first, and eventually to each home."

"If everyone is in agreement, we can trust you with that and we will see how it turns out." Jenyin looked around at the rest and they nodded their agreement. As they started getting up, he called, "Lyamy, Freyie, please feel free to drop the children off with us from time to time. Daret and Chelic seem past their time, but Karis thinks she may be having her last chance."

"Me too," Freyie stated, Lyamy already knew, but everyone else looked surprised.

"I know three of us that will not be fighting on the beach in forty days." Lyamy looked at Marrianne.

"I know, I will behave." she rubbed her belly that did not even hint at growing yet.

Lyamy went back to their den with Freyie and the children. She grabbed some leather strapping before kissing Freyie and the children good night and heading up for her watch. She sat down and placed her hand upon the ground. She needed a second weapon, and it was time to experiment. She reached deep, feeling for the hardest natural metal she could find. She drew the metal from the ground in the shape of her clan sword, except she made the metal of the blade thinner and sharper, sharp enough to cut thought she laughed at herself.

She looked at the blade, the metal was probably too thin. She stabbed the blade deep in the ground and pulled sideways against the blade. With all her strength she could barely make it bend and when she let up it sprang back. She was amazed, she could bend a steel blade with much less effort.

She pulled the sword back out of the ground and examined it. The hilt was eleven inches long, she could wield it one handed or two handed the blade was thirty-six inches long the last twelve inches were edged on both sides. The width of the blade from strong to edge was an inch and a quarter and curved back subtlety to a point similar to a katana with a double edge at the end. The thickest portion of the blade was less than a quarter inch, but more than an eighth inch. The blade, hilt and guard were all one piece.

She laid the sword on the ground and produced another following that with two scabbards of the same material, remembering to shape the squared loops for fastening the bindings. The blades fit just less then tight in the scabbards, held upside down they would slide out. She pulled a small quantity of gold from the ground and bonded it like a ferrule about an inch and a half up the blade from the guard. Now the sword had a snug hold in the scabbard. She bound the hilt from the guard to the suggestion of a pommel with leather stripping to form a grip on each sword. She used additional leather straps to bind the scabbards and form fastenings to attach them to her belt.

She laid them all on the ground in front of her and placed a droplet of her own blood on each. Using the old magic, she bound her blood to the metal giving it a reddish hue. She attuned the blades to herself first with the old magic and then with the magic of the ancients. She equipped both blades and stood to finish her watch practicing dual weapon forms to become familiar with the weight and balance of her new blades.

She heard Jenyin approaching to relieve her shift and made sure that she had pulled all magic to a calm and her eyes were no longer lit with fire. "It is a nice night." she said before turning and facing him.

"It is, and you standing there a vision against the ocean stirs the savage urges, but I will not keep you from your sleep."

"You should know by now; I really don't need sleep beyond an occasional nap." She twitched her tail.

It was late and Jenyin would be done with his watch shortly, by the time she made it back to her den. She did not need sleep, but she liked to cuddle with her den.

*   *   *   *   *

Merkyet looked at Cantese still cowering and subject to her any whim. "Get up and pull yourself together, Khandric must have no clue you tried to dominate me and had it turned back on you. We were brought together for the good of both our peoples to become one, not fight."

"Khandric will know I tried; he knows who I am."

"Then let him know you failed, just leave out the part that you belong to me now."

"How could she do that?"

"She is the Avatar of the ancient that brought us together. She can do what ShadowDancer has given her to do. You only succeeded to start with because I trusted you and had my guard down. Now I will question trusting any of you and keep my guard up at all times. In causing division you have succeeded."

"I cannot face Khandric now, bound and owned."

"I have had enough. You will go out and act like nothing has changed. If I must I command you to do so." Merkyet had received the part of Cantese when Lyamy reversed the bond, but she remembered the lessons she had been taught and it gave her control over the lust and hunger. She followed Cantese out and they headed back to the office of the leaders.

Before they stepped in Merkyet pulled Cantese back, "What?"

"You will defend Yaun from any attack." Merkyet saw fear passed through her eyes. They had indeed plotted to take control of everything, against the instructions of ShadowDancer.

The order that does not exist responded to the messages they received from Merkyet and protective forces surrounded the offices. Inside Merkyet and Cantese took their places. There was a thump outside the door and Khandric was quick, lunging at Yaun with his sword drawn. Cantese slammed him face first against his desk as his sword was deflected by the magic shield protecting Yaun. The door opened and Khandric looked up Yaun's protectors dragged Khandric's oversize guards in with arrows through their legs bound with rope.

Khandric let his sword drop. "We should have continued to avoid you."

"If we wanted you dead," Yaun picked up Khandric's blade, "you would already have been dead. You can let him sit back down Cantese."

Khandric looked at Merkyet, Cantese had been the most powerful with the old magic he had ever met. His power base was removed he no longer had the backing he would need to take control. "So, what will you do with me now?"

"Put the guard in cages and give them the mark of shame." Yaun instructed Merkyet.

"Cantese will do that for us." Merkyet motioned and she obeyed.

"For now, Khandric you still have a job to do and perhaps eventually you can earn enough trust to carry a weapon again. For now, your guards carry your shame this time, next time it will be your den, maybe your son? Or you can choose not to commit any more crimes."

"You know if you had kept your word, you would be under the protection of ShadowDancer, even as your clan still is." Merkyet looked hard at Khandric, "You live now only out of our hope that you might find the error in turning against that which will save your people." Her eyes lit with fire for a moment, "It is still an option for me to claim you too."

Cantese and Khandric both looked at each other, defeated and ashamed of their failure. They could not look more shamed if they bore the mark.

"You will stand tall Khandric, you will lead your people into the peaceful merging of our clans. The first rule you follow is to do whatever it takes for the survival of your race and people." Yaun looked him in the eyes, "We are not the white leopard clan or the bob tail clan or whatever other division there is. We are the surviving Shadowkyn clan. We cannot survive fighting each other."

They stepped out; the over-sized guards were already hung in cages. The arrows had been pulled from their legs and wounds tended. Other than the bandages there was nothing else in the cages with them. There was a mixed crowd gathering, followers of both leaders, and tension was filling the air. Yaun addressed the gathering, "Do you all like having a place to live without fear of being attacked by savage beasts? Do you like the idea of being part of a clan that will survive? There may be subtle differences in the codes we followed before and the way we understood things, but here and now everyone is required to read and learn the expanded code, expounded on by Lyamy for our better understanding. We were brought together by ShadowDancer to give us all the strength to survive."

"Our intent was to merge clans, not to dominate, yet not even here a day and we have twice had to thwart attempts to undermine the mutual benefit of our clans becoming one." Merkyet reached out with the old magic to get a sense of the feelings in the crowd, "It is still our intent to merge clans. There is a lot that we can learn from each other. However, we will not force you to join us, nor will we hunt or pursue you should you choose to leave. For this to work we need to all agree to want it and be willing to put in the effort to make it work."

"We follow our leader." one of the newcomers said with her hand on the hilt of her sword.

"Then it is a good thing we did not kill him for attempted assassination, or you may have had to follow him to death." Merkyet's eyes blazed, "If we had wanted you dead, you would already be there. Make your choice, by sunset tomorrow it will be stay or go after that those who stay are committed and will be treated as members of the clan."

"Khandric and Cantese you must choose now so your people can choose to follow you or not." Yaun demanded, "We will not force you to choose either way, but you are committed to the choice you make now."

Khandric knew he had already failed if he was going to try to be the top leader for his people, they would replace him if they left now and if he stayed it would be with diminished respect. "I will stay. Our people need the strength of the combined clan."

Cantese knew she could survive in the wild using old magic, but she could not keep more than a few protected or alive. "I will stay and do my part to unify our clan."

Hands in the crowd let go of their weapons without drawing them. The tension eased some, but so did clarity of purpose. It was apparent there had been a consensus of the clan to take control when they first came. They did not plan on joining, they planned on taking. A wind twisted through the crowd and came to a stop on the platform between Merkyet and Yaun. The image of ShadowDancer appeared floating about a foot form the ground, "The decisions are made already, and you all know the choice you will make. Do not press this matter again or I will not be as lenient as your leader and your first. Khandric and Cantese have already forfeited the authority they were given; it is at the mercy of Yaun and Merkyet that they have any place at all. The next hand raised against this unity will be removed." ShadowDancer vanished with the wind. The crowd quickly dispersed and went about their business.

Merkyet turned to Cantese, "Summon your bound student or students if you have more than one." she could sense she had just foiled Cantese again, "Do you really want me to increase the bond, so I know your thoughts without looking? I command you not to plot against me anymore."

Two of the new members came up and bowed their heads slightly to Merkyet. She performed the ritual and bound them both as her students also insuring that Cantese did not use them against her. She enjoyed the breath of power a little more than she meant to but kept her outward appearance under control.

"Why don't you relish the power you drink from us?" Cantese asked, confused by Merkyet's control.

"Because I do not wish to indulge in the death of Shadowkyn anymore then I have to even if it is just the partial death of a bond."

"Death" Cantese seemed puzzled

"Yes. The piece of the spirit you pull when making a bond is part of the life, if you take life away you are causing death." Merkyet paused, "and when you take away freedoms, you are also taking away life. Losing the freedom to function outside of my knowledge was death to part of your freedom. The bond of a student is a trade-off, some freedom dies in exchange for access to knowledge. Trade-offs are a part of life, but to dominate for the sake of dominating is not a trade-off."

"You could still make me grovel for what I have done to you or tried to do. You have actually not punished me at all. I would have done worse to you without having as much reason as you have."

"My teacher taught me to think and do that which is good for the clan. As 'first' you are supposed to give yourself for your clan. They do not serve you; you are the servant to all of the clan. With power comes responsibility. My maser of old magic sacrificed herself to save the future of our clan and all Shadowkyn."

"That sounds just foolish, even if you put the clan first ahead of yourself like that and do not make them serve you, if you die you can no longer serve them either so what is the point. If you are gone, why would you care if the clan lived or died unless it was for your own children and even then, what is the point if you are not going to be there to enjoy them."

Merkyet thought maybe surviving in the wild required such a calculated coldness, but she did not need to be a part of this kind of thinking. The majority of the new members were more concerned with settling in and finding a place in their new world than with any power struggle. Merkyet wandered the village, helping the newcomers and making sure things were going peacefully. She left Cantese with the clan supply coordinator to help distribute blankets and household goods the new arrivals might be lacking in to help them get started.

She paused at the statue of Lyamy, "I knew you were still alive. I don't know how you pulled it off, but I am glad you did." She had not been surprised Lyamy was alive when she appeared, but she came back as an avatar for ShadowDancer not as clan. The way she appeared and left would let the clan continue to think she was dead and returning as a spirit avatar of ShadowDancer. Merkyet knew she was teleporting in and out, but she would not blow her cover. It would not be good for the clan right now to know she was alive still.

"I miss her too." Nelk said standing next to her looking ad the statue.

"She is ShadowDancer's avatar now." Merkyet smiled, "She has not left us unprotected."

"I have trained others; I am not really needed here anymore."

Merkyet took a deep breath, "It is time for me to report in to Yaun. You can stop by my place and visit any time you like." she turned and headed up the steps.

She paused before going in and walked up to one of the guards hanging in cages. Even up close they looked like a crossbreed with the savage cats. She looked in his eyes and gently probed the thoughts. The intelligence seemed lower than the mind of a Shadowkyn and he seemed more concerned about the female in the other cage then his own good. She could feel the loyalty to Khandric, a sense of obligation and debt though, not a bonded loyalty. Merkyet pulled large pieces of meat out of her hidden pocket and fed both of the off breeds.

She could sense there was an ability to manipulate old magic within them. In silence she offered to help build the thread between them. They latched on to her effort and completed the weaving so their minds could touch no matter where they were. They both looked at her she could feel the swelling of appreciation, "Thank you for your kindness." She placed her hand on the guard and then turned and went inside.

Yaun looked up when she walked in. "Is everyone settling in?"

"They all have places, Cantese is helping make sure they have comforts from the supply houses. It will take a little time, but for the most part we are one clan now." She looked at Khandric, "What will we do with him? We have permission to do whatever we want. Although the pets in the cages outside have a very strong loyalty to him, a sense of obligation for something he did. I am going to guess he killed the leophardeg that was their mother and claimed it was what killed their mother and he got revenge for them."

She got the response she wanted, he confirmed her suspicions with his reaction although contradicted with his words, "They are my children, I would never lie to them."

"It worked well for you, and they became your personal guards and protectors. Did Cantese tell you they can use old magic? Or was she keeping that one to herself."

"They cannot." his expression made it clear he did not know before she told him.

"Maybe Cantese was just too stupid to know. It is not polite to listen at the door Cantese, please do come in."

Cantese opened the door and stepped in, "I never looked close enough to see if they knew magic, but they are born of him and a beast, how could they be worth the time of old magic?"

"And the horvalka release old magic in waves." Merkyet stated, "You living in the savage jungle know that, though, don't you? Or did you never look close enough at them to help your clan? Or maybe your selfishness made you blind to the obvious around you?"

Yaun looked back and forth between Khandric and Cantese, "You failed each other and your clan long before you ever came here. You were too busy serving yourselves to even see what was around you that could have given you more power?"

"We did the best we could with the hand we were dealt." Khandric objected.

"I had nothing to do with breeding with a beast and then killing the mother."

"No, Cantese, I am sure you didn't," Merkyet snapped, "You were too busy with yourself to care what happened around you, when you were the key to warning your clan to get out of the way of what was coming."

"We are never stuck with the hand we are dealt." Yaun looked calm, "You made choices and they were bad choices. Unless you can see that, then you cannot learn and move forward again. Another choice you have to make, take the second chance you are being given or continue down the path of self-destruction."

"That applies to you also, Cantese. You are getting a second chance. You are already dead living for yourself. Maybe you can learn to live, giving your life to others like your clan." Merkyet turned to Yaun, "Khandric's guards are too big for our cages. They will obey me and sit out their punishment if we let them out. I don't think they would kill Khandric if I told them to, but they will obey me in other things over him. It turns out they can actually think and have emotions."

"I will try." Khandric said.

"Good." Yaun responded, "You still have some respect of your people and they need to be represented in decisions we make."

Cantese crossed her arms I frustration, "So I have freedom as long as I stay within the bounds you set for me. Obviously, I will try whether I want to or not. I understood that Lyamy better than you, she smacked me down for crossing her, you I don't know what it is you do."

Yaun looked at Merkyet questioningly. "Lyamy, avatar of ShadowDancer popped in earlier dealt with Cantese and then vanished again. That is how I wound up having this bond over her. I am protected by ShadowDancer."

"Then the Ancients took her spirit when she left us." Yaun said, seemingly proud of Lyamy.

"What are you talking about?" Cantese looked confused, "I saw her."

"She was burned alive in a hero's sacrifice in front of twelve hundred witnesses. They all saw her plunge herself upon Yaun's sword and climb the pyre and burn." Merkyet looked hard at Cantese, "You saw Lyamy the avatar of ShadowDancer, dead to the clan, yet living for an Ancient."

*   *   *   *   *

The third day came and Wujin called the clan together, "It is time to decide, are we ready to meet the leaders of this place? We have already been told we are welcome to stay here even if we do not join their community. I feel if we are going to learn more and make any further decision we will need to meet and get to know these people."

"I am in favor." Shenji spoke up.

One at a time they went around and each agreed. "Then it is done. Lyamy would you let them know we are ready?"

Lyamy gathered and led the leaders of the sanctuary to officially meet the golden tiger clan. When she arrived facing herself, she stepped together and became one in front of everyone. Everything became so much simpler, she had not even realized how complex everything had been until she was back in one body, with one mind in one place.

"Welcome to Jenyin Sanctuary, I am Jenyin. This place is dedicated to the Ancient or goddess depending on your preference ShadowDancer. You know our first, Lyamy, avatar of ShadowDancer. These others are council, starting with my den Daret, Karis and Chelic. Freyie is den with Lyamy. This is Freldin and Chineene, of elven descent, Desdin, dwarvish, and Grimble gnome"

"I am Wujin and this is my first Shenji," he made a sweeping gesture, "We are the remnant of the golden tiger clan."

"You are welcome to come and go as you like. We have few rules, I am sure Lyamy has briefed you on those. We expect you to honor those rules when deeper than your area of the caves or established sanctuary areas. This area is yours as long as you want to remain a separate entity governed by your rules." Freldin summarized in brief.

"We thank you for your hospitality." Wujin bowed his head slightly acknowledging their authority, "We accept your invitation to stay and mix with your people until such point we decide to stay or go. If we stay, we will be one with your community or extended clan. It would not be right for us to impose and not fully merge, although we would keep this area for those things that are Shadowkyn and stay Shadowkyn, even as you have kept your dens apart from the others."

"We accept the openness of your invitation and the protection we can offer each other. I will submit to your first in matters of the greater community and reserve my place with my people if we do or do not merge with your community." Shenji bowed her head slightly.

The rest gave their formal greetings and then turned to more general and curious conversation. Teas were served and a generous midday meal was shared. Wujin and Shenji were invited to join the evening meetings and brought into the shadow bond with the counsel. They both knew now to break the bond, so it was a voluntary bond, not one of obligation.

Per previous agreement by counsel, Marrianne gave them a quantity of coin for each of the members of the clan so they could exchange them for goods or services. Their knowledge was a historical knowledge of currency, there had been no practical use as nomads in the savage lands. When they were ready to return to other business, the golden tiger clan was ready to mix and meet. Wujin chose to go with Jenyin. Some of the others went with other members of the leadership, some went to explore on their own. Nunji with her cubs and Shenji wanted to meet Lyamy's children, so they went with Lyamy and Freyie

As they walked, Freyie turned to Lyamy, "I have been meaning to ask, you are carrying new swords that did not come from storage. I looked at one on the shelf this morning, the design is similar to our clan swords, but different. They are attuned to you, I can use them, but there is more to them then I can do. Where did you get them?"

"I made them and used the ritual to attune them to me. We are still one, so you can use them, and they are attuned to you also, but they are avatar blades which would be the powers you cannot activate. I can make you a pair tonight if you would like, only without the avatar power."

"I would love that." Freyie smiled

"You have this wonderful shelter; do you still need weapons to defend yourselves?" Nunji asked, checking her cubs. She was carrying them in the basket to avoid the chance of one getting lost on the way.

"We do not often need weapons inside, but everyone is trained to ward off any attacks from the outside. There are communities that number in the tens of thousands or greater and we have to be prepared if a war on another continent overflows to here or if greed or hate drive some to attack here from land or sea... We also still have the savage beasts from the jungle that can stray this far and also be a threat." Lyamy paused, "For the most part we are safe, but it is better to be prepared even for that which may never come."

They turned up the hall form the residential area, "Are these new swords better than the one you already had?" Shenji asked.

"I will let you look at them when we reach the den. We are almost there."

Freyie opened the door and went in and the rest followed, "Children we have company, you can share things you have learned with the younger cubs."

The children ran out and hugged Lyamy and Freyie and were introduced to Nunji and Shenji and the cubs. Lyamy instructed them, "Go play in the bedroom." then turned to the adult company and laid her weapon belts on the table, "You can examine everything. There are twelve throwing knives, two daggers, my clan sword, my two new swords and five throwing stars" she pulled the swords out and laid them next to their scabbards.

"The clan sword is just like mine." Freyie said

"It is similar to the ones she made for us, only ours are single pieces of metal and we had to craft and bind our own grips." Shenji said, "These new swords, the metal is different, and the blade is thinner, ouch, and sharper." she set the sword down and clamped down on her cut finger until it stopped bleeding.

Lyamy touched her hand and healed her, then wiped the blood from her blade with a small piece of cloth and gave the cloth to Shenji, "Please be careful. I can pull the metal from the ground and have it form to a blade or scabbard. This metal is harder and stronger than any that can be forged." She knelt on the floor and summon the metal blade and scabbard for Freyie and did it again so that she also could have two. She pulled the gold from the ground and molded it to the metal like a ferrule so the blades would hold snug in the scabbards. "You can bind your own grips and harnessing, Freyie."

"Thank you."

"Can you make anything that way? Well, anything out of the materials of the earth?" Shenji asked

"I am not sure what I can make until I try. So far, I made the swords for the clan, the swords for me and now these for Freyie. I have seen bars of different metals made this way and coins."

"I may ask you to craft a couple items for me in the future if that is alright."

"I am sure I will do what I can." Lyamy replied

Nunji was exploring the den and looking at the way they had the walls set up to divide the section of the cave and the furnishings and decor. "This is nice I understand we will actually be building structures inside the large cavern, similar to the residential area. I wonder if we could put caverns like this in the walls of the main cavern."

"I would consult Desdin and Grimble before doing anything like that, they know about keeping the structure of a cave safe and they might even want to help you if it will work. One of the drawbacks here is when we need more space there is no room for expanding."

Shenji, laughed, "But you know ways around that, using magic similar to the hidden storage spaces we can make."

"I did not think about that, but you are right, we could use that, but to others it would look like we were walking through walls."

"Unless you held the portal open with a physical frame then they would not even know they were stepping through dimensions."

"I like the way your mind works, Shenji." Lyamy smiled, "You see use in a practical way as easily as I have seen the change in social and political events." Lyamy pulled a square metal frame from the metal in the wall of the cave and held it up pressed against the wall. She cast the locational storage container spell on the frame and pressed it about halfway into the wall. It held the chamber open so anyone could see inside. A small person could actually crawl in if they wanted to through the two-foot by two-foot opening. The space inside was about two and a half feet wide, ten feet high and ten feet deep. The sides bottom and top were all a gray stone.

"It works." Freyie said excitedly

"With that you actually have almost unlimited space." Shenji looked inside the space, "And as long as it is open there will be a continuous flow of air. You will want a bigger space if you are going to use it for added living area. This is good for a storage area though."

"This gives me an idea for our defenses when the armies coming by ship get here. I have been put in charge of our strategies for defense." Lyamy created an illusion in the air of the beaches, ocean and outside area of the sanctuary, "We don't know how many are coming or how many ships. I have already started planting devices along the beaches and sands to put them asleep using magic and gases that we will release, but we could also put traps in place for any that make it by the sleep using these storage spaces in the ground. I am hoping to win without a fight. I appreciate any insight you may have. We are fighting an enemy we do not know."

"It sounds like they have lost the element of surprise meaning you will have that advantage on them. What else do you know about them?" Shenji asked

"They are coming in ships across the ocean." She made the image of ships appear in the illusion, "I am going to assume they have weapons like the only ship I have seen before that can shoot projectiles of various types from a distance out, but not out of range of magic. They are coming from an area which apparently does not have as much magic usage as others, but that is still a possibility. We will know better when the get closer. The other races cannot see as far as we can, so we will see them long before they see us."

"The Magus from Kelleeshia has agreed to help us with defense if we ask him." Freyie offered.

"We better bring that up at our dinner meeting tonight. We need a consensus before we let someone from the outside use that kind of power here. I don't even know if we will need any outside help but might not be a bad idea to have back up just in case we do."

"We could help you make drop pits out of locational storage pockets." Shenji offered, "It looks like a good addition to what you are doing. We can also offer our services defending the ridge if any get that far."

"We can talk about this further later with everyone. This is a social visit, seeing the open pocket distracted me with the idea. This is supposed to be a friendly social visit." Lyamy laughed. She moved her weapons to the shelf by the door with her other garments and gear. "If you want to get comfortable while you visit, we do have guest shelves." Lyamy slipped in the other room and checked on the children and cubs. It seemed two of the cubs took a liking to Nelk who was showing them number manipulation. The cubs still did not have fully developed hands and with their paws could not hold the charcoal pencils well enough to write for themselves yet. The others were all playing other games, but everything they played was designed to teach and instruct also.

"They seem to really like each other." Nunji said over her shoulder.

"As it should be." Lyamy smiled and returned with Nunji back to the other room.

"May I look at your alchemy room? I suspected you had one, being a master of old magics there is a lot we do with studying the interaction with natural elements." Shenji said looking around another partition.

"Shenji we are close enough; you are welcome to explore anything you like in our den." Lyamy gave Shenji a kiss of a den mate, Freyie seeing it did the same giving her open access to their den. "Wujin will have the same welcome to our den when he stops by to visit."

Shenji smiled, "You make the merge more tempting; I will talk with Wujin. You have three distillers and a still, these are things we could not do constantly on the move. I had to find ways of doing different types of processing to get extracts."

Lyamy used their student and master bond and shared the distilling processes and examined the processes that Shenji was using, "Were you getting consistent clean results from the buried fermentation?"

"Normally, unless we did not come back to the same area soon enough, but then it breaks down into other things we could use."

The four of them mixed and went form one subject to another with their shared or separate discussions late into the day. Nunji offered to feed and take care of the children while the others attended the evening meal and meeting.

There was some discussion at the meeting about what would be gained and what trade-offs would be involved in merging the clan with the sanctuary. Plans and preparations for the coming attack were discussed and adjusted. Chelic just smiled and said, "We will be ready."

When they were done, Shenji and Wujin walked Freyie home before heading their own way and Lyamy went out to take her watch. She examined the coast, looking for any details she may have missed. The enemy would be coming from the south, the boats of the sanctuary would be either up the river or north around the coast, but all out of sight. They would have minimal activity where it could be seen, but some activity so as not to arouse suspicion. Everyone would be pulled in for the evening and they would be ready and hidden on the ridge in the morning when the first soldiers touched the beach. They would be ready.

Lyamy sniffed the air, nothing unusual, but her senses tingled. Someone was standing behind her hidden to sight and normal senses, even hidden from old magic perception, but not hidden to her heightened senses laced with the power of the ancients.

*   *   *   *   *

Admiral O'Drell pulled out of the port of Ehrbron four days earlier. It was the only port city in the southern kingdom of Ehrbron and a safe harbor for pirates and marauders. They really had no respect for anyone else and were spared piracy by being their friends. After the embarrassment of their involvement in the war on ShadowKeep, King Tagmerian had ordered armor and swords for three thousand soldiers. Granted they had not yet paid for it, but the shipment was lost and never made it to their soldiers.

Agents in Kelleeshia reported that the Magus had discovered his belongings from the same ship recovered by a small colony on the savage continent. Agents in Ehrbron found out the location of the colony from pirates and the population was around twenty. King Tagmerian did not believe that the Magus would have done business with a population that small so estimated there had to be at least two hundred. One hundred soldiers should have been able to take control of a colony of two hundred civilians, but he was sending a thousand.

It was General Brakhardt's job to take the army in and claim the colony and all its possessions for King Tagmerian and Ehrbron. It was Admiral O'Drell's job to get them their provide cover with cannon fire while they made shore. After the colony was secured, he would provide transportation of surplus troops and recovered cargo back to Ehrbron. The sun was high, and the sails were full. He was getting paid a year's earnings for this three-month job. He and his crew received a third of the payment in advance.

Most of the soldiers were starting to get over being seasick. They only lost three that fell over the rail before the General order them not to wear their armor until they were close to their destination. They sank like rocks when they hit the water and there was no way to bring them back. The Admiral also had the soldiers start using buckets and the crewmen dumping it overboard. He did not want to take a cut for soldiers that didn't make the trip.

The Admiral captained the lead ship with nine others to complete a fleet of ten. On each ship there were smaller boats designed to bring the soldiers to shore in groups of twenty-five. They were designed to be fast and had some kind of magic used so they would go as directed without sail or row. It was a little creepy to the crewmen and captains, but they had all seen them used before. The boats would run completely up onto a beach and the troops would not have to get out in the water. The boats would be lowered when the reach their destination and wait until instructed before launching to the shore. Frequently they would run through the first line of defense and take them out from behind.

Ten ships and one hundred soldiers on each ship. The plan was to have two waves of two hundred soldiers followed by a wave of six hundred. It was expected that any fighting would be over before the third was reach shore. With a cargo of three thousand swords and sets of full plate armor and whatever other loot they could salvage; the troops would have plenty to do. A token force would remain behind to run the colony for the king.

*   *   *   *   *

With the apparent acceptance of the unity of their clans by their leaders, acceptance seemed to go smoothly for everyone else. Not being abused and being allowed to operate independently as long as she did not act against the unity of the clans Cantese seemed to actually be adjusting to her position. Khandric found he was still busy enough doing his share of the coordinating justification for leading any fight against the way things were diminished with each passing day along with motivation. Everything was stacked against success of any undermining operations even his own guards were now working for the current order of things.

Khandric's beast off-spring were let out of the cages at Merkyet's word and stood their punishment for five more days before Yaun spoke with them and released them from further punishment. They had taken to protecting Merkyet and Yaun as leaders of their pride. Merkyet and Yaun never yelled at them and gave them praise for the things they did well and comfort rewards. They seemed almost docile and cute unless something threatened their leaders.

Merkyet and Yaun got word from Serine and Peltrhak of the merging of the lion clan with the western white leopard clan and shared what was happening back home. They actually teleported back with the leaders of all the clans and agreed to rename the clans to the united Shadowkyn clan. They also agreed to call the regions they lived in eastern Lyamy and western Lyamy. The total lack of hostility between all of the other leaders seemed to impact Khandric enough to actually willingly start cooperating in establishing the unity. Settlements spread out within the protected land area and villages formed taking on their own names.

The people were much happier raising their own cubs and children. The schools were still kept busy as children grew and learned more quickly with the knowledge of their dens and wanted to expand beyond their family knowledge. Somewhere along the way they learned that the long ear clan actually had offspring and family too. They had names and secrets of their own. The generosity of change extended to the harvesters and they were invited to participate in community planning meetings and have greater rolls in the clan society.

Merkyet stepped into Yaun's office. "You know more then you tell me, Merkyet."

"What do you mean?" she asked. There were lots of things she knew and did not tell him. She was not going to start guessing what he meant.

"Lyamy was seen in the western clan also. She seemed as alive as ever with new scars and you don't get new scars if you are dead." Yaun looked at her accusingly

"She has the marks of acceptance of the ancients Darvel and ShadowDancer on her shoulders, and the symbolic claw marks of the Shadowkyn on her cheek. So, she is an avatar and a guide to all our people not just us. Do we know what a hero's sacrifice does beyond the death we see?" Merkyet knew she had not answered the question he had not asked.

Yaun sighed and was not really mad anyway, "I would like to tell her to her face she did great things for us. I have followed her instructions as best I could, and things have gone well, and I wish there was a way she could know the good she did."

"I am sure she knows, Yaun. Perhaps the avatar of ShadowDancer may call upon you again sometime." she knew she was feeding his dreams, but they were not bad dreams, "Now what I came for. They all have clan swords and they have been attuned to each individual. It makes a bond of sorts. We should have a celebration and gather everyone for a feast. When the darkest hour reaches under a new moon, everyone lifts up their sword and light them ablaze in a wave moving out from the center."

"That is an excellent idea, it will build on a sense of unity and strength to the clan."

*   *   *   *   *

Lyamy used her power and her eyes turned blueish white with flame. As she turned, she could see the individual before she locked her arms and pinned her to the ground, snarling, "Who are you stalking me in the dark?"

"Avira of the ghost cat clan. How do you see me, we do not even see each other when we are hidden?"

"Appear and let me see you through normal eyes." Lyamy sensed no threat and stood up helping Avira to her feet. She looked around and there were easily over a hundred of the ghost cat clan standing around watching her. "You are not alone, tell them to stay hidden so as not to cause an alarm." Lyamy tried to subdue the flames in her eyes without letting go of the vision it gave her, "What color are my eyes?"

"Green tinted with gold, why?" Avira gave her a totally confused look.

"Not important. Why are you stalking me?"

"We have been watching you since we discovered you here. You mix with others not even from our lands, you have taken in a dying clan of our cousins and given them protection. You are of the clan that almost destroyed us all, but your blood runs different. You care for anyone who you touch. Even those who do you harm you give opportunity to change. It is like you and your friends are atoning for the ills of the past and making things right again in our lands."

"That is your observations, not an answer to what I asked." Lyamy insisted.

"Very well. I came to speak with you this night. Look around you and what do you see?"

"Cousins hiding in the shadows?"

"Female cousins. Oh a few males, but the numbers are dwindling. Our off-spring have always favored female over male, but the number has shifted instead of four or seven to one, the birth rate is close to twenty to one and the mortality of the male cubs, well less than half make it to adult."

"You have no idea why? The food you eat, the magic you use, maybe this improved invisibility you use?"

"We think it has to do with our breeding. We always favored the strong for producing our off-spring and we fear that maybe something was there we could not see, and we were too late to change it. Now as our males diminish in number more and more of us are born of the same sires. So, we cannot help but breed the weakness upon weakness."

"And you think I can help you with this?"

"You took in a clan of our cousins small in size but almost all males. If they have twenty males and we join them it will shift the balance to seven to one which is closer to normal and it may save us all from diminishing for lack of mates of opposite genders."

"So, you are asking to join our clan, er community?"

"I Avira of the ghost cat clan humbly submit our request to become one with your clan. Hania, first of the ghost cat clan will confirm my request for all." she bowed her head to Lyamy even lowering her eyes in submissions showing the desperation of her request.

Another of the clan stepped forward, "I Hania of the ghost cat clan confirm the request of our leader for all and submit to your acceptance."

"The two of you come with me." She led them down to the front entrance and instructed a guard to take her place above. As the passed Jenyin's den she opened the door and called for him to meet her at the golden tiger clan cavern and led the leader and the first of the ghost cat clan to meet Wujin and Shenji. As she entered the large cavern, she called out with thought to Shenji and Wujin who met them as they approached the structures being built for the clan. Jenyin arrived as she was finishing the introductions, so she continued introducing Jenyin also to Avira and Hania.

"They wish to join our clan or community." in thought Lyamy asked Shenji *'Are you decided on whether you will join?'*

'We were going to tell you in the morning and Wujin and I would like to be one with your den' Shenji thought back.

'Yes, yes and yes.' Lyamy thought with excitement

"What is your number?" Wujin asked

"We are two hundred seventy-one females and eighteen males."

"If the four of us agree," Jenyin looked at Wujin and Shenji, "Then it is done."

"Then it is done." Wujin smiled, "they can stay here with us starting now."

"Let's lead your people in the back entrance." Lyamy pointed to the tunnel leading directly out. "Hania your first, Shenji and I can discuss any clan bonding we need to do in the morning. For now, I invite you two to the shadow bond we have among leadership." she performed an abbreviated version of the ceremony where they stood, and Avira and Hania were part of their circle. As they were led in the ghost cat clan dropped their invisibility and were greeted and welcomed. The ghost cat clan appeared to have no markings and their coloring was a translucent gray, giving them a ghost like appearance when they were visible.

Two hundred and eighty-nine members added to the sanctuary. They had grown quickly from the original eleven that governed, then eight more gnomes, then the castaways from the ship and the mixed races that joined through the portal from Kelleeshia bringing the population over five hundred. Now adding the Golden tiger clan and the ghost cat clan they were somewhere between eight and nine hundred in total. With the materials warehoused they would still have a surplus after building and providing for the Shadowkyn.

Lyamy noted how the ghost cat clan was equipped as they appeared. Everyone one of them had a bow and quiver, a long sword of some kind and a dagger. The carrying bags and backpacks they had varied as did any additional weaponry and miscellaneous other gear. "You have someplace where you were settled not far from here?" she asked Avira.

"We have places in the canopy of the forest not far from here. We are limited in what we can do there. This will make a much better home, we are not like the winged folk, if we fall, we hit the ground below. The cubs and children were not part of the count I gave you for our clan"

"Do you or Hania have any of your own?"

"I have three children and Hania has two cubs."

"I have five children," Lyamy purred slightly, "two are male."

"You should get home to them. We can settle in for the night and do what we need to tomorrow."

Jenyin and Lyamy walked back together, "We intimidate the others, because of what we are." Jenyin said, "I hope the increase in our number does not cause tension with the others that have moved here."

"They will adjust." Lyamy put her hand on his shoulder, "You are just thinking like a leader again." she snickered softly.

"Avira seems really nice." Jenyin commented

"And she thinks you are nice too." Lyamy stopped at her door, "I am turning in, there is a guard up covering my shift and it seems the first few minutes of yours. Give him this and tell him I appreciate what he has done." She handed Jenyin a coin. Jenyin looked at it, it was not a sanctuary coin it was a Platinum coin of the followers of ShadowDancer. She stepped through her door and into her den.

Freyie and the cubs were asleep. With Shenji and Wujin joining their den, they would want more space. Lyamy laughed at herself she wanted to play with her magic anyway her den growing just gave her an excuse. She pulled a thin frame out of the stone; made of the strong metal she had discovered. It was about eight feet by eight feet, and she pressed it against the wall, the bottom flush with the floor and began casting the same spell she used for the storage area she had put in the other wall. She applied more power and added depth and width to the container she put behind the frame.

The frame held it open, and the space was a ten-foot cube. Lyamy stepped in and out, she could sense a passage between locations, but it was minor and if she was not paying attention, she would miss it. The walls were gray stone, the same as the storage space she had made. Lyamy summoned her power and reshaped the wall making it ten feet deeper, doubling the size of the space. She pressed her hand on the wall and reached out to feel what elements were behind the stone wall, expecting to feel something like she did from the ground or walls of the cave. What she felt was undefined and she pulled back.

"Opening dimensional pockets and containers is an interesting process." ShadowDancer said as she appeared, "You will be better at it then most though. So, what did you feel behind the wall?"

"It was not defined, neither space nor solid with no clear structure. Something I don't understand." Lyamy looked troubled.

"Sometimes a dimensional pocket opens into an existing dimension somewhere randomly borrowing space, but sometimes it creates a never before existing dimension. See the number of possible dimensions is unlimited. Say there are eleven structural measures to dimensions, and we are familiar with a few, like height, depth and width. Some say time and gravity are also dimensional measures, maybe, maybe not. If you only knew two dimensions you would be living in a layer of what we see and touch now. But the three dimensions may be only a layer in the next measurable dimension and those layers can be infinitely thin. If you trade one of our dimensions for one of the others, then what we see would vanish and the perception of the alternate measures would be different. Adding just one more measurable factor adds an infinite number of possible layers to what we knew and then you multiply that by the number of possible measures and the possibilities are limitless."

"Something like a book full of pages." Lyamy shifted to a perception she could understand, "each page is stacked against the next, but what they contain may be totally different."

"It may be like that or it may be like a glass of water with lots of layers stacked on top of each other, but what happens in one layer, effects the layers around it. Drop a touch of color in the water and each layer sees it differently, but similar to the layers next to it."

Lyamy could see that too. "Does that mean we might exist in dimensions we are not aware of or copies of us infinitely dividing based on decisions we make?"

"I don't know everything Lyamy, use care not to get lost in speculation on things you cannot touch or effect. I don't mean to abandon entertaining those thoughts but keep them in control, so they do not steal your life. The point I was getting to is you have either found a dimension that has never been touched before, of you have created one with this space."

"Then what holds this space together so that I can use it and stand on the floor?"

"You have defined the characteristics of the space you created, and you can control the space around it. You already pushed the one wall back doubling the space. You have the ability to define that which is undefined around you also. Try forming a crystal in the wall from the undefined material that glows and lights up the space. Or push the side wall back and double the space again. These gray walls are still undefined, you can define the substance as whatever you want. Make a door and then define a room behind it."

Lyamy did as ShadowDancer suggested searching for the image of a room, she pictured Nelk's Laboratory behind the door. When she opened the door, every detail that she could remember was there, except nothing living. "You have given me the power to do this?"

"Not exactly, you are more proficient, but actually anyone who creates a pocket into a new dimension has the ability to form and shape that dimension, depending on their skills at controlling the and articulating the powers of their mind. You were good to start with and you have gotten better and had your powers enhanced with knowledge, training and access to greater power."

"So, am I becoming like you?"

"Not exactly. In here the dimension you have found or created in this pocket of space, maybe a lot like me, but out in Ethar the other side of that door and the world around it no. I think things and they happen, like you did the copy of Nelk's laboratory. You have to practice the manipulation of the powers to do things"

"Darvel told me I could teach Shenji everything I knew. At that point in time, I knew the magic of the Ancients already, the blue-white fire. I only knew then how to empower my sword, but did he intend for me to teach that to her also. Is it allowed for me to share that with Freyie or Hania?" Lyamy looked at ShadowDancer, she really did hate hiding anything from Freyie.

"Do you trust these three not to abuse or get lost to the power of what you can teach them? Once you share it, they will be responsible for what they do with it. I am sure you know how to make them think before they act, you have done a good job so far.”

“What about the rest that you taught me with the blink, or is that something you just gave me the ability to do?”

ShadowDancer smile, “That was a gift. I can teach you this though, even though I do not have to perform the manipulation I can show you how.” she pulled Lyamy into her mind and showed her how to step out of time, not quite capturing the moment, but compressing eighty minutes into one second, and how to step back out. “You can teach that to your students. They will be able to get a full night’s sleep in 5 seconds. Although they may want to sit or lay down when they do it.”

“Yeah, some practical wisdom, not falling down.” Lyamy realized she was exposed again to volumes of what ShadowDancer knew.

“Yes, I know you see and learn things I am not teaching you when I do that, but even as you trust Freyie, I trust you. You are my avatar, when you go places as you did back to Merkyet you should dress as I do to reinforce that point, it is a simple illusion and you already know how.”

“So, I saw a piece of the mind of Hania in your thoughts and she wants me to own her even as I owned Freyie for a while. Why would someone who does not even know me want me to own them like that?”

“She has shame and guilt that she has not been able to purge. So she wants someone to control her entirely so she cannot do evil again. The fact that she is that repentant makes it so she will not lose control again. I think you can teach her to overcome her past. Perhaps Freyie should take her as a student, then both of you could teach her. Her heart is good.”

“I will tell Freyie when things settle.”

“No, tell her tomorrow. She will be helpful when you face your small war in thirty-nine days.”

"I will do as you say. Can you tell me what is with Chelic, randomly predicting pieces of the future, seeing things that will happen as though they were already done?"

"I am the first Ancient in thousands of years that has the ability to glimpse into the future. The future has not happened yet though, so we cannot see everything, what we know can change things, so we see shadows and riddles of what is to come. Chelic died. I brought her back from the threshold before she crossed all the way. She surrendered to death before your dagger touched her and did not know she still had reason to live. I had to give her a piece of me for her to live. So, she gets random bits of future events. A part of her has moved partly on but stays as a guardian of the time-lines. She does not know what she is. I do not know if I made a mistake not letting her go."

"She seems happy, and her den is happy she is still with them." Lyamy looked around the empty gray room, "So any Shadowkyn can do this or could someone like the Magus do this with arcane magic too?"

"If they can make a dimensional pocket, they have the potential of doing this with any magic. Remember what I said about you never know when you open a dimensional pocket, what if you open a pocket and it happens to be too close to a sun?"

"That would be a hot pocket, maybe you could use it to cook things?"

"You get my point there are risks involved in multidimensional spacial spells of any kind. There is risk of reaching into a location you really do not want like a sun something worse. There is always a risk of having something cross over from the dimension your reach into ours. Or perhaps a time distortion. You reach in your pocket and pull something out and your hand has aged fifty years."

"That sounds awful. The first thing I teach anyone is to make a hidden pocket, I didn't know it was that dangerous."

"It is rare that things go wrong, I am surprised with over a hundred you have not experienced any mishaps, but you have also had some fortune on your side, luck."

"I am going to leave you to your experimenting. And yes, go teach Freyie, but give her all the warnings too." ShadowDancer vanished.

Lyamy ran to Freyie and woke her up, "I don't have to keep secrets from you." Freyie was disoriented and looked at Lyamy as if she was crazy, "First you need to learn this, I need you rested so we can talk." She pushed the spell for stepping out of time to Freyie and she went back to sleep for several seconds and woke up.

"Ok, that was nice." Freyie looked at Lyamy, "You can tell me your secrets?"

"Yes, I have permission to teach you anything you want to learn, I just have to give you all the warning that go with each." She opened the doors in her mind to Freyie.

Freyie felt her opening up but did not explore her knowledge. She stood up and gave Lyamy a big hug and held her for several minutes. "It is not important what I don't know, it is important to me that we are one, no secrets to keep us apart."

"Well, there are a few things I need you to know," she paused, "if you are willing to learn the ancient magic?"

"The magic that is so dangerous I should not want to know it?" Freyie hesitated, "If you think I need to know or you need me to know, I will accept your judgment."

"It comes with a warning, absolutely make sure you have thought through anything you do with the greater magic. I need you to be able to wield the power in your sword, see with the greater magic vision, use the greater teleport, and enhance your old magic."

Lyamy showed her pushing herself into Freyie's mind how to use the ancient magic to empower her sword, "How did we not know this was here before?" Freyie asked astonished, "There is nothing we can do without it being interwoven."

"Now that you have touched it, it will work very much like the old magic, but with subtle differences. You never want to use it to remove something, not even a grain of sand, only use the old magic for that. Old magic will only remove it from the present and actually move that which makes up the object, where the ancient magic will remove it from the beginning and will impact everything that grain of sand touched throughout all existence and time."

"It is beautiful." Freyie said looking around with the enhanced magic vision, "You can see the underlying power in everything. You did that?" Freyie walked over to the dimensional expansion of their den.

"Yes, I was experimenting. If you do not want it I can remove the changes. "

"No." Freyie opened the door out of curiosity, "Really? Nelk's lab?"

"It was the first room I could think of that had no windows."

"Well, it seems you managed to bring in a collection of his handiwork too."

"Yeah, looks exactly like it did last time I saw it. I have not looked in any of the drawers of cabinets or secret compartments he may have. I wonder if it only did what I could see or where I could fill in the blanks or if it actually replicated even what I did not know was there?" Lyamy's curiosity was getting the better of her. She opened a drawer and to her delight it was filled with a variety of vials and instruments. "It seems even what I could not see is here."

Freyie held her hand on the wall and got dizzy and looked ill for a moment, Lyamy caught her, "There is nothing there, well something, but not anything at the same time."

"It is the undefined existence of a new dimension, totally mine to manipulate into anything I want, well as long as it is not something living." Lyamy walked Freyie back out of the dimensional space. And sat her down. "You relax, I'll fix you something to eat, it may have been only a few seconds, but you got a full night's sleep and should be hungry."

"Thank you." Freyie sat, "I think it was just a reaction to feeling what was or wasn't on the other side of the wall. I was expecting rock and minerals and metals."

"I was uneasy the first time I did that too. ShadowDancer explained it to me." Lyamy fixed a plate of breakfast foods and brought it back out to Freyie. She placed a hand on Freyie's shoulder after handing her the plate and pushed healing energy into her.

"I am lucky to have you." Freyie purred as Lyamy set out bowls of food and sat down and ate with her. "The children are getting up and you already have breakfast ready for them too."

"Shenji and Wujin will be joining our den today. You will take Hania as your student and I think she will be joining our den also."

"That will change the name of our den, you know." Freyie teased.

"Yes, we will officially be Wujin's den as the first adult male, but it may be hard to get those who have known us from referring to us as Laymy's den." Lyamy heard the children moving, "Come out and eat, children." The children rushed out with hugs for both of their moms and sat down to eat.

*   *   *   *   *

Brelk had asked her to join his den. He knew she had a wolf companion that would come with her. She like him and his den mates and Chayrn the younger male taken into their den was nice too. They had been apprentices at the same time. She was already spending three nights a week there, and she decided she would start moving in, but did not want to let go of her own place yet.

Merkyet had not yet given cubs to the clan, but she would soon and being part of a den would help. She had offered Cantese the chance to live with her, but it did not matter what she did, Cantese was filled with hate and anger. Now she was glad she had been turned down; the cubs would have learned from that bitterness. Brelk already knew some of the old magic, so Merkyet becoming a part of their den would not be as out of place as other dens. The children and cubs of the den would all start learning old magic, just because she was part of the den.

Treska was her student, but at least one of the children of her own den would be a student also. Cantese was cut out of the training and her students went straight to Merkyet for training. Merkyet had scribed the pages from Cantese book into her own that contained the spells she did not have. She did not share back but told Cantese if she chose to give up her hate and anger, she would consider doing so. Cantese was with cubs, and Merkyet knew she was considering running away and raising them on her own in the jungle. She would not try to stop her.

Khandric had taken up leading hunting parties and they were providing a wealth of food for the clan. Merkyet had noted that now he was not worried about leading the clan, he was actually finding he enjoyed more time doing less stressful things. The fact that Khandric was finding happiness not being the leader, seemed to push Cantese deeper into her private darkness. Khandric seemed to lose interest in caring about what Cantese thought and without him, she had no other friends and nobody that was sympathetic to her downward spiral.

The rest of the wild clan had blended in and they were all a functional part of the same clan. The bobbed tailed members still caught her attention. She was also intrigued by the variety of sizes and colors and patterns. Once in a while Merkyet caught herself staring at someone intrigued by the colors and patterns and actually had to apologize a couple times, although they seemed to take it well. Overall things were going well with the new combined clan.

Word from Serine indicated that their clans were merged without incident and they were headed for a population boom. The land was friendly, and they were in no rush to build the fortifications with no enemies attacking, no savage beasts. After thorough discussion they did decide to build defensive measures after they had completed buildings for civil needs. They even were working on the idea of boats something to float or travel on the water of the river, maybe even the sea.

*　　　　*　　　　*　　　　*　　　　*

Freyie left with the children they were going to spend the day with Jenyin's den. Lyamy went back to the facsimile of Nelk's laboratory when she felt Merkyet tugging at the thread that joined them. '*Nelk is ready to leave here. He has trained others to fill his roll. You know he never has felt like he belonged here.*'

'*I can come get him, but how will you explain his absence?*' Lyamy inquired.

'*It doesn't really matter. He will probably be gone a few days before anyone notices he is missing. He is liked, but he disappears for days to his work.*'

'*Let him know I will come to his laboratory tonight and pick him up.*'

'Thank you. I will not be there; it would get suspicious. Wish you could come visit openly.' they broke off conversation.

Lyamy left the laboratory and grabbed her clothing and gear from the shelf by the door. When she was dressed and cinched up, she stepped out into the hall and met Freyie coming back down with Jenyin. Traveling through the residential area they got more looks then normal and there was a tension in the air. Lyamy reached out with her mind and picked up on the fact there were rumors of more Shadowkyn moving in and there was some discomfort, even fear.

"They are afraid of more Shadowkyn." Lyamy said, "We will have to work on fixing that."

"They will get over it with time." Jenyin stated.

"We did have to accept it when more of them came and we adjusted." Freyie added.

"True, but we were never afraid of them. I am sure there is something we can do to ease everyone's discomfort." Lyamy smiled, "We have something more important to do today."

They arrived early at the Shadowkyn cavern, but not before Desdin, Grimble and their teams. There were caverns cut in the sides of the larger cavern and slopes and stairs leading to a second level of caverns cut into the walls. The walls were marked out and it appeared that there would be enough caverns for more than the number of dens that would be formed. Other buildings were also being built in the central area.

"We are well on our way to settling in." Wujin walked up leading Shenji, Avira and Hania, "If we are ready our people are expecting the ceremony this morning."

"We actually have a series of ceremonies to do today." Sheji smiled at Lyamy and Freyie

They gathered the Shadowkyn clans. The ceremonies were not long, but both Avira and Wujin turned leadership of their clans over to Jenyin. Shenji and Hania official submitted to Lyamy as first. They sealed the agreements as one clan as Jenyin's sanctuary clan. There was a period of celebration and then more announcements. Avira was joining Jenyin's den and Wujin, Shenji and Hania were becoming one den with Lyamy and Freyie. They would move to Lyamy and Freyie den and then be known as Wujin's den.

It was after midday meal when the leaders went down to the meeting hall in the residential area of town and met with the rest of the leadership and who ever wanted to attend the meeting. They went through all the announcements and answered questions. There was celebration and some of the tension went away. It would take time for the two totally different social orders to mix and become comfortable with each other. The meeting disbursed and everyone went back to their own business.

As Hania was placing her gear on the shelf set aside for her just inside the den, Lyamy noticed her carefully place a tube and a couple belts or straps strung with feathered tufts in the same place as her weapons. "What do you do with the tube and feathers?"

Hania picked up the tube and one of the belts with feathers, "These are blow darts. The darts themselves do not do much of any damage, but they carry what we want them to do. These with the brown feathers will put a leophardeg to sleep so we do not have to worry about them catching our scent when we stumble across one. The ones with the red feathers can cause a permanent sleep in most creatures. We carry those little vials in case of accidental pricking from the red darts. You must be drink it before falling asleep, it will save you from the poison."

"You will have to show me how they work." Lyamy was intrigued.

"Sure, we can use them while we are invisible to others. The sleep works immediately." she dropped a dart in the end of the tube, "You just put the dart in, take a deep breath and blow a quick burst in the tube to shoot." she took a few steps back from her garments on the shElf and blew the dart into her tunic. Then she went over and picked it up. "See the dart will go through most softer materials and still penetrate depositing the powders into the blood."

Under close examination the sides of the dart tips had small pockets containing pressed powder. "I know how to aim a bow; how do you aim these blow darts?"

"It takes practice, but you keep both eyes open. It will look like you have two dart tubes so you center your target between them, then the height part you guess, based on your experience and what feels right." she handed Lyamy the dart gun and one of the brown-feathered darts, "I'll hang my tunic on the back of the door, and you can give it a try"

It took five attempts and then Lyamy was able to hit her exact mark every time. As they were putting them up Hania added, "You will have to add height for greater distances and adjust if there is a breeze."

"We can use these in our defense." Lyamy smiled, "This solves what I think was my last problem. We need to grab Freyie and Shenji and go up to the beach, should probably invite Jenyin too." She sent out the messages and the two of them slipped into their gear and headed up the hall and out the entrance of the cave.

"What are we doing?" Hania asked

"Testing a theory. I'll explain the details when everyone is here" Lyamy looked and there was one of their larger boats on the dock. It was a reasonable distance from where they were for testing. She had already arranged the items for transport to test.

The rest were emerging from the door of the cave together. "What are we doing?" Jenyin called out as they closed the distance to where Lyamy and Hania stood.

"I wanted to test our teleport skills, if everyone is willing to try with me. Jenyin, I'll have to teach you how to alter time, I have taught this to my den mates already." She touched his temple and pushed what she knew from student to master. He sat down and tested it.

Five seconds later he stood up fully rested. "I am impressed."

"Alright, at first we are doing this all, in regular time. See our biggest boat at the docks? First, we will teleport to the deck, then to the big cavern next to the Shadowkyn cavern. Once there we will each touch a cannon barrel and teleport back here." Lyamy looked at everyone to make sure they understood, "I will give more instructions then."

"The crew of the boat looked a little surprised when they appeared on the deck, nobody was in the large cavern. Each of them touched a cannon barrel there was an extra they left behind, and they all had their canon barrel with them when they landed on the beach.

"That was fun." Jenyin laughed.

"I think we are only just beginning." Sheji suggested.

"You are correct." Lyamy touched one of the other's cannons. "One at a time we will teleport with two cannon barrels to the boat deck and back." Lyamy went first and stepped aside, Jenyin went next and each of the others in turn.

"What's next?" Freyie was enjoying playing with teleportation.

"I am going to make four hops and you each have to follow." Lyamy smile, "Are we all ready?"

They all nodded, Shenji answered, "We are."

Lyamy teleported three miles up the coast, then to the boat, then the beach where they had been and finally to the cavern where they had picked up the cannon barrels. "Now for the part I needed everyone to test the most. Alter time, go invisible and follow me." She gave everyone enough time to cast and teleported to the beach, then the boat, then three miles up the beach, to the river about a half mile upstream and back to the cavern.

Jenyin was actually the straggler, but he did not have as much experience with slowing time, "That was more difficult." he stated, "I have never tried to follow someone else teleporting before, then to do it carrying a load and with altered time. So, I am guessing there is a purpose to this exercise?"

Lyamy gestured and the cannons returned to their places for defending sanctuary. "There is. When our enemy arrives, they are coming in ships by sea. They are military, so it makes sense that they will be armed ships." Lyamy laid out for them the plans she had for the ships and their crews. She brought up the illusion of the beach and their preparations for battle.

"You plan on keeping the five of us very busy." Hania stated, "We have five others of the ghost cat clan who are already proficient at this type of activity although not with ships. If it is allowed to teach them the time trick."

"We are adding it to our books of old magic, we measure our trust with every spell we share." Lyamy stated. "Who are the five you would train?"

"Avallach, Uberto, and Muhjah, males, Arima and Kachina female." Hania responded.

"Rukyo and Nunji also know everything except the time altering part." Shenji offered.

"Very well, however since we seem to have plenty to join us, Freyie and Nunji will stay in reserve. They are going to be significantly along with cubs and need to stay out of harm's way if possible." Lyamy looked apologetic at Freyie, then back to addressing all of them. "I want every Shadowkyn trained in using those blowguns and equipped with them and sleep darts as a backup for anyone they find that is not effected by other efforts.

When they were back in the den, Lyamy disappeared into the room that appeared as Nelk's laboratory. Shenji walked in, "What are you up to now?"

"A promise to an old friend. This was what his laboratory looked like when I left, and it is time for me to go get him." Lyamy faced Shenji, "You are welcome to come for the ride?"

"I am not saying I object, but you are bringing someone from outside into our den. We are a den now, so shouldn't we at least talk about things that effect the rest of the den?" Shenji was obviously trying to, not be confrontational.

"You are right, Shenji. I apologize. Nelk is waiting for me already, I think he can wait a little longer. I need to bring him here tonight even if it is not to our den. Everyone is home, we can meet and discuss this right now?"

"Still a little imposing, but better." Shenji smiled and walked back to the main den and called to everyone.

As they all gathered, Lyamy spoke, "I am not used to being in a full den yet, so allow me to apologize for presumptuous behavior that I may be guilty of imposing on everyone. I will attempt moving forward to defer the proper respect to the order of the den. I have made a commitment tonight without having consulted the den to bring someone here, Nelk, an old friend from my prior clan. I am due now to pick him up. My intent was to bring him back here, but only one of you knows him, so I would need your permission before bringing him into our home."

"What other option is there at this late a point?" Wujin asked, "Even if you bring him back outside our den, he needs a place to stay at least for the night?"

Sheji put a hand on Lyamy's shoulder, "We are a family and of course your friend can stay the night. We just need to consider the family when we do things inside the den. I know it is a change for most of us, not just you."

"You were correct, Shenji. It is probably more comfortable for everyone that I am the example to present the issue and I am probably the guiltiest. Is everyone alright with Nelk coming here for the night?" They all conceded.

"I will go with you, if you do not mind." Shenji said as they walked back to the laboratory.

When they arrived Nelk was busy working away at one of his benches, "I should never doubt you will be there when we need you." He set down what he was doing.

"Hello Nelk, Shenji, Nelk." Lyamy introduced them quickly, "Do you have everything together?"

"I am ready, this bag is all I should need." Nelk had his clan sword, but nothing else that could be construed as a weapon. He was not a fighter. "You know once I have seen your community, I will want to move on and explore the world." He paused with a trouble look, "I assumed you would have access to the rest of the world, do you?"

"We have a means of passage for you." Shenji laughed, "He is kind of cute."

"I am standing right here." Nelk winked at Lyamy.

"Let's not waste time and avoid making enough noise to attract attention." Lyamy said looking at the door. She teleported the group back to the laboratory in the den.

Nelk did a double take of the room, "For a second I thought you made a mistake." He opened a couple draws. "This is very good; it is like you turned back the clock in making this replica. But why would you make my laboratory?"

"I happened to be the only room with no windows I could think of at the time." Lyamy felt slightly embarrassed, "I am sure Jenyin will want to know you are here, but that can wait until morning."

"I look forward to spending time with him." Nelk nodded

Shenji lead the way back to the main den, "I am sure you will be welcome to stay with us as long as you need. It is time for me to turn in." She slipped back in the bedroom with most of their den, adding as she walked off, "He is our guest and as is custom, welcome to our bed."

Nelk fit in quickly and moved in with Jenyin's den until after the coming battle. He helped develop some devices for their plans and suggested improvements on others. He was very impressed with the work of the gnomes and wound up spending a lot of time with them learning from their work.

Lyamy started teaching combat classes in the large unused cavern between the Shadowkyn cavern and the residential cavern. Everyone was welcome and the classes got very large. There were trainers from other races that offered to assist with training. When she was teaching techniques that took advantage of having a tail, they came in quite helpful at teaching alternatives for those who did not.

One night a knock came at the door of their den, Nunji happened to answer and came to Lyamy. "There is a cloaked figure, happens to be human who is requesting to speak with you in private. He is trained to conceal his thoughts and not with magic."

"Thank you." Lyamy went to the door and stepped out into the hall closing the door. "How may I be of assistance to you." He was alone and she sensed no threat.

"Can we go somewhere private?"

"As you wish." Lyamy teleported them to the jungle where the gnomes used to have their village and put them under a dome of concealment.

The man pulled back his hood, "Forgive the cloak and dagger, I am Hue Alastor of secret order of the Guardians of Honor. Our purpose is to watch for events that can create a threat to honorable people of the world. It has been determined that your sanctuary is honorable people. First business is to warn you. The Southern Kingdom of Ehrbron has sent ten ships with a thousand soldiers to come and take this place. I would guess from the preparations I have seen you are already aware of at least some kind of threat. I hope this information is useful."

"How do I know you are not a party to this threat either over stating to cause fear or understating to cause overconfidence? Why me, why now?"

"You seem responsible for security. Now is the soonest we could get someone here assess the situation and sound the alarm so to speak. We discovered the potential threat, but then we had to get someone here and evaluate it takes time. Our organization is out of ShadowKeep. I have no means for you to verify who I am."

The voice of ShadowDancer whispered in her thoughts, '*He is who he says he is. He servers under the kingdom run by an Ancient who is my friend. You can accept his invitation without any risky obligation.*'

"You have received the highest verification. I accept your information. So, what is your second order of business?"

"I have been asked to invite you to join the order. We ask that you share information when it can help others, but you are not obligated. We do ask that you carry this medallion, it gives you the means to communicate to the order at any time."

"I will accept," she said examining the medallion, "but I will turn off the tracking ability in the medallion."

"It was not put there to use against you, but rather so we could locate you if we had need to ask about events."

"I am reachable, just broadcast the request and I will respond as soon as reasonable depending on what I am doing at the time."

"You are good," He looked at her, "Forgive me, that was all the official business, but I have watched you training, you have a wide range of skill and techniques that do not belong to a single school of training. Perhaps someday I will have a chance to receive training from you in private."

"We shall see, for now I must get back to my den."

He did not know she had altered time and they arrived within seconds of when they left. He vanished in the shadows and she went back into her den.

"That was quick." Nunji stated, "What was it about?"

"A messenger letting us know that there are ten ships coming filled with one thousand soldiers."

"Can we trust the information?" Shenji asked overhearing the conversation.

"He was confirmed as a reliable source. It means we have a little more than we expected to deal with but does not change our plans. If Marrianne is correct, we are sending back a bigger message and they will not

be likely to try again, because they are not ready to commit to a costly war."
Lyamy placed her gear back on her shelf, "We can tell Jenyin and the counsel
tomorrow. We have a couple weeks, and this really will not change
anything."

"We have three crew of our own waiting for ships to be built." Freyie
said letting it hang in the air.

"Nice thought, we should have them waiting in the cavern between
the residential areas." Lyamy laughed. "It would be worth our time if we
could acquire a ship or two form an attacking enemy."

"The safety of our people first." Shenji pointed out.

"Of course." Lyamy agreed, "All of our people." she knew Shenji was
still not including those who were not Shadowkyn in her thinking. It was still
a difficult step to accept other races as being part of the clan.

Shenji sighed, "Yes, All of our people." They laughed and hugged, it
was better to be reproved within the den then make the mistake in public.

*   *   *   *   *

They could see the land line in the distance. They were well out of
sight of anyone looking out to sea. They had four days travel north and then
three towards land. They would start turning when they saw the gap formed
by the river just south of the cave settlement. How many people could
possibly live inside coastal caves? It would be all lights out once they turned
towards land. The plan was to be unseen until the morning they launched to
shore. The ships would drop their masts and use the power of the galleon to
row towards shore. With no lights and no sails anyone on shore would have
to be deliberately looking for them and know where they were coming in to
see them before the night of the attack. Then darkness would be their cover
until it was too late.

No one had ever before tried to settle these lands. According to all stories the beasts of the land were too savage, and any settlement would be destroyed before they could be securely fortified. There were sailor stories of beasts that picked up entire ships and threw them back out to sea. The fact they were going to overthrow an existing settlement and expected to do so with ease indicated to Admiral O'Drell that these stories were overstated if not totally fabricated by pirates and sailors reaching the bottom of a good bottle of rum.

He smiled to himself, they had their victory rum stashed in the bottom deck. If all went according to plan in nine days, they would be telling their own tales from the bottom of a bottle. Admiral O'Drell was hoping there would be resistance already on the beach when they arrive, shouting out warnings and giving him an excuse to unload a volley of cannon fire on the beach and test the new hardware. After this mission the crew would get a month or two off to spend with their families, there was no better way to get a man ready to spend time at sea then time with their family, that Admiral laughed at the thought.

General Brakhadt's thoughts were not too far from the Admirals. This was going to be an easy win and the army needed a win to help with morale. His troops would be the first to wear the new armor and wield the new swords. The men were in the army for several reasons. Some were here for what they saw as the honor and glory of war. Most of the men were here because they had families that needed to eat and survive. There was a portion of the troops that were here to avoid prison or worse. About two hundred were mercenaries hired for this mission. They were not even the mercenaries best; they were discounted new mercenaries out to get some experience themselves.

The newest troops would be in the first wave. This should be an easy fight and the only way they will get experience in battle is if they are in the front line while there are still enemies. Each ship held eighty swordsmen and twenty archers. Each of the first two waves would be 160 swordsmen and forty archers. General Brakhardt hoped there would be at least some resistance, but he would take an immediate surrender. They would still have to kill most of the leaders and soldiers as an example to prove they were there for business. They would exercise a firm hand of control and eventually the people would accept their rule. That is how they maintained as much control as they did back in Ehrbron and the lands around it.

They were the most powerful of the southern kingdoms and their neighbors paid them homage to keep the peace. They would build a colony of equal power here in these new lands. He would be staying; it was his job to rule the new colony with military order and discipline. Two of the ships would stay as part of their defenses and they would be putting major weaponry on the beaches to defend against anyone attempting to take the colony away from them after it was captured. There were a few wizards on consignment with the army, they were not that powerful, for that matter they did not get accepted at the academies of they would not be serving with the army.

General Brakhardt did not much like casters or spooks, but they did let him know they were not detecting much if any arcane magic in use as they passed along the continent. They might not be close enough to tell though, but if he caught them telling lies to him, they would be dead. At the very least they would give their best guess. They also told him there is a certain amount of arcane power that would be detected anywhere residual like light and air. They would not be able to get a better picture for him until they were close enough to see something they could target to scry effectively. Casters always seemed to be a lot more powerful when they were fighting against you, but pretty wimpy when they were on your side.

He would lead the third wave. Six hundred, one hundred twenty archers and four hundred eighty swordsmen. If the first two waves failed, he would not. These were his men, they had fought and won battles together. They were not part of the contingents that were sent against Shadow Keep and failed before ever getting close. He had called that a fool's errand before they even left. This was by far a more intelligent military move. The next generation would want to join the army for the glory and to spare their families harder taxes. Eventually the next generation would be the advocates of the kingdom, maybe empire if they had enough successes.

Eight days prior to the expected arrival the fleet of mixed boats was split, half went up the river and the larger vessels up the coast. They had been well supplied with food and what they needed to lay low for two weeks if they had to. They had the tools and resources to disappear and begin new survival tribes just in case things got out of control. It was part of the code of all clans and they by nature honored it.

Kachina was on watch when Lyamy received the message she spotted ships out at sea to the south. They had teams of fifteen to twenty people who were out where they might be seen from the ocean. Doing tasks like net fishing off the docks or working on building little row boats.

"There are ten ships, we have seen all of them now." Lyamy was saying,

"You people see an impossible distance," Marrianne laughed, "I am glad I am on your side." she rubbed her belly and groaned a little. She was showing more than the others.

"Based on where you say they are now; they should start turning towards land sometime tomorrow." Grimble stated, plotting their course on a piece of paper

"We are as ready as we can be." Lyamy stated, "So far it looks like they are coming with only physical force, scrying the ships we see minimal magic and what we see is arcane only."

"We are prepared if we have to retreat also." Desdin added. "Some will escape through the teleport room and it will be sealed, then we will use sealing portions of the tunnels as a means of trapping soldiers if they make it far enough to try and pursue."

"If we are forced to the tunnels, they are restricted in how many they can attack with at a time, and we have mechanisms in place to clean the tunnels when we are clear." Jenyin noted.

"It should not get that far. I would like to win with nobody dieing, but if things push far enough, we will unleash devastation on the beaches. They have numbers, but we have surprise and the advantage of the battlefield." Lyamy smiled, "And we are not playing fair."

"Don't get overconfident, Lyamy." Jenyin borderline scolded, "You have a scar on your chest that you did not know you were going to get and if you had lost control both you and Freyie would have been dead. Do not drop your guard now, there are a lot of people at stake depending on your plan being successful."

"I will reign in my celebration until after we have succeeded and exercise proper caution. You were kind in not pointing out that my mistake killed Chelic even though ShadowDancer brought her back." Lyamy had done special training with those who would be teleporting other people, the others did not know what they could actually do. He was right, she had to stay focused and not get distracted.

The next three days moved slow and everyone in the sanctuary was on edge. Almost everyone was prepared to do what they could in defense of the sanctuary. The women with children were all moved to the Shadowkyn cavern where they could escape if things got that urgent. They would be safe and out of the way of any battle. The forces ready to engage were not that far out of balance, over eight hundred to ward off a thousand. The Magus of Kelleeshia came the last day and selected where he and his contingent would conceal themselves up on the ridge and help if they were needed. Everyone slept early with guards on alert. With the approach of midnight everyone was awaken and moved to their positions, ready for the attacking forces to reach the beach."

*   *   *   *   *

Masts down and lights out they worked their way towards the coast. The peasants fishing off the beaches did not seem to notice their approach. General Brakhardt waited until they had gone in for the night before loading the troops onto the fast boats. The ships stopped a safe distance out and lowered the fast boats to the water.

They used hand signals and ordered and formed up the boats. Around midnight, they ate their last per-battle meals and rested awaiting the signal to go in. The ships were at an angle out from the shore in a diagonal row. The fast boats were all inside from the nearest ship to shore. The signal came and the first wave of fast boats headed to the beach. Everyone was focused on watching events unfold.

Lyamy and her teleporters altered time around them as soon as the first wave started for shore.

The captain of the farthest out boat felt a touch on his hand. In a moment he was naked in his own brig, surrounded by his crew in the same condition. They felt the boat rise in the water as though a large amount of weight had been removed. He started to move, and the crew of their sister ship was also naked in their brig.

Everything from the five ships farthest out was in the cavern between residential areas, including the crew's weapons armor and anything not nailed down. It was not sorted or placed in any order. They waited for the first wave to reach the shore.

The wave of fast boats hit the shore propelled up onto the beach. The soldiers stepped out, no targets in sight for the archers, they started to form up. There were clicking sounds around them a tainted mist rose up and a magical wave accompanied it. The soldiers slumped to the ground asleep. Ghosts touched the sleeping soldiers and the armor collapsed empty as they were teleported naked to the last two ships and left sleeping on the decks.

They waited, there was no signal back from the first wave and no sound of fighting. General Brakhardt assumed they had entered the tunnels and were busy with the sleeping colony. He signaled the next wave. They shot forward stopping between the other boats. The soldiers were out and formed up and moving up the beach. When one of the archers called something out and they stopped the second burst of vapors and magic higher up the beach put the majority of the soldiers to sleep. Two of the archers were too far back to get caught in the gas or spells that were released. They both yelled out before the darts found their marks and they too went down to sleep. The armor collapsing as the bodies inside were teleported away.

With the sound of yelling, unable to see events on the beach in the dark General Brakhardt commanded the rest of the boat's forwards in a hard final attack to overcome whatever obstacle the rest had encountered.

The rest of the boats were emptied rolling the crew from each boat back naked onto a previous boat. The closest two boats were left completely empty. Everything was removed from all the boats except for the naked crewmen and captains which were shuffled and sleeping on eight of the ships.

When the last six hundred soldiers landed and started up the beach, they halted seeing the armor and weapons of their comrades laying on the sand. When they turned towards their fast boats, the boats were gone. Suddenly there were several flares in the middle of their ranks followed by cannon blasts from the face of the cliffs above the beach. The soldiers charged up the beach, but most were caught in the burst of gas from the projectiles that hit the beach. Those that escaped the gas fell into the ten-foot-deep pits in the sand. There were only about fifteen soldiers that managed to avoid gas and drop pits, but the unseen enemies did not miss with their darts.

There were eight ships filled with sleeping solders by the time the sun was lighting the beach. All the armor and weapons were cleaned off the beach and it looked as if nothing had touched the beach. Those injured by the pitfalls were healed before being left naked with their peers. The Admiral and General were on the same ship. Lyamy woke them up, just the three of them at least visible on the deck.

"You have attacked the wrong people. Your lives have been spared this time." She glared at them letting her flesh ripping cat teeth show and flexing her claws threateningly.

The general started to retort, as he was waking up, but realized his situation. An enemy that had total advantage just woke them up back on their own ships with no weapons or even clothing. "How have you done this?"

"That does not matter. You have eight of your ships left to carry you all home. We will give you food to make the journey and ask our Ancient to watch out for you. Heal on your journey home."

"We cannot, ..." Captain O'Dell lost interest in his protest. "We have little choice but to accept your generosity in sparing our lives. As a military leader I will point out that letting your enemies live leaves you open to another attack from a wiser enemy."

"You have not even begun to tax what we could have done. What do you think you know about us?" Lyamy looked at him hard, "You can certainly know this, once we can forgive you your transgression, a second time we may explore how much pain your form can tolerate."

The ships were filled with more than enough food to get them home. The two empty ships were crewed and brought to the docks to refit. They watched the ships from shore. There were three that took off on their own. It was after midday when the remainder of the fleet took off as a group. The last five ships were monitored until they vanished from sight. The spoils were tallied and made available for the people or the sanctuary as long as nobody was excessively greedy with what they took, they were allowed to take pretty much anything they wanted. Anyone who wanted had weapons and armor.

The Magus was in attendance at their evening meeting meal, "I am impressed. I think this is the first war I have seen where one side overwhelmingly won and nobody died. You really had no need of my power. I dare say there are those among you who exceed anything I could do."

"I have something for you Magus, I am giving it to you with permission. If you learn and master this, the only request is that you use wisdom before considering a student." She pulled out a ring, simple brass, with a flame embossed in it like a seal.

He put the ring on. "Simple, but I cannot feel any power."

"Focus on the ring, just clear your mind and focus." A small flicker of fire appeared out of the ring. "When you can feel the power, you will wonder how you ever did not feel it."

The Magus was filled with excitement, "This is the best single gift I have received in years. This alone will pay for any services your sanctuary might ever ask of me."

"So, we drove them off," Jenyin had some concern in his voice, "but will this keep them from trying again. We may not always have warning and we need our defense to be dependent on something more than the right person or people being here. I know that what was done was a group effort and there was back up if things went wrong."

"I agree with your concern." Marrianne added her voice, "We also have a fairly open door for anyone to come join us. We could have spies on the inside next time, or a better planned assault that includes forces coming by land. I am not saying we should be paranoid every step, but I would suggest we may want to set up perimeter watches and scout our coasts for any unusual activity."

"It is not hidden knowledge in Kelleeshia that we have at least some degree of wealth." Freldin agreed, "Rumors can spread and grow, we could find ourselves the target of militant operations with world dominance as a goal, thinking we may have the wealth they need to finance their delusion."

"There are defensive steps that can be taken," The Magus pulled his eyes from his new ring, "We have taken many measures in Kelleeshia and I can share at least some of our measure with your security team. This was a small army movement. I can assure you if there is a massive enough army movement to be a real threat you will have warning now that you are plugged into the rest of the world."

"This will be an ongoing project, protecting our sanctuary and keeping it secure from threats from the outside and the inside." Jenyin stated, "but isn't that true of every place?"

"We have a sizable fleet of boats now." Freyie offered, "with those forty fast boats we could keep a pretty good patrol of the coast and rivers. They are low profile and fast if patrols need to outrun anything."

"I have some ideas for the ships we captured also. We can give them an armament that includes magical weapons" Lyamy was obviously rolling thoughts over in her head, "I have some ideas for protecting the vessels also. I am responsible for security on land at the sanctuary. Jenyin is in charge, the leader of sanctuary. I would suggest we put someone else in charge of our water-based operations."

"Keeping power divided." Freldin contemplated, "There is wisdom in that. For now, though I think we should keep that division among those who founded the sanctuary. Desdin and Grimble are in charge or building operations within sanctuary limits. I would like to nominate Marrianne to be in charge of our naval operations."

The evening discussion continued along the path of organization. Freldin and Chineene were placed in charge of social and political relations both internal and external. Freyie was put in charge of internal investigations. Avira was assigned to set up intelligence gathering working with Shenji. All areas were to recruit members from other races to help build confidence and a sense of teamwork.

Sanctuary lands expanded northward, avoiding encroaching on territory of allies. The navy had an instant size, but they expanded its capabilities. They had the two captured ships and built two additional warships. Lyamy plated the outside of the warships with the metal she used for her sword. Every boat was given at least some defensive capabilities. They had at least ten fast boats patrolling the coasts at any given time monitoring hundreds of miles of coast in either direction. They also built two merchant ships although the nearest port was Kelleeshia and they had a portal to support that trade.

Freyie, Avira and about a quarter of the Shadowkyn population had cubs within two months of the beach skirmish. Some were half breeds with other races that appreciated the difference in customs while visiting. Marrianne went three weeks longer then the Shadowkyn and Lyamy and Shenji were in Jenyin's den to help when the time came.

Shadowkyn normally used cleaned cured leather, but per her request Marriannne had linen and silk over the top of the hide. Lyamy had her hand placed on Marrianne's swollen tummy, "Well, they are all facing the right way, that will make it easier."

"We have a human medical person coming." Shenji said "We are not familiar with any subtle differences, so felt we could use more expert consultation."

"This way." Daret said in the other room and then as they walked into the bedroom, "This is Doctor Michelle Grimes."

"How close are the contractions? You are blowing them off until it is time, right?" Doctor Grimes knelt down between Marrianne's legs.

"Glad you are here." Lyamy said, "We do not have to do this blowing off contractions you are speaking of we just have them when it is time."

Doctor Grimes examined Marrianne and stated, "She is ready, if each of you could hold her feet up about here, it will make it easier for her. Do you have warm water and towels for cleaning the newborn?"

Chelic brought a basin in with towels soaking in it, "I knew you would ask. Your ways are different, we will still have to do some cleaning the clan way to trigger the clan maternity bonds."

A contraction started, "Push!" Doctor Grimes was almost not ready for how fast the first cub came out. Doctor Grimes seemed not pleased for a moment but put her professional face back on.

"They are big." Lyamy said noting they were more than twice the size of her cubs.

"They are more developed." Shenji said as the second cub came out, "and you can see the effects of mixed blood already. They are cute."

The women of the clan were gathered around and insisted on licking each cub at least once and having Marrianne do the same. Doctor Grimes was obviously disgusted by the practice but maintained her silence.

When they were done, there were four human Shadowkyn cubs. Each cub nursed from Marrianne first and then from each of the den women Daret, Karis, Chelic and Avira. Doctor Grimes could not get out of the den fast enough, although they all thanked her. They all laid down with Marrianne while she slept and fed her cubs and the other cubs of the den. The new cubs were as big as the ones that were a month old and at least as alert.

Lyamy and Shenji pushed healing magic to Marrianne and then left returning to Wujin's den, their home. They all crawled in cuddling with their own den cubs and children. The voice of ShadowDancer whispered in her ear, Lyamy opened her eyes and listened, '*There are more of the lost clans to be gathered. I would also have you visit my followers in my homelands. Rest tonight, but we still have a lot of work ahead of us.*'

'*The clan and sanctuary are bound to meet soon. They will learn that Jenyin, Freyie and I live still and have prepared the way for alliances if they are ready.*'

'*They are ready. Yaun and Merkyet will be glad you are alive and allowed once again to commune with the clan. They will also understand that I called all of you out.*'

'*They will know that I deceived them.*'

They will know that you acted under my instruction and for the good of the clan and future of the Shadowkyn. We will just make sure it does not become a public issue. I will visit them and prepare the way. They do not need to know more then I reserved you all for my purposes.'

It was about a week later when ShadowDancer pulled Peltrhak, Yaun, the leaders of the clans that joined and their firsts to a meeting at the sanctuary. Merkyet explained that Cantese had chosen to return to the savage jungle on her own and was raising her cubs in the wild.

They met in the meeting hall in the residential area of Jenyin's sanctuary. There were many of the leaders and firsts that Lyamy had not previously met. There turned out to be five other settlements of Shadowkyn and other indigenous races to the savage continent. Two settlements were on the northern coast and three on the southern coastal regions. The civilized or more civilized races surviving on the continent were led to the nearest colonies, the population of the sanctuary exceeded five thousand in six months and was the largest community. The winged folks of the canopy forest allied for mutual protection associated themselves with Jenyin's sanctuary.

Lyamy found herself frequently called upon as the Avatar of ShadowDancer to travel and help settle situations. She discovered by accident one day that she could actually split herself a second time and be in three places at the same time. She considered the difficulty of being in three places at once and decided not to try any further and only use that in emergencies. She was able to spend time with her children and the children of her clan while still traveling, helping the Shadowkyn centered cultures to prosper and grow strong.

Nelk was the first Shadowkyn to leave the savage continent. He wandered the world an anomaly everywhere he went. He was accepted because he was unique and gained a reputation for solving problems. It would be a while before Shadowkyn became comfortable enough to leave their homelands and mingle further with other races outside the comfort of their communities.

The children of Lyamy Avatar of ShadowDancer would eventually become well known among her people around the world.

DEDICATED WITH LOVE TO MY LATE WIFE,
TAWNIA MARIE TREMAINE

* 9 7 8 1 9 6 6 9 5 4 3 9 2 *